HIS CRUEL OBSESSION

THE HIS OBSESSION SERIES
BOOK ONE

A DARK BILLIONAIRE ROMANCE

FREYA LOCKE

HIS CRUEL OBSESSION
A STEAMY DARK OBSESSIVE
BILLIONAIRE ROMANCE

Julian Blackwell waited seventeen years to claim Clara Hayes. Now he owns her debt—and he's collecting.

Clara is days away from losing everything. Her family's ranch is drowning in debt, foreclosure is imminent, and pride is the last thing she can afford. Salvation comes from the one man she swore she'd never accept help from—**Julian Blackwell**, the ruthless billionaire who dismantled her father's empire and never forgot the girl who laughed at him in high school.

His offer is simple.
One year. Complete submission.
In exchange, Julian will save her ranch—free and clear.

The contract gives him total control. Her time. Her obedience. Her body. Julian doesn't want a temporary arrangement—he wants Clara on her knees, bound by rules he's been perfecting for seventeen years. What begins as blackmail turns into something far more dangerous as forced proximity, obsession, and undeniable desire blur the line between captivity and craving.

Julian Blackwell is everything Clara should fear—possessive, calculating, and devastatingly dominant. Yet the more she resists, the more her body betrays her. Because the terrifying truth is this: part of her has always belonged to him.

Now Clara must decide whether to fight for her independence—
or surrender to the man who built an empire just to own her.

A dark enemies-to-lovers billionaire romance featuring blackmail, forced proximity, obsession, and power exchange.
This full-length standalone delivers high heat, emotionally intense dominance and submission dynamics, and a morally gray hero who takes what he wants—until she realizes she wants to be taken.

No cliffhanger. Guaranteed HEA.

CONTENT WARNING
READER ADVISORY

ALSO BY FREYA LOCKE

Dark romance.

Dangerous obsession.

Power that cuts both ways.

Series Overview — The Obsession Series

The *Obsession Series* is a collection of standalone dark romances centered on men who do not fall in love gently and women who refuse to be broken by them.

Each story explores desire sharpened into obsession, control forged into intimacy, and the dangerous space where power becomes connection.

These are high-heat, emotionally charged romances where surrender is chosen, redemption is earned, and love is never soft—but it is always complete.

CRUEL OBSESSION

Julian Blackwell & Clara Hayes

Seventeen years after walking away, Clara is forced to confront the man who never stopped claiming her—only now, survival means surrendering to the obsession that owns them both.

SINFUL OBSESSION

Kael Draven & Lila Chase

To save her forest, Lila strikes a bargain with a man who doesn't negotiate mercy—and Kael intends to bind far more than land before he's finished.

RUTHLESS OBSESSION

Damian Stryker & Avery Donovan

Damian destroyed the monster who hurt her, but salvation comes at a cost—and Avery must decide whether true surrender can exist without lies.

DARK OBSESSION

Colton Wolfe & Ivy Monroe

Colton dismantled her father's empire piece by piece, and now Ivy is the final acquisition—eight years of obsession coming due.

TWISTED OBSESSION

Nathan Cross & Sera Winters

She's determined to expose his dangerous research; he's determined to prove her desire is darker than her fear—and neither of them plans to lose.

SAVAGE OBSESSION

Sebastian York & Chloe Henderson

To save her brother, Chloe signs a contract with a man who doesn't
forgive debt—and Sebastian always collects in full.

***

Start at the Beginning

Begin with **CRUEL OBSESSION**, or read the Obsession Series in any
order—each novel is a standalone with its own dark romance,
guaranteed HEA, and no cliffhangers.

Visit: www.freyalocke.com

DEDICATION

For the ones who love recklessly, even when it hurts.
For the broken, who find beauty in the fire.

And...

For the women who've ever been told they were too much, too loud, too complicated—may you always find a hero who sees you as just enough.

If this dedication feels a little too close to home...

If something in your chest tightens instead of pulling away—

Go on...

I DARE You

Turn the page.

Be brave enough to keep reading.

GOOD GIRL...

CHAPTER I
CLARA HAYES

One look at the ink on the paper and my spine goes rigid.

The devil doesn't need to sign his name for me to know who sent it. Every curve of every letter drips with Julian Blackwell's brand of precision—controlled, taunting, deliberate.

Like he's reaching through the page to remind me he's watching.

Black ink. Heavy paper. My name carved across the envelope like a verdict: *Clara Hayes.*

The wind catches it, slapping the letter against the screen door again and again—impatient for me to accept my fate. I stand frozen on the porch, heart a slow, brutal drum.

Only one man writes like he's signing a sentence instead of a signature.

Julian Blackwell.

Seventeen years since high school. Six months since my father died. His last words were to warn me to stay away from Julian. And now Julian is reaching for me—from a distance, through debt and paper and ink.

I tear the envelope open with shaking fingers.

Your debt has been purchased by Blackwell Holdings. You have seven days to vacate or accept alternative arrangements.

The words coil through me like smoke—soft, poisonous, promising ruin. Heat stirs low in my belly—nerves, or something far more dangerous—a shiver caught between fear and fascination.

The wind scrapes across the high plains like sandpaper, grit settling into the cracks of my lips and the folds of my clothes, and the dust blurs the horizon into a wavering line where the sky presses down hard enough to smother. The barn looms in the distance, weather-beaten boards silvered by too many summers. The earth around it is dry and split, veins of dirt running jagged in every direction.

Once, this land fed cattle and horses. Now it's a husk, clinging to life the way I do.

My palms are raw from pulling weeds that aren't worth pulling. My mother's roses—her breath of beauty in the middle of all this roughness—have gone feral. Thorns crawl along the fence line, petals burning crimson against the gray of everything else. The scent lingers, stubbornly sweet, mixing with sweat and old hay. It feels wrong that the roses thrive while the ranch starves.

The letter shakes in my hands. The roses shiver in the same wind, as if they know what the paper means.

My mother's roses. Her ranch. Her legacy. I've lost it all.

The memories come anyway: my father's voice, slurred with whiskey, muttering how the Blackwells stole everything—his business, his pride, and his will to keep breathing.

Martin Blackwell made the first cut. Julian sharpened the blade his father wielded so well.

The headlines from years ago: "Heir apparent turned ruthless mogul." The boy turned man, with a wolf's smile and eyes like winter storms.

Six months since Daddy died, and his last words still echo: *That Blackwell boy... he watched you in school. Still watches you. Don't let him close. Promise me.*

I promised. And I kept it—at least in the flesh—but not in my dreams.

Julian Blackwell has lived there rent-free for seventeen years, a ghost of what-ifs and forbidden dreams. In his senior year, he cornered me at my locker—quarterback shoulders, dangerous charm—and asked me to Homecoming in front of everyone. I laughed instead of crying. I didn't mean to be cruel. It was a shield.

But he took it as defiance. A challenge.

He kept asking—after practice, after class, in the parking lot, when the air smelled like woodsmoke and possibility.

Every time, I said no.

Not because I didn't want to. God help me, I wanted to say yes. But my father's voice always drowned out my own: *You'll have nothing to do with a Blackwell.*

So I denied Julian, over and over, pretending I didn't ache from the way he looked at me like I already belonged to him.

And the cruelest twist?

Seventeen years later, he's still the one boy I can't forget. The one man who stalks my dreams, who makes me imagine things I shouldn't want.

Dirty. Filthy. Savage things.

I've followed him quietly from the sidelines—headlines first, then glossy profiles. Blackwell heir in tailored suits. A half-smile that never reached his eyes. Acquisitions with sharp verbs: *absorbs, consolidates, takes, demolishes, destroys.* The "restructured" deal that gutted my father's business. The refinancing that finished it.

I told myself I hated him for it, but hatred never erased my curiosity. It only inflamed my dreams, dark, obsessive dreams of him doing things to me that would make my father roll in his grave.

Scout's bark snaps me back to reality. Gravel spits. A car—sleek, black, wrong for this road—slides into view, eating the distance like it owns it.

Heat and dread coil in my gut. I don't need to see his face. My body knows before my mind catches up.

Julian Blackwell.

The boy I refused.

The man I've secretly followed for seventeen years.

And now—for the first time since high school graduation—he's here.

The engine's purr dies, leaving the world too quiet. Even the wind forgets to move.

The car door opens.

Julian Blackwell steps out.

For a heartbeat, everything inside me stops. Seventeen years should have softened him, blurred him into memory, but the man standing on my dirt road isn't memory—he's retribution in a thousand-dollar suit. Every sharp edge of the boy I knew has been tempered into something harder, colder, breathtakingly dangerous.

Broad shoulders fill the cut of his jacket, as if it were made to contain power. The dark fabric drinks in the light, the wind teasing a single silver thread in his hair. His jaw—razor-clean, shadowed just enough to promise sin.

And those eyes. Storm-gray, the color of the horizon before it breaks. The same eyes that used to follow me down high-school hallways now rake over me with slow, proprietary precision, mapping the places I've changed—and the ones I haven't.

My thighs clench. Reflex. Recognition. My body remembers before my brain can lie.

He doesn't smile. Doesn't need to. His silence does all the talking, the kind that hums with ownership.

"Clara Hayes."

Just my name, low and deliberate. But the way he says it feels like possession—like he's been keeping it caged behind his teeth for seventeen years, tasting it every night, waiting for this moment to let it free.

The wind moves again, spinning dust around us, but I don't hear it. There's only his voice—dark, velvet, inevitable.

Heat blooms low and hot, traitorous and humiliating. I hate that my skin flushes, that my pulse hammers, that every cell in me still remembers him. He was the boy every girl wanted. Now he's the man no woman can deny.

And he's standing here.

On my road.

On my land.

I should slam the door. Scream. Throw something heavy. Anything but this. Instead, I lean toward him—helpless, traitorous—before my brain can form a single word.

"You're trespassing." The words come out thin. Raw.

"Not anymore." He climbs the porch like he owns the rhythm of the world—slow, deliberate, every step a quiet assertion of dominion. "I own the note. Which means I own the deed. Which means this ranch is mine."

"You can't just—" The protest dies on my tongue, brittle as glass.

"I can. I did. It's done." He lays the papers on the porch rail like a gauntlet. The legalese glints in the sun: signatures, seals, the kind of certainty that eats hope. "Every acre. Every building. Every blade of dead grass."

My hands go numb. "Why?" The syllable cracks in my throat. "Your father already destroyed mine. Wasn't that enough?"

A flicker of something dark crosses his face—not sorrow, not hesitation. Something older, colder, welded from patience and purpose.

"Our fathers are dead. This is between us now."

"There is no *us*." I spit the word like a curse.

His eyes darken, the faintest smile curving like a blade. "There's been an us since you were seventeen in that white sundress." He says it slowly, savoring the memory like a weapon. "The one that turned transparent in the rain after graduation. You walked past me like I was nothing, but I saw everything. The shadow of your bra. The way your nipples pressed through the fabric. I went home and jerked off three times thinking about it."

Heat and shame flare through me, molten and sickening. It should humiliate me. Instead, it wakes something feral I've kept buried. "That's—you can't just—"

"I can do whatever I want." He closes the space between us without hurry, until his scent—cedar and dark smoke—wraps around me like a tether. His hand dips into his pocket, fingers closing around something unseen before withdrawing empty-handed, as if reminding me he carries secrets, weapons, and time.

"I've waited seventeen years. Planned for the last three. Every loan your father couldn't pay, every buyer who mysteriously backed out, every contractor who suddenly couldn't work for him —that was me. Setting the stage."

The words land like blows. Not shouted. Not dramatic. Just facts. Balanced accounts.

"Setting the stage? This is deliberate?" My voice shakes with rage. I want to rip the papers from the rail, shred them, tear into him—kiss him. God help me, I've lost my mind.

"It was inevitable." The calm of a man who wrote the ending years ago. No anger. No triumph. Just inevitability.

"You destroyed him. He died thinking he'd failed—" My voice breaks on my father's memory.

"He died knowing he couldn't protect you from me." He doesn't look away. The statement isn't cruel; it's a verdict. "And now here we are."

My fists clench on the rail until my knuckles blanch. Rage crawls up my throat, hot and acrid. "I'll burn it down before I let you have it."

He studies me like a man weighing the last sliver of resistance in a prize he already owns. No smirk, no sneer—just quiet, merciless patience. He doesn't need to stop me. Power radiates off him like heat from a forge: immovable, inevitable, terrifyingly calm in the ruin he's engineered.

"The ranch?" His smile comes slowly, predatory, as though the question amuses him. "You think I went to all this trouble for land and run-down buildings?" He steps closer until my back hits the door, until his presence becomes a wall. His cologne swallows the air. "The ranch is bait. You're the prize."

"God, you're insane."

"No." His voice is a low blade. "I'm a man who takes what he wants." He lifts his hand, fingers ghosting along my jaw without quite touching, and the lack of contact makes every nerve in my body spark. "And I've wanted you since you laughed at me in front of my entire team when I asked you to the homecoming dance. Since you walked past me at prom with Marcus Henley's hand on your back. Since you left for college without looking back, while I stayed here, building an empire, always knowing I'd use it to bring you home."

My heart thunders so loud it echoes in my ears. "That's not love, Julian. That's savage."

"I prefer *obsessed*." He brushes his thumb across my lip, devastatingly gentle. "I never said it was love. Love is too soft. What I feel for you has teeth."

"Julian—"

"I'm going to make you an offer." He steps back, voice steel. Somehow, the space feels worse than his nearness. "But first, you'll call me Mr. Blackwell."

Arrogant ass. But then his words sink in, and my breath catches. "An offer?"

"One year." Each word is precise as a signature. "You come willingly. Live in my house. Submit to my will. Share my bed."

"This is about sex?" Barely a whisper. "You're crazy."

"It's about much more than sex." He holds my gaze, gray and endless, swallowing every breath I try to take. "This isn't about a night in my bed. It's about possession." He drags his thumb once across my bottom lip, slow and deliberate. "No more refusals. Not this time. Not ever again."

My mouth goes dry. "That's not a deal. That's slavery."

"It's a negotiated exchange." Each syllable lands like a clause. "In return, the ranch comes back to you free and clear."

"You can't be serious."

"I've never been more serious about anything in my life." He stares me down. Merciless. "Submission for salvation. You'll hate it at first, but you'll embrace it in time."

A bitter laugh tears out of me before I can stop it. "You're out of your mind." The words come out shaking. "You can't think I'd agree to that? You can't walk onto my land, after destroying everything I've fought for, and expect me to—"

He turns toward the steps, his retreat somehow heavier than his presence. "There's a gala next Saturday—an agricultural preservation fundraiser. Ironic. You'll attend as my guest and give me your answer."

"And if I say no?"

"Then the next day, the sheriff arrives with an eviction notice." His smile is sharp as frost. "Everything your family built will be bulldozed for a shopping center."

"You wouldn't—"

"Try me." He pauses at the edge of the porch, quiet. Absolute. "One week. Lose your ranch and keep your pride... or keep your ranch and submit to me. Choose wisely."

He's in his car before I can breathe, before I can throw something, before I can scream every curse I know—leaving only dust and the echo of his words coiling through me like smoke and a promise I shouldn't want.

The sleek black car glides down my dirt road like a predator melting back into the woods.

I sag against the door, palms flat to the wood, trembling. I want to run inside and scrub myself raw under the shower, and wash his cologne off my skin. I want to scream until my lungs empty.

And I want *him*.

That's the part that guts me. That's the part that makes my knees weak. I want what he's offering even as I hate him for offering it. My mind chants *No, no, no*, but my body is already whispering *Yes, yes, yes*.

I press the heels of my hands against my eyes like I can erase the image of him—dark suit, darker eyes, words cutting as deep as any touch. Seventeen years, and he still knows exactly where to strike, even from a distance.

"I hate you." The words break in the empty air.

But when I stumble inside and slide the bolt home, my skin is still humming. The truth terrifies me more than eviction notices and bulldozers: It isn't hate making my hands shake.

It's hunger.

CHAPTER 2
SUNDAY

I DON'T SLEEP. THE HOUSE IS DARK AND ECHOING, AND I STALK IT LIKE A caged animal—bare feet on cold tile, pacing until my arches ache. Every number I run, every desperate calculation ends in the same cold truth.

The bank won't return my calls. Every lawyer in three counties is suddenly in trial or booked solid. It's as if Julian reached inside my life and salted every field before I could even think to sow my desperation into infertile ground.

By dawn, I'm at my laptop, blue light slicing through swollen eyes. I type his name with shaking fingers. *Julian Blackwell.*

The business articles are what I expect—hostile takeovers, brutal efficiency, a man who dismantles companies like he's playing chess. Photo after photo of him: storm-gray eyes, gray suit, the expression of someone building a beautiful, merciless future.

But then there are the other stories, buried in comment sections and anonymous blogs—women who dated him briefly, leaving with dazed expressions and airtight NDAs. The same words repeat: *Intense. Dominant. Demanding.* One even called him *a lesson in being undone.*

I slam the laptop shut like it burned me. Too late. The images are already branded behind my eyes: Julian's hands on my wrists. His mouth closing over mine. His voice telling me when to breathe. When to beg. The command he gave me on the porch still reverberates through my bones—*You'll call me Mr. Blackwell.*

The humiliation of it makes me burn. The heat of it makes me ache.

I throw myself into work until my muscles scream—mucking stalls, fixing fence posts, hurling hay bales harder than necessary —anything to outrun the obsessive thoughts. But my traitorous body keeps circling back, feeding on what I swore I wouldn't imagine.

By nightfall, the barn is silent, my hands blistered and filthy, my body trembling with exhaustion. It isn't enough.

The shower becomes my confessional. Steam blurs the mirror, water roars down, and still I can hear him in my head. *You'll call me Mr. Blackwell.*

I brace my palms against the tile, my forehead to my forearm, trying to scrub him off me. Instead, my fingers slip lower, driven by a hunger I can't name.

I come fast and hard, shuddering against the slick tile, a choked sound tearing free from my throat. The shame hits just as sharp as the release—water mixing with tears, humiliation knotting with need until I'm shaking.

I slide down to the shower floor, curl into myself, and cry.

Not because of what he's done.

Because of what I want.

CHAPTER 3
MONDAY

THE KNOCK COMES AT DAWN. A BLACK BOX WAITS ON THE STEP, TIED with a blood-red ribbon, my name slashed across it in his unmistakable hand.

I shouldn't open it, but curiosity gets the better of me.

Inside: a book—*The Story of O*. First edition. Leather soft as a whisper, pages faintly perfumed with age. Between the leaves, a card in the same sharp, slanted script:

So you understand what you're accepting. Pay attention to how she finds freedom in surrender. — Mr. Blackwell

The book is heavy in my lap, the note fluttering between my fingers like a dare. *Freedom in surrender.* He thinks he knows me. He thinks I'll read and break.

The worst part is that he's right.

I hurl the book across the room so hard it slams into the far wall and drops with a thud, the sound echoing through the kitchen like a gunshot. My hands shake. My pulse hammers. My fingers itch to turn the pages.

Then, like a lunatic, I crawl after it—fingers closing around the leather cover, dragging it back to me like it's alive. Like he's inside it.

I open to the first page. Then the next. And the next.

I don't skim. I devour.

Every scene feels like it's his hand on my skin. Every act of surrender crawls beneath my ribs and nests there, humming. I see myself in the pages—stripped, collared, kneeling.

I see Julian—*Mr. Blackwell*—towering over me, voice like velvet drawn across steel, hands turning my body into something pliant and trembling.

By the last chapter, my thighs are slick, my breathing ragged. Shame and hunger twist together until I can't tell them apart. I slide my hand between my legs like a thief, furious and desperate at once.

I come hard, knees drawn to my chest on the kitchen floor, Julian's name—no, *Mr. Blackwell's*—ripping from my throat. The sound shatters the air.

I hate myself for it.

I want him more for it.

A strange fog settles over me, making the shame feel distant, almost euphoric. I curl on the kitchen floor, blinking through the drowsiness, convincing myself it's just fatigue.

What is wrong with me?

CHAPTER 4
TUESDAY

HE DOESN'T SEND A BOX. HE SENDS AN ARMY.

Stone-faced men unload a catered feast into my kitchen as if I'm not standing there in my father's threadbare flannel, barefoot, arms crossed, staring.

Filet mignon. Truffle risotto. A chocolate soufflé that looks like a mortal sin. Wine that costs more than my truck.

A card propped against the soufflé:

You're too thin. Eat. I intend to grab those hips when I fuck you, and I want something to hold onto. —Mr. Blackwell

My stomach knots. I should dump it all in the trash. I should send it back.

Instead, I sit at the table and eat every bite.

The food is rich and obscene on my tongue. Each mouthful feels like a line I can't uncross. The wine is heavy and lush, loosening things in me I've kept bolted down for years.

By the last glass of wine, a warmth uncoils in my veins, loosening thoughts I've kept chained. The wine feels unusually potent, leaving me languid, emotions heightening in a way that borders on unnatural—but I blame the richness of the meal.

I want him. Have wanted him since high school.

And the fact that he's orchestrated this nightmare? It should make me sick. Instead, it makes me want things that terrify me—wanted enough to be hunted, cornered, and caged.

By him.

What kind of wanting drives a man to such extremes?

CHAPTER 5
WEDNESDAY

"CLARA HAYES?"

The woman at my door is elegant and cool, the kind of voice used in places with marble floors and no prices on the menus. She carries sleek black cases I recognize instantly as couture.

"Mr. Blackwell sent me." She steps past me without asking. "For measurements."

"Measurements for what?"

"Your wardrobe." She's already snapping open her case, laying out measuring tapes like scalpels. "He's particular about fit."

I stand frozen as she moves around me, brisk and impersonal. Bust. Waist. Hips. Inseam. Neck.

Then wrists.

"Why my wrists?" My voice is barely a whisper.

Her smile is small and knowing. "Mr. Blackwell didn't specify. I've learned not to question his requirements."

The tape glides around my wrists like a premonition, and a peculiar calm washes over me—resistance dulling into accep-tance, my pulse steadying unnaturally. Leather. Buckles. Cold metal. It should terrify me; instead, the thrill is quiet but unmistakable, like standing on the edge of a cliff and leaning forward.

When she's gone, the house feels hollow. My wrists tingle. I'm wet. The thought of what he's planning should terrify me.

Instead, it makes me ache.

Again.

CHAPTER 6
THURSDAY

THE SECOND PACKAGE IS HEAVIER—SOFTER SOMEHOW. I TEAR THE PAPER with shaking hands and find a nest of black tissue. Inside: lingerie. Not trashy—exquisite. French lace that feels like a whisper against my fingers. Garters that frame rather than confine. A corset designed to cinch my waist and lift my breasts like an offering.

A note slips from the lace:

These are for you to wear under your clothes. So you remember who you're dressing for, even when I'm not there. —Mr. Blackwell

I tell myself I won't. I'll box it up, send it back, burn it if I have to. But I can't stop myself.

I slip the corset around my waist, hook the garters, and smooth the lace over my hips.

When I see myself in the mirror—soft turned sharp, plain turned powerful—I understand exactly what he's doing. He isn't diminishing me. He's reshaping me. Showing me who I could be in his world. Not hidden.

Displayed. Desired.

I wear the lingerie under my work clothes while fixing the barn door. The secret of it—the silk scraping against my skin as I hammer a nail, the corset biting faintly at my ribs—makes me hyper-aware of my body in ways that have nothing to do with shame and everything to do with anticipation.

By dusk, I can smell my own arousal beneath hay and sweat. My hands tremble when I button my shirt.

CHAPTER 7

FRIDAY

Nothing arrives.

The absence feels like withdrawal, like he's pulled a drug from my system without warning. I check the door obsessively, hating myself for the disappointment when nothing appears.

He's trained me in six days to expect him—to crave whatever he'll send next like a fix.

That night, my phone rings. Unknown number. My pulse spikes before I even answer.

"Have you decided?" His voice is dark velvet through the speaker.

"I haven't—I need more time to—"

"You need more time to what? Pretend you haven't already made your decision? That you haven't been wet all week thinking about submitting to me?"

My breath catches. "How do you—"

"Because I know you. I've had seventeen years to study you." His voice is slow, deliberate, sliding between my ribs like a blade wrapped in velvet. "I know you touch yourself with your left hand. I know you bite your lip when you come. I know you arch your back right before you fall apart."

"You've been watching me?" The words hiss out, but my pulse betrays me.

"No." Low and rough. "But I've imagined it so many times it might as well be memory."

Silence stretches—only his breathing coming through the line, dark and hungry.

"You want to know what I'm doing right now?" It's a dare.

I swallow. "What—"

A soft laugh. Dangerous. "I'm stroking myself. Thinking about tomorrow night. About that red dress clinging to your body. About the moment at the gala when no one will know..." His voice drops to a growl. "They won't know when we slip away that I'll make you kneel for me. My hand in your hair. Your lips wrapped around me. My cock slamming into the back of your throat. They won't know that while they sip champagne, you'll be on your knees, serving me."

I press my knees together hard, heat pooling between them, shame and want tangling until I can't tell them apart.

"They won't know," he continues, slower now, "that I'll be fucking you for the first time. That while they're toasting their causes, I'll have you bent to me—your body open, your mouth eager to please me, your pussy weeping to take what I've been waiting seventeen years to give." His breath hitches. "No more jerking off thinking of you. I'll have you there—present, open to me, available whenever I want."

A ragged sound escapes me, and for a moment, the world blurs at the edges, his voice echoing in my head like it's inside me, amplifying the heat between my thighs. I shake it off, but the haze lingers, making his imagined touch feel too vivid.

His breathing turns rougher, deeper—the sound of him on the

edge. "I can't wait to come inside you. To stop fucking my fist thinking of you and fuck you instead."

A low groan comes through the speaker. Then a sharp exhale, like a man spending years of patience in a single breath. When he speaks again, his voice is almost gentle. Almost.

"Midnight. Wear what I send. Be ready. And, Clara?"

"What?"

"Don't touch yourself tonight. That orgasm belongs to me."

The line goes dead, leaving only my own pulse in my ears, my thighs slick, my body already obeying a command I haven't even accepted yet.

I throw my phone across the room. Then retrieve it. Then spend the entire night aching, needy, and obeying his command even though I haven't agreed to anything.

CHAPTER 8
SATURDAY MORNING

The final box is massive, as if a whole world fits inside. Black box. Blood-red ribbon. His handwriting on the label.

I should leave it. Pretend I never saw it. But desperation always outweighs pride.

My bare foot connects with the side—a dull thud satisfying for half a second before regret crawls in. Of course, I pick it up. Of course, I tear the ribbon like it's a tether binding me, only to find another leash inside.

A dress that looks like liquid fire. Red silk that will cling to every curve, reveal every secret. The neckline plunges, the back is nearly nonexistent, and the slit rises high enough to make me blush. It's a dress designed to make me feel naked while clothed.

Shoes that are architectural marvels—delicate straps, impossible heels that will force me to walk slowly, deliberately.

And at the bottom of the box, wrapped in tissue: stockings, garters, and nothing else.

The note, in his sharp handwriting:

No panties. I want nothing between you and me when you say yes.

Because you will say yes. You've already said yes in every way but words. Tonight you'll feel me inside you—fucking you. Making our bargain official. A car will arrive at seven. Drink the champagne. You'll need it. —Mr. Blackwell

My heart hammers so hard it hurts. The silk slides like liquid flame over my palms.

Then I start getting ready.

Because he's right.

I've already decided.

I decided the moment he stepped out of that car, bringing seventeen years of want with him.

God help me, but I'm going to say yes.

CHAPTER 9
SATURDAY NIGHT

THE DRESS FITS LIKE SIN DISGUISED AS SALVATION. SILK GLIDES OVER MY skin like a lover's palm, clinging to every curve, making a secret of my bare body beneath—only stockings and garters, no panties, as commanded. Each shift of my hips sends a whisper of fabric between my thighs, a taunt that reminds me exactly who I'm dressing for.

In the mirror, I'm a stranger. Not Clara Hayes, the ranch girl. Not the daughter of a man who lost everything to a Blackwell. This reflection is expensive, dangerous—a woman who might kneel for Julian Blackwell and crave the moment he fists her hair.

The thought makes me wet. Again. Still. My body's been in a low burn for a week, a constant throb bordering on madness.

The car he sends is obscene—black, sleek, predator-silent. The driver doesn't speak, only opens the door with a gloved hand to reveal an interior that smells of leather, smoke, and money. A bottle of champagne waits on ice, a card tied to its neck with a blood-red ribbon:

Dutch courage, if you need it. Though I suspect you need something else entirely. Something only I can give you. —Mr. Blackwell

My hands tremble as I pour a glass. The first swallow burns sweet. The second pools heat low in my belly, spreading like warm oil, softening muscles, blurring edges. I tell myself it's the alcohol, but the precision of the calm—the way my nerves uncoil just so—feels too deliberate, like a drug designed to lower inhibitions.

Every mile brings me closer to a choice that isn't really a choice at all. Because he's right—my body already decided. It decided the moment he said *You'll call me Mr. Blackwell* in that voice that brooks no argument.

Butterflies turn to ravens in my stomach, wings beating against my ribs.

Memory floods in—senior year. Julian in worn jeans and a football jersey, shoulders filling doorways, that lazy confidence that made teachers forget to scold him. He leaned against the lockers like he owned them, crooked smile undoing cheerleaders, math teachers, and anyone in his line of sight. But he always looked at me. Always tracked me through the cafeteria. Burned into my back during calculus.

"Lost another case to Martin Blackwell. That whole family's poison, Clara. You stay clear of that boy." Daddy's voice echoes in my head, breakfast, his newspaper crumpled in his fist.

"I don't even talk to him."

"Good. Keep it that way. Bad blood between our families goes back before you were born. No good comes from mixing with Blackwells."

But God, how I'd wanted to mix.

I'd watch Julian during practice from the library windows, pretending to read while he threw—shirt clinging to his back, muscles coiling and releasing with the same controlled power he brought to everything.

Girls whispered about what happened in his truck after games. Sarah Michael emerged from the equipment shed with beard burn on her neck and a secret smile. Rebecca Anston sobbed in the bathroom after he ended things, mascara streaked like war paint, while her friends promised he wasn't worth it.

He went through them like tissue paper. Used. Discarded.

And still, when he cornered me by my locker, caged me in with one arm while reaching for a book he didn't need, my whole body would light up like struck flint.

"Hayes." His voice would drop to that register that made my knees weak. "Come to the party tonight."

"Pass."

"You're scared of me."

"I'm smart enough to avoid you."

"Same thing." His breath would stir the hair by my ear. "One day you'll say yes."

"One day, you'll get bored of asking."

But he never did. Three years of high school, and Julian Blackwell kept asking. Kept watching. Kept wanting what he couldn't have—the only girl who wouldn't give in.

And the whispers were darker than the gossip. Rumors that he didn't just break hearts—he broke spirits. That the girls who lasted longest were the ones who liked to be held down. That his appetites ran toward things nice girls didn't even have words for.

"He likes control." Sarah whispered it once in the locker room. "Like, *really* likes it."

"Control how?" someone asked.

Sarah's cheeks had flushed deep red. "Just... control."

I press my thighs together now, silk riding higher, pulse drumming steady between them. It's just sex. One year of sex. People do worse for less. And it might even be good—God knows the girls didn't look unhappy, just wrecked and dazed, like they'd been stripped bare and rebuilt. They'd go back for more until he cut them loose.

Now look at me. Dressed in his color. Sitting in his car. About to sign his contract. Ready to become his.

CHAPTER 10
THE GALA

The hotel blazes against the Montana night, all crystal and light. Valets scramble for cars worth more than houses. Women drip diamonds while men carry themselves like weapons in expensive suits.

And at the entrance—waiting like he's been standing there for seventeen years—is Julian Blackwell.

The sight of him stops my heart. Black tuxedo tailored to perfection, highlighting broad shoulders, narrow waist—the body of a man who wields power like breath. But it's the way he pins me with a look—storm-gray, patient as winter, hungry as a wolf. He tracks me from the car, cataloging every inch of exposed skin, every place the dress clings.

When I reach him, he doesn't speak immediately. Just extends his hand and waits. The choice. Take it and seal my fate, or turn and run.

I take his hand.

He strokes his thumb over my knuckles, and that single touch sends electricity straight to my core.

"Red suits you." He leans close enough that his breath warms my ear. "Tell me, Clara—did you follow all my instructions?"

"That's none of your—"

He tightens his grip around mine, not painful but inescapable, steering me off the marble entryway toward the hall leading to the gala. The heat of his palm burns through my skin.

"Everything about you is my business now." Low. Certain. "Answer the question."

The chandeliers scatter light like shards of ice. My cheeks burn. "Yes."

He stops walking and turns slightly. "Yes... what?"

The words snag in my throat. I want to rebel, to keep a shred of dignity. "Julian—"

He narrows his eyes, the name hanging between us like a blade. "That's not who I am anymore." Quiet. Final. "Julian was the boy you knew in high school. The one who asked you to the homecoming dance. The one you laughed at. I am not that boy."

My pulse jumps. "It's a bit much, having to call you..." I fight to steady my voice. "You already have what you want. Do you really need..."

"Need? No. I don't need it. I *want* you to call me Mr. Blackwell." His voice remains low and even. "Because the boy you knew is gone. The man standing here built an empire, waited seventeen years, and orchestrated everything to bring you to me. Because when you call me Mr. Blackwell, I want you to taste that power and remember exactly what you agreed to—and who you serve." The hallway falls away. There's only him. "Now, try again."

My heart slams against my ribs. "Yes... Mr. Blackwell."

The flicker of satisfaction in those eyes makes my knees weaken. "Good girl." He brushes the back of my hand with his thumb.

The praise shouldn't affect me, but it does.

He leans down, his breath warm against my ear. "Are you wet for me yet?"

Heat bolts through me; I press my thighs together. "Julian, please, don't be vulgar."

His smile curves, dark and slow. "Julian is not how you address me." It's a gentle correction wrapped in steel. "Say it."

"Mr. Blackwell..." My voice catches. "People will hear."

"Let them." He slides his hand to my lower back, just above where the red silk plunges scandalously low. The touch is proprietary—a warning and a promise. "Though I think you're more worried about me discovering how wet you are than them discovering what you call me."

He doesn't stop walking. Doesn't look back. Just guides me toward the music, each step his, each breath mine, the name still burning on my tongue.

"Now answer me." His lips brush the shell of my ear as we step into the gilded glow of the ballroom. "Have you been wet for me all week?"

I stumble. He snakes his arm around me, catching me before I fall, pulling me flush against the hard, unyielding wall of his body. The ridge of his arousal presses into my hip—thick, insistent, demanding.

"How—" The word breaks, breathless.

"Because I know you." His voice drops, dark velvet edged with steel. "Seventeen years of studying you. I know the way your pupils blow wide when you're turned on. The way your breath hitches and your lips part. The way your thighs are pressed together right now, chasing friction you can't have. You've been aching for me every day this week, haven't you?"

"Yes." It rips out of me, raw, unwilling.

He brushes his lips against the angle of my jaw and tightens his grip on my back. "Yes... what?"

Heat scorches my face. The chandeliers blur. Trembling, I whisper, "Yes, Mr. Blackwell."

"Good girl." The words land like a caress and sting like a whip —pride and possession entwined. He slides his grip lower, almost indecent, almost claiming. "You should know that I'm hard and aching for you. I intend to take what I've been waiting for tonight."

We step into the glittering crush of society's elite—politicians, bankers, ranchers' wives dripping in jewels. Laughter and music swirl around us, but all I feel is him. His hand on my back. His voice in my ear. His cock thick against me, promising what's coming.

No one here knows I've already said yes. That I'm already burning, undone. That every step deeper into this ballroom is another step under his control.

The orchestra plays something slow and sultry. He pulls me onto the dance floor, one hand at my waist, the other holding mine. We fit together perfectly, like we were designed for this. His thigh presses between my legs with each turn, and I have to bite my lip to stay silent.

"All these people," he murmurs against my temple, "and none of them know that under this dress you're bare for me. Wet for me. Ready for me to claim what's been mine since you were seventeen."

"I was never yours—"

"No?" He spins me, pulls me back tighter, his thigh sliding higher. "Then why are your nipples hard against the silk? Why did you spend all week reading that book I sent, touching yourself, imagining submission?"

"How could you possibly—"

"Because I did the same." The confession is rough, a growl in his throat. "Seventeen years of fantasizing about you. Do you know what I thought about most?"

"I don't want to—"

"The first time you'd call me Mr. Blackwell while on your knees." He tightens his grip at my waist, guiding me through the steps, seducing me in plain sight. "The look on your face when you finally understand that submission isn't weakness—it's power. The power to give someone what they need. The power to choose surrender instead of having it taken."

"That's not what this is. I'm not choosing. You're forcing me—"

"It's exactly what this is." He pivots us toward the edge of the dance floor, into shadows cast by massive flower arrangements. "You could have found another way to save the ranch. Sold something else. Begged from someone else. But you came to me."

"Because you made sure I had no other choice."

"Because your body recognizes its master even if your mind rebels."

We're in an alcove now, hidden from view but not truly private. He slides his hand down my hip, catches the slit of my dress.

"Shall I prove it?"

"Here? People could—"

"See? Yes, some might see." He slides his fingers higher, finding the lace edge of my stocking. "They'll watch me claim what's mine." Higher still, finding bare skin. "Will I care? Not even slightly."

He ghosts his fingers over my inner thigh, and I grab his shoulders to stay standing.

"Please—"

"Please what? Stop?" He brushes his thumb so close to where I'm aching that my knees go weak. "Or don't stop?"

"I—I don't—"

"You do." His breath is a threat at my ear, his fingers a promise at my thigh. "You've known all week. Fighting it is just exhausting you."

He finally touches me, finds me soaked, and we both inhale sharply.

"Christ." His voice is dark with triumph. "You're drenched."

As he curls his fingers inside of me, pleasure surges sharp and hot, a rush of heat floods me, making submission feel inevitable and euphoric. I bury my face against his shoulder, wondering why it feels so profound so fast.

"A week of denial has you ready to break."

He slides one finger inside, curling it with devastating precision. I bite down on a moan, breath catching against his collar.

"This is what you are." He adds a second finger, pumping them in a slow rhythm that matches the music. "Wet and willing and mine. You just need permission to admit it."

"I can't—not here—"

"You can." He finds my clit, circles it with his thumb once, twice, sending shocks through me. "You will. Because your body already obeys me. Has since the moment I told you not to touch yourself last night."

His voice drops to a low, dark rasp meant only for me.

"They won't know when we slip away that I'll make you kneel for me. That you'll take my cock in your throat before I fuck you for the first time. That it won't be a fantasy for either of us anymore. It'll be real. You'll be right there—present, open, mine. No more imagining. Just you."

The words batter me like a storm. I press my thighs together on instinct, his fingers still inside me, his thumb still circling. And over the roar of blood in my ears, I hear it—his breath breaking, rough and uneven—the sound of a man stroking himself with his free hand, coming undone with the picture he's painting of me.

"I can't wait to come inside you." A groan, so low only I can hear. "To finally stop fucking my fist thinking of you. To finally have you."

And even surrounded by society's elite—under chandeliers and champagne—I'm trembling, coming apart on his fingers. Responding to his voice, his promise, and his power.

Knowing what's coming next.

CHAPTER II
THE GALA

He works me with expertise that speaks of those seventeen years of imagining. Pleasure builds, a strange warmth floods my veins, making the vulnerability feel safe, almost euphoric. My resistance melts into an unnatural calm I attribute to the alcove's shadows.

I'm climbing toward an edge I haven't reached all week. Just as I'm about to shatter, he withdraws, leaving me gasping against his shoulder.

"No." He brings his fingers to his mouth, tasting me while maintaining eye contact. "Your first orgasm belongs to me, properly. Not hidden in an alcove like we're teenagers."

"Then why—"

"Because I wanted to know if you taste the way I imagined."

Something shifts in his expression—darker as he lifts his hand between us. The scent of sex hangs heavy in the air—warm and forbidden.

He slides his fingers between his lips, slow and deliberate, and curls his tongue around them, tasting every trace.

A low sound escapes him, half growl, half sigh.

"You taste better. Like want and shame and need, all tangled together. Like surrender."

A waiter passes. Julian snags two champagne flutes and hands me one. My hand shakes as I take it.

"Why did you always say no?" The question comes suddenly, his voice different—younger somehow. "In high school. Every time I asked."

The memory surfaces sharply. Julian, at seventeen, golden and confident, backing me against my locker. "Come to the party with me. Let me take you out. Just once." And behind him, down the hall, my father picking me up early from school, looking at Julian, his face hardening.

"My father." The admission comes quietly. "He saw you that day, sophomore year. When you had me against my locker."

"I remember." His jaw tightens. "He looked at me like I was already inside you."

Heat floods my face. "That night, he sat me down. Told me about the Blackwells. How your grandfather destroyed his father's business in the '70s. How your father was doing the same to him. He made me promise to stay away from you."

"And you always were daddy's good girl." There's bitterness there, old hurt. "Even when you wanted to say yes."

"I didn't—"

"Liar." He sets down his champagne and crowds me against the wall. "Junior year. After the homecoming game. I found you under the bleachers, crying because Marcus stood you up. I gave you my jacket. We talked for two hours about everything except what we both wanted. When I leaned in to kiss you, your whole body leaned toward me. Then you remembered daddy's rules and ran."

The memory crashes over me. His letterman jacket smelled of cologne and sweat. The way the moonlight caught in those storm-gray eyes. How badly I wanted that kiss, how I touched myself that night imagining what would have happened if I'd stayed.

"That's when I decided." He continues. "If I couldn't have you then, I'd have you later. When daddy couldn't protect you anymore."

"So you destroyed him." Anger rises, mixing with arousal in a cocktail that makes me dizzy.

"He was destroying himself. Bad investments, worse decisions. I just... *accelerated* things." No apology in his voice. "And now here we are. No father to forbid it. No rules except the ones I make. No barriers between what we both want."

"I haven't said yes."

"Your body has." He leans in, breath warm against my ear. "Your pussy is dripping down your thighs. Your nipples are hard enough to cut glass. Your pupils are blown wide with need. Every cell in your body has already submitted. We're just waiting for your mind to catch up."

"Mr. Blackwell—" The title slips out unconsciously, and his whole body reacts, pressing harder against me.

"Say it again."

"Mr. Blackwell."

"Good girl. Now come with me. It's time to make this official."

He leads me through the ballroom, past faces I recognize—the bank manager who wouldn't return my calls, the lawyer who was suddenly unavailable, contractors who mysteriously couldn't work. They all watch us, knowing something is happening but not what.

"Did you pay them all off?"

"I didn't have to. They know better than to cross me. Your father learned that lesson too late."

We pass through a side door into a hallway that grows

progressively quieter, darker. My heels click on marble, then carpet, the sound swallowed by wealth and distance. He stops at a heavy wooden door and produces a key.

"Last chance to run."

"Where would I go? You've made sure I have nowhere else."

"Then I guess you'd better come inside and accept my terms."

The room beyond is all masculine luxury—dark wood, leather, and crystal decanters catching the low light. A judge's chambers or a king's study. He closes the door with finality, and turns the lock.

My cheeks burn. "We need to discuss—"

"Alternative arrangements?" He steps closer, voice dropping so only I can hear. "A payment plan? Higher interest rates? Different terms?"

"Yes. Something reasonable—"

"No." The word slices through mine, clean and final. "The terms are what they are. One year. In exchange, your ranch is saved, your debts cleared, your legacy preserved."

"A year of what, exactly?"

His smile curves, slow and lethal, like a man savoring a checkmate. "Of belonging to me. Whatever I want. Whenever I want it. However I want it." He tilts his head, a glint in those storm-gray depths. "Was the book not clear enough?"

The memory of the leather cover, the trembling pages, slams into me. "*The Story of O*."

He leans in just enough for his breath to brush my ear. "I sent it for a reason. So you'd understand the shape of what you're agreeing to."

My hands shake. I press them against the silk, trying to steady myself, but the fabric reminds me I'm already wearing his choices.

"I need to hear you say it." His voice is quiet. Absolute. "Here. Now. That you accept my terms."

"Julian—"

Something dangerous flashes across his face. "That's not what you call me."

A chill runs down my spine. "What does that mean?" My breath catches, half-fear, half-something darker.

"You'll address me properly."

I shake my head, disbelieving. "You can't be serious. That's—"

"*That* is one of my rules." He tilts my chin higher, forcing me to meet the implacable weight of that gaze. "Mr. Blackwell. Nothing else."

"Why?" The word tears out of me, equal parts protest and plea.

"Because it establishes what we are." He drags his thumb across my lower lip, slow, deliberate. "It reminds you of the bargain you made. Of the power flowing between us. You give yourself to me. This isn't about fair. This is about being mine."

My lips part, a shaky breath escaping. "I can't just—"

"You can." His voice softens, dropping to a velvet growl. "And you will. Because every time my title leaves your mouth, you'll remember what you agreed to. You'll feel it here." He presses his hand flat against my sternum, right over my racing heart. "And here." He cups his palm between my thighs, heat blooming where his touch lands.

A tremor shudders through me. My mouth shapes his name, the one I've always known him by, but the look in those eyes burns it away. My throat works, tight, then loosens on a whisper.

"Please..." My voice breaks. "Don't make me do that. It's humiliating."

He traces his thumb in a slow line over my lip, then down the side of my neck. "Doesn't matter." His tone is low, velvet, and steel all at once. "Or maybe that's the point."

He leans in, his mouth so close to my ear that each word drags a shiver down my spine. "I want you always to be aware of our bargain. Of what you're willing to do to save your land. To remind you," he tightens his grip just enough to make me gasp—"that you belong to me. Say it. Show me that you understand exactly what you're agreeing to."

A sudden wave of warmth floods me; his presence feels like gravity rather than a chain, pulling me toward him even as every instinct says *run*. My emotions sharpen, heighten, tipping from fear into something dangerously close to craving. But I shove it aside, blaming adrenaline, blaming anything but him, forcing myself to focus on the moment instead.

"I hate you for this."

"Doesn't matter how it makes you feel, only that you obey. Say it now. I won't ask again."

Heat blooms low in my belly, shame and want spiraling together until I can't tell them apart. My lips part again, breathless. "Mr. Blackwell..."

Satisfaction flashes in those eyes, a dark spark under the controlled mask. He tilts my chin higher, the pad of his thumb dragging across the pulse hammering at my throat. "Say it again."

"Again?"

"Are you already defying me? Are you so eager to lose your land for good?"

"You don't have to be an ass about this."

"I get to be whatever I want to be. That's how this works, and you do whatever I tell you."

I swallow hard as he leans in.

"And right now, I want to hear you call me Mr. Blackwell."

"Fine. Mr. Blackwell..."

"Good girl." His voice dips lower, a growl of possession. "That's how it starts. That's how you remember who you are in this room. And who I am. We are no longer equals, and it's best you accept that." He brushes his thumb over my lower lip. "You have no idea what you've given me, do you? Seventeen years of wanting. Seventeen years of watching you pretend I don't exist. And now..."

"Now what?"

"Now I have 365 days to make you pay for every single moment of denial. Do you agree to my terms?"

"Fine." A whisper.

He arches an eyebrow. "Fine?"

"I agree to your terms."

"All of them? Say it properly. Tell me exactly what you're agreeing to."

Each word feels like glass in my throat: "I agree to be yours. For one year. Whatever you want, whenever you want it, however you want it."

"And if you refuse me? Even once?"

"The deal is void."

His smile spreads slow, satisfied. "Good girl."

"Don't call me that." The phrase sends unwanted heat through me.

"You're mine now." He steps close enough that I smell cedar and smoke. "I get to call you whatever I want. That's what you agreed to." He takes my hand—firm, possessive, final. "Now, take off the dress."

CHAPTER 12
THE GALA

The command hangs between us. This is it—the moment of true choice. I could still leave. Face eviction, lose everything, but keep my pride.

I move my hands to the zipper.

"Slowly." He settles into a leather chair like a king on his throne. "I've waited seventeen years for this. I want to savor it."

The zipper whispers down. The silk puddles at my feet, leaving me in stockings, garters, heels, and nothing else. The cool air makes my nipples tighten further, and he tracks every response.

"Christ." The word escapes him. "You're more beautiful than I imagined. And I imagined you constantly. Turn around."

I do, hearing his sharp intake of breath.

"The first time I saw you," his voice is rough, "you were fourteen. First day of high school. You wore a yellow sundress and had your hair in a ponytail. You smiled at everyone except me. I knew then I was fucked."

"We barely talked—"

"Because your father already warned you. But I watched. I memorized. The way you bite your lip when you concentrate. How you twist your hair when you're nervous—like you're doing now."

I drop my hand, not realizing I'd been doing it.

"Come here."

I cross to him on unsteady legs, hyperaware of my nudity, his gaze, the contract we haven't signed but might as well have.

"On your knees."

The carpet is soft, but the angle makes me vulnerable, looking up at him, neck exposed, everything exposed.

"Do you know what I thought about most?" He slides his hand into my hair, not pulling, just holding. "This moment. You kneeling for me, understanding that submission to someone who truly wants you—needs you—isn't degrading. It's powerful."

"How is this powerful? I'm on my knees."

"Because you chose to kneel." He traces my jaw. "Because you're giving me something I've craved for nearly two decades. Because your surrender has the power to bring me to my knees once you learn how to wield it."

"I don't understand—"

"You will. Over the year, you'll learn exactly how much power you have over me. But tonight..." His other hand works his belt, the sound loud in the quiet room. "Tonight, you learn what it means to be mine."

He frees himself, and my breath catches. He's bigger than I expected, harder, already glistening with need—seventeen years of wanting made manifest.

He trails his hand down my throat, fingertips barely grazing skin. "Your body already knows who it belongs to." His voice is low and certain. "Even if your mind is still fighting."

"I don't belong to anyone—"

A dark, knowing laugh. "Lie to yourself if you need to, but your body?" He rests his palm against my racing pulse. "Your body tells the truth. Tell me what you're thinking right now."

It's not a request.

"I hate you."

"No, you don't. Try again."

"I hate that I'm here."

"Closer, but still a lie." He hovers an inch from my mouth. "The truth, Clara."

The words tear from somewhere deep: "I hate that part of me wants this."

"There it is." Satisfaction colors his voice. "Was that so hard?"

"You're enjoying this. My humiliation."

"I'm enjoying your honesty." He rests his hand over my racing heart. "Do you know what I'm going to enjoy even more?"

I don't answer. Can't.

"Every wall you've built, I'm going to tear down. Every defense, every carefully controlled response—gone. By the end of this year, you won't remember why you fought this so hard."

"Never."

"We'll see." He leans closer, cedar and smoke and danger filling my lungs. "Do you want to know what I thought about? All those years?"

"No."

"Liar." He brushes his mouth against my ear. "I thought about this moment. Having you at my mercy. Making you admit what your body already knows—that you've wanted this as long as I have."

"That's not—"

"Your pulse says otherwise. Your breathing says otherwise." He spans his hand across my waist, thumb stroking through the silk. "The way you're trembling says otherwise."

"I'm trembling because I'm angry."

"You're trembling because you're fighting yourself, not me." He pulls back to study my face. "And you're going to lose that fight. Tonight. Tomorrow. Every night for the next year until fighting becomes surrender, and surrender becomes craving."

"You're so sure of yourself."

"I'm sure of this." He traces my cheekbone with unexpected gentleness. "I'm sure that you wouldn't be here if part of you didn't want to be."

"I had no choice—"

"You needed an excuse." He pins me as effectively with his gaze. "You needed me to choose for you. To take control so you didn't have to admit you wanted to give it up."

The truth of it steals my breath.

"That's what I'm going to give you. For one year, you don't have to be in control. You don't have to make decisions or maintain walls or pretend you don't feel anything." He hovers his mouth over mine, not quite touching. "All you have to do is surrender."

"I can't—"

"You already have. The moment you put on my dress, you surrendered." He frames my face, thumbs stroking my cheeks. "Now comes the interesting part."

"Which is?"

"Teaching you to love it."

Satisfaction flickers across his face, sharp and predatory. He closes the last inch between us, and his mouth descends—not soft, not coaxing, but claiming. It's a kiss that devours.

Possession in its purest form.

And I don't hate it.

He crushes his lips to mine, sweeping his tongue in to taste, to take, to own. My head tilts under his hand as he sweeps deeper, claiming everything I tried to hold back. My resistance frays, and I lean in to him, every nerve betraying me.

When he finally pulls back, I'm gasping, lips swollen, pulse hammering against my throat. He trails his fingers down the side of my neck, a languid stroke that sends shivers over my collarbone. Then, his fingers drift lower, brushing the upper swell of my breast.

"Open your mouth."

I part my lips, and he traces them with the head of his cock, painting them with his precum. The taste is salty, musky, and male.

"Wider."

I obey, and he slides in slowly, letting me adjust, watching my face intently. "That's it. Take me in. Show me that mouth I've been dreaming about."

He goes deeper, not forcing, but insistent, until I have to breathe through my nose and relax my throat. He tightens his grip in my hair.

And I *like* it. I *love* it. There's just something about *everything* that I love, and I hate that I do. I hate that he's right. I crave whatever *this* is.

"Look at me." A command. "I want to see your eyes when you realize this is where you belong."

I meet that gaze as he starts to move, shallow thrusts that gradually deepen. His control is fraying—I can see it in the tension of his jaw and the roughness of his breathing.

"Seventeen fucking years. Do you know how many women I fucked, imagining they were you? How many times I came with your name on my tongue?"

He pulls out suddenly, hauling me to my feet, spinning me to face the wall. He's everywhere—rough, desperate, seventeen years of patience finally snapping.

"Hands on the wall."

I brace myself as he kicks my legs wider, sliding his fingers through my wetness.

"You're dripping." A growl. "You love this. Being commanded. Being claimed."

"I—"

Heat lances through me at the warning, equal parts fear and want. My hips twitch into his hand without my permission. Then he slides a second finger inside me, slow and inexorable. He curls his fingers, finding that spot inside me, stroking it with maddening precision.

A whimper escapes before I can stop it. My knees threaten to buckle.

He licks up the column of my throat; his teeth catch my earlobe. He presses his fingers deeper, thumb relentless. I gasp, hips jerking against his palm.

The pressure builds to breaking. He's everywhere—mouth at my neck, fingers inside me, palm grinding me against the wall until I'm trembling.

"Are you going to come for me?" His voice is rough velvet against my ear. "Here, against this wall? Don't lie."

"Please—" I can barely shape the words.

"Please, what?" He presses his thumb harder, relentless. "Stop?" Another curl of his fingers. "Or don't stop?"

"Don't stop." The words come out like a sob. I'm past caring about pride.

"Then come. Now."

The command shatters something inside me, pleasure rips through every nerve as he swallows my cry with another crushing kiss, taking everything—my breath, my control, my pretense that this is just business.

He slips his fingers free, and I bite back a whimper at the loss.

My forehead lowers to the wall, cool wood against my heated skin, and I tremble, half-afraid, half-desperate. There's no coming back from this.

"I've waited seventeen years for this." His voice is a low growl, rough with need. "Seventeen years of being hard for you. Of watching you walk away."

He spans his palm across my lower back, warm and implacable, holding me in place.

"Tonight, you don't walk away." His breath is at my ear, harsh and shaking. "Tonight, I make you mine."

The first press of him steals my breath—hot, thick, impossible. He pushes in slowly, inch by devastating inch, until I'm gasping against the wall, nails scraping for purchase.

"God..." The sound that rips from his throat is low and wrecked. "Better than I dreamed. So tight. So perfect."

He begins to move—long, deliberate strokes that build from controlled to demanding. He slides his free hand up my spine to the back of my neck, fingers splaying until they curl around my throat. Not squeezing, just holding.

Claiming.

My pulse hammers under his hand; I'm pinned, tethered to him, every thrust pressing me harder into the wall. Fear flickers, swallowed by a rush of molten heat. My hips roll back onto him before I can stop myself.

"Say it." His voice snaps like a whip. "Say you're mine."

"I'm—" The words break on a moan as his hips grind into me.

"Say it." He tightens his grip just enough to make my breath catch.

"I'm yours."

We both groan—him finally inside me, me finally filled by him.

"Mine." He pulls out and slams back in. "Say it."

"Yours." The word comes out in a gasp.

"What's my name?"

"Jul—Mr. Blackwell."

"Good girl." He sets a punishing pace, one hand on my hip, the other sliding around to find my clit. "This is what you've been missing. What we've both been missing. Fighting it was pointless."

He works my clit as he fucks me, and the dual sensation is overwhelming. I'm climbing fast toward an orgasm that feels like it might destroy me.

"That's it. Let go. Show me how you fall apart."

"I can't—it's too much—"

"You can. You will. Because I command it." His voice drops to that tone that brooks no argument. "Come for me. Now."

The orgasm hits like a lightning strike, violent and absolute. I scream into my arm as my body convulses around him, the intensity almost painful.

He follows immediately, grinding deep as he comes with a guttural groan, flooding me with heat. "Fuck, Clara. Fuck."

We stay frozen for a moment, both panting, bodies locked together. Then he withdraws slowly, turns me to face him. He traces my swollen lips.

"That is just the beginning." A promise. "We have a year. And I plan to use every minute of it."

He helps me dress with surprising gentleness, but doesn't let me clean up. "You'll wear me the rest of the night." His voice is low. Proprietary. "My cum dripping down your thighs while you smile at my guests. A secret between us."

"That's—"

"—what you agreed to." He straightens his clothes, looking perfectly composed while I'm thoroughly debauched. "Complete submission. Starting with this."

He reveals a box and opens it with reverence. Inside, nestled in black velvet, lies a diamond choker. At first glance, it's exquisite—delicate white fire winking from every facet, the kind of piece worn with couture gowns and cameras flashing. To the world, it's elegance. Refinement. Beauty.

But when Julian lifts it from the velvet and turns it, the underside reveals its truth. A band of platinum against the skin, engraved letters so sharp and deep I can almost feel them without touching: *I belong to Mr. Blackwell.*

My breath stutters.

He holds it up between us, diamonds catching the light, the hidden words gleaming darker in the shadows.

"To them," his voice is a low rasp, "it's an ornament. Something beautiful around your throat. To us? It's a truth no one else can see."

I hate how it makes my pulse spike, how the words seem to sear themselves into me before he's even fastened it.

"Why?"

His smile is slow, deliberate, cruel. "To remind you every second of every day who you belong to. Every time it brushes your skin, you'll feel the letters cut into you. You'll remember."

My throat is dry. "Is that a lock?"

"It is." He lifts the clasp, revealing the small, intricate mechanism. "And only I have the key." He grazes his thumb across the back of my neck, possessive. "Because choice matters. Once you submit, once you let me lock this on you, you can't undo it. Not until I say so."

"Why now? You already have me for the year." A whisper.

"Because a contract is paper. This—" he presses the choker against my throat, cool weight promising heat—"this is flesh. This is truth. We've shifted, Clara. We're no longer negotiating. Tonight, you stop being a debtor. Tonight you become mine."

The lock clicks shut. The sound is soft, but it detonates inside me. The weight settles, diamonds glittering for the world, the words etched against my skin for me alone.

And when his mouth claims mine, I know I'll never be free. The collar's weight settles like a drugged haze, my mind swimming with unnatural contentment, memories of the night blurring at the edges. I dismiss it as the intensity, but a nagging unease stirs.

We return to the ballroom, and I understand what he meant. Every step reminds me of what just happened, what I've agreed to. His hand at my back is possessive, claiming, and everyone who looks at us knows something has shifted.

"Three months from now," he murmurs during a slow dance, "you'll beg for this. In six months, you'll crave it as much as air. By the end of the year, you won't be able to imagine life without me controlling you."

"You're very sure of yourself."

"I'm sure of us." He tightens his grip on my waist. "I've had seventeen years to be certain. You've had a week. But you'll catch up."

The terrible thing is, he might be right. My fingers go to the choker at my neck.

I'm already catching up.

CHAPTER 13
THE GALA

The rest of the gala passes in a haze. Julian parades me through conversations with people who matter, his hand never leaving my body—my back, my waist, my neck. Each touch a claim. Each gesture a reminder that I've agreed to this, even if we haven't signed anything.

"Judge Morrison." Julian greets an older man with silver hair and calculating eyes. "You know Clara Hayes."

"Ms. Hayes." The judge's gaze flickers over me, noting the dress, Julian's possessive stance, and the way I'm standing slightly behind him. "I heard about your father. My condolences."

"Thank you." I barely manage the words.

"The judge is an old friend," Julian explains, though his tone suggests *friend* might not be accurate. "He's agreed to witness our contract signing. Make it official."

My stomach drops. "Now?"

"Why wait?" He strokes his thumb across the nape of my neck. "Unless you're having second thoughts?"

The judge watches with interest. This is a test. Backing out now, in front of a witness, would be worse than never agreeing at all.

"No second thoughts, Mr. Blackwell."

The title makes both men react—the judge's eyebrows rising, Julian's hand tightening possessively.

"Good girl," Julian murmurs, just loud enough for me to hear. "Judge, we'll meet you in an hour."

After the judge leaves, Julian leads me to a quiet corner. "You're doing beautifully."

"I feel like everyone knows."

"Knows what? That you're mine?" He brushes his lips against my ear. "Good. Let them know. Let them see that Clara Hayes belongs to Julian Blackwell now."

"Only for a year."

His smile is dark. "We'll see."

The hour passes too quickly. Soon, we're back in the private room, but now there's a desk with papers spread across it, and the judge is waiting.

"The terms are straightforward." The judge's tone suggests he finds them anything but. "One year of... personal service in exchange for the ranch's return and financial compensation."

I pick up the contract and scan the legalese, which boils down to my complete surrender. "This says I'll reside at Mr. Blackwell's primary residence."

"You'll live where I live, sleep where I sleep,"—Julian confirms.

"And this clause about 'complete obedience in all matters'?"

"Means exactly what it says." Julian's voice brooks no argument. "You obey my commands, follow my rules, submit to my will. In return, your ranch is safe and profitable."

"And if I refuse a command?"

"Then you're in breach of contract, and you lose everything."

The judge shifts uncomfortably. "Ms. Hayes, I should remind you that you're under no obligation—"

"She knows her options." Julian cuts him off. "Don't you, Clara?"

I do. Submit or lose everything. Pride or land. Freedom or heritage.

I pick up the pen.

"Wait." Julian moves behind me, his chest against my back, his hand covering mine on the pen. "I want you to understand exactly what you're signing. No confusion, no claims of coercion later."

"I understand—"

"Do you?" He slides his free hand to my throat, fingers resting against my pulse. "You're agreeing to call me Mr. Blackwell always. To wear what I choose or nothing at all. To kneel when commanded. To come only with permission. To be used however I see fit, whenever I desire."

Each word makes me wetter, my body betraying me even as my mind screams warnings.

"Say yes if you understand."

"Yes, Mr. Blackwell."

"Sign it."

I move my hand under his, signature flowing across the page that signs away my freedom. Julian signs below, his name bold and confident. The judge witnesses, looking like he's attending a deal with the devil.

Which he is.

"It's done," the judge says. "The contract is binding for one year from today."

"Thank you, Judge Morrison. That will be all."

The dismissal is clear. The judge leaves quickly, apparently used to what he witnessed.

As soon as the door closes, Julian spins me to face him. "Mine now. Legally. Bindingly. Completely."

"For a year—"

He kisses me, cutting off my correction. But this kiss—God, this kiss is nothing like before. He slides his hand into my hair, gripping just hard enough to angle my head where he wants it, and the dominance in that simple gesture makes my knees weak.

This is possession. This is claiming, and as his kiss deepens, a rush of security floods me, unnatural in its suddenness, making the surrender feel right, inevitable, though part of me wonders at the ease of it.

This is seventeen years of want condensed into a single, devastating moment.

He bands his other arm around my waist, pulling me against him until there's no space between us, and I can't help the sound that escapes me—part protest, part surrender. He swallows it like he's entitled to it, like every breath I take belongs to him now.

And the worst part—or maybe the best part, I can't tell anymore—is how my body remembers. Remembers being seventeen and watching him command a room. Remembers the dreams I tried so hard to forget, where his hands held me exactly like this, where I gave him exactly this power over me.

I'm kissing him back before I can stop myself, my fingers curling into his suit jacket, and I taste his triumph in the curve of his mouth against mine. He knows. He's always known what I wanted, even when I was denying it to myself.

When he finally pulls back, I'm gasping, lips swollen, my carefully constructed walls in ruins at his feet. He traces my bottom lip, proprietary and tender at once.

"A year." His voice is rough. "More than enough time to make you admit you've wanted this all along. When I said you belong to me, I meant it. Tonight, you learn what that means."

I back up a step, bumping into the wall.

"I won't force you." Calm. Deadly. "You're free to walk out. Walk away and lose the land. But if you stay, you'll obey. All of it. No half-measures."

He holds my gaze—dark, knowing, patient, like he can see straight through to that locked room in my soul where I've hidden seventeen years of want.

Everything inside me swirls—fear, anger, the memory of his hands and mouth, the heat that caught me off guard. But underneath all of it, something else unfurls.

Something dangerous.

Something that tastes like those nights I spent awake at seventeen, imagining what it would be like if my father hadn't interfered. If I'd been the one Julian pulled under the bleachers, pressed against the wall, claimed with that same commanding certainty he wears now like a second skin.

He's not that boy anymore. This Julian—Mr. Blackwell—is something else entirely.

Powerful. Ruthless.

The kind of man who bends the world to his will with a look, a word. And he's offering me the perfect excuse. I can tell myself he's forcing me. I can pretend I have no choice. I can let him take what I've always wanted to give and never admit the truth—that this is every dark fantasy I've buried come to life.

He's a devil, but a devil who tells the truth. And the truth is, I'm not moving. Can't move. Won't move. Because I need to know what comes next. What he'll demand. What he'll make me become.

As we step back into the ballroom, sudden fatigue crashes through me, my limbs heavy, the high of submission fading into an odd emptiness I blame on the evening's intensity.

He settles his palm against the small of my back, firm and guiding.

Music swells; a string quartet slides into something slow and shimmering. Laughter ripples through the crowd. The ballroom smells of polished wood, perfume, and money.

Julian's hand stays at the small of my back, the weight of it unyielding, a leash made of heat and command. My skin is still damp beneath the silk of the dress, his come leaking between my legs.

No one else knows—but I do.

A hidden brand.

"Head up," he murmurs. "Shoulders back. Smile."

My spine stiffens. His voice is soft enough for only me, but it's not a request. I force my lips into something polite, brittle. I press my thighs together with every step; each movement drags the silk against my nipples, makes me tremble.

Julian steers me through the crowd as if we're a single body. He dictates our pace with the subtle pressure of his palm—slowing to greet an oil magnate, tightening when he wants me to pivot. My own will dissolves into the choreography of his.

"Look at me when I introduce you. Then look at them and smile. That's all you have to do."

His gaze drops to my mouth, then back up. The briefest flash of a smirk crosses his face—an unspoken reminder of where that mouth just was.

I do as I'm told. I look, I smile, I nod. Every "pleasure to meet you" tastes like iron. My pulse hammers at my throat. No one notices that my fingers dig into my clutch until the knuckles whiten. No one notices how hard it is to breathe.

"Beautiful, " Julian murmurs as we drift away from another cluster of guests. He strokes his thumb along the base of my spine, a caress disguised as guidance. "Do you know how long I've wanted this? To walk into a room with you on my arm, everyone knowing you're mine?"

"I'm not—" My voice snags.

"You are." He cuts me off gently, his smile a weapon for the room but a blade for me. "Seventeen years ago, I asked you to the homecoming dance, but your father interfered. I had it all planned—I wanted to parade you in front of everyone, so they'd all see you were with me. Then I was going take you under the bleachers, mark you in every way that mattered, and afterward..." His breath warms my ear. "Afterward, I'd walk you back into that gym, your hand in mine, both of us knowing what we'd done while everyone else danced, oblivious."

He tightens his fingers possessively on my waist. "This isn't homecoming. It's better. Because now, when I take you home after this, when I do everything I've imagined for seventeen years, it won't be for just one night. You're mine for a year. And everyone in this room can see it, even if they don't know you're already shaking and wet under that dress, doing exactly what I tell you."

Heat climbs my neck. I swallow hard. The humiliation coils tighter with every step. But so does the ache. My body hums, slick and restless, denied release.

Julian leans closer, ~~his~~ lips almost brushing my ear. "Smile wider." A whisper. "They think it's charming. Only I know it's because you're desperate to come again."

I can't stop the shiver that ripples through me.

"Good girl," he says softly. "We'll leave after the last toast. Then you'll learn what kneeling really means."

He straightens, mask of perfect host back in place, and raises his champagne glass to a passing guest. I stand beside him, glittering under the chandeliers, a porcelain doll in a red dress. Inside, my pulse is a drum. My skin is a fuse. My body is a storm he's holding by the throat.

And no one—not a single soul—can tell.

94

CHAPTER 14
THE GALA

THE CAR RIDE TO JULIAN'S ESTATE TAKES THIRTY MINUTES THAT FEEL LIKE hours. Julian's hand rests possessively on my thigh, fingers drawing lazy circles through the silk. Every touch reminds me of what I've signed, what I've agreed to, what's about to happen.

"You're thinking too loudly." He doesn't look at me.

"How can you possibly—"

"Seventeen years. I know every expression, every tell." He strokes his thumb higher. "Right now you're warring between anger at what I've done and curiosity about what comes next."

"I'm not curious. I'm trapped."

"Liar." He turns to face me fully, storm-gray eyes seeing straight through me. "You're wondering if I can really make you crave submission. If the book I sent you was a promise or a threat. If the wetness between your thighs means you've already lost."

Heat floods my face. "That's just biology. Physical response. It doesn't mean—"

"It means everything." He slides his hand higher, fingers ghosting over where I'm embarrassingly wet. "Your body recognizes what your mind fights. You were destined for this. Made for me."

"You destroyed my father for this." The anger feels safer than the arousal. "You planned his downfall to get me in your bed. I'm not going to forget that."

"Your father kept us apart when we should've been together from the start, and it's not just my bed." His voice darkens. "You're in my life now. Under my control. My possession. And yes, I orchestrated everything. Your father's loans being called in. The buyers who mysteriously backed out. Every contractor who suddenly couldn't work for him."

"Why?" The word comes out broken. "Why go to such lengths?"

"Because you were always supposed to be mine." Real emotion bleeds through his control. "Senior year, when I had everything—captain of the team, acceptance to Harvard, my father's empire waiting—the only thing I wanted was you. And you laughed at me."

"I didn't laugh—"

"October fifteenth, senior year." His recall is precise, painful. "In front of the entire cafeteria. Down on one knee like an idiot, holding those yellow roses because I noticed you drawing them in your notebook. You looked at me, looked at everyone watching, and laughed."

The memory rises, jagged and hot, but from my side, it looks nothing like the story he's telling. I can still see the cafeteria floor, the glossy linoleum, the smell of fried food, and teenage sweat. His knees on the tile. The roses trembling in his hand. Everyone holding their breath. My heart pounding so hard it hurt.

I wanted to say yes so badly I could taste it—yes to him, yes to the roses, yes to the boy who made my stomach flip every time he looked at me, but that morning, my father's voice had been in my ear, venomous and absolute: *Stay away from the Blackwell boy. His father will destroy us if you don't.*

So when Julian looked up at me with those storm-gray eyes, all I had left was the brittle laugh I'd been taught to use as armor. It came out instead of tears. A shield instead of a confession.

"I wanted to say yes." The ache of it curls under my ribs even now. "I wanted you so badly it felt like dying. I'm sorry." The words scrape my throat raw. "It wasn't meant to be cruel. It was the only way I knew to keep from falling apart in front of everyone."

"But it was." He tightens his grip on my thigh. "The golden boy brought low by the ranch girl. Do you know what that did to my reputation? My father called me weak. Said a real Blackwell would have taken what he wanted."

"So you waited seventeen years to take it?"

"I waited until I could take you perfectly." The car pulls through gates that close behind us like a trap. "Until you had no choice but to come to me. To need me. To beg me for salvation that only I could provide."

The house rises from the darkness—all glass and stone and modern angles that speak of money and power. Nothing like my warm, worn ranch house. This is a fortress. A beautiful cage.

He helps me out of the car, his hand at my lower back as he guides me inside. The foyer soars three stories, all marble and crystal, designed to intimidate.

"Welcome home." The words carry weight.

"This isn't my home—"

"It is for the next year." He turns me to face him, his hands framing my face. "Every room. Every surface. Every inch of space will know you before we're done."

Fear and heat twist in my stomach. "You can't really mean to—"

"I mean to do everything." He traces my lower lip. "Everything I've imagined. Everything you've feared. Everything your body is already begging for despite your protests."

He leads me upstairs, past closed doors that could hide anything, to a master suite that's larger than my entire house. He pauses to pour a glass of red wine from a decanter on the sideboard.

"Drink. You'll need it."

CHAPTER 15
THE GALA

THE WINE IS RICH AND VELVETY, WARMING ME FROM WITHIN WITH AN ease that feels too quick, loosening my fears unnaturally as we enter the suite.

The bed dominates—massive, four-posted, with rails that could hold restraints. I shiver.

"Cold?" He knows I'm not.

"Julian—"

He cracks his hand across my ass, sharp even through the dress. "What did you call me?"

"Mr. Blackwell. I'm sorry, I keep forgetting—"

"You'll learn." He turns me to face a mirror that runs the length of the wall. "Watch yourself. Watch what you become when I touch you."

He stands behind me, sliding his hands up my sides, cupping my breasts through the silk. I see everything—my flushed face, hard nipples visible through the dress, the way I arch into his touch despite my mind's protests.

"You're already different from how you were this morning."

He observes, his fingers finding my nipples, pinching just hard enough to make me gasp. "Already responding to my commands. Your body is a faster learner than your mind."

"This is just sex." Even as I protest, heat pools between my thighs. "Physical response. Biology. It doesn't mean anything."

"You keep saying that, but I disagree." He slides the dress straps off my shoulders, lets the silk puddle at my feet. I'm naked except for stockings and heels, exposed in the harsh light. "Look at yourself. Really look."

I see a woman I don't recognize. Lips swollen from his kisses. Beard burn on my throat. Thighs glistening with arousal. But it's my eyes that shock me most—pupils blown wide, hunger visible even to me.

"This is who you are when you stop fighting." The words land against my ear. "Beautiful. Needy. Mine."

He spins me around, his mouth claiming mine with brutal intensity. I moan, melting into his, hands gripping his shoulders, nails digging into flesh. The sound that rumbles from his chest is pure predator.

He breaks away, trailing his mouth down my neck—teeth scraping, marking. I arch involuntarily as he moves lower, finding my nipple. The combination of bite and soothe makes me gasp. He gives the other breast the same treatment while I writhe beneath him, fingers tangled in his hair.

Lower still, his mouth maps a path down my stomach. He kneels before me, gripping my hips, breath hot against my sex. When he meets my gaze, the hunger there steals my breath.

"Remember." Low. Commanding. "You don't come until I allow it."

He circles my clit, thrusting his fingers deep while pressing his thumb just right, building the pressure until my muscles clench and I teeter on the edge. But every time I peak, he withdraws, leaving me trembling, my core throbbing with unfulfilled ache.

What follows is exquisite torture, each denial building a pleasure. Something almost chemical floods through me—my body enduring the edge with unnatural resilience. I attribute it to his expertise.

He edges me repeatedly, bringing me to the precipice of orgasm only to deny me, until I'm sobbing, begging, promising anything if he'll just let me come.

"Please, Mr. Blackwell—"

"Earn it." He stands, towering over me. "Show me how badly you want it."

His mouth descends, and I nearly come apart immediately. Just as I reach the edge, he stops. Pulls back. Watches me with dark satisfaction.

He spins me around, bends me over the bed. I hear his belt, his zipper. The head of his cock teases my entrance, but he doesn't enter. I push back against him, and he pulls away with a dark chuckle.

"Beg properly."

"Please." A sob. "Please, Mr. Blackwell, I need—"

He slams into me in one brutal thrust that steals my breath. But he doesn't move. Holds himself perfectly still while I clench around him, desperate for friction.

Pain flares at the sudden fullness—it's too much, too fast after the edging. He wraps his hand around my throat, not squeezing hard, but enough to remind me of his control, the pressure building my pulse to a frantic beat.

As I coil tighter, chasing the release he's withheld, he slows, pulling back until only the tip teases me.

"Not yet." A growl. He delivers a sharp slap to my ass that

makes me yelp, the sting pushing me closer to the brink before he stops again.

He repeats it—thrusting deep, building me up, then denying, his fingers digging into my hips hard enough to bruise. The pain keeps me grounded, sharp and insistent, heightening every denied wave until tears stream down my face.

"Please." My voice breaks. "I need to come."

"That is how I felt." Against my ear, the heat of his breath makes me shiver. "Every day in high school. Watching you. Wanting you. Hard and aching with no relief. You made me suffer. Now it's your turn." His words hit like blows, twisting the knife of our past while his cock drives deeper.

He pulls almost all the way out, then drives back in slowly. Torturously. Each thrust is calculated to keep me on edge but never push me over. His control is absolute.

He pulls out, flips me to my back. The pain of his grip on my wrists—pinned above my head—blends with the ecstasy building again.

He leans over me, his breath hot against my ear, his pace unrelenting, but still controlled.

"You have no idea how long I've waited for this. Back in high school, I fantasized about you every fucking night. You'd walk by in those tight jeans, that ponytail swinging, and I'd be hard under my desk, imagining bending you over the bleachers after practice, fucking you until you screamed my name instead of laughing it off. The library stacks—pushing you against the bookshelves, your skirt hiked up, taking you right there while everyone else studied. The back of my truck at a bonfire party, spreading you out under the stars, claiming what your father tried to keep from me."

"I didn't know."

His pace increases slightly, but still not enough. Not nearly enough.

"I imagined you on your knees in the parking lot, my cock filling your mouth. Bent over in the gym. Spread out in the football field under the lights. Every fantasy starred you, and I had to settle for pale substitutes. Do you know how many girls I fucked, pretending they were you?"

His voice is rough. "In the locker room after practice, thinking of you. In my car after seeing you at your locker. In empty classrooms, imagining it was you bent over the desk. They were tight, willing, but never you. I had to grab them rough and fast, because the need you built in me was too damn great. But now? Now I have you. And I'll make you pay for every denied fantasy." He punctuates each confession with a thrust that makes me whimper.

"Please, please, I can't—please let me come." I'm sobbing now, my body wound so tight I might shatter.

"Not until I decide you've earned it."

He fucks me harder, his control slipping, but still he won't let me come. Every time I get close, he changes angle or speed, keeping me suspended in exquisite agony.

"Do you understand now?" A demand. "Do you understand what you did to me?"

"Yes. Yes, I understand. I'm sorry, please—"

He bites down on my shoulder, and the pain peaks hard enough to draw a gasp that borders on a scream.

"Come." A command, and my body obeys instantly.

I come so violently my vision blurs, stars exploding behind my eyelids, my walls clenching around him in spasms that milk every drop from him. He follows with a guttural groan, filling me as my body convulses, the mix of agony and bliss leaving me shattered.

When I can breathe again, his expression is fierce and possessive. "I can't believe you're finally mine."

I want to argue, but he's already pulling me to the bathroom. He starts the shower. Under the hot spray, he washes me with surprising gentleness before taking me again—this time allowing my pleasure, praising each response, and rewarding my submission.

By the time he carries me back to bed, I've lost count of how many times he's claimed me. He takes me once more in the soft sheets, drawing out my pleasure until I'm boneless and sated. His mouth finds that spot on my neck that makes rational thought impossible, his dominance sealing the moment like a brand.

The afterglow wraps me in a hazy contentment, memories of the night's events fading at the edges, leaving only a satiated warmth that I don't question.

CHAPTER 16
DAY 1

I wake to sunlight and soreness. Every muscle aches, compounded by a lingering fatigue that weighs down my eyelids, making them bounce between open and closed. It's a crash from last night's intensity I blame on lack of sleep, though it feels deeper, more drugged.

My throat is raw from screaming—his name, his title, pleas for more and less, and everything between. The bed beside me is empty but still warm, and the smell of coffee brewing somewhere in the house drifts on the air.

I stretch carefully, cataloging the pleasant soreness throughout my body. Evidence of everything that happened. Everything I agreed to.

Everything I'm terrified I might actually want.

"Awake?"

Julian stands in the doorway, already dressed. He looks perfectly composed while I'm thoroughly debauched, marked by his mouth and hands and his ownership.

"How do you feel?" It's not really a question—he can see the bruises on my thighs, the bite marks on my shoulders. Evidence of a night that redefined everything I thought I knew about myself.

"I hate you." The words come out hoarse.

"No, you don't." He crosses to the bed, sits on the edge, and traces a particularly dark mark on my hip. "You hate that I was right. That your body craves submission. That you came harder from being commanded than from any lovemaking in your past."

"It was just—"

"If you say 'just sex' one more time, I'll prove otherwise." Something glitters in those eyes. Promise. "Last night was educational. You learned what your body is capable of when you stop fighting. How many times did you come? Six? Seven?"

Eight, but I won't give him the satisfaction.

"Today, you learn the rules of your new life." He stands, all business. "Shower. Dress in what I've left out. Breakfast in thirty minutes."

"I need to check on the ranch—"

"No."

"But the animals—"

"Are being tended by the crew I hired." His tone brooks no argument. "Your only responsibility for the next year is to me."

He's at the door when I find my voice. "It won't work. You can't make me want this."

He turns, smiles that dark smile that makes my stomach flip. "I already have. Your body sang for me last night. Begged. Pleaded. Came apart over and over at my command."

"That's different from—"

"From what? Emotional submission? Psychological need?" He leans against the doorframe. "Give me a month. In a month, you'll crave my control as much as the air you breathe. In two months, you'll kneel without being told. After three months, you'll forget why you ever fought this."

"Never."

"We'll see." He taps his watch. "Twenty-eight minutes now. Don't be late. Tardiness has consequences."

After he leaves, I lie in his bed—my bed now, technically—and catalog the damage. Not just physical marks but something deeper. The way my body heats, remembering his commands. The way "Mr. Blackwell" feels more natural on my tongue than his first name. The way disappointment mingles with relief at waking alone.

What scares me most isn't what he did to me last night.

It's how much I want him to do it again.

The shower is marble and glass, with more settings than my ranch has rooms. I stand under water hot enough to burn, trying to wash away the feeling of his hands, his mouth, his complete possession.

But the marks remain.

Evidence of what I've become: Julian Blackwell's property.

The clothes he's chosen are a revelation. Not the jeans and flannel I prefer, but not the overt sexuality I expected either. A simple sundress in soft blue, modest enough for the day but clearly expensive. Flats instead of heels—a small mercy. No panties.

I find him in a dining room that overlooks the valley, morning light making everything golden. He's reading something on his tablet, coffee steaming beside him. A place is set next to him—not across. Beside. Close enough to touch.

"Sit."

I do, hyperaware of his presence, his scent, the way he tracks my movements.

"Eat."

The breakfast is simple but perfect—eggs, fruit, and toast. Things I might have chosen myself if I still had choices. He doesn't speak as I eat, but his hand lands on my thigh under the table, possessive and casual.

"Today you learn the house rules. Where you can go. What you can do. How to behave."

"I'm not a child who needs rules—"

"You're mine, which means you follow my rules." He tightens his fingers slightly. "Rule one: You address me as Mr. Blackwell. Always. The only exception is if we're in public and the situation demands otherwise, but even then, your tone will remain respectful."

"For a year—"

"Rule two: You don't speak of this as temporary. For the next year, this is your life. Your reality. Mentioning the end date constantly only makes you miserable."

"You can't control what I think—"

"Rule three: Complete honesty. You don't lie to me about anything. What you feel, what you want, what you hate. I want your truth, even when it burns."

"Then here's the truth—I think you're a controlling bastard who—"

"Who made you come eight times last night." He slides his hand higher on my thigh. "Yes, I counted. Your body is very honest even if your mouth isn't."

Heat floods my face. "That doesn't mean—"

"Rule four: You wear what I choose. Every day, I'll select your clothes. Sometimes modest, like today. Sometimes... not."

"I won't—"

"You will." His voice carries that implacable certainty that makes my stomach flip. "Rule five: You come only with permission. Your pleasure belongs to me now."

The words should terrify me, but a peculiar serenity settles, resistance dulling like fog, my mind swimming slightly as if I've drunk something soothing I can't recall.

"That's impossible. You can't control—"

"I already have. Last night, how many times did you beg? 'Please, Mr. Blackwell, please let me come.'" His imitation of my desperate voice makes me want to disappear. "Your body already knows who owns its pleasure."

He continues to list rules—about privacy (I have none), about punishments (swift and memorable), and about the West Wing (off-limits without him). Each one another bar in my cage, another reminder of what I've signed away.

"Questions?" He asks when he's done.

"What about my life? My friends? The ranch? What about Scout?"

"Your life is here. Your friends can visit with my permission, but only after the third month. The ranch is being managed. Scout can live with us." He pulls me up with him. "Your only concern for the next year is me. My pleasure. My satisfaction. My complete ownership of you."

"You can't really expect—"

He silences me with a kiss that's all dominance and control. When he pulls back, I'm gasping, my body already betraying me by wanting more.

"I expect everything, and you'll give it to me. Maybe fighting at first, but eventually, you'll be willing, eager, and desperate to do so."

"Never."

His smile is knowing, confident. "You're already halfway there. Your body surrendered last night. Your mind is following, even if you don't see it yet. Fighting me is just exhausting you."

He steps back, checks his watch. "I have business calls this morning. You'll stay in the library—there's a selection of books you might find... educational. We'll have lunch at noon, then I'll show you the West Wing."

"The forbidden wing?" I can't keep the sarcasm out of my voice.

"The wing where you'll spend considerable time learning exactly what submission means."

The words stir an odd craving, a heightened anticipation, my pulse races as if already under his spell.

Something darkens in his expression. "Last night was just an introduction. Your real education starts today."

Fear and anticipation war in my chest. "What kind of education?"

"The kind that will have you begging to call me Master by month's end."

"I'll never—"

"You will." He heads for the door, pauses. "Oh, and Clara? That wetness between your thighs right now? That's your body telling the truth your mouth won't speak. You want this. You want me. You want to know how deep this rabbit hole goes."

He leaves me standing in the dining room, shaking with anger and arousal in equal measure. Because he's right—I am wet. Have been since I woke up. My body is betraying me, craving what my mind knows is dangerous.

But what terrifies me most is the small voice in my head, wondering: What if he's right about everything else? What if I am meant for this? What if seventeen years of denying him one postponed the inevitable?

What if I don't want to leave after a year?

I push the thought away, but it lingers like his cologne on my skin—present, persistent, and impossible to ignore.

CHAPTER 17
DAY 1

THE LIBRARY IS NOTHING LIKE THE CRAMPED ROOM AT THE RANCH WHERE Daddy kept his farming manuals and Mom's dog-eared paperbacks. This is a temple—floor-to-ceiling shelves, leather spines, the clean bite of furniture polish. Sunlight spears through tall windows, turning dust motes into slow, captive stars.

On the central table, five books. Beside them: a crystal decanter filled with water so clear it looks like air made liquid, two heavy-cut tumblers beading with condensation. A folded note rests on the top book in Julian's unforgiving hand:

Education comes in many forms. These will help you understand what you've agreed to, what I expect, and what you might discover about yourself. Read them in order. Be honest about your reactions—I'll know if you're not. Remember: arousal is not betrayal. It's recognition. —Mr. Blackwell

My hands shake as I lift the first title—*The Psychology of Power Exchange*. Academic. Clinical.

I pour a glass of water. It's cool, faintly sweet with the tang of lemon from a thin slice floating in the decanter. The first swallow

119

slides down like velvet; the second leaves a low, spreading warmth in my chest, a hush at the edges of my nerves.

I read.

The author discusses the paradox of surrender—how control can be ceded without being lost, and how a submissive chooses the terms of their own yielding.

I snort, reach for the glass again—another sip.

The room sharpens and softens at once: letters go crisper, thoughts go quieter. My shoulders unclench without permission.

The second book, *Negotiated Dominance*, is part memoir, part manual. Boundaries. Safewords. Ritual as a way of telling the body it's safe to let go.

My mouth goes dry; I take another drink. A pleasant heaviness pools low in my belly, a buoyant calm lifting the edges of my doubt. It feels...nice. Too nice.

I set the tumbler down, then pick it up again to feel the cool weight in my hand.

By the third—*Physiology of Arousal and Obedience*—my cheeks are warm, my pulse steady as a metronome. I'm rereading phrases I meant to mock. *Cortical quieting. Pleasure-trust feedback loops.*

The words should infuriate me. Instead, they hum through me like a chord I half remember. I pour more water. The crystal catches the light; the ripples look like silk.

I move to *Contracts of Desire*, legalistic and precise.

Clauses about consent, exit terms, and restitution. Somewhere between "consideration" and "specific performance," my breathing is deep and slow, my body loose as if I've just woken from a perfect nap.

A lazy certainty settles in my bones. I can do this. I want to try. I take another sip, chasing the calm as if it were courage in a glass.

The last book is thinner and more personal—*The Art of Yielding*. It reads like a prayer. *Kneeling is not a sign of smallness; it is a sign of focus.* I trace the sentence with my fingertip, swallow the final mouthful from my tumbler, and close my eyes. The world tilts almost imperceptibly, not dizzy—buoyant.

My doubts feel far away, as if someone set them on a high shelf I can't quite reach.

When I look down, the decanter is lighter, the lemon slice adrift near the crystal lip. I tell myself the warmth in my veins is only sunlight and study. I tell myself it's only water.

And I keep reading.

I'm so absorbed I don't hear him enter until his hand lands on my shoulder.

"Which one affected you most?"

I jump, the book falling closed. "How long have you been standing there?"

"Long enough to watch you shift in your seat three times during that last chapter." He moves to sit across from me, studying my face. "You're flushed. Pupils dilated. Breathing shallow. The books are having an effect."

"It's warm in here—"

"Rule three, Clara. Complete honesty."

I look down at the scattered books, unable to meet his gaze. "Fine. They're... informative."

"And?"

"And they make me think about things differently." The admission burns. "About power. About choice. About... us."

"What about us?"

A memory surfaces unbidden. "Senior year. After you asked me to the homecoming dance and I... laughed. You cornered me by my locker a week later. You didn't say anything, just looked at me. And I wanted to apologize, to explain, but my father was coming down the hall and I couldn't—"

"You wanted to say yes." Not a question.

"I wanted a lot of things I couldn't have." The truth spills out like water through a broken dam. "Do you know how many nights I lay awake wondering what would have happened if I had said yes? If my father hadn't forbidden it? If I'd been brave enough to defy him?"

"And now?"

"I'm here because you orchestrated it. Because you took the choice away." I finally meet that gaze of his. "Which should make me hate you."

"But?"

"But there's something... freeing about it. About not having to choose. About being forced into what I wanted anyway." I gesture at the books. "According to these, that's common. The need for an excuse."

He leans forward. "What else did you learn?"

"That safe words exist. That limits are negotiated."

"Is that what you want? A safe word?"

I consider. "Would you respect it?"

"Always, but at a cost." No hesitation. "I have a proposition."

My pulse quickens. "What kind of proposition?"

"For our year together, I'd like for you to agree not to use one. Full surrender to the contract we signed."

I sit up straighter. "That's—you can't be serious."

"I'm entirely serious." His gaze holds steady. "You can leave at any time. You always have that choice. Walk out the door, void the contract, keep your freedom. You can use a safeword if you truly need to, but that also voids our agreement. The land reverts to me."

"Why?" My voice comes out breathless. "Why would you want that?"

"Because I want complete power for these first months. I want you to understand what it means to truly submit, without having an easy out. I want you to know that when you stay, when you obey, it's because you're choosing to honor what we've agreed to."

An odd openness settles, making the idea of full surrender feel right. My emotions intensify in a way that's almost too much, but I nod, attributing it to the book's influence.

He pauses. "And because I think you need an excuse to let go completely. To not have control. To blame the contract for what you secretly desire."

"But you orchestrated my falling—"

"I orchestrated the opportunity. You chose to fall." He stands and extends his hand. "Come. It's time to see the West Wing."

My hand trembles as I take his. "The books talk about dungeons, about Red Rooms—"

"Mine is both more and less than what you've read." He pulls me up, keeps my hand in his. "It's where you'll learn the difference between fantasy and reality. Between what you've imagined submission to be and what it actually is with me."

We walk through corridors that grow progressively quieter, the house itself seeming to hold its breath. At a black door with a biometric lock, he stops.

"Last chance to ask questions about what you've read."

"Is it real?" The question bursts out. "Those relationships, that dynamic—people don't really live that way, do they?"

"Yes, they do." He presses his thumb against the scanner, and the lock clicks open. "I've been living it in my mind for seventeen years. Every woman I've been with has been practice for you. Learning what works, what doesn't, what makes someone truly surrender versus just playing at it."

"That's—"

"Obsessive? Extreme?" He pushes the door open. "Yes. But also real. More real than anything else in my life." He pauses at the threshold, turning to face me fully. "The rule I set for you—

complete honesty—it applies to me as well. That's a promise I'm making to you. You ask me anything, at any time, and I'll tell you the truth. No games, no deception. You deserve to know exactly who has this power over you."

He holds my gaze, his expression intense and unwavering. "I won't hide what I want from you, or why, or how long I've wanted it. That's the trade—you don't get to hide behind pretense, and neither do I."

He pushes the door open, and the room beyond makes my breath catch. Not because it's shocking but because it's beautiful —red walls that pulse with contained fire, dark wood gleaming under soft lighting that casts everything in a warm, intimate glow. Equipment that could be art if you didn't know its purpose: padded benches with rings for restraints, walls lined with implements—floggers of supple leather, coils of silk rope, crops with handles carved like sculptures—displayed with museum-like precision.

This is a space built for the fulfillment of obsession. The air smells of polished leather and faint incense, stirring a haze of unnatural calm from the books' lingering effect, but beneath it, fear coils—yet so does curiosity, the paradox Julian promised.

"This is where you'll learn that everything in those books is possible." His hand rests at my lower back, grounding the whirlwind in my chest. "Where you'll discover which parts appeal to you. Where you'll understand the difference between reading about submission and living it."

I walk to a wall displaying various floggers, whips, and crops. "Have you used all of these?"

"Yes. But not all will be used on you. Everyone's different. Some prefer sting, others thud. Some need pain to find subspace, others just need control."

"Subspace." Another term from the books.

"You were there last night." He moves behind me, not touching but close enough that I feel his heat. "When you stopped saying no and started saying please. When your eyes went soft, and your body went pliant, and you looked at me like I was your whole world."

"That was just—"

"If you say 'just sex,' I'll demonstrate right now how wrong you are." His voice carries a warning. "What happened last night was you letting go for the first time in your life. Stopping the constant control, the rigid responsibility. You surrendered, and your body rewarded you for it."

I turn to face him. "The books say the Dominant has as much responsibility as power. That they have to earn the submission. Forcing me into this isn't earning anything."

"I will earn your willing submission. That happens when you accept what you are."

"Which is?"

"Mine." Simple. Absolute. "But more than that, you've been waiting seventeen years for someone strong enough to take what you've been afraid to give."

"That's not—"

He steps closer, backing me against the wall. "Stop fighting just to fight. Try actual submission instead of grudging compliance. If after three months you still insist this is 'just sex,' I'll revise our contract."

"Revise how?"

"We'll discuss that in three months." He traces my jaw. "But I'm betting by then, you'll be begging me to remove the time limit altogether."

"Never."

"We'll see." He steps back. "For now, we're done here. Dinner's at seven. Wear the green dress. No panties."

"Julian—"

"What did you call me?"

"Mr. Blackwell." I correct it, hating how natural it's becoming.

"Good girl. Tonight after dinner, we'll discuss which of those books' scenarios you found most intriguing. So think carefully about what you want to admit to wanting. I'll leave you to explore."

He leaves me in the Red Room—because that's what it is, despite his prettier words. I stand surrounded by beautiful instruments of control, my body humming with possibility and dread. The air feels charged, heavy with intention, with all the things that have happened and all the things that will happen to me.

The books made it seem like fantasy. Safe words and negotiations, careful boundaries drawn in ink and conversation.

But this is real.

The leather is real—I can smell it, rich and dark.

Julian is real—I can still feel where his hands gripped me earlier, phantom pressure points that pulse with my heartbeat.

And the most terrifying truth is that my body's response is real as well—the heat pooling low in my belly, the way my breath comes shorter just looking at these beautiful, terrible things.

I spend another minute studying the room, but I'm no longer seeing it as it is.

I'm seeing myself in it.

Restrained on that bench, wrists bound, completely at his mercy. Decorated with those ropes, red lines crisscrossing pale skin like a map of surrender. Marked by those implements, each one leaving its signature, claiming territory.

And then it hits me—what I've agreed to.

An entire year of this without a safeword.

Looking at this room, at these instruments of pleasure and pain, I finally understand the choice he's forced on me. I can't tap out, can't call yellow or red, can't negotiate in the moment. I either accept everything he delivers, submit completely to whatever he decides I need, or I walk away and lose the land forever.

He would never force me—Julian made that clear. But he has forced this choice: absolute surrender or absolute loss. No middle ground. No safety net.

I wait for the fear to come. For the revulsion. For my mind to rebel against these dark imaginings and the complete power I've handed him.

Instead, my fingers tremble with the effort of not touching. Instead of disgust, I'm flooded with something far more dangerous—recognition. Like my body has been waiting seventeen years for this exact room, this exact man, this exact moment when I stop pretending I don't want to know what happens next.

The books were right about one thing—the journey from resistance to acceptance is not a straight line. It's a spiral, circling closer to the truth with each turn.

And I'm already dizzy from the spinning.

CHAPTER 18
DAY 1

The green dress is a weapon designed specifically to destroy me. Silk that clings to every curve, backless to my waist, a halter neck that makes wearing a bra impossible. I look expensive. Owned. His.

No underwear, as commanded. Every step reminds me of my vulnerability, my forced obedience.

I find him on the terrace, the evening light casting a golden glow over everything. The table is set for two, but only one chair is at the table. He's changed into dark pants and a white shirt, sleeves rolled up, looking deceptively casual.

"You're wondering about the missing chair."

"Let me guess—another power play?"

His jaw tightens at my tone. "Sit." He indicates his lap.

"This is ridiculous—"

"This is what you agreed to." His voice sharpens. "Or do you need reminding that breach of contract means losing everything?"

The threat hangs between us. I perch stiffly on his lap, maintaining as much distance as possible. He wraps his arm around my waist and pulls me back against his chest. Then, he hands me a glass of wine and waits for me to take my first sip.

"Tell me about the books." A command.

"They were interesting fiction."

"Fiction?" He tightens his grip on my waist.

"Yes. All those women choosing submission, finding freedom in surrender—it's erotica. Fantasy. Nothing like reality."

"And what's your reality?"

"My reality is being blackmailed by a man who destroyed my father to get to me." The words taste like copper. "Those women in the books had a choice." A fleeting haze crosses my mind, making the lack of choice feel oddly secure, my trust in him surging too strongly, stirring vague unease. "Safe words. The ability to walk away."

His body goes rigid behind me. "You have choice in this, and the ability to walk away."

"Comply or lose everything isn't a choice, it's coercion." I turn to face him. "Which makes me nothing like those willing submissives you had me read about."

Something turns winter-cold in his expression. "Is that what you think?"

"What else would you call it?"

"Inevitability." He shifts me roughly, making me face forward again.

The wine's lingering warmth deepens, loosening my defiance into an unnatural calm, making his words sink in without the usual fight.

"You think those women started out eager? Read closer. Each of them began resistant to the idea. Fighting their own desires."

"Their own desires. Not desires forced on them by circumstance."

"Tell me," his voice drops dangerously, "when you touched

yourself after reading about O's submission, was that forced? When you got wet reading about power exchange, was that coercion?"

Heat floods my face. "Physical response doesn't equal consent."

"Doesn't it? You want to hate this. Hate me. It would be simpler."

"I do hate you."

"Liar." He slides his hand to my throat, not squeezing, just resting there. "You hate that your body responds despite your mind's protests. You hate that part of you that wonders what complete surrender would feel like. You're exhausted. Bone-deep tired from carrying everything alone. Fighting every battle. Making every decision." He eases his grip slightly. "I'm offering you a year of not having to be strong."

"By forcing me to be weak?"

"By forcing you to let go." He studies my face. "The women in those books found freedom in submission because they chose it. You'll find it because you have no choice but to discover it."

"That's insane logic."

"Is it? Or is it exactly what someone as stubborn as you needs?" He slides his hands to my waist. "You'd never choose this on your own. Too proud. Too controlled. So I removed the choice."

"And you think that makes you some kind of savior?"

"I think that makes me the only person strong enough to give you what you need." His certainty is absolute. "In three months, you'll understand. In six, you'll be grateful. In a year..."

"Yeah, yeah. In a year, I'll leave and never look back. You're like a broken record with that. In a year, I'll walk away."

Something flickers in that gaze—hurt? Fear? It's gone before I can identify it.

"We'll see." He stands abruptly, setting me on my feet. "Dinner's over. You clearly need another lesson in what you've agreed to."

He clamps his hand around my wrist—not hard enough to hurt, but firm, unyielding—as he leads me from the dining room. The estate's grand staircase looms before us, and he pulls me up the steps with controlled strides, his grip a silent command.

I stumble once, but he steadies me without breaking stride, his silence thick with restrained anger. My heart hammers, defiance warring with the unwelcome heat low in my belly—this man who ruined me for his obsession, yet my body anticipates what that look promises.

In his bedroom, the door shuts with a decisive click, sealing us in the opulent space. The bed waits like a battlefield, black sheets stark against the dim light. He releases me only to shrug off his jacket and loosen his tie, pinning me with that gaze in place.

"Strip." His voice is a low growl edged with authority. I falter, and he steps forward, crowding my space until his chest brushes mine. "Now. Or I'll rip it off you myself."

Trembling, I obey, the fabric whispering to the floor until I'm exposed, vulnerable under his scrutiny. He circles me once, a predator assessing prey, then grips my shoulders, maneuvering me onto the bed with unyielding hands. "Arms up. Now."

I raise them, and he fetches silk scarves from the nightstand—deceptively soft, but their knots will be ironclad. He binds my wrists to the headboard, pulling the silk taut until my arms strain, every tug met with his warning glare.

"Struggle all you want." His voice is laced with dark promise. "It changes nothing. This is my domain, and you're here to learn mastery—starting with addressing me as Mr. Blackwell. Every time you forget, you'll pay for it."

He starts slow, deliberate, lips brushing the inside of my knee, climbing higher with open-mouthed kisses that tease without satisfying. He pins my thighs wide, thumbs pressing bruises into the soft flesh.

When his mouth reaches my core, he doesn't ease in—he dives deep, tongue thrusting before flattening against my clit in broad, insistent strokes.

The pleasure builds fast, a coiling fire, but as my breath hitches and hips buck, he withdraws, teeth grazing my inner thigh in a sharp nip that draws a hiss from me. Pain blooms, hot and grounding, sharpening the ache of denial.

"Not yet." His breath is hot against my skin. He returns, mercilessly—sucking my clit hard enough to make stars burst behind my eyes, fingers plunging inside to curl and stroke that devastating spot. Tension winds tighter, and I arch, pleas for *more* and *don't stop* bubbling up—

"Julian, please"—but he stops again, this time biting down on the sensitive fold of my labia, the sting making me yelp as he soothes with a languid lick.

"Wrong" he snaps. "Mr. Blackwell. Say it, or you'll stay denied."

"Mr. Blackwell..."

The edging drags on, endlessly, his mouth a weapon of torment. Fourth denial: tongue flicking rapid circles while teeth scrape my clit, the edge of pain pushing me to the brink, only for him to pull back, leaving me shaking, sweat-slicked, restraints biting into my wrists as I strain.

Fifth: he adds fingers, three now, stretching me to the point of burn, mouth latching on to suck with bruising force, nipping intermittently until tears stream down my face.

"Mr. Blackwell." The words rasp out, raw. "Please..."

"Louder. Beg like you mean it." His eyes lock on mine, unblinking, as he edges me a sixth time—tongue delving deep, teeth tugging my clit just shy of too much, fingers thrusting in a rhythm that has me sobbing.

I quake, my core clenching on nothing, the void of denial is a physical agony.

"Admit your body craves this."

I hate him for making me beg, but I'm too far gone not to give in. "Mr. Blackwell, please—let me come."

He doesn't yield immediately. Seventh build: his mouth devours without restraint, teeth marking the tender skin, pain threading through the ecstasy until I'm a trembling wreck, every nerve alight.

"Say it again." He pauses with me teetering. "Your body wants this."

"Please, let me come." I'm broken and desperate.

Only then does he relent, mouth sealing over me, tongue and teeth working in furious tandem—sucking, biting lightly, fingers pounding until the orgasm erupts, a shattering wave that convulses me against the bonds, screams tearing from my throat.

He draws it out, prolonging the bliss-pain until I'm oversensitive, begging him to stop.

But he doesn't. Leaving me shaking, body limp and quivering, he climbs up, shedding his pants in one fluid motion. His cock, hard and insistent, presses against me as he positions between my spread thighs, pinning my hips.

He thrusts in deep and hard, forcing a gasp from my raw lips —the stretch borders on too much, my recent climax making every inch burn with overstimulation. He sets a brutal pace, hips slamming forward, the bedframe rattling with each forceful drive. He grips my throat, thumb pressing my pulse, his steely gaze boring into mine.

"Take it." A growl escapes him. "Take all of me."

I can't stand it—the intensity overwhelms, pleasure crashing into the raw edges of my body, tears mixing with sweat as he fucks me relentlessly, refusing to slow.

"Mr. Blackwell." The title slips out with a whimper, instinctive now, a plea and submission all rolled into one.

He growls approval, thrusting deeper, one hand sliding to pinch my nipple sharply, the pain spiking the ecstasy until I shatter again, clenching around him in uncontrollable spasms. He follows with a guttural roar, spilling deep, but even then, he grinds through it, drawing out my pleasure until I'm boneless, my vision blurring at the edges.

He collapses beside me, chest rising and falling in ragged bursts, the air thick with heat and salt and the raw pulse of what he's just taken.

My wrists strain against the bindings, the ropes still biting into skin gone tender. I'm trembling, every nerve strung tight, and yet—that look sparks an unbearable ache all over again.

Without a word, he releases one restraint, just enough to move me. He slides his hand beneath my shoulder, rolling me to my side.

He leans over me, a shadow of heat and intent. The pad of his finger traces the slope of my spine, slow enough to make me shiver.

Down, down, following the fine trail of goosebumps he leaves in his wake. He pauses at the small of my back, then dips lower, circling the one place he's avoided thus far—the one that's still mine.

His voice drops to a low, dangerous purr against my ear. "If I want to take you here..." The circle tightens. "...are you going to refuse me?" He pauses, letting the implication of refusal—and what it would cost—hang in the air. "Or are you willing to let me claim this too?"

Fear crashes over me like ice water. I've never done that. Never even considered it. The idea alone makes my stomach twist, panic rising sharp and immediate.

Every muscle in my body locks, caught between fear and a hunger that feels dangerous. He presses just enough to make me gasp—not entering, just reminding me how he could.

"You're trembling." His voice is rough silk. "But you're not saying no."

"Please don't." My voice is hoarse and cracking, twisting my hips away despite the bonds that hold my wrists taut. My heart races, breath coming in shallow gasps, the room spinning as terror claws up my throat. "I've never... Mr. Blackwell, no. I can't. Please—not that."

His touch pauses, but doesn't retreat, his finger pressing lightly, testing. He meets my gaze steadily, his expression a mask of calm dominance.

"You can refuse. Always. But it voids the contract. You'll lose everything I've dangled as salvation. Is that what you want? Back to scraping by, fighting alone again?"

The words hit like a blow, amplifying the panic until I'm on the cusp—chest tight, vision tunneling, tears spilling hot and unchecked. The ranch, my father's legacy, the fragile lifeline he's twisted into chains... gone. All because of this. I shake my head wildly, sobs hitching.

"You can't... I'll hate you for this. It's too much. I'll never forgive you. Never. You're a monster."

He doesn't flinch, his voice low and unyielding, laced with the weight of years.

"I don't care about your forgiveness. I've waited seventeen years to have you in every way—every inch, every surrender. This is happening tonight. You'll learn to take it, just like everything else." He shifts, his free hand untying the scarves just enough to flip me onto my stomach, my cheek pressing into the sheets, arms stretched forward as he rebinds them to allow the new position without escape.

The vulnerability hits harder now, my ass raised slightly by the angle of my hips, exposed completely.

Panic surges again, my body rigid, but he soothes with a firm hand on my lower back.

"Please, don't...please don't make me...Julian—Mr. Blackwell, I'm scared—"

"Breathe. I'll be gentle. I'll prepare you properly." He reaches for the lube on the nightstand, coating his fingers generously before circling the tight ring of muscle, pressing just the tip of one inside. The intrusion is foreign, a slow burn that makes me clench and whimper, fresh tears soaking the pillow.

"Relax." He holds still until my trembling eases, his other hand stroking my hip in rhythmic circles. "Good girl. Just like that."

He works the first finger deeper, inch by inch, the stretch uncomfortable but not unbearable, his thumb occasionally dipping to my clit to spark distracting pleasure that wars with the fear. Minutes pass—five, ten—as he crooks and twists gently, whispering commands to breathe, to push back against him.

"I hate you." The gasp is muffled against the sheets, body tensing as the burn builds. "Please."

But he doesn't stop, adding a second finger, the added girth drawing a sharp cry from me, the burn intensifying to a point that has me biting the sheets.

"Almost ready." His voice is rough with restraint. "You've taken worse tonight. Trust my mastery—let it happen." He stretches me further, the discomfort blending into a deep ache that he counters with firmer strokes to my front, building reluctant arousal until my hips twitch involuntarily.

"No... please." The words dissolve into blubbering whimpers

as strange sensations stir, pleasure threading unbidden through the pain.

By the time he withdraws his fingers, I'm a mess of sweat, tears, and conflicting sensations—fear still thrumming, but resignation settling like lead in my chest.

He slicks his cock, positioning himself behind me, knees nudging my thighs wider. The head presses against me, blunt and insistent.

"Eyes forward if you can't look at me**." One hand fists the sheet near my head for leverage, the other guides himself. He pushes forward incrementally, the pressure immense, a tight burn that steals my breath and reignites the panic—my muscles clench instinctively, resisting.

"Breathe out." He pauses as I gasp and sob, tears blurring everything.

"I hate you." My voice fractures into incoherent cries as he advances, inch by agonizing inch, holding still each time I whimper, his fingers returning to my clit to ease the way with building tension.

When he's fully seated, the fullness is overwhelming, a deep, invading pressure that borders on pain, leaving me trembling uncontrollably.

"Mine." The word is strained, giving me moments to adjust before he begins to move—shallow thrusts at first, each one a careful invasion that stretches me to my limits, the fullness bordering on too much, a deep, insistent pressure that makes my breath hitch in shallow, panicked gasps.

He steadies me with his hand on my hip, fingers splaying wide to hold me in place, but there's no escaping it—the way he fills me so completely, so intimately, in this forbidden way that terrifies me. I squeeze my eyes shut, fists twisting in the sheets, hating the vulnerability, the way my body clenches instinctively against him, fighting even as a traitorous heat begins to flicker at the edges.

"Relax for me." His voice is a low rumble against my ear, gentle yet unyielding, like silk over iron. "Breathe with me—feel how I'm taking you slowly. You're safe under my control."

He slides his free hand between my thighs from the front, fingers tracing feather-light circles over my clit, not demanding but coaxing, building a spark of pleasure that wars with the burn. The contrast is maddening—the slow drag of him inside me sending unfamiliar ripples through my core, a deep ache that shifts from sharp discomfort to something warmer, more insistent, with each measured rock of his hips.

I whimper, tears pricking my eyes, torn between pushing back and pulling away, the fear coiling tight in my chest even as his touch ignites a low, building throb that makes my toes curl.

The burn fades gradually into something fuller, more consuming, his hand between my legs now pressing firmer, circling with expert rhythm that draws a reluctant gasp from my lips.

Pleasure teases at the fringes, unbidden waves lapping at the edges of my resistance—each shallow thrust pressing deeper, the friction igniting sparks that travel up my spine, making me tremble despite myself.

"That's it." His breath is hot on my neck, pace steady and unrelenting, forcing me to feel every inch as his fingers quicken, pinching lightly at my clit to send jolts of heat coiling tighter.

I hate how good it starts to feel, the pressure building in layers —fear melting into haze, my body betraying me with soft, involuntary motions, rocking back against him, chasing the edge even as my mind screams no. The fullness overwhelms, pleasure threading through the ache like fire through shadow, pulling a broken moan from my throat as the first tentative spasm grips me.

"Oh God... no, yes... I—ahh." Words tumble into senseless

moans as the tight friction ignites, pleasure overtaking the edges of pain, my body betraying me with building spasms.

"Come for me," he says. Low. Final.

It crests—a tight, intense orgasm that pulls a shocked, broken wail from deep in my chest, my body clenching around him in waves that leave me shuddering and incoherent.

He groans, thrusts faltering before deepening, chasing his release until he spills with a low, possessive growl, grinding through it as if to seal every claim.

Finally, he stills, withdrawing carefully before untying the scarves with surprisingly gentle hands, massaging the red welts on my wrists.

I curl into myself at first, but he draws me to his chest, encircling me firmly, his breath steady against my hair. Emotions crash —fury boiling over as reality seeps back in.

"You're a bastard." I shove weakly at his chest, tears still falling. "You forced me. I hate you for this—for everything."

He holds me tighter, unfazed, his voice a calm rumble. "You always have the ability to walk away. The door's right there."

"That's an illusion of choice." Anger sharpens through the haze. "You know what it would cost me—the ranch, my father. It's not real freedom; it's just another cage you built."

He strokes his hand down my back in soothing circles. "I don't care. Besides, I felt you come on my cock when I was in your ass. Hard. You can't deny your pleasure in it."

"I hate you." The words come out weaker now, tangled with the lingering throb of satisfaction.

"No, you don't." His tone shifts to insistent command, tilting my chin up to meet his gaze.

"You're wrong."

"Underneath the fight, you're discovering what you need. What you've always needed." He strokes his hand down my spine.

"You can hate me all you want. You can curse my name every time your body betrays you. But we both know this ends the same way."

"With me leaving after a year?"

"With you understanding that you were always meant to be mine. That every relationship you've tried, every man you've dated, failed because they couldn't give you what I can."

"You're insane." I want to argue, but my body is too satisfied, my mind too fuzzy. "Nobody wants this."

"Perhaps." He pulls the covers over us both. "But, you're not nobody. You're mine, and I'm the only honest one here. Time will tell. You love that I took control and didn't back down. That I pushed you past what you thought you couldn't handle. Tell me the truth—did you hate what I did to you?"

I hesitate, the weight of that look pressingdown on me, remembering the contract's clause on honesty, the invisible chains it weaves. Swallowing hard, voice barely audible, I admit, "No... I didn't hate it. Obviously. I came."

His smile is triumphant, soft in the dim light, as he kisses my forehead. "That's my girl. Resistance is expected." His voice softens. "But it's futile. You can resist me, but your body's already yielded. And soon, the rest will."

"Why?" Anger and confusion tangle with the afterglow. "Why push this far?"

"Because this is best for both of us." He tightens his hold possessively, the afterglow wrapping me in a hazy contentment, details of the pain fading too quickly, leaving only a warm, lingering trust I don't question. "I've engineered everything to claim you fully—not just your body, but the freedom you deny yourself. You've shouldered too much alone. Under my mastery, you'll learn to let go, whether you fight it or not." He traces the line of the choker he locked around my neck.

A collar that says I belong to him.

I'm physically wrecked and oddly anchored by his warmth, hating him even as I melt into his embrace.

Later, I lie in his bed, wrists still marked from the scarves, body humming from release I didn't want to want. He's beside me, one arm possessively across my waist, his certainty as solid as his presence.

"The books were right about one thing." he says.

"What?"

"True submission can't be forced. But it can be... awakened." He splays his hand across my stomach, proprietary. "You'll stop fighting what you crave. And when that happens..."

He doesn't finish, because he doesn't need to. The implication hangs between us—that my resistance is temporary, my surrender inevitable.

"You've dragged me, kicking and screaming."

"Have I?" He tightens his hold around me. "Or have I removed all the obstacles you put in your own way?"

I don't answer because I don't know anymore. The woman in those books chose to surrender. I'm being forced into mine. But my body doesn't seem to understand the difference.

And that terrifies me more than anything else.

"Stop fighting just to fight," he murmurs against my hair. "Give me three real months of honest effort."

"And if I still hate you after three months?"

"Then we'll discuss adjustments."

"What kind of adjustments?"

"The kind we'll discuss in three months." He brushes his lips against my shoulder. "But by then, you won't want adjustments. You'll want more."

"You're wrong."

"We'll see."

His breathing evens out, but I lie awake for hours. The books make submission seem like a gift freely given. Mine is being taken, molded, and shaped by hands that orchestrated my downfall to possess me.

But the worst part—the part I'll never admit aloud—is that my body doesn't care about the distinction. It responds to him like those willing submissives responded to their dominants.

I wanted to date Julian way back then. When we were young, and the world wasn't so complicated. Now, I crave the callousness of Mr. Blackwell and the way he brings my body to life.

And I hate him for knowing that would happen.

I hate myself more for proving him right.

CHAPTER 19
DAY 14

Fourteen marks in my journal. Two weeks of waking to Julian's hands, his mouth, his commands. Two weeks of my body betraying me every single day.

"We're going to the ranch today." Julian's voice slices through the quiet like the edge of a blade—smooth, inevitable.

He sits across the table, reading the morning news on his tablet, a study in composed dominance. Coffee, black. Posture perfect. Every movement is efficient, deliberate, and contained.

I look up from my breakfast—one he's watching me eat, as always, tracking every bite like it matters.

"What?"

"The improvements are ready for inspection." He sets down his coffee with that deliberate precision that means he's already planned every moment. "You should see what I've done with your inheritance."

"It's not yours to improve—"

"Everything of yours is mine to improve for the next year." His tone carries that edge of authority that makes my stomach flip. "The sooner you accept that, the easier this becomes."

"Easy was never your goal."

"No. It's not."

At my feet, Scout shifts, toenails tapping lightly against the marble.

Julian never planned to allow him here. "He's a distraction," he said when I first asked. "Animals are unpredictable." But after a pause—one of those long, assessing silences where he seemed to measure the weight of my soul—he added, "If it makes you more... compliant, then fine. But he follows my rules."

That's how Scout came to live here—a concession, not compassion.

Now he lies half under my chair, head resting across my bare feet, a low sigh vibrating through his chest.

I've caught Julian reaching down more than once to scruff his fur in passing, his hand rough but controlled.

The gestures aren't affectionate. They're possessive—like everything he touches eventually becomes his.

Breakfast is quiet except for the clink of silverware and the steady rhythm of his scrutiny. I push a piece of bacon around my plate. Scout lifts his head, tail giving a hopeful thump.

When Julian glances back at his tablet, I risk it—breaking off a small strip and slipping it under the table. Scout takes it gently from my fingers, warm tongue brushing my skin. The smallest rebellion, the faintest reclaiming of control.

The sound of metal on porcelain freezes me.

"Did you just feed the dog?" His voice is soft, too soft—the kind that makes the air turn electric.

"He's used to breakfast scraps." I try for casual.

Julian lowers the tablet, folds his hands, and studies me over the rim of his coffee cup. "Not at my table."

A tremor moves through me. "It was just bacon."

"It was defiance." He leans back, voice smooth as silk and sharp as a knife. "And defiance has a price."

Scout's ears flatten, a quiet whine escaping him.

Julian flicks his gaze to the dog, then back to me. "Do you want me to take you to the Red Room?"

My breath catches. "For feeding him?"

"For disobedience." He sets the cup down, not with force, but solid. Sure. Absolute. "You know how we correct that."

"Julian—"

"Careful." His voice drops. "That's not what you call me."

I swallow hard. "Mr. Blackwell."

"Better." He studies me, every inch of him calm, controlled, and dangerous. "Now tell me, if I decide to take you there right now, are you going to refuse me?"

The question lands like a blow. The meaning beneath it is clear: refusal means breach. Breach means everything is gone.

I glare at him over my fork, heat rising in my cheeks. "No." Sullen. I stab at my eggs. "Of course, I won't refuse you. You know I won't."

He knows precisely what that defiance costs me.

Ever since he introduced me to the Red Room, he's been peeling me open, one layer at a time. Not just punishments, but other things as well. Pain that blurs into pleasure, boundaries bent until I can't tell where one ends and the other begins. Each lesson leaves me trembling, wet, ashamed, and coming back for more.

But this? Feeding Scout under the table? He never said a word about it. No rule. No warning. My fingers tighten around the fork.

"It's not fair," I mutter under my breath. "You never said it was against the rules."

"Consider it a new rule." Julian leans back, watching me with that unhurried, predatory patience, like a man already deciding what lesson to teach next.

Scout whines again, nudging my leg. I start to reach down, but Julian's voice cuts through the air like a command.

"Don't."

I freeze midair, a strip of bacon hovering over Scout's waiting muzzle.

Julian doesn't even look up from his tablet. "Finish your breakfast. Drink your orange juice. Then you can feed the dog. Not before. Obedience first. Indulgence second."

The glass of orange juice sits by my plate, bright and cold, beads of condensation sliding down the sides. I've never liked orange juice—too sweet, too acidic—but every morning since I signed his contract, it's been there waiting. Every morning, he insists I drink it.

I lift the glass, swallowing back the bitterness, trying not to make a face.

Julian returns to his tablet as if the conversation never happened, perfectly composed. The only sign he's paying attention at all is the subtle flick of his eyes toward the glass to make sure I keep drinking.

Scout whines softly, tail sweeping the floor. Even he seems to sense the rules here.

I force myself to chew, the bacon tasting of salt and submission. Across from me, Julian looks every inch the man who owns the house, the table, and the woman sitting at it.

Under the table, Scout presses his head against my ankle—a quiet reminder that something in this house still belongs to me.

"Wear jeans. Boots." Julian's voice breaks the silence. "You'll need them."

The idea of real clothes—ranch clothes—feels like freedom. "What, no silk dress with strategic gaps?"

"Not today." He moves behind my chair, hands on my shoulders. "Today, you see that I don't just take. I also give. Even when you're too stubborn to ask."

The drive to the ranch is silent except for my heart hammering. Julian drives himself today—no driver, no buffer. His hand rests possessively on my thigh, thumb stroking through denim in that absent way that suggests ownership has already become habit.

When we crest the last hill, I gasp.

The ranch is transformed.

New fencing stretches in perfect lines. The barn has been completely rebuilt—same footprint, but with fresh lumber, modern ventilation, and a roof that won't leak. The pastures are green despite the season, and new irrigation systems are visible. Equipment that would have taken me twenty years to afford sits ready for use.

But it's the roses that break me.

I stare at them through the car window as we pull up to the ranch house, the sight hitting like a gut punch.

My mother's wild, chaotic roses—untamed tangles of thorns and blooms that she let sprawl freely across the fence, a riot of color mirroring her own fierce, unapologetic spirit—have been transformed. Someone has carefully tended them, trained the unruly vines onto sturdy new trellises that arch elegantly over the garden path.

They've been pruned, deadheads snipped away, encouraging vigorous new growth that spirals upward in controlled loops. They're still wild at heart, those blood-red petals defiant and fragrant, but now they're supported, guided by the wood's unyielding frame, channeled into something beautiful yet contained. Allowed to thrive, yes—but within a structure they never asked for.

A metaphor for me, unbidden and unwelcome, blooms in my mind. I was choking on my own freedom, scrambling for survival after Mom's death, after Dad's decline, thorns out to protect the fragile heart beneath. Independent to a fault, blooming in chaos because that's all I knew.

And now?

Under Julian's hand, I'm being reshaped—pruned of resistance, tied to his rules, forced to climb higher not on my own terms, but his. The thought twists like a thorn in my chest.

Is this thriving, or survival in a prettier cage?

"You touched her roses." My voice cracks, raw with accusation and something deeper—grief for the woman who planted them, for the girl I was tending them beside her.

"I saved them." He parks the car smoothly, turns to face me, his gaze steady and unrepentant. "They were choking themselves, growing wild without direction. Now they have structure. Support. They'll bloom better than ever. Like you under my control."

The words land like a slap, slicing through my defenses. *Like me.*

My breath catches, a wave of hot denial crashing over the chill of recognition. He's not tending plants; he's claiming the symbolism, weaving it into his narrative of ownership.

I want to scream that I'm not a flower to be tamed, that my wildness isn't a flaw to fix—it's survival, it's me. But deep down, a traitorous whisper wonders: What if he's right? What if the structure he's imposing is the trellis I needed all along, lifting me from the dirt instead of letting me sprawl and wither?

The parallel terrifies me, because if the roses can be beautiful this way... what does that make me become under him? Caged. Controlled. His.

"You had no right—" I start, voice trembling, fists clenching in my lap to hide the shake.

"I had every right. This is mine for the year, remember?" He gets out and circles around to open my door with that infuriating courtesy. "Come. There's more."

"Julian—"

"Mr. Blackwell." He corrects me sharply by placing his hand on my throat, fingers tightening just enough to emphasize the shift. "Say it properly, Clara. Or this lesson starts now."

My pulse flutters under his fingers, but I force the words out, defiance lacing them. "Mr. Blackwell."

"Better." He releases me, stepping back with a nod toward the door. "Follow."

He leads me into the barn, the scent of fresh hay and polished leather enveloping us. The improvements unfold like a cruel gift: climate-controlled air humming softly, keeping the space cool and dust-free; modern stalls with padded floors and automatic waterers gleaming under LED lights; a tack room where saddles and bridles hang in neat rows, organized bins holding every tool a rider could need.

It's everything my father dreamed of—whispered plans over late-night coffee, sketches on napkins that never materialized because the money dried up after Mom's medical bills, after the droughts, after his pride kept him from loans. Now, it's realized, but not by him. By the man who broke him.

"Why?" I turn on Julian in the feed room, now stocked with premium grain in sealed containers, supplements lined up like soldiers. "Why spend this much on something you'll give back?"

"Because it's yours." He closes the distance, backing me against the rough wooden wall, his body a wall of heat and intent. "And I take care of what's mine."

"I'm not yours—"

"You are." He brackets my face, thumbs brushing my cheeks with deceptive tenderness. "You're completely mine. And when this year ends, you'll have a ranch worthy of your family's legacy."

"This doesn't make up for destroying my father—"

"Nothing makes up for that." The admission surprises me, a crack in his armor. "But I can give you a future even while I take your present. Do you remember Junior year? The agricultural science project."

"Mr. Patterson paired us together. You were furious."

"I was thrilled." He traces my cheekbone. "Three weeks of sitting beside you, close enough to touch. Three weeks of watching you bite your lip when you concentrated, smelling your shampoo when you leaned over the microscope."

"You complained to Patterson. Tried to get a different partner."

"Because I knew I'd give myself away." His voice roughens. "Do you know what torture it was? Having you that close but untouchable? Your father picking you up every day, glaring at me like I defiled you just by sharing air?"

The memory surfaces—Julian was cold, distant, and barely spoke to me, except to work on the project. But underneath...

"The last day." A whisper. "When we were alone in the lab..."

"You dropped the slides." He slides his hands to my throat, not squeezing, just holding. Fingers playing with the diamond choker. "Glass everywhere. You cut your hand trying to clean it up."

"You wrapped it with your shirt."

"And you let me." Something darkens in that gaze. "For thirty seconds, you let me take care of you. No walls, no distance. Just my hands on yours, stopping the bleeding."

"Then my father walked in."

"Then your father walked in." His jaw tightens. "Called me a predator. Said I was just like my father, taking what wasn't mine.

" I decided that day," he continues, voice dropping to that dangerous register, "if I was going to be accused of taking you, I might as well be guilty of it."

"So you waited seventeen years—"

"I waited until you needed me." He presses closer, pinning me completely against the wall. "Until fighting me would cost more than surrendering to me."

"That's not healthy."

"That's obsession." His lips hover over mine. "And now, in the barn your father built, on the land he died trying to protect you from me, I'm going to remind you who owns you."

CHAPTER 20
DAY 14

Before I can respond, he spins me around, pressing my chest to the wall while his hands work at my jeans, shoving them down along with my panties in one swift motion. Cool air hits my skin, and I gasp, hands scrambling for purchase on the wood.

"No, not here. This is my father's—"

"Your barn now." A growl. "Improved. Like you."

He reaches for a coil of soft rope from the newly organized tack hooks—barn-grade nylon, sturdy yet smooth—looping it around my wrists, securing them to a high ring meant for tying leads. The position forces me to stand on my toes, arms stretched overhead, body arched and exposed.

I tug, but it's secure, the rope biting just enough to remind me of my place.

"You can fight me with words, but each refusal to acknowledge my gifts is a strap from my belt later—a punishment you'll earn. You'll learn gratitude one way or another."

He slides his hand between my thighs from behind, fingers

parting me without preamble, finding me already slick despite my protests—a betrayal that burns hotter than shame.

He circles my clit slowly, building pressure with expert strokes, his free hand roaming my hip, then delivering a light smack to my ass that stings through the vulnerability. Pleasure coils fast, my breath hitching as I near the edge.

"Thank me for the climate control." His voice is rough. Demanding. "Say it—Mr. Blackwell, thank you for keeping this barn perfect for my horses. For us."

"No." Even as I say it, my hips buck involuntarily, heat flooding my core. "I won't play your game. You're twisting everything—"

He withdraws his fingers abruptly, leaving me throbbing and empty, a whine escaping despite myself.

"That's one stripe."

He waits, while my body aches for more, then returns, two fingers thrusting deep while his thumb presses my clit, the rhythm relentless. The build is quicker this time, my traitorous nerves firing hot and insistent, teetering on the brink.

"Thank me for the stalls now. Mr. Blackwell, thank you for making them safe and modern."

"You're a monster." My voice fractures as denial looms. "Ruining my home for your ego—ahh—I hate you for this." The words sharpen my defiance, even as my thighs tremble.

He pulls back again, the sudden void making me clench on nothing, frustration boiling into tears.

"Two stripes. Keep fighting—it only makes the lesson sweeter." The third time, he adds his mouth, dropping to his knees behind me, tongue laving broad strokes over my folds while his fingers curl inside me, hitting that spot unerringly.

Pain mixes in—a sharper nip to my inner thigh, his teeth

grazing sensitive skin—amplifying the torment. I'm shaking now, breath ragged, so close I can taste release.

"The tack room," he murmurs against me, his voice vibrating through my core. "Thank me for organizing it. Say the words."

"Fuck you." Tears spill now, my body arching back despite my venom. "It's not yours to fix. You'll never break me."

He stops, mouth withdrawing with a deliberate slowness that leaves me sobbing softly, the ache a physical torment deeper than the rope's bite.

"Three."

Four, five, six—he repeats the cycle without mercy, edging me with fingers, tongue, the heel of his hand grinding against me in turn. Each time, he demands thanks for another improvement—the premium feed, the automated systems, the reinforced fences—his voice a steady drumbeat of command. And each time, I fight: "You're destroying me," "This isn't care—it's control," "I won't thank you for stealing my life."

My verbal barbs grow weaker, laced with moans and gasps, my body is a live wire of desperation, but I don't yield, don't give him the satisfaction. By the tenth denial, I'm a wreck, sweat-slicked and trembling, my core pulsing with unmet need, tears streaming freely down my face.

"Ten stripes, then." He rises behind me, voice thick with restrained hunger. "Punishment for your stubbornness."

I hear the clink of his belt buckle, the whisper of leather sliding free, and panic spikes through the arousal.

"No—please." A whimper. But it's too late.

He folds the belt over double, the first stroke landing across my ass with a sharp crack that blooms into fire, the pain jolting through me like electricity.

I cry out, body jerking against the restraints, the sting confusing—raw and humiliating, yet it sharpens the ache between my legs, making me clench around nothing, desperate for him despite the tears.

"One." Calm as ever, he delivers the second stripe lower, overlapping the first, the heat layering until it's a throbbing inferno. "Two."

Sobs rack me now, the pain blurring with the frustration of denial, my skin is hypersensitive, every nerve screaming for release—his touch, his cock, anything to fill the void he's carved.

"Three." Each lash is controlled, not brutal, but unyielding—the belt whistling through the air before snapping home, welts rising in neat, punishing lines.

By the fourth strike, I'm blubbering, my cheek pressed against my bound and raised arms. Confusion overwhelms me. Why does the fire from his belt make me ache for him more? Why does the pain twist into something almost like need, my hips twitching back involuntarily as if begging?

"Four. Five."

Tears soak my face, voice hoarse with cries—"Stop. It hurts," —but he doesn't. The sixth, seventh, and eighth strikes land with heat, the burn so intense it steals my breath, leaving me limp and quivering on the edge of collapse. Arousal and agony tangle until they're inseparable.

"Nine." A growl. The ninth strike cracks across my already throbbing skin like lightning, sharper than the last, sending fresh fire lancing through me.

I clamp my thighs together as a ragged, unintended moan escapes, the pain shoving me closer to the release he denies.

I hate it, hate how my core clenches emptily, the sting radiating inward to pulse hot need between my legs, arching despite the sobs wracking my chest. He presses his hand firmly at the small of my back, holding me open, unyielding, as if savoring every tremor.

"Ten" The final blow falls with deliberate force, a searing whip that blurs my vision, the impact jolting through my spine like an electric current, forcing a broken gasp from my lips as the burn peaks, white-hot and all-consuming.

My knees buckle, hips bucking back in desperate, shameful invitation, pleasure coiling tight from the denial now unraveling in waves of humiliated want—tears streaming, breath shattered, reduced to nothing but his to command.

He discards the belt, gripping my hips as he frees his cock, thrusting into me in one deep, claiming stroke that rips a shattered cry from my throat—the fullness a brutal mercy, stretching me through the haze of pain and denial.

He fucks me hard against the wall, hips slamming forward with possessive force, the welts on my ass igniting with every impact, blending the hot sting into a building wave of ecstasy—a punishing rhythm that drives me higher, the fullness of him stretching me relentlessly, my bound hands straining against the rope as pleasure coils tighter, hotter, from the denial that's left me so raw.

I teeter on the brink, body trembling, my core clenching around him in desperate, fluttering pulses that beg for release, but I can't—I won't—Rule Five burns in my mind like the welts on my skin: no coming without permission.

My breath hitches in sobs, walls of ecstasy pressing in, threatening to shatter me, but I bite my lip, whispering, frantic, "Please —please let me come," through the haze, terrified of the consequences if I break without permission.

"Scream for me." He tightens his grip, thrusting deep with savage intent, like he's unraveling me thread by thread. "Come now—come for me."

The command unravels everything, permission flowing through me like liquid fire, and I shatter at last, the orgasm crashing over me like a dam breaking—waves of blinding release convulsing through my bound form, clenching around him as sobs turn to moans.

He doesn't stop, driving deeper, chasing his own peak until he spills with a guttural groan, grinding through it to wring every aftershock from me, leaving me boneless and spent.

Finally, he stills, withdrawing slowly before untying the rope, rubbing the red marks on my wrists. He turns me gently to face him, my legs unsteady, and pulls me into his chest, one arm banding around my waist while he soothes the welts on my ass with light, cooling strokes—his touch firm but tender, tracing the raised lines without flinching.

I wince at first, fresh tears spilling, but the contact grounds me, the pain easing into a dull throb under his care.

"Breathe." His voice is low and steady, the aftercare a stark contrast to the storm he just unleashed. "Punishment isn't cruelty—it's structure. Each denial you threw at me, each refusal to see the gifts I've given this place, earned a stripe to sharpen your focus. Pain to cut through the fog of your resistance, to make you feel my control in every inch of you. It's how you learn: the sting reminds you that fighting only heightens what you crave. And now? You throb with it, don't you? Marked inside and out as mine."

I bury my face in his shirt, a fog settling over the pain, making the welts throb with a strange contentment, memories of the denial blurring into acceptance I can't fully explain.

My sobs quiet to shaky breaths, the explanation twisting deeper into my confusion—resentment flaring even as a traitorous part of me leans into his hold, the warmth seeping through the ache.

No words come; I nod faintly, too raw to argue, the welts pulsing like echoes of his words.

Satisfied, he helps me pull up my jeans over the tender skin, the fabric rough against the marks, then guides me—arm secure around my shoulders—to the small office off the tack room. The space is spotless now, a far cry from the cluttered chaos it once was.

He flips open a heavy ledger on the desk, the pages filled with neat columns of meticulously documented expenses: dates, vendors, amounts for materials and labor, every cent poured into the ranch's revival.

"All accounted for." His voice is steady as he traces a line with his finger. "Transparent. And after the year ends? It's all transferred to your name. The improvements, the land, the future—yours free and clear. No strings, no liens. I've made sure of it. This, me taking your farm..." he gestures around us. "It isn't theft; it's an investment. In you."

The revelation stuns me, a mix of unwanted gratitude and seething fury twisting in my chest, his hand still warm on my back as the implications sink in. The diamond collar around my neck burns.

He's not just taking; he's rebuilding. But on his terms. Always his terms.

Later, I sit on the new porch steps—reinforced, level, safe—watching the sunset paint everything gold. Julian sits beside me, possessive hand on my thigh, surveying his improvements like a king reviewing his kingdom.

"There's going to be a business dinner tomorrow night." He doesn't look at me. "Investors from Tokyo. You'll attend as my companion."

"Your property, you mean."

"My business partner." He turns to look at me. "I want them to see what I've acquired."

"An unwilling woman you've blackmailed?"

"A brilliant woman who understands land management better than any consultant I could hire." He stands, pulls me up. "Wear the black dress. The one with the pearls."

"More commands."

"Always." He leads me back to the car. "That's what you are learning to love about me."

I don't argue. There's no point, and no way I'll confirm or deny what he says. I can't, because I'm not willing to face the truth he's showing me. I'm not ready to face that yet.

As we drive away, I look back at the ranch—transformed, improved, but somehow still mine underneath. Like the roses, I'm being trained, guided, forced into a shape someone else decided I should take.

The terrifying part is that it might actually be making me stronger.

"Stop overthinking." Julian's hand lands back on my thigh. "You'll drive yourself crazy trying to hate something your body already accepts."

"My body's responses don't mean—"

"Your body's responses mean everything." He squeezes gently. "Your mind will catch up eventually. It always does."

Fourteen days in. Three hundred and fifty-one to go. But who's counting?

And he's right. My mind is already catching up and accepting that this might be something I truly crave.

CHAPTER 21

DAY 15

THE BLACK DRESS WITH PEARLS IS ARMOR MADE OF SILK. IT COVERS everything while revealing everything—the way fabric clings, the way the pearls draw attention to my throat, the way the slit allows glimpses of ~~creamy~~ thigh.

I am what I appear to be: an expensive acquisition.

"Perfect." Julian appears in the mirror behind me, already in his tuxedo, his reflection exuding that effortless command. "They'll be impressed."

"By your pet?" The words slip out sharper than I intend, my gaze locked on the diamond choker around my neck—Julian's mark of ownership.

He brings his hand to my throat, fingers curling lightly over the necklace, not squeezing, but possessive enough to send a shiver down my spine.

"My partner." He leans in close, his breath warm against my ear, voice dropping to that low, intimate rumble that always unravels me. "You can be my pet in private—but for this? Tonight?

I need a partner. Show them the mind I own, the one that tames empires like our ranch."

I meet his gaze in the mirror, the weight of it all pressing in—the ranch, the contract, this twisted life he's woven around me.

"The ranch I lost." My voice is quieter now, laced with the doubt that's gnawed at me since signing away my freedom. "If I couldn't save that, how can I possibly hold my own in your world?"

He straightens slightly, but his hand stays firm on my throat, thumb tracing the choker like a promise—or a threat.

"You have what it takes. More than enough." His gaze intensifies, dark and unyielding. "You didn't lose the land—your father did. He let pride and ruin bury it. But you? You're rising from it. Under me." His other hand slides to my waist, pulling me back against him, solid and unmovable. "Now go show them why I chose you."

"Then why parade me like—" I trail off, glancing down at the gown he's chosen: a sleek, deep black silk that hugs my curves, a neckline plunging deliberately to draw the eye, paired with the diamond choker that feels like a leash disguised as luxury. It's stunning, but it makes my skin crawl—am I arm candy for his empire, or something more?

"Because I want them to know you're mine." He steps around to face me fully, raking his gaze over me with that predatory satisfaction, honest and straightforward in its raw possession. "In every way that matters."

He brushes his fingers against my neck again, a subtle reminder of the choker locked on—the one etched with the words *I belong to Julian Blackwell*, until the year's end. But then his expression shifts, softening just a fraction, though the dominance never fades.

"Tonight, they'll see a sharp and brilliant woman who knows

markets and legacies better than those peacocks in their suits. You hold the keys to deals they'll envy—agricultural empires, sustainable yields, the futures they're scrambling to buy. You're valuable to me for that mind, for the way it challenges and completes mine. But make no mistake—they'll sense it all: the fire I control, the body I claim. You'll be the envy of the room, my partner in public... my everything in private."

His words land like a velvet command, easing the knot of confusion even as they tighten the invisible bonds around me. I belong to him—utterly, unmistakably—and tonight, the world will glimpse why that ownership is his greatest triumph.

The Obsidian eClub is the kind of place that doesn't display prices on the menu. Our table overlooks the city lights, and three Japanese executives wait with their translator. They stand when we approach, but their eyes linger on me in a way that makes Julian's hand tighten at my waist.

"Gentlemen, may I present Clara Hayes." He doesn't say girlfriend or companion. Just my name, his hand on me saying everything else.

"Ms. Hayes." The oldest, Mr. Yamamoto, bows slightly. "Julian speaks highly of your expertise in land management."

I glance at Julian, surprised. Has he discussed me professionally?

"The Hayes ranch has been in successful operation for three generations." Julian pulls out my chair. "Clara understands sustainable agriculture in ways that can't be taught in business school."

The dinner progresses with a discussion of their potential investment—a massive agricultural development. They defer to Julian, but increasingly, they ask my opinion.

"What do you think of water rights in this region, Ms. Hayes?" Yamamoto asks.

I start to answer, then feel Julian's hand on my knee under the table. A warning? No, it's encouragement. He strokes his thumb once: *go ahead.*

"Water rights here are complicated by historical usage claims." I warm to the subject. "The Hayes ranch, for instance, has senior water rights dating to 1892..."

I talk for ten minutes about something I understand and am passionate about, something that isn't about submission or control. The men listen intently and take notes. Julian's hand stays on my knee, both proud and possessive at once.

"Fascinating." Yamamoto nods. "Your practical experience is invaluable."

"She's invaluable in many ways." Julian's voice carries layers of meaning.

The conversation shifts to Japanese, and the executives discuss among themselves. Julian leans close, breath warm against my ear.

"You're doing beautifully."

"I'm performing as commanded."

"You're being yourself. That's what I wanted them to see." Julian's voice is a low murmur beside me, pitched just for my ears amid the clink of silverware and the executives' drone about tariffs and yields.

Hidden beneath the heavy linen tablecloth, his hand slides higher along my thigh, fingers tracing the hem of my short black dress—silk that barely skims mid-thigh when I sit, leaving me exposed, no panties as per his standing rule.

I shift in my chair, pulse quickening, but force a steady smile for the table. The Obsidian Club gleams like everything else in Julian's world—crystal, candlelight, and power polished to a mirror sheen. On the surface, it's where executives broker mergers over Bordeaux, where fortunes change hands between courses. Everyone knows the Club by reputation—its membership is envied and whispered about in private. Its invitations are coveted.

But sitting here, surrounded by powerful men, I feel the current beneath the civility. The kind of quiet dominance that doesn't need to be spoken to be understood.

Tonight, they're here for Julian's latest venture: a sustainable model for drought-resistant farming. My input on soil integration and market projections has them leaning in, impressed despite themselves.

"Yes, integrating those hybrid grains could offset the water costs by twenty percent." I keep my voice even as dessert arrives—chocolate torte sliced with precision, mirroring the way Julian's fingers part my folds under the table.

He dips in without warning, one thick digit circling my clit in slow, deliberate strokes, slick from my earlier arousal during dinner debates. Heat floods me, traitorous and insistent, but I clench my napkin in my lap, nails digging into my palms.

"We've run the numbers—it's viable if we—"

His touch quickens, thumb joining to press and rub, building friction that makes my thighs tremble. I bite the inside of my cheek, tasting blood, as an executive nods approvingly.

"Impressive foresight, Ms. Hayes. Your family's land must've given you real insight."

Julian's free hand lifts his wine glass in a toast, utterly composed, while his hidden fingers plunge deeper—one, now two—curling inside me, pumping in shallow rhythm that grazes that spot, driving me toward the edge.

My breath hitches, disguised as a sip of water, my core clenching around him as pleasure coils tight, unbearable.

"It did." My voice thins. "Hands-on... experience."

The double entendre burns my cheeks, but Julian's eyes flick to mine, dark with amusement and hunger. He's enjoying my fight to stay poised, the executives oblivious across the table.

Dessert forks scrape plates, conversation turning to logistics, but Julian doesn't let up. His circling intensifies, thumb grinding my clit while his fingers thrust relentlessly, the wet sounds mercifully drowned by the ballroom's hum.

I'm soaked, hips twitching involuntarily under the table, orgasm hovering like a threat—right there, if he doesn't stop, I'll shatter in front of them all.

"Tell them about the yield projections again." Casual as ever. His command is iron.

I open my mouth to respond, but a gasp escapes instead, thighs clamping on his hand.

The lead executive pauses, eyebrow raised. "Everything alright, Miss Hayes?"

Julian withdraws his fingers abruptly, leaving me throbbing and empty, a whine dying in my throat.

"Actually." He signals the waiter. "I think we've covered enough for now. Clara, you look flushed—perhaps a moment to freshen up?" He stands, all urbane charm, extending a hand to help me rise.

My legs wobble as I take his hand. The gown rides up dangerously short, but I nod, excusing myself with a murmured apology. Julian waits a beat—long enough for decorum—before following, the executives chuckling about "young stamina" as the door swings shut.

The private bathroom down the hall is lavish, marble and gold, but I barely register it before the door locks behind me. I whirl, heart pounding, leaning against the sink to steady myself, and Julian looks at me with heat and hunger.

"What the hell was that?" The ache between my legs betrays me, body still humming from his touch.

Julian stalks forward, caging me against the wall with his body, tuxedo pristine despite the feral glint in his eyes.

"That was a reminder." He fists his hand in my hair, tilting my head back as the other hikes my gown, exposing me fully—no barriers, just slick need. "You hold your own out there, brilliant as ever. But you don't get to forget who owns you." He grinds his palm against my core, rough and demanding, and I arch despite myself, a moan slipping free.

"Please—" It's half-protest, half-plea, but when he frees his cock—hard, thick, straining against his slacks—and notches it at my entrance, I don't push away.

Instead, my legs part wider, hips tilting up to meet him, pulling him in. Surprise flickers in his eyes as I wrap my thighs around his waist, locking my ankles behind him, the stretch burning sweet as my walls flutter around his length.

God, I want this

I surge up, capturing his mouth in a tentative kiss—my first real reciprocation—lips parting under his, tasting the wine and dominance. He grips my ass to pin me against the wall, thrusting deep and possessively.

"That's it, Clara—take every inch. My cock filling your pussy, stretching you just right." His pace turns savage, grinding against that spot with each drive, the wall cool and unyielding at my back as my gown bunches at my waist.

He kisses me—claiming my lips, nipping my neck—but this time, I respond, nipping back, my tongue tangling with his in fleeting hunger.

"Harder." I gasp. Nails dig into his shoulders through the jacket, meeting his rhythm with a roll of my hips, my core clenching greedily around him. "Deeper, please, I need it harder."

The words tumble out, raw and unfiltered, my body arching to take more, passion blooming fierce and surprising even to me.

He groans, his pace stuttering at my plea before he obliges, pounding relentlessly, one hand bracing by my head while the other slides between us to circle my clit—adding that final spark.

"Greedy for it, aren't you? Your pussy gripping me like it never wants to let go—fuck, so perfect, taking me all."

But then it slips: "Julian—oh God, Julian, please let me come." His name on my lips, forbidden and intimate, hangs in the air.

He stills for a heartbeat, buried deep, eyes locking on mine—dark with shock, but not anger. No correction comes. Instead, a low, possessive rumble vibrates through him, as if the slip unlocks something deeper, a new layer of connection between us.

He surges forward again, thrusts turning wilder, almost reverent in their intensity.

"Come for me, Clara—milk my cock, show me how much you need this."

Pleasure shatters through me, my walls pulsing around him as I cry out, legs tightening, body shuddering against the wall. He follows with a guttural groan, spilling hot and deep, grinding through the waves until we're both trembling, locked together.

He pulls back slowly, easing me down but keeping me steady. His eyes search mine—still dominant, but laced with something deeper, like triumph edged with wonder at this shift.

"Good girl." He straightens my gown with surprising tenderness, thumb brushing my swollen lips. "Now let's seal that deal."

We return to the table, a subtle crash leaving me fatigued, wondering why the peak felt so enhanced. The executives pretend nothing's amiss—though their knowing glances suggest the club's undercurrents run deep.

Over coffee, they agree to the terms: Investments flow.

Julian's hand finds mine under the table once more, squeezing possessively, and for the first time, I squeeze back.

In the car afterward, I'm shaking—from anger, from arousal, from the complexity of what just happened.

"You used me to close that deal."

"I showcased you." He drives with one hand, the other possessively on my thigh. "Your intelligence closed the deal. Your submission to me just... sweetened it."

"They knew what you were doing."

"They suspected. Japanese business culture understands power dynamics better than most." He squeezes my thigh. "They saw a man in control of his acquisitions. It impressed them."

"I'm not an acquisition—"

"Aren't you?" He glances at me. "Bought and paid for with your ranch as currency?"

The truth of it stings. "You're sick."

"I'm honest." We pull into his garage. "And you performed perfectly tonight. As a business partner and as mine."

"Don't—"

"What? Don't acknowledge that you came in that bathroom while I fucked you against the wall? That you bit my shoulder to stay quiet? That you loved every second of being commanded in public?"

Heat floods my face. "That's not—"

"Rule three. Complete honesty."

He gets out, comes around to open my door. When I don't move, he exhales, a sound more tired than angry. The shift in his expression catches me off guard—less predator, more man remembering something he can't quite let go.

"A memory for you—Senior year. The winter formal you attended with Marcus Henley."

I look up, surprised by the sudden shift in conversation.

"You wore silver. Hair in some complicated updo that left your neck bare." He looks distant, lost in the past. "I spent the entire night watching you dance with him, laugh with him, let him touch what should have been mine."

"Julian—"

"I got drunk. First and only time in high school." He helps me out of the car and holds my hand. "Drove to your ranch at two AM. Stood in your driveway throwing rocks at your window like some pathetic Romeo."

"I never knew—"

"Your father knew." His jaw tightens. "Came out with his shotgun. Not loaded—I found out later—but effective enough. Told me if I ever came near you again, he'd destroy my family the way my father was destroying his."

We're in the house now, moving through familiar halls.

"So I waited." He continues. "Graduated. Built my empire. Watched from a distance as you struggled. Waited for the perfect moment to make you mine without interference."

"And destroyed my father. We've been over this Jul—ummm, Mr. Blackwell." I shake my head in frustration. "I wish you would lift that rule."

"I won't. As for your father, he was destroying himself. Bad investments, worse loans. I just..." He pauses at his bedroom door, "directed the destruction to my benefit."

"That's savage."

"That's strategy." He opens the door and guides me inside. "And it worked. You're here. Mine. Wearing a collar I locked around your neck. I took you to a dinner where I commanded you in public. And with you by my side, I closed a deal worth billions. My obsession for you may not be healthy, but it has its uses."

I want to protest, to fight, to maintain some dignity. But he's right. About all of it.

"Fifteen days," I say quietly. "That's all it's been."

"Fifteen days of you learning what you really are." He moves behind me, hands rubbing my shoulders.

"I'm counting each one."

"So am I, but for different reasons. You're counting down toward freedom. I'm counting how many days I have to convince you to stay."

"I'll never—"

"Never say never." He turns me to face him. "You've already broken so many of your own rules. What's one more?"

He's right, and I hate him for it. Hate myself more for the small voice asking, *What if I stayed? What if this is what I've always needed?*

But that's exhaustion talking. Stockholm syndrome. It has to be.

Doesn't it?

And if I stay, will he still force me to call him Mr. Blackwell? And why does thinking that name make me wet?

CHAPTER 22
DAY 18

I can't sleep. Again.

Julian's breathing is deep and even beside me, one arm thrown possessively across my waist, even in sleep. I've learned to move carefully, incrementally, to escape without waking him.

Tonight, I have a destination.

The library calls to me—specifically, the books he left for my "education." The ones I dismissed as fantasy. The ones that have been haunting my dreams.

I curl into the leather chair, pulling *The Loving Dominant* into my lap. The chapter on psychological surrender falls open—clearly well-read, though not by me. Julian's notes fill the margins in his sharp handwriting.

Clara will fight this—her nature demands it—but once she understands surrender is strength, not weakness...

I slam it shut, grab another. *Power Exchange in Practice*. This one has sticky notes throughout, marking passages. I read one:

The submissive often takes months to understand their true power in the dynamic. They control the pace, the intensity, the very existence of the exchange through their consent.

Julian's note beneath: *She hasn't realized yet that she could destroy me with a word. That her surrender is what gives me life.*

My hands shake. Is that true? Do I have power here that I don't recognize?

"Interesting reading?"

I jump, the book falling. Julian stands in the doorway, silk pajama pants low on his hips, chest bare. He looks like sin incarnate.

"I couldn't sleep—"

"So you came to read about what you claim to hate?" He moves into the room with predatory grace, picks up the fallen book. "Page 247. Read it aloud."

"Julian—"

He narrows his eyes, and I correct myself.

"Mr. Blackwell, I don't—"

"Read it."

My voice shakes as I read: "The Dominant may choose to demonstrate control through denial—keeping the submissive at the edge of pleasure without release, building need until the submissive understands that their pleasure belongs entirely to—"

"Enough." He takes the book and sets it aside. "Is that what you were hoping to understand? Why I control your orgasms?"

"I was trying to understand all of it." The admission burns. "Why does my body respond when my mind says no. Why I get wet when you command me? Why I—" I stop, having said too much.

"Why you what?"

"Why I dream about you." The words barely whisper out.

Something dark shifts in his expression. "Tell me about these dreams."

"No."

"Rule three."

"Fine." Anger is easier than vulnerability. "I dream about kneeling for you. About wanting it. Are you happy?"

"I'm intrigued." He pulls me to standing, backs me against the bookshelf. "In these dreams—do I hurt you?"

"Sometimes." I can barely breathe with him this close. "You... take care of me. Control me but... lovingly. Like in the books."

"And you hate that."

"I hate that I don't hate it." The truth spills. "I hate that those women in the books found freedom in surrender, and part of me wants that. Wants to stop fighting everything. Wants someone strong enough to—"

"To what?"

"To make me stop being strong all the time." Tears prick my eyes. "I've been the strong one since Mom died. Since Dad got sick. Making every decision, fighting every battle. And these books talk about the relief of letting go, and I want that so badly it terrifies me."

He frames my face, thumbs wiping tears I didn't know were falling. "That's what I've been trying to give you."

"Through force."

"Through removal of choice." His voice gentles. "You'd never choose submission freely—too proud, too conditioned to be the fighter. So I removed the option. Made it a business transaction. Gave you an excuse to surrender."

"That's manipulation—"

"That's understanding you better than you understand yourself." He pulls back slightly. "Which scene were you reading when I found you?"

Heat floods my face. I hesitate, gaze dropping to the floor—anything to avoid the specifics burning in my mind.

"The one about... restraint." It's a partial truth, skirting the deeper pull toward the pain-laced scenes that had my pulse racing.

He tilts his head, reading me like an open book, thumb tracing my jaw with deceptive gentleness.

"Restraint is broad. Be specific."

When I stay silent, lips pressed tight, he steps closer, his bare chest brushing mine, voice dropping to that commanding timbre.

"Page 186? Where the Dominant ties the submissive to the bed and worships her body for hours without letting her come? Or 193, where the Dominant ties his submissive to the cross and whips her?"

I squirm against the shelf, throat tight, trying to hold back the flood. "I... don't remember the page."

His gaze sharpens, unfooled. "Liar. There's nothing wrong in wanting to explore this—I've seen you tremble at my touch, felt you arch into the bite of it. Tell me. Is it the pain you want to explore? Or, like in the barn, is it the punishment you crave—the structure of it, the release?"

The barn. The memory hits like a lash—his belt across my skin, the sting blending with something darker, more needed. My breath hitches, and the dam breaks.

"Yes." A whisper. Then louder, meeting his gaze. "To both. The pain... and the punishment. I want to know why it feels like... like breathing again."

He nods slowly, a flicker of pride softening the intensity in his eyes. "Thank you for being honest with me. That's the first step." He places his hand on my cheek, the touch almost reverent. "Would you like to experience that? See if reality matches fiction?"

There's an eagerness in his voice—not just dominance, but a genuine hunger to guide me through this, to fulfill every shadowed fantasy I've buried, to explore the depths of what we could be together.

"I—I don't—"

"Yes or no. Would you like to understand why the woman in that scene cried from joy, not pain?"

I swallow hard, the pull of it too strong to deny anymore.

"Yes."

The word hangs between us, a key turning in a lock.

His smile is slow, triumphant, as he takes my hand—firm, but not crushing—and leads me from the library, down the shadowed hall to the Red Room.

The door clicks open. The St. Andrew's cross stands in one corner, a padded bench nearby, coils of silk rope, and implements arranged on a side table. The air smells faintly of leather and sandalwood, charged with possibility.

"Trust me tonight." He guides me to the center of the room, his voice a steady anchor. "We'll go slow. Red for stop, yellow for pause."

I hesitate, the weight of our contract pressing in—the one that made safewords a trapdoor to everything crumbling.

"And if I use it... I void the contract?"

He pauses, cupping my chin to lift my gaze to his face. His gaze is steady and sincere, the dominance tempered by something deeper.

"For tonight only, you may use your safewords. I want to free you as much as I can, so you can embrace this without fear. Use them if you need to; I'll honor them as I honor you."

"Thank you."

He brushes his thumb over my lower lip, a promise sealed—tender, almost gentle in the dim light of the Red Room. But then his voice firms, the dominance threading back through like steel beneath silk.

"Come morning, my control resumes as always." His gaze holds mine, unyielding yet laced with that rare warmth, a reminder that his tenderness is granted, not surrendered—his dominance eternal, even in vulnerability.

He selects a bundle of silk ropes—soft, crimson strands that whisper against my skin as he begins.

"Arms above your head." He wraps the first loop around my wrists, explaining each knot. "This is a single-column tie—secure but not biting. It holds without harm."

He threads the rope through an overhead ring, pulling my arms taut but not straining, my body stretched vertically.

"It holds you in place, in a position where you can't escape the lash."

My nightgown rides up, exposing me.

"Beautiful. Now, breathe. Feel the support."

He doesn't rush. Pleasure builds as my body relaxes into the ropes. He focuses on worship—kneeling before me, hands gliding over my thighs, lips following in feather-light kisses that trail upward.

"You're mine to cherish." His voice is husky as his mouth finds my core, tongue lapping slowly and deliberately.

Pleasure builds like a tide, my hips bucking instinctively, but he pulls back just as I crest, denying me with a soft chuckle.

"Not yet. Let it build." He repeats it—twice, three times— teasing with fingers, mouth, the heat of his breath, each edge leaving me gasping, body quivering in the ropes, slick and desperate.

My mind fractures under the intensity, surrender inching closer.

Sensing my readiness, he rises, selecting a deerskin flogger from the table—soft suede tails, light and snappy—or so I've read.

"Sensation first." He trails the falls over my skin like a caress.

The first strike is gentle, a warm sting across my breasts, just shy of pain, sending sparks through my nerves.

"How's that?" He watches my face, attuned.

"More." The word surprises me.

He nods, building rhythm—snaps against thighs, stomach, the undersides of my arms—each one a thrum of heat that blurs into pleasure. My skin heats under the onslaught. He finds my limits, testing with firmer lashes, pausing at my winces.

"Yellow?" His hand soothes the reddened flesh. When I shake my head, eyes locked on him, he presses. "Tell me—are you interested in why pain brings such pleasure? How it unlocks you like this?"

"Yes." My voice is raw, the vulnerability stripping me bare. "I want to explore it."

Something ignites in his eyes. "Then we go deeper."

He sets the flogger aside, picking up a crop—leather tip for pinpoint strikes. It cracks lightly against my inner thighs, a sharp bloom that makes me cry out, then moan as endorphins flood in.

Next, his belt doubled, swung with controlled force across my ass, the impact deeper. Finally, his hand—bare palm meeting flesh in rhythmic strikes that leave handprints, each one drawing whimpers that turn to pleas.

Pain and pleasure entwine, while my body comes alive, every nerve singing his name.

He unties me with deliberate slowness, but only to reposition me—dropping me to my knees before him.

"Please me first." There's no gentleness now.

I free his cock from his pants, and it's thick, hard, and already leaking.

My denial throbs, but I lean in, mouth opening eagerly despite the ache. He fucks my mouth hard, fisting my hair, thrusting deep and unyielding, making it last—slow drags, then relentless pumps that hit the back of my throat, tears streaming as I gag and take it, hollowing my cheeks to please him.

His groans fill the room, control fraying, but he draws it out, hips snapping until he's on the edge.

Before he comes, he spins me roughly, forcing me up and against the cross—wrists rebound swiftly, ass presented. His hand cracks down a few more times, spanking the already tender flesh until it's fire-hot, then he notches at my entrance from behind.

"What do you want? Say it."

"You—inside me," I beg, no fight left, only need. "Hard—please."

He thrusts in with a growl, filling me completely, the stretch exquisite after the denial.

"Fuck, so tight—taking me like you were made for it." His pace is punishing, hips slamming against my reddened ass, one hand gripping my hip while the other snakes around to circle my clit.

I push back, meeting him, the cross biting into my palms as passion surges—raw, unfiltered. "Yes! Harder," I gasp again. "Deeper—God, please let me come."

"Admit it," he demands, voice strained. "You crave this—surrender, pain, my cock owning every part of you."

"Yes—yes to all of it." The words tear free as an orgasm crashes through me, my walls clenching around him in waves, milking him until he roars, spilling deep, grinding through the aftershocks.

He unties me, gently, carrying me to the padded bench. There, he places cool cloths on my skin, soothing lotion massaged into welts and rope marks, water sipped from his hand.

We discuss the books in hushed tones, wrapped in a blanket, his arms a rare, protective cocoon.

"The reality is more intense than the fiction," I admit finally, tracing a fading line on my thigh. "Deeper. Like it rewires you."

He presses a kiss to my temple. "I learned these techniques specifically for you. Read every book, trained in ropes from a master in Japan, flogging from masters in elite clubs. All to understand how to give you what you need, even before you knew it yourself."

I nestle closer, the terror ebbing into tentative peace. For the first time, surrender feels like coming home.

CHAPTER 23
DAY 19

The red dress he's chosen for tonight is different from the first one. This has structure—a corset-style bodice that cinches every-thing, a full skirt that moves like liquid fire. I look like something from a fairytale. Or a nightmare, depending on the perspective.

"The surprise at the ranch," I say as he zips me into it. "You never said what it was."

"Horses." His hands smooth the fabric at my waist. "Two Arabians. Bloodlines you researched seven years ago when you thought the ranch might expand into breeding."

My breath catches. "How could you possibly know—"

"Your browser history at the library was hardly private." He steps back to survey his work. "I told you—I studied everything about you."

"That's invasion of privacy—"

"That's thorough preparation." He produces a long velvet box. "For tonight."

Inside is a necklace that makes my stomach drop. It's beau-tiful—garnets that match the deep crimson gown laid out on the bed—but it's also clearly more. The width, the weight, the way it will sit at my throat like a constant, unyielding claim...

"This is—"

"A collar disguised as jewelry." He takes it from the box, the garnets catching the light like drops of blood, his fingers deft as he unclips the heavy silver chain. "You'll wear it tonight instead of the diamonds. Feel it every moment. Remember what it represents—your surrender, your place at my side."

"Julian—it's..."

Stunning?

His eyes narrow at the name slip, a flicker of warning in the dark depths, but he lets it pass without correction, his focus shifting to the velvet pouch beside the box.

"It complements your permanent collar nicely, but there's more."

I watch, my breath shallow, as he reveals the "something special" he mentioned earlier. It's a small, sleek vibrator—curved for proper placement, remote-controlled, with a harness of silken straps designed to nestle it intimately against my body beneath the gown. No panties, as always, but this... this is deliberate torment wrapped in luxury.

"Hold still," he murmurs, kneeling before me in the vanity's soft glow.

His hands are steady, almost reverent, as he parts my thighs and secures it in place—the cool silicone pressing against my clit, the internal piece sliding deep with ease, my body still sensitive from last night. He adjusts the straps, hidden under the gown's folds, then stands, pocketing the remote with a satisfied smile.

"Perfect. You'll feel me with you all evening."

The drive to the Obsidian Club's gala is tense, the city lights blurring past the tinted windows of the Maybach. I shift constantly in the leather seat, hyperaware of everything—the collar's cool weight encircling my throat, the vibrator's insistent presence humming faintly even now on its lowest setting, and Julian's profile beside me, utterly composed, exuding that predatory satisfaction that makes my pulse race.

The gown clings like a second skin, the garnets winking at my reflection in the partition—elegant from afar, but up close, a mark of ownership.

He glances over, eyes glinting. "Comfortable?"

Before I can answer, he clicks the remote. The vibration surges to life—strong, rhythmic pulses that target my clit with unerring accuracy, the internal arm curling just right. My body responds more intensely than before.

"Tonight," he says, voice low and intent, watching me with that mix of command and care, "I will drown you in pleasure. A reward for what you gave me in the Red Room last night—your honesty, your surrender."

"Oh God—" The first wave builds fast, my thighs clenching as I grip the door handle, trying to stay silent amid the driver's discreet presence up front. But he doesn't edge me this time; he pushes, ramping it higher, the vibrations intensifying into a relentless buzz that has me arching, a gasp escaping despite my bitten lip. "Are you going to let me come? Or torment me all night?"

"Yes." His dark eyes twinkle with wicked intent, a smirk curling his lips as he leans in, voice dropping to a velvet murmur laced with promise. "To both. Go ahead. You're free to come... all night long. I'll flood you with pleasure until you're begging for mercy, every secret spot of you owned by pleasure you can't escape."

The words paint dark delights in my mind—endless waves crashing over me in public, his control turning ecstasy into an exquisite overload—and a flicker of fear twists in my gut, the vulnerability of it all too raw. But the need is stronger, a desperate pull that drowns out caution; I need this release too much to care, to stop.

Pleasure coils tight, shattering through me in seconds—my first orgasm of the night, walls fluttering around the intruder, slick heat soaking the seat. I shudder, head falling back, but he doesn't stop, dialing it back just enough to let me breathe before surging again.

"Again," he commands softly, his free hand claiming mine, thumb stroking my knuckles in a grounding contrast to the torment between my legs.

The second orgasm comes harder, my body betraying me with a muffled whimper, hips bucking involuntarily as ecstasy rips through, leaving me trembling and dazed. By my third climax of the night, I'm panting, tears pricking my eyes, the collar suddenly feeling tight around my throat.

"It's too much..."

"Yes."

He eases it then, but only to a teasing hum.

"Don't think I didn't catch that slip earlier with the collar." His voice is laced with dark amusement, and he leans closer so his breath fans my ear. "Remember how you address me—we are not equals in this relationship." He clicks the remote, the vibrations pulsing faster than before, forcing the pleasure to rebuild despite my shudders. "You will take it for me. Every wave, every release— surrender to the pleasure."

The fourth orgasm crashes over me like a storm, my nails digging into his hand as I convulse silently, body writhing in the seat, a choked cry swallowed by the roar in my ears.

He holds me through it, murmuring praises—"Good girl, just like that"—before intensifying once more, the toy's dual action grinding against my g-spot and clit in merciless harmony.

The fifth release builds slower but deeper, my vision blurring as I teeter on the edge of overload, every muscle taut until it snaps —waves of bliss so intense they border on pain, leaving me limp and gasping, slick thighs pressed together in futile resistance. Finally, as the sixth orgasm looms, he dials it down to a faint buzz, my body a quivering wreck, utterly spent before we've even arrived.

"Stop fidgeting." As we near the venue, the vibrator finally quiets, though my body hums with aftershocks.

"Please, no more. I can't—this is too much—"

"It is exactly enough." He takes my hand, thumb stroking over my pulse. "Tonight, you learn the difference between public and private submission."

The Morrison Foundation gala is old money trying to look progressive. The same families who've run this state for genera- tions, pretending they care about preservation while buying up land for development.

"Julian Blackwell." Judge Morrison greets us at the entrance— the same judge who witnessed our contract. "And Ms. Hayes. Lovely to see you again."

I manage a smile while the collar feels like it's burning my throat.

We're barely inside the grand ballroom of the Obsidian Club when the whispers start rippling through the crowd, heads turning our way. Everyone knows something: that I'm living with Julian now, that the ranch debt was mysteriously transferred to him, that we're together in some twisted capacity. But they don't know the truth—the contract, the collar hidden as jewelry at my throat, the vibrator still nestled inside me, a silent threat of plea- sure under his control.

The air is thick with crystal clinks and murmured speculation, the deep crimson of my gown drawing eyes like a flame.

"Clara Hayes?" The voice slices through, saccharine sweet with an undercurrent of venom.

I turn to find Melissa Conway—high school's queen bee, now a polished realtor who probably helps men like Julian acquire failing properties and shatter families like mine. Her blonde waves are artfully tousled, her smile all teeth as she sips champagne.

"Melissa. It's been years. You look well."

She catalogs everything in a single sweep—the expensive silk of my dress hugging my curves, the garnet necklace gleaming like a subtle shackle, Julian's proprietary hand resting at the small of my back.

"I heard you two finally got together. Only took what, seventeen years? From awkward high school crushes to... this." She gestures vaguely between us, lingering on his touch with poorly veiled curiosity.

Julian's fingers press a fraction firmer, a silent claim. "Some things are worth the wait."

She laughs lightly, but there's a probing edge to it. "High school seems like a lifetime ago. Remember all that drama back then? Prom, especially—God, the tension around you two was thicker than the fog machine at the dance."

The mention of prom hits like gasoline, igniting old memories I buried deep.

Julian's voice cuts in smoothly, conversational but laced with intent. "You were dating Tyler Henderson, weren't you?" He traces a subtle circle against my skin that sends a shiver up my spine. "Didn't he break up with you at prom?"

"Oh God, that was brutal." She tosses her head back with genuine amusement, oblivious to the way my breath hitches as Julian's free hand slips into his pocket. "But it looks like you finally got the girl." She shifts her attention to me.

I feel it immediately—the remote clicking under his thumb, the vibrator humming to life inside me on a low, insistent thrum that targets my clit with precision.

Pleasure coils low in my belly, the vibrations building stealthily, forcing my thighs to press together beneath the gown's folds.

I grip Julian's arm for balance, trying to keep my face neutral as Melissa rambles on, but he's merciless, ramping it higher with a subtle twist of his wrist.

The pulses intensify, a rhythmic assault that has my inner walls clenching around the toy, edging me right to the brink— heat flooding my core, breaths coming in shallow, quick gasps. I bite the inside of my cheek to stifle a whimper, the edge so sharp it borders on torment, my body trembling against him.

Julian's hand tightens imperceptibly at my waist, his expression unchanging—cool, engaged.

"Playing the long game, were you? All those years must make this moment all the sweeter." Melissa eyes me knowingly, sipping her drink as if she senses the undercurrent but can't place it.

"Something like that." Julian's voice is steady, but I feel the smirk in the way his fingers dig in, holding me upright as the vibrations throb relentlessly, keeping me teetering on that exquisite precipice.

Sweat beads at my temples; I'm seconds from shattering right in front of her, the public humiliation a dizzying mix of fear and forbidden thrill.

Finally, Melissa drifts away with a wave and a parting quip about "old flames reigniting." Her laughter fades into the crowd, leaving us amid the swirling guests who now cast lingering glances our way.

Before I can catch my breath or beg for mercy, Julian turns me toward him, sliding his hand up to cup the nape of my neck, pulling me into a deep, possessive kiss.

He claims my lips with unapologetic intensity, an explicit declaration that we're not just together; we're entangled. As our mouths fuse, tongues brushing in a dance that's equal parts passion and control, he clicks the remote higher. The vibrations explode into a fierce, grinding rhythm, pushing me mercilessly over the edge.

The orgasm rips through me, the undulating waves prolonged, pleasure so intense it disorients me.

My body shudders uncontrollably in his arms, walls spasming around the toy in wave after wave of blinding ecstasy. I nearly cry out—gasping, whimpering—but his kiss swallows it all, muffling the sounds against his mouth, his body shielding the subtle arch of mine from prying eyes.

Slick heat floods me, thighs quivering as the pleasure peaks and drags, leaving me limp and dazed in his hold.

He doesn't pull away until the aftershocks fade, breaking the kiss slowly, his gaze locking on mine with that triumphant gleam, as if to say, *See? You come for me anywhere, anytime.*

Around us, a few approving murmurs ripple—the kiss sealing our facade, the power play hidden in plain sight.

Melissa is gone, but others approach throughout the cocktail hour, each with their own memory of our high school dynamics, drawn like moths to the flame of our history.

"Remember when Mr. Peterson made you lab partners? You two could barely look at each other without sparks flying."

"That time at the winter formal when you threw rocks at her window, Julian—romantic or creepy, depending on who you ask."

"Your fathers never did get along, did they? All that bad blood... makes this reunion poetic, almost."

Each comment builds a picture I never saw entirely—Julian's obsession was never a secret, just a patient one.

Everyone knew. Everyone watched. Everyone waited for us to inevitably collide, like stars too close to orbit without crashing.

"I need air." I whisper, during a break in conversation, the vibrator now a low hum.

"No, you don't." His voice is steel. He guides me toward the dance floor instead. "You need to stop running from the truth."

"What truth?"

"That we were always going to end up here." He guides me toward a quiet corner. "That every person in this room saw it except you."

A new voice interrupts. "Clara? Clara Hayes?"

I freeze. Marcus Henley—the boy who took me to prom, whom I dated briefly before college. He looks good, but is softer than Julian.

"Marcus."

"I heard you were back." He shifts his attention to Julian with barely concealed dislike. "And with him."

"Problem, Henley?" Julian's voice carries a warning.

"No problem." But Marcus looks at me with concern. "Just surprised. Clara, are you... okay?"

"No problem." But Marcus looks at me with concern. "Just surprised. Clara, are you... okay?"

The question holds weight. He's asking if I'm here voluntarily, if I need help. For a moment, I consider it. Consider telling the truth—that I'm being blackmailed, controlled, held by contract rather than choice.

"She's perfect." Julian answers for me, sliding his hand to my throat, thumb resting against the collar.

As if to underscore his words, his other hand dips into his pocket, and suddenly the vibrator surges to life at its highest setting—a bald power play, the relentless pulses slamming through me like a shockwave, reminding me exactly who holds the reins.

My knees buckle slightly, but his grip keeps me upright, the intensity coiling heat low in my belly even as humiliation burns my cheeks.

"Aren't you, Clara?" Julian demands. The unspoken command echoes in my head, daring me to contradict him in front of Marcus.

But something rebels in me. Perhaps it's seeing Marcus—a reminder of normal choices and normal relationships. Maybe it's the weight of everyone's assumptions. Maybe it's just exhaustion from pretending.

"Actually," I step away from Julian's touch, forcing my voice steady despite the toy's merciless assault, "I need to powder my nose."

I leave before he can stop me, moving quickly through the crowd toward the bathroom, the vibrations making every step a torment of building need.

Heart pounding, I slip into the dimly lit hallway beyond the ballroom doors, my heels clicking urgently against the marble floor as I pick up speed, desperate for even a moment's space to breathe, to think without Julian's shadow looming.

A place to remove the distraction between my legs threatening to drop me to my knees. I weave past a cluster of waitstaff, my breath coming in shallow gasps.

Then I feel it—Julian's presence, like a chill down my spine. The air shifts behind me. Footsteps, measured and unhurried, echo closer, and I know without looking that he's there, closing the distance.

I don't make it far. Julian's hand catches my elbow in the hall-way, grip firm but not painful, steering me away from prying eyes into a shadowed alcove near a service door before pulling me through the door into a small, unused antechamber—likely a storage space for the venue, dimly lit and mercifully empty. The door clicks shut behind us, muffling the gala's hum.

"That was a mistake."

"Was it?" Defiance feels good after days of submission, even as my body betrays me, thighs slick and trembling. "Or was it the first honest thing that's happened tonight?"

"You want honesty?" He backs me against the wall, caging me with his body, his presence overwhelming in the dim light. "Here's honesty—you're wet right now despite your little show of rebellion. You're thinking about what I'll do to punish you. Hoping that not only will I punish you, but that I'll make it hurt enough to make you forget you want it."

"You don't know—"

"I know everything." He slides his hand to my throat, over the collar, pressing just enough to make my pulse thunder beneath his fingers. "I know you read the chapter on discipline this afternoon."

Heat floods my face. "That's not—"

"Rule three, Clara."

He doesn't wait for my protest. With a swift motion, he bunches the fabric of my dress around my waist—no panties to contend with, just bare skin and the humming toy he inserted earlier.

Exposing me fully, he eases the vibrator free with a deft twist, setting it aside on a nearby shelf—the sudden emptiness leaves me aching, clenching around nothing as the vibrations fade.

"Skirt up." His tone brooks no argument, though it's already done.

He spins me to face the wall, one hand pressing between my shoulder blades to bend me forward. The first spank lands sharp across my bare skin—a crack that echoes in the small space, the sting blooming hot and immediate. I gasp, fingers splaying against the cool plaster.

"Count them." Another strike, harder, the pain radiating like fire.

"One." My breath hitches on the word.

He delivers nine more in quick succession—each one measured, controlled, turning my ass a throbbing red that I can feel even without seeing. The pain twists into something darker, needier, my body arching into each blow despite myself. By the tenth strike, tears prick my eyes, but so does the ache between my legs, every throb amplified without the toy's distraction.

After the last strike, his hand soothes my heated flesh, fingers dipping lower to circle where I'm drenched. He frees himself, thrusting into me in one deep, claiming stroke that has me crying out.

He fucks me hard against the wall, each snap of his hips a punctuation to his possession, fisting in my hair to hold me in place.

I shatter around him twice before he follows, spilling inside me with a guttural groan, his body pinning mine as we both come down. But he doesn't pull away immediately.

Instead, he reaches for the vibrator, slicking it briefly with my arousal before sliding it back into place, seating it firmly. He adjusts the remote to a low, teasing hum—not enough to push me over, just enough to keep the edge sharp and unrelenting.

"No more free orgasms tonight." His voice is low and commanding as he straightens my dress, though his eyes gleam with satisfaction. "This is part two of your punishment. You'll beg for release from here on out... or suffer in silence. Your choice."

My legs are jelly as he leads me back to the ballroom, the low vibrations a constant, torturous whisper that makes every step a secret battle, building need without mercy.

When we return, I'm shaking. My lipstick has been reapplied, but my eyes tell the story—pupils blown, cheeks flushed, that look of someone who's been thoroughly claimed.

Marcus is still there, watching with growing concern. "Clara—"

"Is fine." Julian finishes, his arm possessively around my waist. "We were just discussing ranch business."

"Ranch business." Marcus's tone suggests he knows exactly what happened. "Clara, if you need anything—"

"What she needs," Julian cuts in, his voice dangerous, "is for people like you to mind their own business."

"Maybe we should ask Clara what she needs."

The two men face off, seventeen years of rivalry condensing into this moment. The room notices, conversations quieting, attention turning.

"Stop." I say quietly, then louder: "Stop. Both of you."

They look at me—Marcus with hope, Julian with warning.

"Marcus, thank you for your concern, but I'm exactly where I choose to be, with the person I want to be with." The words taste like truth, the low hum of the vibrator underscoring every sylla-ble, weaving desire into conviction despite the contract that binds me. "Julian and I have an... arrangement that works for us."

"An arrangement?" Marcus steps closer. "Clara, that doesn't sound—"

"It sounds like none of your business." The words surprise everyone, including myself. "I'm not seventeen anymore. I can make my own choices."

Even if those choices aren't really choices.

Marcus retreats, hurt and confused, his shoulders slumping as he mutters a goodbye and fades back into the crowd. Julian's satisfaction radiates from him like heat, but there's something else beneath it—surprise? Pleasure that I defended our arrangement, even if it was laced with necessity?

"Well done." His voice is a low rumble against my ear. "You're learning to play the game."

"I'm learning to survive it."

"Same thing." He guides me toward the dance floor, his hand firm at the small of my back. "Dance with me."

"I don't want—"

"I wasn't asking."

He pulls me into his arms as a slow song begins, the orchestra's strings weaving a languid melody through the room. We move together, bodies close in the sway of the crowd, and I'm transported back to senior year—the last dance before graduation, watching him with another girl from across the gym, wondering what it would feel like to be in his arms like this, enveloped and claimed.

"You wanted to dance with me then." He reads my mind as easily as ever, his breath warm against my temple. "I saw you watching that last dance at prom."

"Everyone was watching. You were the golden boy."

"I was watching you watch me." He spreads his hand across my lower back, pressing me flush against him, the heat of his palm seeping through the fabric of my dress.

With a subtle shift, his other hand dips into his pocket, and I feel it immediately—the low hum between my legs intensifying to its maximum. A furious, unyielding vibration slams through me like lightning.

I gasp sharply, my body jolting in his hold, fingers digging into his shoulders as the pleasure coils viciously tight.

He knows exactly what he's doing—forcing me to the edge, testing my resolve, making me beg right here, amid the glittering crowd. The toy pulses relentlessly, every nerve alight, but I bite down on the plea rising in my throat.

Not yet. I won't give him the satisfaction so easily.

"You wore navy blue." His voice stays steady as if he hasn't just turned my world into a storm of need. "Hair down for once. You looked like you wanted to be anywhere else."

"I did." My words come out breathy and strained as we turn in time with the music.

The vibrations are merciless, building pressure low in my belly, my thighs trembling against his. I press my face briefly to his chest to muffle a whimper, but he only holds me tighter, guiding our steps with infuriating calm.

"Liar." He brushes his lips against my ear, amusement threading his tone. "You wanted to be in my arms. You just couldn't admit it. Do you remember my letter?"

"The one you slipped into my locker the day before graduation?" I look up at him, forcing my eyes to meet his despite the way the toy is unraveling me from the inside out.

The conversation anchors me, a desperate distraction, even as sweat beads at my temples and my breath comes in shorter, sharper gasps.

"I never opened it."

Something flashes across his face—hurt? Regret? The vulnerability there almost makes me forget the torment between my legs, but the vibrations don't relent, pushing me closer to the brink with every sway.

"Why not?" His voice is quieter now, the hand at my back tracing slow circles that only heighten the ache.

"Because I was scared of what it might say." The truth surprises me, spilling out amid the building desperation. "I threw it away unopened."

"It said I loved you." The admission is quiet, almost vulnerable, his gaze locking onto mine with an intensity that pierces through the fog of pleasure-pain. "That I'd wait for you. That someday you'd be mine."

The music swells around us, the crescendo of violins and piano rising like a tide, mirroring the unbearable urge cresting inside me. I can't hold it back anymore—the vibrations have me teetering on the razor's edge, arching involuntarily against his, every fiber screaming for release. Defiance crumbles under the onslaught.

"Please." The word breaks free at last, my voice a ragged plea muffled against his shirt. "Please, let me come. I can't— I need it."

"How do you address me?"

"Mr. Blackwell, will you please let me come?"

"Of course, my pleasure." He smiles down at me, dark and triumphant, his arm tightening to shelter me from the room's eyes. "Come for me. Now."

The permission unleashes it all. I shatter against him, the orgasm ripping through me in shuddering waves, my nails biting into his back as I bury my face in his chest to stifle the cry that escapes.

He holds me through it, unyielding, his body a shield as the tremors fade, the world narrowing to the steady beat of his heart under my cheek and the low thrum of satisfaction humming in my veins.

CHAPTER 24
DAYS 20–22

The days blur after the gala.

Every morning begins the same: breakfast at his table, orange juice I don't like but drink because it's expected. Then hours in his study, books waiting in precise stacks—psychology, power dynamics, memoirs of women who've written about surrender. Some clinical. Some erotic. All curated for me.

Sometimes Julian sits with me while I read, silent except for the occasional note scrawled in his leather-bound journal. At other times, he disappears for meetings, leaving instructions on which pages to study and what reflections to write. At night, he returns and questions me, coaxing out my reactions.

My answers are measured at first, but he always finds the cracks—an unguarded breath, a shift of my thighs, a tremor in my voice.

He hasn't taken me fully since the gala. Not the way he promised. He's content to keep me on a leash of denial, using his fingers, words, and the occasional brush of his mouth to keep me desperate.

Always stopping just before I break.

Always whispering that it's my choice to cross the line.

But while he denies my release, he never denies his own.

He uses me when he wants—his hand in my hair, his voice low and absolute. I'm on my knees more often than I'm on my feet.

Sometimes he wakes me with a touch to my throat and a quiet command; sometimes he draws me to him mid-afternoon, between meetings, using my mouth like it exists for no other purpose.

He never thanks me. Never asks. Just watches, silent, until his control frays and his release floods my tongue. Then he wipes his thumb across my lips, smearing what's left, and tells me I'm learning.

By the third night, my desperation is a kind of ache that has nothing to do with him and everything to do with me. My body thrums with need, hypersensitive, my skin too tight for the heat beneath it. Sleep won't come. My mind spins with contradictions —resentment and craving tangled into something I can't separate.

The books he assigns are starting to work their way under my skin. Words I once thought were rubbish now echo in my head when I close my eyes.

Power in surrender.

Choice in submission.

It isn't that I'm starting to believe them; it's that I can't stop thinking about them.

When he's gone, I spend hours with Scout curled at my feet— the one piece of the ranch he allowed me to keep. Julian calls him a distraction, but he hasn't sent him away.

Sometimes I catch Julian watching us, something unreadable flickering in his gaze before he looks away.

By the time Day 23 arrives, something new has crept in—something more complex than lust. My body still obeys him, but my mind claws at the edges. I wake already bristling, patience threadbare, denial turning to quiet rebellion. I want to defy him, to test the boundaries of this cage he's so carefully built.

So when he sits across from me at breakfast, when he orders me to eat, to drink, to obey, some part of me wants to push back—not to win, but to test. To see what happens when the girl he's been training stops behaving.

CHAPTER 25

DAY 23

"You're sulking." Julian's voice cuts through the quiet like a blade. Controlled. Unyielding.

"I'm complying." I push eggs around my plate without lifting my gaze. "Isn't that enough?"

"No." The word is flat, absolute. "Compliance without intent is still rebellion."

"Add it to my list of infractions." The words come out bitter.

His jaw flexes. Then his eyes drop to the untouched glass beside my plate. "Drink your orange juice."

I glance at it, grimace. "I don't like orange juice. Too acidic. Too bitter."

"That's not relevant." His tone doesn't waver. "You eat what I provide. You drink what I provide. That's one of your rules."

"It's breakfast, not boot camp."

"Drink it." The command lands soft but final, leaving no room for refusal.

I meet his gaze, defiant for one beat too long, before I lift the glass. The juice burns across my tongue—bright, bitter, cloying. I swallow anyway. His eyes follow every movement of my throat.

When I set the glass down, his lips curve—not warmth, not affection, but satisfaction. "Good girl."

The praise slides under my skin, unwanted and electric. I hate that. I hate how those two words, said like *that* make me hot. I'm a grown woman, not a girl. Yet, when Julian says those two words to me...something lights up in my brain.

He leans back, studying me like I'm a problem he's already solved. "What's going on with you?"

I stare at the empty glass, hating the tremor in my voice. "I want my life back."

"Then stop fighting the one you've chosen." He smiles faintly, but the smile doesn't reach his eyes. "Your prior life was failing. The ranch was dying, and you were drowning in debt—"

"At least it was mine." The words crack through the morning. "My failure, my choice, my consequences. Not this... choreographed existence where you control everything."

"I don't control everything."

"No? Then I can leave right now? Visit friends? Make my own choices? Not drink the damn orange juice?"

His silence is answer enough.

"That's what I thought." I push my chair back and stand.

"Sit down."

I stay on my feet, arms crossed, chin lifted.

"Sit. Down."

The command slices through the air, low and absolute.

For a beat, the only sound is the clock ticking. Then he moves —slow, unhurried, a predator closing distance. In two strides, he's before me, and suddenly the world narrows to the space between us, to the gravity he radiates.

Before I can step back, his hands are on me—not rough, not

cruel, but unyielding. One arm locks around my waist, drawing me flush against him; the other captures my wrists behind my back, pinning me effortlessly.

"Stop fighting." The words land warm against my ear. "Feel what happens when you do."

I do feel it. The heat, the tremor, the pulse that betrays me. Every breath shallow, every nerve tuned to him.

"Let me go...please." I whisper, though even I can hear the lack of conviction in my voice. I crave these moments when he asserts his authority over me.

"No." His tone is a quiet command, threaded with dark amusement. "You can hate the rules. You can hate me. But your body doesn't lie." His hips roll once, deliberately, the hard line of his cock pressing against my belly. "Every time I take control, it responds with heat and hunger, need and desperation."

"Stop—"

"You don't want me to stop." His breath skims the curve of my neck. "You want to know which will break you first—my discipline or my control." His voice drops lower, dangerous, intimate. "Tell me, do you need the punishment that reminds you who you obey..." His teeth catch my earlobe. "...or the command that makes you surrender?"

My pulse stutters. His words are a blade drawn slowly.

"I don't—" My voice catches. "I don't know."

He exhales, slow and satisfied, his mouth brushing my throat. "An honest answer at last." He flexes his fingers against my wrists, not releasing, not hurting, just holding. "Until you do, I'll decide for you. I'll give you both until you remember why you chose this."

"I didn't choose this. You forced this on me."

"I created the circumstance where you could experience what we can be together. Force is as much a part of it as choice." The words settle like a promise—or a sentence. He doesn't take me upstairs. He doesn't even glance toward his bedroom.

He carries me through the house instead, past polished wood and muted art, to the door I dread.

The Red Room.

Each step is unhurried, deliberate. By the time he pushes the door open and the scent hits me—leather, oil, something metallic—my pulse is frantic.

The Red Room, with its deep red walls, dark floors, and glints of chrome and velvet, isn't a dungeon, not exactly.

It's a stage.

A place where he teaches and takes. Punishment. Training. Pleasure so intense it borders on pain.

He sets me on my feet but doesn't release my wrists. "Strip." The single word lands like a command.

I obey, clothing falling away until I'm bare beneath the low red light. His gaze stays fixed on me—dark, intent, assessing.

"This is what you need." He circles me once, fingers brushing the inside of my elbow, down the curve of my hip, not tender but not cruel. "My authority when you resist. My discipline when you forget. And both..." He stops behind me, his mouth at my ear. "... when you defy me."

A shudder moves through me, not only fear but something sharper—anticipation. This is where he recalibrates me. Not punishment for punishment's sake, but a reminder of the bargain I made. The walls, the restraints, the implements on the velvet-draped table—they're as much ritual as they are threat.

He doesn't immediately bind me. Instead, he moves me into position with steady hands, guiding rather than shoving. Leather cuffs slide around my wrists, snug but not cutting, pulling my arms up and slightly apart. My spine curves, my breasts are exposed, my breaths turn ragged.

Julian steps in front of me, thumb brushing my bottom lip. His eyes search mine, calm and unreadable. "Look at me." The command brooks no refusal. "Right here. Only me."

I lift my gaze. The world narrows to his eyes, the red glow, the faint clink of buckles as he adjusts the cuffs.

"This is where you learn." His voice drops, low and intimate. "That obedience isn't just about rules. It's about surrendering the chaos in your head so I can take it from you. Punishment is the frame. Control is the art. Do you understand?"

I swallow hard, my pulse racing. He hasn't told me what's coming. He hasn't even touched me beyond arranging me. And yet the space between us vibrates with promise.

When he finally lays his hand on me—low on my back, not striking but steady—it feels less like domination and more like inevitability. A warning. An anchor.

My body trembles, but my voice is a whisper of truth: "I understand."

Julian tilts his head, a faint smile ghosting across his mouth— not victory, not cruelty, something more dangerous: satisfaction.

"Good. Now let me show you."

What follows blurs into sound and sensation—leather sliding through metal, the whisper of my own breath, his voice low and precise.

A command.

A gasp.

The sharp crack of control met with the ache of release.

Punishment and pleasure coil together until I can't tell one from the other. Until I'm not sure if I'm trembling from pain, relief, or something darker that feels too close to need.

When it finally stops, silence rushes in, thick and humming. My arms tremble, heavy in the restraints, and I barely register the soft click of buckles before my wrists are free. He catches them before they fall, his fingers tracing the tender skin where the leather bit. Warmth follows in gentle circles, grounding me in touch instead of command.

A soft weight settles around my shoulders—a throw, smooth and cool against overheated skin. I sink back into him, boneless, my pulse still a wild stutter beneath the quiet. He tightens his arm around me, not in restraint this time, but something steadier—grounding, unshakable.

"You're released, for now." His lips brush my temple. The words shouldn't soothe me, but they do. They hum low in my chest, warm and deep, sinking into a place that should stay locked. "Rest. Think about what happened here. We'll talk when you're ready."

I nod, or maybe I just breathe. It's hard to tell where I end and he begins. My body feels both lighter and heavier at once—emptied out, yet full of something molten that moves slow and sweet through my veins.

My thoughts quiet. Resistance dulls at the edges, dissolving into something dangerously close to peace.

His scent—cedar and smoke—fills my lungs, and suddenly, leaning into him doesn't feel like submission.

It feels like safety.

Like home.

My muscles loosen against his chest. I let him draw me closer, too tired to fight, too calm to care why the air feels thick and shimmering, why every beat of my heart seems to echo his.

Whatever he's done to me in this room, it lingers—under my skin, in my blood, in the slow rhythm of breath that somehow syncs with his. And though I tell myself it's exhaustion, or adrenaline, or the strange afterglow of surrender... deep down, a quiet, unsettling truth takes root.

I want to stay in his arms.

I curl into the sheets, spent and strangely adrift, the ache of release mingling with the remnants of my resistance. For the first time in days, the silence between us feels less like a wall and more like a bridge—fragile, but there.

Later, I'm in the library, the hush of it pressing close around me. The smell of old leather and furniture polish should calm me, but my nerves are frayed, brittle as glass. Julian's voice drifts faintly from down the hall—low, sharp, handling some urgent call—and for the first time all day, I'm alone.

My phone buzzes.

The sound jolts through the quiet like a gunshot. I freeze, staring at the screen.

I shouldn't answer. I don't remember Julian saying I couldn't accept calls, but he didn't say I could, either.

My fingers hover, my heartbeat tripping faster, a flush of guilt rising before I've even done anything wrong.

The phone keeps buzzing. Louder. Insistent.

I swipe before I can talk myself out of it.

"Clara? It's Frank."

My old neighbor's voice is like a lifeline thrown across a storm. "Frank? What's—"

"There's been an incident."

My blood goes cold. "What kind of incident?"

"Fire in the east pasture. Controlled now, but... it was deliberately set."

My stomach knots so hard it hurts. "What? Who would—"

"That's something you need to discuss with Blackwell." His tone carries weight. "This is bigger than burnt grass."

The line clicks dead just as movement fills the doorway. Julian. He's there, leaning against the frame, his expression unreadable but heavy, like he's been standing there long enough to hear everything.

A rush of guilt hits me so fast it's dizzying. It's not just fear—it's that low, insistent tug under my skin, the one that makes honesty feel like survival. I scramble to explain before he can even speak, words spilling out too quickly.

"That was Frank—my neighbor. He said there was a fire in the east pasture. It's out now, but... he said it was deliberate."

I'm babbling. My heart's hammering like I've been caught doing something wrong. All I did was answer my phone, but it feels like a breach. Like I need to confess before he asks.

Julian steps into the room, the shadows moving with him. His eyes flick to my phone, then to me.

Calm. Assessing. Dangerous.

"Handled." The word is clipped, final. "I knew before Frank called."

"Someone tried to burn my ranch—" My voice shakes. "Why didn't you tell me?"

"Because it wasn't meant for you." He crosses the space between us with slow, deliberate steps. "Someone sent a message. To me, through you."

He lifts his hand, brushing a thumb across my cheek—not gentle, exactly, but steady. Grounding. My chest trembles.

"You're frightened," he murmurs. Not a question. "And you're explaining yourself to me like a schoolgirl caught sneaking out. Do you know why?"

"I—" The word dies. The truth presses against my tongue, terrifying and intimate.

"Because you're learning." His voice softens. "Because the rules, the structure, the way I hold you—all of it's starting to strip away the lies you tell yourself. You don't hide from me anymore. You come to me." He strokes his thumb once more before dropping. "Even when you're scared."

His gaze pins me. I should be furious. Instead, the warmth

curling low in my belly makes me sway closer, like my body's been trained to reach for him in moments of crisis.

I hate that about myself.

I can't stop it.

"From now on," his voice dips lower, "if there's a call, a message, anything—you come to me. You tell me first. You don't hide. Understand?"

I nod, throat tight, the thought of defiance suddenly unbearable. "Yes... Mr. Blackwell."

His eyes darken, satisfaction flickering there. "Good girl."

But the haze doesn't last. It never does. It thins like mist burned off by sunlight, leaving me staring at him, heart thudding. A fire. Deliberate. Someone tried to send a message through me. Through the ranch.

"Who?" My voice comes out quieter than I intend, a thread pulled taut.

"Business competitors." The words are sharp and biting. "People who think attacking my acquisitions will give them leverage." His gaze hardens. "They're wrong."

"Your acquisitions?" The haze is gone now, replaced by a cold knot of dread. "That's my home—"

"Which is under my protection for the next eleven months." He pulls out his phone and types, not looking up. "Security will be increased. No one will touch the ranch again."

"This is because of you. Because of your deals, your enemies—"

"Being mine comes with risks."

"You never mentioned that in your contract."

"I protect what's mine." He lifts his gaze from his phone, locking on me. "That includes you."

The words land heavy, deeper than they should, and something old stirs—like a hand dragging through the silt at the bottom of a river. *I protect what's mine.*

It yanks me backward before I can stop it. "Junior year. The fight the day before the Winter formal."

He looks up sharply. "You remember that?"

"Three guys jumped you in the parking lot. Everyone said it was about a girl—"

"It was about you." He sets down his phone. "They heard I was planning to ask you to the dance. Wanted to warn me off. Your father put them up to it."

"Who were they?"

"Does it matter? They failed." His smile is cold. "Though not for lack of trying."

"You went to the hospital."

"Three cracked ribs. Concussion." He shrugs. "Worth it to prove I wouldn't be scared off."

"But you never asked me to the dance."

"Your father visited me in the hospital." His voice hardens. "Made it clear that if I pursued you, he would ensure my father's business suffered. And he had enough connections to do it."

"So you backed off?"

"I waited. Learned patience. Built my own empire so no one could threaten me again." He stands, moves closer. "And now here we are. You're mine, the ranch is protected, and anyone who tries to hurt either will regret it."

"This isn't protection—it's possession. Obsession."

"Sometimes they're the same thing."

My phone buzzes. Text from Marcus: *Coffee? Need to make sure you're okay.*

Julian reads it over my shoulder before I can hide it.

"No." Simple and final.

"You can't—"

"I can. I will." He takes my phone. "You don't meet with other men. Especially not ones who've touched you."

"Marcus and I barely—"

"You dated for three months during your senior year. He was your first kiss." His voice carries dangerous edges. "Did you think I didn't know? Didn't watch him put his hands on what was meant to be mine?"

"I wasn't yours back then."

"You were always mine. You just didn't know it."

CHAPTER 26
DAY 24

The ranch is crawling with security when we arrive—black SUVs lined like sentinels, earpieces flashing in the sun. Men in dark suits nod at Julian and glance at me as though I might be a threat instead of a woman in boots and a borrowed sweater.

"This is excessive." I mutter and hug my arms across my chest.

"This is necessary." Julian's hand rests at the small of my back, a subtle pressure guiding me past them. "Someone needs to understand you're off-limits."

The burnt pasture spreads out before us—black earth, charred fence posts, smoke still clinging to the air. But it's already being rebuilt, crews moving with a determination that reeks of unlimited budget and absolute orders.

"Why do you care so much?" My eyes stay fixed on the workers hammering new rails. "It's just property to you."

"It's yours." His voice is quiet but unyielding. "That makes it important."

I stop walking, turning to face him fully. "But why? Why does what's mine matter so much to you?"

"Because I've loved you for seventeen years."

The words hit like a blow. My lungs stutter, my pulse hammering against his fingers where they cradle my jaw. "You don't love me. You're obsessed—"

"Both can be true." He steps closer, closing off the space between us until there's nowhere left to retreat.

He slides his hands from my cheeks to the sides of my neck, thumbs grazing the spot where my pulse pounds, a hold that feels both reverent and possessive. His smirk blooms—slow, predatory, inevitable.

"It's the thing you hate," he murmurs, eyes locked to mine, "and the thing you crave. It's why you fight my discipline, but desperately crave it. It's why you tremble when my hand closes on your throat while I'm fucking you. Why you arch into me when I yank your hair, why you come harder after I edge you, deny you, then obliterate you with pleasure. You can pretend you hate it, but your body has already accepted its master."

My breath comes ragged. "None of that is healthy."

"Who says?" His grip tightens just enough to make my breath catch, but not enough to hurt. "You? Them? People who think love only comes soft and safe?"

His smirk tilts darker. "In my world, I'm not just dominant in bed. I'm this way everywhere. In my business. In my life. In my relationships. You can call it an obsession. You can call it control. But it's still love." He strokes his thumbs over my pulse, coaxing it faster. "I've always been in love with you. I've just stopped apologizing for how I express my devotion."

My voice breaks. "This isn't love. This is—"

"—you learning how much you need to surrender to me and desire a man with authority over you." His eyes darken, his mouth hovering a breath from mine. "Stop telling yourself it's wrong. Feel it. Embrace it. Whether you call it control or obsession, it's the only kind of love I know how to give. And it's the only kind of love strong enough to match what you need."

My knees tremble despite myself, my body leaning infinitesimally into his grip even as my mind claws for distance. "I can't—"

"You can." His voice is low, dark, unshakable. "And I'm going to show you exactly what I mean."

He lets the weight of the words sink in, his smirk fading into something steadier—promise, threat, vow. Then, he slides his hands from my neck down to my waist, guiding me with that same unhurried inevitability he always has.

"Come inside." Soft, but not a request.

I move, unsteady, my pulse a drum under my skin as he leads me up the porch steps, through the hall that smells of ash and polish, his palm warm at the small of my back. The house feels different with his security swarming the property, like a fortress instead of a home.

"Where are we going?" My voice is smaller than I want it to be.

"Upstairs." He doesn't look at me. "We're staying at the ranch tonight. I want to oversee the protection myself." He glances down at me, eyes glinting. "And it means I finally get to take you in your own bed."

The words land like a brand. My breath catches. "Julian—"

His hand tightens at my hip. "Careful."

I swallow hard. "Mr. Blackwell."

"Better." His smirk curves again, dark and slow. "Now come upstairs."

I follow him. I always do.

The rest of the night unfolds like a lesson—one I never asked for, and one he's determined I learn. He keeps every promise he's ever made about control, patience, and pain. He takes what he wants in his own time, methodical as ever—no chaos, no mercy, no release until he decides I've earned it.

By the time he's done, I'm trembling, wrung out, and finally, he lets me come. His voice is the last thing I remember, quiet and commanding in the dark.

"Now you understand."

CHAPTER 27
DAY 25

The morning after, I wake sore, heavy, the sheets tangled around my legs like restraints that never fully let go. Pale light filters through the curtains, gilding the ranch in gold and smoke. Somewhere downstairs, I hear him moving—precise, deliberate, already in control of the day.

It shouldn't feel like peace. But somehow, it does.

I slide out of bed, every muscle stiff from the night before. His shirt lies draped across the chair, but instead of slipping it on, I open my old dresser. My fingers brush denim. Cotton. Things I haven't touched since the contract began. Things he hasn't explicitly forbidden but hasn't exactly allowed either.

Act first. Permission later.

I pull on a faded T-shirt and worn jeans, my boots muffling against the rug. The clothes feel alien on my skin—looser, rougher, mine. A ghost of my old life clings to them, making my chest tight.

I tiptoe down the stairs, heart hammering. His voice carries from the kitchen, low and clipped: "...tell them the shipment leaves Friday, or they'll regret it—"

The sound cuts off. He's looking at me now. Phone still in his hand, his gaze sweeps over the clothes, the boots. His expression doesn't change, but the temperature in the room does.

He lifts a finger to whoever's on the other end of the line. "Hold." Then, to me: "Going somewhere?"

"I just... want some air. Walk the grounds." The words come out smaller than I want.

One brow arches. "That's not how you ask."

My throat works. "I—"

His head tilts, patience gone predatory. "Say it properly."

"Mr. Blackwell..." The words scrape coming out. "...may I go outside?"

His mouth curves, slow and dark. "Better." He glances at his phone, then back at me. "You can go. You have thirty minutes. Stay within the perimeter."

He pauses just long enough for the weight of it to settle. "And Clara?"

"Yes?"

"If you run, I will catch you." His voice is quiet, lethal.

A tremor races down my spine. "I wasn't going to run." The words come out barely above a breath.

He brings the phone back to his ear, his gaze still fixed on me. "Go." A command, not permission. "Thirty minutes."

I step out the door, the sound of his voice resuming behind me as the screen clicks shut, the open air feeling like a dare more than freedom, every breath tinged with the knowledge that somewhere behind me, the predator is waiting.

The paths wind toward the back acreage, where Mom's garden used to sprawl—wild roses and lavender she'd coax from stubborn soil, a riot of color against the plains' monotony. I half-expect weeds and neglect, but as I round the corner, my breath catches.

It's there, meticulously restored: the flowerbeds edged in reclaimed stone, perennials blooming as if she'd just tended them yesterday. Yellow roses climb a trellis—my favorite, the one detail I buried deep.

He must have consulted old photos, hired landscapers who knew her varietals by heart. It's not just preservation; it's resurrection, a quiet claim on my grief. Sitting on the stone bench she'd carved initials into, I trace "C.H. + M.H." with my finger, tears blurring the petals.

Julian didn't touch this for control—he did it because he knew it would heal something in me, emotional threads woven into his possession as surely as the physical ones.

When I return to the house, he's in the study, but he doesn't ask where I've been. His eyes flick to the dirt smudged on my jeans, and a faint smile tugs at his mouth.

"It looks good out there." As if reading my silence. No gloating. Just acknowledgment.

I nod, the warmth in my chest unwelcome but undeniable.

We stay for two days.

Two days of quiet oversight—of him moving through the house while men in dark jackets test alarms, rewire sensors, and sweep the perimeter. I catch glimpses of him outside, phone pressed to his ear, every motion efficient, controlled.

And during those two days, he lets me roam.

No questions, no guards trailing at my back. Just me, Scout at my heels, the wind combing through the tall grass.

I walk every fence line, every path I used to ride as a girl. I visit the barn, stroke the necks of the stallions he purchased for me—his gift, his mark, his claim—and try to imagine this life without the shadow of his rules.

Maybe freedom was never the absence of strings. Maybe it was learning to live with them—how they stretch, tighten, loosen —always there, invisible until I tug too hard.

At night, I hear him moving downstairs, his voice low in the study. On the second evening, I almost go to him. Almost.

But instead, I stay in my room, staring out at the pastures gilded silver by moonlight, wondering which feeling will devour me first—the craving for his control, or the illusion that I still have any at all.

CHAPTER 28
DAY 27

On the twenty-seventh day, we return to his mansion. Night falls heavy, the house silent except for the creak of floorboards under my feet.

I can't sleep—restless, the kind of itch that isn't just physical. My body hums from everything he's done these past nights, but my mind won't settle.

He let me walk the ranch alone again that afternoon. No guards shadowing my every step, no Julian pacing beside me. Just the wind in the pasture, the smell of ash where the fire had been, the familiar dirt under my boots.

My land. My air.

It felt like breathing for the first time in weeks.

Now, padding down the hall in a silk robe, I head to the library, drawn by the soft glow of lamplight spilling from the cracked door.

Julian's there, reclined in the leather armchair, a book open on his lap—one of the BDSM manuals from his collection, pages marked with tabs. He doesn't look up as I enter, but his awareness shifts, like a radar locking on.

For a moment, I hover in the doorway, every instinct telling me to retreat. But another part of me—the part that felt wind on my face today and remembered who I was—wants to cross the distance on my own terms.

I step inside, silent on the rug. His gaze flickers upward, unreadable.

"I wanted to thank you." My voice is low but steady. "For taking me to the ranch with you. For letting me... walk it. Without you."

His brow arches a fraction, as if waiting to see what I'll do with this sliver of freedom.

Before I can overthink it, I'm kneeling before him, silk pooling around my knees. My hands lift to his belt, deliberate, unshaking. The buckle clinks softly as the zipper rasps down.

He's already hard, as if he's been waiting for this moment.

I free him, lean in, and close my mouth over him—not out of command, but out of something that feels frighteningly like choice. Like gratitude. Like hunger that's mine alone.

He hovers his hand above my head but doesn't push, doesn't guide. He lets me set the pace, his eyes darkening as he exhales slowly.

His head tips back against the chair, a low groan escaping as his fingers thread gently into my hair—not guiding, just holding.

He doesn't speak, doesn't rush; he simply enjoys it, every swirl of my tongue, every hollow of my cheeks, his breath coming ragged until he tenses and spills down my throat with a shuddering exhale.

When I pull back, wiping my lips, his eyes meet mine—dark, approving, a rare softness edging the satisfaction.

"You're full of surprises." He helps me up and into his lap. No punishment, no analysis. Just the weight of his arm around me as we sit in the quiet, the book forgotten on the floor.

He slides his fingers through my hair, slow and steady, like he's petting a tamed thing. "Just breathe." His thumb brushes the edge of my jaw. "I like you soft like this."

He reaches for the glass on the table and tips it to my lips. "Drink."

The water is cool, metallic on my tongue. I swallow without thinking, the simple act leaving me weak, pliant.

"Seventeen years." His voice is a low rasp that vibrates against my spine. "That's how long I've been waiting. Waiting for you to fall to your knees by choice. To open that pretty mouth, suck my cock without me having to tell you." He drags his thumb down to my throat, pressing lightly over the frantic flutter of my pulse. "It's everything I've ever wanted."

My breath hitches. He isn't whispering it like a confession; he's laying it out like a claim, rough and unvarnished, forcing me to hear what he is.

"You offering yourself like that—" his grip at my nape tightens, just enough to make me shiver "—that was a gift. And I don't take gifts lightly." He tilts my face until our eyes lock. "I'll remember this moment. I've waited years for it, and I won't forget it."

The words slam into me, crude and reverent at once, leaving me trembling with the dangerous realization of just how much power I've handed him—and how much of me wants to keep handing it over.

CHAPTER 29

DAY 29

The morning sun slants across the kitchen, honey-gold and soft, painting everything in warmth that feels almost domestic. The scent of batter and burnt edges hangs in the air, the kind of imperfection that shouldn't exist in Julian's world—yet somehow, here, it does.

He's a beautiful mess. Sleeves rolled up, hair mussed, flour streaked along his forearms. When he flips the pancake too early and splatters the stovetop, he mutters a curse under his breath, and it makes me laugh. Really laugh. The sound startles both of us.

"You're a disaster." I dip my finger into the bowl and flick a bit of batter at him. It lands just below his cheekbone.

He freezes for half a second, the commander of empires caught mid-ambush. Then one brow lifts, slow and dangerous in mock offense.

"Are you challenging me in my own kitchen?" Before I can retreat, he swipes a fingertip through the batter and smudges my nose. "Payback."

237

The moment stretches, ridiculous and sweet. My pulse kicks. I smear another streak on his jaw.

He lunges—not with menace, but mischief—and I dart around the island, laughing, heart pounding in that delicious way that has nothing to do with fear. His footsteps follow, unhurried but certain, the hunter pretending to give chase.

When he catches me, it's gentle. He slides his hand around my waist, his thumb brushing the batter from my nose, lingering along the curve of my cheek. The laughter drains from my chest, replaced by a quiet that hums with something else—want, yes, but something softer too.

His mouth finds mine. Slow at first, a tasting, exploring kiss that deepens with every breath. He cradles my face, steady, reverent, as if I might vanish if he lets go.

When I tug him closer, it's instinct. He lifts me easily onto the counter, the marble cold against my thighs, my robe slipping open. The heat between us takes over—urgent but not harsh. His body presses to mine, each movement unhurried, deliberate, as if he's memorizing rather than claiming.

When he thrusts inside, it isn't dominance; it's connection—slow, deep, a rhythm that says *I'm here. You're mine. And I'm in charge here.*

My arms lock around his shoulders, his mouth buried in my neck, both of us moving together until the tension shatters.

After, he stays inside me, breathing hard, forehead pressed to mine. And then—it happens. A smile. Not his usual sharp, knowing smirk, but something unguarded, boyish, almost tender.

"You're trouble." His voice is rough with amusement.

"And you're terrible at pancakes."

His laughter rumbles against my chest. The sound warms me more than the sunlight ever could.

We clean up together, side by side. He rinses dishes while I flip the few survivors, both of us stealing quiet glances, brushing hands, sharing burnt edges and sticky syrup.

He's still in control—he always will be—but it feels different today. Softer. Balanced. Like we've both stepped into something fragile and real, something that could almost pass for normal.

When he reaches across the counter to tuck a strand of hair behind my ear, his fingertips linger, tracing my jaw in a touch that says what neither of us dares to voice.

For the first time, the contract doesn't feel like chains. It feels like a choice—dangerous, complicated, maybe even real.

The tenderness lingers long after the batter's been wiped away.

All afternoon, Julian moves through the house differently— still precise, still in control, but softer somehow. When I brush past him in the hall, his hand catches my waist, not to correct, but to hold. When I laugh at something small, he laughs too—low, quiet, a sound that feels like sunlight after a storm.

We spend the day in this fragile rhythm of almost-normal. Sharing coffee on the terrace. Reading in silence. His fingers trace idle patterns on my thigh while we eat dinner by the window. Every touch is gentle, reverent, threaded with something that feels dangerously close to affection.

And maybe that's why, when the shift comes, I feel it before he speaks.

The way he sets down his glass. The way the air stills around us. The way his eyes darken—not with anger, but purpose.

"Stand." Quiet, but absolute.

I do, heartbeat thudding, the warmth in my chest cooling into anticipation.

He rises, stepping closer until the scent of cedar and smoke fills my lungs.

"You've done well these past days." His voice is measured.

"Better than I expected." He presses his thumb lightly beneath my chin, forcing my gaze up. "But pleasure without purpose dulls the edge. You need to remember what surrender feels like when it costs you something."

I swallow hard. "What are you saying?"

"I'm saying…" He leans in until his breath warms the corner of my mouth, "Tonight, we go back to the Red Room."

The words slide through me like a current—half dread, half longing. The Red Room is where he resets me. Where rules stop being abstract and become flesh, sound, and breath.

He studies me for a long moment, searching for resistance. Finding none, only the tremor that betrays both fear and want.

"I want you naked and waiting for me there in ten minutes." His tone is calm, absolute.

"Yes, Mr. Blackwell." My voice comes out softer than I mean it to.

Something flickers in his eyes—satisfaction, maybe even pride. "Good girl."

He steps back, giving me room to move, to prepare, to think. But even as I walk toward the hall, I can feel him watching me, the weight of his gaze as binding as any restraint.

Because tenderness never means relinquishing control with Julian. It only means he's decided to take me apart slowly, piece by piece, until I forget the difference between love and surrender.

That night, the Red Room is waiting—dimmed lights, leather and steel glinting in the low glow like the promise of a storm. His softness from the kitchen is gone. In its place is precision. Command. Every movement deliberate, every instruction calibrated to strip me down to nothing but breath and nerve.

He takes his time, circling me, making me wait. The blindfold goes on. My arms are positioned. My body becomes a canvas for his restraint, his voice the only thing anchoring me.

Not a single touch is casual; every sound he makes is measured—soft leather sliding, a low hiss of breath, a command whispered just before it lands. Punishment, denial, sensation—woven so tightly I can't tell them apart.

By the third hour, I'm trembling so hard my knees barely hold me. My safeword hovers on the back of my tongue, a lifeline I'm terrified to use. If I say it, I lose everything. If I don't, I might lose myself.

Julian knows exactly where I am; I can feel it in the way his hand lingers at the back of my neck, the way his voice dips lower when I shudder.

"You're on the edge." Not a question. "Right where you're supposed to be." His tone isn't cruel. It's inexorable. A promise that he will take me apart but not break me—unless I choose to break.

Somewhere in the haze, I realize how close I am to begging, how deep the hunger has dug its claws into me. My body aches, nerves stretched thin, every inch of me attuned to his control.

When he finally lets me go—lets me shatter, lets me come—it's like air after drowning. The sound I make isn't a scream; it's a sob. Release, relief, surrender all at once.

Afterwards, he unfastens the cuffs himself, lowering my arms carefully and massaging my wrists where the leather had been. A throw wraps around my shoulders, cool against overheated skin. He draws me back against his chest—not possessive, but firm, grounding me, his heart steady against my spine.

"You're right where I said you'd be." His lips brush my temple in a tender kiss. "You crave my control."

I want to deny it, but the soft haze in my veins makes the words lodge in my throat. All I can do is breathe, trembling, while his fingers stroke slow circles on my arm and the Red Room fades around us.

CHAPTER 30

DAY 30

The first month hits like a quiet earthquake.

Thirty days in this house, this life, and something shifts—not a break, but a hairline fracture in my resistance. It's subtle, but I feel it in the way my body fits the rhythm of his world. In the silence that no longer feels suffocating. In the warmth that lingers, unwanted, after his touch.

I wake tangled in his sheets, the weight of his arm heavy across my waist, the steady rise and fall of his chest against my back. His scent—cedar, smoke, the faint salt of skin—wraps around me, and I don't pull away. My fingers trace the edge of his jaw, the hollow beneath his ear, memorizing the man I swore I'd never submit to.

His voice drifts through memory, clear as the morning light spilling through the window:

"By Day 30, the walls you've built will start to crack. You'll crave the structure, the certainty of my commands. You'll seek my touch not out of fear, but because you've learned it's your anchor—the only thing that quiets the chaos inside you."

How I laughed and told him he was delusional.

Now the laughter feels far away, almost cruel. Because lying here, I can't deny how right he was.

I crave the structure he surrounds me in.

I crave his power and control.

I crave him.

The realization leaves an odd taste in my mouth. Not bad. Not good. It's fear, longing, and surprise. If he can make me bend this far in a month, what will a year do to me?

What will be left of the woman who signed that contract in defiance, who thought she could outlast him?

He stirs, eyes opening, silver-gray and sharp even in half-sleep.

"Good morning." His voice is rough and intimate.

"Morning." I'm unable to hold his gaze. I can't let him see the truth on my face. He's been right all along. This is where I belong.

Over coffee, he studies me in that quiet, unnerving way he has. "You're different today." The observation lands soft.

I try for nonchalance, but my pulse betrays me. "Maybe I'm tired of fighting."

Something flickers across his expression—a ghost of a smile, part satisfaction, part something softer. "Tired," he repeats. "Or ready?"

I don't answer. Can't.

Later, in the study, he pulls me onto his lap while he works, the movement casual but inescapable. My head finds his shoulder without command. His hand rests against my thigh, not possessive, not punishing—just there. Steady. His thumb makes slow, absent circles on my skin while he scrolls through contracts and messages.

It's not dominance.

It's something worse.

Intimacy.

Voluntary. Quiet. Dangerous.

And as I sit there, breathing in the scent of him, matching the rhythm of his heart, I realize the truth that terrifies me more than his punishments ever did.

I want this. I need him to be in control.

CHAPTER 31

DAY 32

He's leaving for business tomorrow—three days in New York, something about acquisitions. I find him in the shower that morning, steam fogging the glass, his silhouette broad and unhurried. The door's ajar, an invitation or carelessness.

Heart pounding, I slip out of my sleep shirt and step under the spray, pressing close to his back.

My lips find his neck first, soft kisses trailing to his shoulder, then his chest as water cascades over us. My hands roam lower, wrapping around his hardening length, stroking with intent ahead of my mouth.

He stills, then groans, head tipping back against the tile as I sink to my knees, taking him in—slow, deliberate, water mingling with the taste of him.

"Clara..." His voice is rough, fingers in my wet hair, but he lets me lead until he's trembling.

Then he hauls me up, spinning me to face the wall, one hand on my hip, the other sliding to my throat—not choking, just holding, a gentle pressure that grounds me. He enters me from behind in one smooth thrust, the rhythm building fast and fierce, his grip tightening just enough to make me gasp.

I come undone with the water pounding down, him following with a low growl against my ear.

Afterward, he wraps me in a towel and dries me with uncharacteristic tenderness. "Stay in the house while I'm gone." His voice goes firm again. "No leaving. And no orgasms—your pleasure waits for me. Understood?"

I nod, the denial already a twisted thrill. As he dresses and leaves, the house feels emptier, but not oppressive. I head to the library, diving into the shelves—books on dominance, submission, M/s dynamics. Scout, my trusty companion, curls at my feet.

Tucked in one of the volumes on power dynamics, a worn leather notebook slips free and lands with a soft thud on the library rug.

Julian's handwriting—bold and precise—fills the pages, spanning years of notes from adolescence to the present. I trace them with trembling fingers, starting with the early entries, scrawled in shaky ink like confessions from a fever dream.

High school obsessions: the depraved sexual awakening of a boy hurtling into manhood, his urges erupting in unbridled, voracious detail.

Page after page unleashes M/s dynamics through a teenage haze of hormones and fixation—me as his collared property, leashed in the shadows of the school bleachers, the metal ring around my neck yanked taut as he forces me to my knees in the dirt, my mouth claimed while distant cheers mock my degradation.

Punishments spiral into mania: fevered scenes where I'm chained to the ranch's old tractor, naked and shivering under the stars, his improvised whip—his father's old belt—lashing my back until red stripes map my surrender, my cries blending pleas for more with sobs of shame, his boyish scrawl noting how I'd "break beautifully under the pain, mine to mend."

Bondage fantasies dominate the margins—frantic pencil sketches of explicit deviant art, dark and harrowing in their raw intensity: me hogtied on the gym floor after hours, ropes biting into my wrists and ankles until circulation fades, his teenage form hovering with a switchblade to "free" me only after he fucks me raw, cum dripping like a seal of ownership; another, me dragged by iron chains into the family basement, suspended from the rafters like meat, his hands exploring every inch before carving temporary runes into my skin with a scalpel, blood and semen the ink of his eternal claim.

The depravity is unchecked, a storm of lust-fueled violence and possession, every twisted vignette centering on me—his untouchable siren, the one girl who ignited this inferno, driving him to secret nights of edging himself to these horrors, manhood forged in the fire of obsession too potent to quench.

The entries fracture in senior year, a desperate bid to escape the pull: logs of how he fucked his way through school, always ravenous, chasing fleeting highs from one girl to the next in a haze of parties and backseats, vanilla trysts that curdled into half-hearted attempts at control, all to drown out the singular hunger for me.

"Prom night—K., cheerleader, all giggles and short skirts," he starts in erratic script, detailing the hookup in the hotel after-party: her bent over the sink, skirt hiked, him thrusting with teenage force, slapping her ass experimentally like his fantasies demanded, but her moans fake and light, no submission in her eyes—just detached pleasure before she straightened her dress and laughed it off as "wild."

No satisfaction, the echo of my imagined whimpers mocking him as he came alone in his hand later, the chaos unquenched.

Entry after entry piles on the pattern—study sessions turning into blowjobs under desks with the debate team girl, her mouth eager but unskilled, no collared devotion, just sloppy release that left him pacing the halls, harder than before; stolen afternoons in the janitor's closet with the art major, pinning her wrists above her head as he fucked her against the wall, whispering rough commands she ignored with breathy compliance, her orgasm quick and forgettable while his mind overlaid my face.

From one to the next—varsity parties where he'd claim a stranger in the shadows, trying to satisfy his urges with improvised binds from belts or ties, the girls bodies willing but yielding no depth, no fire; always missionary in borrowed rooms or frantic against lockers, positions that hollowed him out, laughter and sighs a pale mockery of the screams and chains haunting his sketches.

"Tried with E.—six weeks, no protocols at first, just sex to forget," he writes in clipped lines, the emptiness glaring: fumbling encounters in her bedroom, her body soft and available but not the fortress he craved, vanilla rides that peaked too soon, leaving him staring at the ceiling, hungry and half-hard.

He pushed it further—slipping a necklace around her throat like a collar during one heated fuck against the wall, growling "mine" as he drove in hard, but she laughed it off, arching for her own pleasure while he faltered, no fire igniting, her climax ripping through without pulling him under; he didn't even finish, pulling out to spill on the sheets, "Clara's ghost laughs louder, every girl a shadow without her spark."

It crashes in a final blowout—arguments over his brooding intensity, her calling him "obsessed with some ex," walking away with a shrug, leaving him alone in the empty house with the sketches and fantasies, the string of conquests sharpening the boy's chaos into a man's unyielding demand: discipline awaited, but the outlet? Only in the one he couldn't have—yet.

College bleeds into post-graduation haze, the notebook dormant for stretches, then reigniting with a shift—late twenties now, the raw frenzy tempered but not tamed.

"Found a Mentor," begins a new chapter, his first real training under a shadowy guide, far from our rural world. No denial of flesh; the sessions are hands-on immersion, sex, and BDSM as curriculum to harness the storm.

Initial notes recount introductory scenes: a submissive woman, experienced and bound in soft cuffs for his practice, her body the canvas for his awakening control—flogger strikes measured under the Mentor's watchful eye, the thud building her subspace while he learns breath play's edge, her gasps teaching him rhythm without ruin. Followed by union: her on all fours, collared loosely as he thrusts from behind, practicing denial —"Hold it, pet," he commands her as she clenches around him, the release his reward only after she shatters, journaling the thrill of guided dominance, how it echoed his fantasies but layered trust over terror.

Progress unfolds in vivid logs: rope sessions evolving from basic ties to full suspensions, his hands steadying a partner mid-air as she wraps her legs around him, the fusion of immobility and penetration a lesson in vulnerability—sex suspended, her moans syncing with the creak of ropes, teaching the exquisite alchemy of dominance and devotion.

Deeper failures punctuate the growth—a brief dynamic with another sub, post-mentor, where he tested full protocols: "Collar exchanged, month-long immersion," but it crumbled under his unspoken comparisons. "Bound her for impact—cane welts perfect, but her subspace felt borrowed; fucked her in the cage, chains rattling, yet empty, like whispering to a mirror. Ended it clean. The pull is singular—I need Clara." The void propels him deeper, manhood crystallizing from boyish depravity into calculated mastery.

As the pages turn, the entries mature, desires sharpening over years of relentless study—notes evolving into methodical research: the art and science of power and control, dissecting the psychology behind the dynamics he craves.

Advanced catalogs from private clubs (dates coded, partners anonymized), experiments in sensation play—trails of ice melting into wax seals on quivering skin, the contrasts forging intimacy through shared extremes, sex as capstone: partners riding him bound, the trust amplifying every clench until mutual release cements the lesson.

Detailed breakdowns of rope play: intricate shibari diagrams annotated with load-bearing physics and emotional aftercare, knots that embrace rather than ensnare, followed by accounts of erotic suspensions—bodies impaled and helpless, thrusts timed to the sway, teaching the exquisite alchemy of dominance and devotion.

Impact play becomes a treatise—implements dissected by sensation. The thud of suede floggers versus the sting of canes, physiological charts of adrenaline rushes into subspace, citations from kink psychology texts on attachment and consent, how calibrated pain rewires devotion into destiny.

Deeper still, explorations of Master/slave relationships— complete power exchange, not mere submission, but a collared life where trust is absolute, every decision a thread in the tapestry of ownership, marriage as the vessel to sanctify it eternally, blending legal vows with ritual oaths of unending surrender.

The planning phase hits hardest: timelines etched in recent ink, once he accepted he'd mastered the craft—financial webs spun around the ranch's debts, psychological maps of my vulnerabilities, contingency contracts refined over sleepless nights, even dialogue trees for seduction laced with strategy.

It's all converging on the end goal, circled on the final page: partnership veiled in total surrender, me not just his submissive, but his in every way—decisions, body, soul—collared at the altar in a ceremony fusing wedding bands with leather and steel, the contract a prelude to forever. Not fleeting control, but eternal, woven intimacy.

Rather than recoil, heat floods me, arousal coiling low and insistent despite his orders. My thighs press together as I envision the collar's click, the chains' intimate weight, the depraved boy forged into this unyielding man who waited nearly two decades to have me.

The depth of it, his patience—from hormonal inferno to disciplined devotion—draws me in. I close the notebook, breathless, the denial sharpening the ache into something exquisite and unbearable.

CHAPTER 32
DAYS 34-35

He returns late, the front door clicking shut like a punctuation to the silence I've wrapped myself in. I'm in the library again, curled in the reading chair, surrounded by scattered books on M/s relationships—protocols, trust-building, the psychology of total exchange. The words blur with my own swirling thoughts, arousal from the notebook lingering like a low hum.

Julian enters, his presence immediate and magnetic. He scans the open pages, the titles, noting everything—the depth I've delved, the tabs on consent, collars, ceremonies—but he says nothing, his expression unreadable, a flicker of approval in his gaze.

He crosses the room in three strides, lifts me from the chair as if I weigh nothing, settling me on the edge of the desk, books tumbling to the floor.

"Missed this." His voice is rough from travel and restraint, his mouth claiming mine in a kiss that's tender at the edges but laced with control.

After days without, he doesn't tease; he frees himself and thrusts in slow, deep, filling me until I gasp against his lips. It's intimate, unhurried—his free hand cradling my jaw, eyes locked on mine as he moves, dominant in every measured stroke, drawing out my need until I shatter around him. He follows with a quiet groan, holding me close through the aftershocks, our breaths syncing in the lamplit quiet.

Day 35

We're back at the ranch for upkeep and maintenance, or so Julian says. I'm out at the barn, a moment of quiet without Julian while he works.

The photo albums nag at me, discovered in the preserved workshop off the barn—Dad's tools still oiled, workbench cleared but for a box of high school yearbooks and faded pictures.

Flipping through, one catches my eye: Julian's father, young and stern even then, arm around a girl in a prom photo. Her face... it echoes Mom's—same dark curls, same tilt to the smile. Scribbled in the margin of a yearbook page: "E.H. + J.B.," her initials with his.

Over morning coffee on the porch, I can't hold it back. "The albums in the workshop...the woman with your father in the yearbook? Was it my mother?"

Julian stills, setting his mug down.

"She was his high school crush—his first love. He never got over it. Dad ranted about her for years, how your father 'stole' her at prom, swept her off with charm, and that damn ranch dream. They married young, had you, and built everything on what my father saw as his loss. Money and land were the excuses—the feud was his heartbreak, poisoned into legacy. But that was his feud, never mine. I didn't use his hate to fuel my desires."

"So the grudge was personal." I stare at the horizon, pieces slotting together, but not fully. Why preserve the albums if he knew?

"Yes." He reaches for my hand, not as redemption or echo, but steady. "I pursued you on my terms. You weren't compensation for his ghosts—you were the one I saw clearly, from the start."

The crack widens—resistance fracturing into possibility. Not surrender, not yet. But the fight feels... optional now.

Dinner feels different tonight. No staff. No contracts spread across the table. Just a meal he's clearly had prepared for us, waiting under the low glow of the chandelier. The house smells like rosemary and garlic; a bottle of red breathes between us, soft candlelight flickering over polished silver.

"There's an agricultural fair tomorrow." Julian breaks the quiet. His fork pauses midair as he watches me pick at my food. His eyes, still sharp, still searching, lock on me until I finally look up.

The past month has woven us tighter. His commands have softened at the edges; my responses come quicker, laced with something warmer than resentment. But the contract still hangs over us, a shadow that won't lift.

"The County Fair?" A flicker of excitement sparks before I can swallow it down. I've been going since I was five—sticky cotton candy, blue ribbons from horse shows, Mom's laughter echoing over the midway.

"Yes." He sets down his wineglass with a kind of finality that vibrates across the table. "Wear the sundress. The yellow one." His voice is low, almost fond, anticipation glinting behind the words.

"Like the one I wore freshman year?" The words slip out before I can stop them. Memories flood: wildflowers in my hair, Julian's gaze lingering from across the quad—a spark that feels almost innocent now.

His eyes darken, pupils dilating with something that isn't just hunger but nostalgia. "Exactly like that one."

The room feels smaller suddenly, candlelight dancing over his face, making him look almost young again. He reaches across the table—not to command, but to touch. His fingers brush mine, a light stroke down the back of my hand.

"I remember that day." His words are quiet, but weighted. "I remember thinking you were the only thing I wanted that I couldn't have."

I stare at him, heart racing. There's no hard edge to his voice— just this strange, dangerous softness between us.

"All because of a feud between our fathers. I'm sorry for that." I squeeze his hand back, tentative. "It feels... different. This thing between us."

His thumb circles over my knuckles, a small, steady pressure. "It does."

We sit like that for a moment, the food cooling on our plates, the wine catching candlelight. For once, it isn't about possession, power, or punishment. It's about memory, anticipation, and the quiet truth of two people sharing a table.

Dinner lingers longer than it should. The candles burn low, their wax pooling into lazy spirals. My plate sits mostly untouched, but the wine... each time it empties, Julian refills it. The deep crimson catches the light like liquid velvet.

Julian leans back in his chair, relaxed in a way I don't often see —tie loosened, sleeves rolled to the elbows, the hard lines of control softened by the glow of the room.

He looks... almost human.

He studies me as I sip, eyes tracing the curve of the glass, the way my lips part with each swallow.

"You're different tonight."

"I'm thinking." The words come out soft.

The warmth of the wine spreads slowly through my chest, loosening something I hadn't realized was tight.

"About what?"

"How strange this all feels."

"Strange how?"

"Like I'm living someone else's life." I swirl what's left in my glass. "Expensive dinners. Tailored dresses. Security details. You." My lips curve faintly. "You most of all."

He smiles, just enough to show the edge of a dimple. "You make that sound like a bad thing."

"It's not bad." I look up at him, the words feeling heavy and honest. "It's just... not what I imagined when I thought about love."

That word hangs between us, fragile as spun glass. I half expect him to flinch, but he doesn't. He watches me, his expression unreadable, before reaching for the bottle again. The neck tilts toward my glass, a slow, deliberate pour.

"Sometimes," ~~he says, "love doesn't look the way you think it should. Sometimes it looks like control. Like protection."

"Or obsession."

His gaze sharpens at that. "Sometimes those are the same thing."

I should argue. But the wine is warm in my veins now, the world soft at the edges. Whatever's in it—whatever makes me pliant and open—dulls the need to fight. The shadows of the contract blur. All I can feel is the steady weight of his eyes, the gentle scrape of his voice when he says my name.

"Come here," he says.

I rise before I've even decided to move. My bare feet whisper across the hardwood. When I reach him, he doesn't pull me down or issue a command—he just opens an arm, inviting me into his lap. I go willingly.

His hand rests low on my back, tracing lazy circles. The silence stretches, intimate. My head finds his shoulder. I can hear the steady beat of his heart through his shirt, and it feels... safe.

Wrongly, impossibly safe.

"Mr. Blackwell?" The name slips out before I can stop it—solid, grounding, like coming home after a storm, even as the wine wraps it in golden haze.

His thumb stills against my spine. "Yes?"

"Thank you." The words spill out heavy with truth. "For showing me this—for showing me that what we have can be beautiful. Nice, even. Like it fits, deep down."

His breath brushes my hair. "You don't have to thank me for that."

But I do. The words catch in my throat. "I just... needed to say it."

He nods once, the motion subtle against my temple. "Good."

Something inside me unravels then—too much wine, too much warmth, too much him. I shift on his lap, the friction sparking heat low in my belly. His eyes darken instantly, sensing it.

"Clara."

"I just want to be close to you."

And it's true. Whatever's in the wine has dissolved the distance between wanting and acting, flooding me with a glorious haze—euphoric, golden warmth that makes everything feel right, perfectly bonded, like he's the missing piece I've craved without knowing.

His heartbeat syncs with mine, steady and possessive, pulling me into a world where we're unbreakable, fused in this intimate glow.

No walls, no doubts—just us.

My hands tremble as they slide up his chest, fingers curling into his shirt, needing more of that connection, that safety only he provides.

He doesn't stop me—his breath quickens, a low hum of approval rumbling in his throat—as I swing a leg over, straddling him fully in the chair, my dress hiking up around my thighs.

The wine's fire surges through me, bold and unhesitating, as I fumble with his belt, freeing him with a needy urgency that feels divine, inevitable.

He settles his hands on my hips, guiding but not commanding, his gaze locked on mine with raw hunger.

I sink down onto him slowly, gasping at the stretch, the perfect fit that sends sparks of bliss radiating outward—our bodies aligning in glorious unity, bonded deeper than words.

I rock against him, riding the rhythm I set, my hips circling with a desperation born of the haze, chasing that euphoric closeness, his groans fueling the fire as I take him, claim this moment as mine in the warmth that makes everything feel eternally right.

Pleasure builds fast under my control, coiling tighter with each grind, the friction pushing me toward the edge where everything shatters—but I teeter there, breath ragged, remembering the rules that bind us like threads in this glorious tapestry, Rule Five holding me back even as I initiate, because yielding to him feels like the deepest connection, the truest bond.

"Mr. Blackwell," I gasp, my voice breaking on the name that echoes like home in my chest, safe and possessive all at once, "please... May I come?"

It's a plea wrapped in acceptance, the wine making it feel

sacred, my acceptance of his control the key to this euphoric fusion.

His eyes flare with dark satisfaction, thumbs digging into my hips as he thrusts up once, deep and claiming.

"Come for me—show me how you belong to me."

The permission crashes through, and when I come, it's not from command but connection, waves of release pulsing around him, glorious and unbreakable.

After, he gathers me close, fingers combing through my hair until the edges of the world blur into drowsy gold, but the haze lingers, pulling me deeper into the bond, making me crave even more of his world.

"Mr. Blackwell." My voice is low, reverent, trembling with need. "Take me to the Red Room. Finish the night with me there— anything you want, anything at all. I want to serve you."

The words hang between us like smoke, soft and dangerous. For a heartbeat, everything stops. His hand stills in my hair. His breath catches against my temple. I feel the shift in him—subtle, seismic—the predator disarmed by the prey offering herself freely.

When I tilt my head up, his expression steals the air from my lungs. Shock first—genuine and raw—cracking through the perfect composure he wears like armor. His gaze searches mine, sharp gray gone wide and uncertain, as if he's not sure whether to believe what he just heard.

"Clara..." My name comes out hoarse, his voice roughened by disbelief. He brushes his thumb across my cheek, tracing the flush that wine and want have painted there. The air hums with it—the tension, the ache, the unspoken possibility of surrendering completely.

Then he exhales, the sound low and uneven. A smile ghosts

over his lips, not the cold, calculating kind I know, but something softer. Almost reverent.

"You have no idea what that does to me." The words come out rough. His gaze lingers on my mouth, then drifts lower, down my throat, my trembling hands still clutching his shirt. "Hearing you say that. Needing to serve me..."

He cups my face in both hands, tilting my chin until his forehead rests against mine. His voice drops to a whisper, unsteady. "You've had too much wine. You're soft, open, pliant... and I won't take advantage of that. Not tonight."

My breath stutters. "I'm not drunk."

His low chuckle vibrates through me.

"No, but you're not entirely yourself either." He tucks a strand of hair behind my ear, his touch tender in a way that feels more intimate than any command. "You think this is what you want— but when I take you there, I want your head clear. I want you to be aware of what's happening and remember every second of our time there."

He presses a kiss to my forehead, lingering there as if grounding himself. "You're more than I ever hoped for." The admission comes quiet. "And far more than I deserve."

I start to protest, but he hushes me with a touch to my lips. "Not tonight. Tonight, I take care of you."

And then he scoops me up effortlessly, the movement both protective and final, carrying me toward the stairs. The world tilts as he carries me through the dim hallways, his scent surrounding me—cedar, smoke, and something unguarded.

When he lays me down, it's not in the Red Room. It's his bed —our bed, now, maybe. The sheets cool against my overheated skin, his hand lingering at my cheek like he's memorizing me.

"I'll take you there another night." His voice is quiet, steady again, but softer than I've ever heard it. "When you're ready. When you know."

He presses one last kiss to my temple. "For now, let me take you to bed."

And as the drugged warmth pulls me under, the last thing I feel is his thumb tracing slow circles over my wrist—steady, protective, and impossibly gentle.

CHAPTER 33
DAY 36

The fairgrounds assault me with nostalgia—popcorn grease in the air, the low bellow of cattle, sun-baked dirt under my sandals. I used to run these paths with ribbons in my braids, Mom pinning yellow roses to my collar like talismans.

The sundress clings in the heat, Julian's hand a warm, unyielding weight at my lower back, guiding me through the crowds. His touch feels like habit—comforting in private, but here, in the open, where no one knows the truth of us, it's a reminder of the invisible chains.

"Nostalgia?" His thumb traces lazy circles on my skin, sending sparks up my spine that are welcome now, though tangled with unease.

"Memories." My voice is softer, glancing up at him with a small smile.

"Good ones?"

"Before you... complicated everything, yes."

But as we weave past the Ferris wheel, his presence steadies me, our intimacy a quiet shield against the town's prying eyes. No one here suspects the contract binding us; they see only rumors of the ranch heir and the Blackwell heir together, whispers of convenience or scandal.

His hand tightens slightly, not painful, but firm—a reassurance I've come to rely on.

Mrs. Patterson, my high school English teacher, with her silver hair pinned back, eyes widening behind wire-rimmed glasses, spots us near the craft booths.

"Clara Hayes and Julian Blackwell." She pronounces our names like a scandalous plot twist. "Together?"

"Mrs. Patterson." Julian extends his hand, his charm a natural extension of him, and his smile easy. "You haven't aged a day."

Her gaze sharpens on me: the sundress's modest neckline hiding the collar's trace, the way I lean into him without pulling away, my body language speaking of something no one can name.

"Clara, dear, are you alright? I remember a girl who swore she'd never let a Blackwell—"

"People change, I suppose."

"They do." ~~Julian's tone is light but edged with confidence. "Sometimes they just need the right motivation."

He draws me closer, arm sliding around my waist in a gesture that's public affection, possessive yet casual—like lovers, not what we truly are.

She nods dubiously and moves on, but her words linger like the fair's dust.

"Clara! Clara Hayes!" Tommy Morrison's voice cuts through—Frank's grandson, my old riding buddy, genuine and uncomplicated. He jogs up from the midway, grin wide, but it falters when he sees Julian.

"Haven't seen you in weeks. Not around the ranch circuits or town." His eyes flick to Julian, hardening.

You work the spread next door." Julian extends a hand, his

voice even, but the challenge is there—alpha sizing up territory without aggression. "

"My family's land." Tommy ignores the hand, crossing his arms. "Still free and clear, no buyouts or strings."

Tension crackles like dry lightning. Tommy's never backed down—not from auctions or arguments.

"How's your grandfather?" Desperate to defuse, my fingers twitching toward Julian's.

"Worried about you." Tommy's eyes lock on mine, ignoring Julian. "Says you haven't been around the ranch much. Disappeared after everything went down with the deed. He said someone got you twisted up, under their thumb. Is it true? Is he forcing you into... whatever this is?"

The truth burns on my tongue—the contract, the loss of choice—but after a month, it's evolved into something I navigate, if not embrace.

"What this is, is none of your business." Julian steps forward subtly, settling his hand possessively on my waist, asserting dominance without raising his voice. "Clara and I are making updates on her ranch together—fixing what's broken, building it stronger." His tone is calm and authoritative, his eyes locked on Tommy's, making it clear that the territory is claimed.

Tommy's jaw clenches, unconvinced, searching my face. "If you need anything, you know where to find us." He shoots Julian a glare and walks away, leaving the air thick with unresolved tension.

Julian doesn't gloat. Instead, he pulls me closer, lips brushing my temple in the fair's bustling noise.

We wander on, his arm around me, feeling less like possession and more like a shield—solid against the world's ignorance of our truth.

We're by the horse pavilion when I spot him: Meteor, my

father's prize stallion, sleek black coat gleaming in the sun. Heart seizing, I move without thinking, hand outstretched. He whickers, nuzzling my palm, as memories crash through me—rides at dawn, Dad's proud grin echoing in my chest.

"He's for sale," the owner says casually. "Prime bloodline. Steep price."

"How much?" Julian's already stepping forward, his body a shield beside mine.

"Fifty thousand."

"Sold." Julian's on his phone before I can blink, transfer complete in seconds.

I whip around. "What? You can't—"

"I can. I did. You sold him to help pay your father's debts." He pockets the device, eyes soft on my tears, voice low amid the animal noises. "Consider it a gift. He belongs home with you."

"Why?" My voice cracks, the dam breaking—anger, gratitude, confusion swirling as I bury my face in his chest, sobbing while strangers glance but keep their distance.

"Because you loved him. Because losing him broke something in you. Because my job is to take care of you." He wraps his arms around me, solid and warm, holding without demand, his heartbeat steady against my cheek.

"I hate you." I whisper, but I clutch his shirt, pulling him closer.

"I know." He kisses my hair, voice low and rough. "But you love the horse and someday... You'll love me too."

He's partially wrong. I'm already in love with him.

Back at the house that night, his ravenous side unleashes. We barely make it through the door before he's on me—sundress hiked, me pinned to the wall, his mouth devouring my neck as he drives into me with desperate thrusts.

"Seeing you there, in yellow, claimed by all eyes but belonging to me." His pace is unrelenting, hands everywhere—gripping my hips, teasing my clit—until I'm screaming his name, the fair's intimacy fueling his hunger. "It was perfection."

He takes me twice more before bed, each time deeper, hungrier, our bodies slick and entangled, whispers of "mine" blending with my moans, ending in an exhausted tangle as moonlight filters through the windows.

CHAPTER 34

DAY 37

MORNING LIGHT FILTERS THROUGH THE BARN AS I BRUSH METEOR, HIS coat shining under my hands. The rhythm soothes—the old normal amid the new chaos we've made our own. Julian watches from the doorway, arms crossed, but his gaze is patient, almost affectionate, a quiet presence I've grown to crave.

"You're good with him." He steps closer—not to interrupt, but to join, his hand covering mine on the currycomb, warm and steady.

"Thank you. I didn't realize how much I missed him." I glance up. A small smile tugs my lips; he nods, understanding the concession.

We ride together—shared silences deepening the bond, transforming the ranch into something shared, even if it remains under his ownership.

Meteor is strong under me. Julian is on one of the other stallions. The land stretches endlessly, wind whipping our hair, and for stretches, it's silent companionship—no commands, just a shared horizon and birds wheeling above.

He points out a hawk circling, tells a story from his own childhood rides—it's a rare moment of vulnerability, his laugh low and genuine when I tease his form.

By dusk, ravenous again, he pulls me from the saddle in a secluded meadow, clothes shed in the grass—slow at first, kisses trailing down my body, exploring with a tenderness that belies his hunger. At the same time, I arch beneath him under the sky, our releases mingling with the earth's pulse, bodies arching in the golden light.

He smiles faintly, breath still uneven as he brushes a strand of hair from my face. "We ride well together—in every way that matters."

The words sink deep, a low hum between us. I trace a finger down his chest, feeling his heartbeat steady beneath my touch. "You mean when you're in control."

"Absolutely, and you love it." His eyes darken, the corner of his mouth curving. "When I'm inside you," his voice rough and reverent, "the world disappears."

For a heartbeat, I can't breathe. The honesty in his tone—raw, unguarded—hits harder than any command. My throat tightens.

"Maybe that's the problem." My eyes stay on the fading light beyond his shoulder. "Because when you touch me, I start to forget where I end and you begin."

His hand finds mine, fingers threading through with deliberate certainty. "That's the point."

CHAPTER 35

DAY 38

AFTERWARD, WE SETTLE THE HORSES, AND JULIAN TAKES MY HAND.

"I want to show you something."

"What?"

"Your mother's garden." **His voice is** even, eyes meeting mine with that quiet intensity.

A memory surfaces—her old vegetable garden, choked with weeds and regret because I didn't have the time to tend it properly.

"What about it?"

"Follow me." He leads, hand light on my elbow—guiding, not forcing, a touch that feels like an invitation now.

Rounding the corner, I stop cold: raised beds brimming with heirloom tomatoes and zucchini, soil rich and turned, hand-painted signs restored and staked. Lavender borders the edges, her favorite scent filling the air.

"How—?" I kneel, touching a leaf as if it's fragile, my heart swelling.

"Photos from your albums, once I had access to the deed.

Frank helped with the layout and planting while you've been here with me."

"Frank? Helped you?"

"I may have had to plead my case, but yeah, he did."

He hands me a worn notebook—Mom's garden journals, pages yellowed but intact, recipes scrawled beside sketches of yields. Her scent almost lingers, lavender and earth, pulling tears to my eyes.

"This took time." **My fingers trace** her handwriting.

"I've been busy." He crouches beside me, not touching, but close enough that his warmth seeps in. "I knew you'd appreciate this. It's part of taking care of what's mine—including you."

"In exchange for total servitude?"

The bite's half-hearted now, softened by the gesture, the care evident in every detail.

"Of course." His hand finds my cheek, thumb wiping a tear gently. "For you. Your surrender—your body, but for your heart, too."

The admission hangs, intimate, pulling me closer despite myself. We kneel there a while, talking about my mother—stories I haven't shared in years, his listening ear drawing out more than I expect, vulnerability flowing both ways.

That night, his hunger mirrors the day's tenderness: in the garden's shadow, he lays me on a blanket under the stars, devouring me slowly—tongue between my thighs until I beg, circling and teasing, then thrusting with restrained ferocity, eyes locked on mine through the dim light.

"I want all of you." **He groans, drawing** out my climax before chasing his own, collapsing tangled and sated, his heartbeat steady under my ear as stars wheel above.

CHAPTER 36

DAY 39

Julian suggests a simple dinner—me chopping vegetables while he tends the stove, attempting a stir-fry that's more experiment than recipe. The oil pops, onions sizzle, and I steal a piece of carrot from the cutting board, sliding it into my mouth with a grin.

He playfully swats my hand, but his eyes darken, pulling me against the counter mid-chop.

"Tease." He kisses me deeply, hands sliding under my shirt to trace my sides.

The moment escalates quickly—no power play, just us: him lifting me onto the edge of the counter, pushing my skirt up, entering me slowly amid the aroma of garlic and herbs. Our passion builds, gasps shared as pots simmer forgotten. My nails dig into his shoulders as we climax together, the kitchen warm with steam and afterglow.

Afterward, we salvage the stir-fry, eating at the island with easy laughter about his "gourmet disaster."

As we linger over the last bites, the warmth between us still humming, Julian sets his fork down, his gaze turning thoughtful, almost tender.

"Clara." He reaches across to trace a finger along my wrist. "Do you remember a few nights ago? Over dinner, the wine... when you asked me to take you to the Red Room?"

The words pull at the edges of my memory—the golden haze of that evening, my bold whispers against Julian's chest, offering myself completely.

It's blurry now, fragments of urgent need and euphoria, my boldness raw and unfiltered.

Heat creeps into my cheeks, but it's not shame—more a flustered warmth, the aftertaste of that night making me feel closer to him, bonded in a way that's intoxicating.

I nod slowly, biting my lip. "Vaguely... I remember wanting it. To serve you. Anything you desired. I was... bolder than usual."

His thumb brushes my pulse, eyes darkening with a mix of recollection and heat.

"You were. You offered everything—beautifully." He pauses, voice dropping lower. "I didn't take you then. You had too much wine, but tonight... will you give yourself to me? As you offered?"

My heart stutters, a wave of struggle crashing through the haze—part of me recoils at the unknown, the kitchen's easy warmth clashing with memories of punishments, the welts that still ache faintly.

But the bond pulls stronger, Julian's gaze holding me steady, the contract's weight reminding me my choices aren't truly mine.

I swallow, voice soft but strained. "The choice isn't mine, Mr. Blackwell? If that's what you want, then that's what I'll do."

"You're right." His finger stills on my skin, tone gentle yet unyielding. "You can't refuse me. But I want to ask—if you're willing. Because when you choose, even within the rules, it means everything."

"How deep do you want to go?" I search his eyes, Julian's intensity flickering with something almost vulnerable, and the words tumble out.

He doesn't look away; his voice is honest, raw. "Deeper than we've gone before. More pain to test your limits—sharper edges, the kind that breaks you open. But more pleasure too, building from it, letting it consume you. And I won't withhold your release; you'll come as many times as you want, no denials tonight."

Fear coils low in my belly, sharp and cold—the thought of that pain... What if it's too much?

But even as dread flickers, something else rises in its wake, warm and unshakeable. He won't let me drown; he'll carry me, as he has before.

"I'm willing." I meet his gaze with quiet resolve.

For a moment, Julian's eyes soften. He rises, extending his hand—palm open.

"Your surrender means everything. Come."

The Red Room door yields, scented with leather and secrets. He undresses me with worshipful hands, the blindfold falling softly over my eyes, plunging me into a world of echoes and touch.

A cool glass meets my lips—"Drink, to ground you"—and the water quenches, its subtle warmth unfurling like hidden sunlight, easing without erasing the edge.

The air inside the Red Room feels different—charged, metallic, as if it already knows what's coming.

Julian moves with unhurried intent, the soft scuff of his shoes against the floor the only sound. His energy hums low and dangerous, all restraint stripped away. The warmth I know in him is gone, replaced by something colder, sharper—a man testing not just my obedience, but my faith.

He circles me like a storm gathering strength. Every brush of air feels deliberate, measured. When his gloved hand skims my shoulder, I flinch—not from pain, but from anticipation. He pauses, noting it. The corner of his mouth curves, not in kindness.

"This is not about comfort," he says quietly. "It's about truth. How deep you're willing to go when everything in you wants to run."

Leather tightens around my wrists. The sound of the buckle closing feels final, like a sentence being sealed. I breathe in— leather, smoke, the faint sweetness of polish and skin.

He binds me standing. Ankles spread, wrists drawn above my head, shoulders pulled tight enough that I rise onto my toes. The first bite of leather around my wrists steals my breath. He fastens me in place, step by deliberate step, until I can't move without feeling the strain, the tension of his design.

"Do you trust me?"

"Yes." The word quivers.

"Say it again."

"I trust you."

"Then you'll take what I give."

A hum, low and dangerous, precedes the first strike. The flogger's tails kiss my back—gentle, testing. The next lands harder. And the next. Heat blooms, sharp, rhythmic, finding a rhythm that forces my body to anticipate pain and crave it in the same heartbeat.

The rhythm builds, methodical and exacting, each strike a question, each gasp a reply. I try to count, to ground myself, but the numbers slide apart, replaced by pulse and breath and the sting that threads through every nerve.

He moves closer, voice low against my ear. "Still with me?"

"Yes, Mr. Blackwell." The reply comes out ragged, trembling.

"Then you'll take more."

He shifts the angle, the tails biting across my thighs, the backs of my knees. I shudder violently, gasping. The leather licks across welts already raised. My body jolts forward, held fast by restraint.

He changes the pattern—faster, sharper, impossible to anticipate. The air whistles between each hit. My body jerks, the restraints creak. The pain crests, then folds into something else entirely—heat, release, wild and consuming.

"Too much?"

I can't speak. I shake my head.

He presses close, breath hot against my neck. "Then take more."

I float in sensation until the next wave of pain hits—deeper, harsher. My thoughts scatter, the sound of my own breath is too loud, too fragile. Panic flares for a heartbeat. I can't. I can't endure this.

And then—his hand, steady at the base of my throat. Not choking, just there. The weight of it pulls me back into my body.

"Breathe." A command. "Don't run from it. Stay."

Something in his tone—steel threaded with desire—roots me again. I obey, lungs trembling as air shudders through. The pain doesn't stop, but it changes. It becomes the language between us —the way he speaks, the way I answer.

He doesn't relent. The pain crests, breaks, reforms. I lose the count. All that exists is heat, sound, and pulsating pain. The sting becomes fire, the fire becomes light, and somewhere inside it, something gives. The part of me that fights, that resists, dissolves.

He studies me with the stillness of a predator deciding when to strike. The faint scent of clove and smoke clings to him, an anchor to something human—but his eyes are no longer gentle. They're black glass, reflecting nothing.

"Do you understand what it means to serve me here?" His voice is quiet, the calm before a storm.

"Yes, Mr. Blackwell."

"Then remember that when you beg me to stop."

He moves closer. The sound of his breath against my neck is the only warning before leather slides around my neck—tight, final.

His touch disappears. The silence grows heavy enough to shake.

Then—impact. Not measured, not patient. The strike cracks through the air, stealing my breath. The next lands before I can recover, faster, crueler, his rhythm precise yet unrestrained, building until the space between hits disappears.

I gasp, stumble against the bindings. He doesn't pause. Doesn't soothe. His control feels different now—frenzied, exacting, stripped of mercy. The air fills with the sharp echo of every blow, every breath he takes through clenched teeth.

Pain blooms and folds into heat, a dizzying blur of sensation that burns too bright. My mind fragments around it, the world reduced to pulse and sound.

When I finally speak, my voice is wrecked. "I can't—"

He's behind me in an instant, his hand firm against my jaw, forcing my head up.

"You will. Don't hide from what you crave. Tonight, you pay for seventeen years of want."

There's no warmth in him now—only fire contained by will. It terrifies me how beautiful he looks like this. How precise. How close he walks to losing control and still chooses to hold it.

The next strike lands lower, sharper, each one breaking something open inside me. Fear rises again, bright and cold—but underneath it, a pulse of something deeper.

Surrender.

My body trembles violently. He catches the sound of my breathing, the tremor, the shift.

"Good." A growl. "Now you're listening. Now you suffer for me. Now, you're mine."

The word detonates inside me. The pain, the fear, the pleasure —they blur until I can't separate them. The world narrows to him. To this. To the way his darkness calls something inside me I didn't know I wanted to answer.

He doesn't stop until I do—until my body folds, my mind empties, and there's nothing left but the sound of his breathing and the steady tremor of my own heart.

When I finally break, it's silent. No scream. Just the release of everything I've been holding. The trembling stops. My muscles soften. The resistance that's lived inside me for so long dissolves into the floor.

He senses the shift instantly. The next strike lands softer. Then softer still, until the flogger trails like silk. I'm trembling, sobbing, undone.

When he finally touches me again, his hands are shaking. He draws me close, his forehead pressed to mine, breath harsh, human again.

"You shouldn't have been able to take that." His voice is ragged. "And yet you did. This is what I want—for you to choose me. To serve, not because you must, but because you will."

I want to tell him I only made it because he needed me to. But I can't speak. The words aren't big enough for what this was.

He releases me slowly, reverently. The ache hums through my limbs, but beneath it lies something astonishingly calm. I sink against him, not in defeat, but in quiet triumph.

But it's not over.

He tilts my chin up, thumb tracing the tear tracks down my face. "You're not done serving, are you?"

The question burns deeper than the welts. My body aches, alive, the pain transformed into something that feels like truth.

"No, Mr. Blackwell."

He pushes me gently to my knees. The sound of his zipper unfurls in the air, low and final.

"This is where surrender becomes devotion. Worship me."

He knots his hand in my hair, guiding—not cruel, not kind, just absolute. The first touch of him against my mouth is heat and salt and command. I open for him because I want to. Because every part of me has already yielded.

He drives the rhythm, relentless but controlled, using me as he said he would. But this time, I'm not afraid. Each thrust is a mark, a claiming, a wordless vow between us. My throat strains, tears slip free, and still I serve, every movement a surrender freely given.

When he finally releases me, he catches me again, pulling me upright, wrapping me in his arms. My body quakes against his, raw and trembling.

He gathers me close, holding me steady while my body remembers how to breathe without command.

"Look at what you give me when you stop fighting."

CHAPTER 37
DAY 41

EMBOLDENED AFTER THE RED ROOM'S INTENSITY, I SLIP INTO THE morning shower, where steam already fills the bathroom.

Julian is under the spray with his eyes closed, water cascading over his broad shoulders. I join him, pressing against his back, initiating kisses down his spine, hands exploring the ridges of muscle. I dip down, wrapping both hands around his cock, stroking him.

He turns slowly, surprise flickering to hunger, but he lets me lead—my lips trailing lower, dropping to my knees under the warm rivulets, taking him in my mouth with newfound confidence, tongue swirling until his hands fist gently in my wet hair, a low groan escaping.

"Clara..." He tips his head back, enjoying the reversal.

The sound of his voice, rough and fractured, vibrates against my lips. It fuels a sudden, fierce possessiveness in me. Last night, he had been the architect of my sensation, dismantling me until I was nothing but nerve endings and need. But here, amidst the rising steam and the deafening hiss of the water, the balance shifts. I am the one unraveling him.

I take him deeper, the heat of the water matching the heat rising in my blood. There is a heady power in this—sensing the tension coiling in his thighs, the way his hips snap forward involuntarily to meet me. I run my hands up his legs, over the hard planes of his hips, grounding myself as I work. I want to taste every drop of his control slipping away. I want to memorize the texture of his surrender.

This...This is the other side of the coin. If the Red Room is about his command and my surrender, this is about my worship, acceptance, and a reclamation of my power.

I'm learning the map of his pleasure just as thoroughly as he knows mine. He likes the heat and the friction, but it's me on my knees that unravels him.

His grip in my hair tightens, turning urgent—an anchor in the storm I'm creating. A massive shudder moves through his massive frame, a tectonic shift in a man usually made of stone. He makes a sound, half-growl, half-plea, that hits me right in the chest. It's a raw, unpolished noise that belongs only to me.

I don't let up. I push him, swirling my tongue, tightening my suction, demanding everything he has. His hips buck, a sharp, jagged rhythm taking over, and then he breaks.

My name tears from his throat, a guttural sound of release that echoes off the tile. The hot rush of his climax fills my mouth, and I swallow it down, drinking in his pleasure, savoring the absolute vulnerability of this man who rules everything else in his life. I don't stop until every last tremor has left his body, until he is utterly spent, his breathing harsh and ragged in the small space.

Only then do I pull back. His hands, still trembling slightly, slide down to cup my face, and he urges me up.

I rise, water sluicing down my face, breathless and aching with satisfaction. He pulls me into him, hard, his wet forehead resting against mine as we just breathe, the water beating down around us. The air is thick, charged with the electricity of what just happened and the ghost of what happened last night.

Steam drifts in lazy spirals, clinging to glass and skin. Julian leans back against the tile, the spray rolling down his shoulders as his heart rate slowly returns to earth. When he finally lifts his head to face me, the distance between us feels non-existent, yet the air tightens like a wire pulled taut.

"Last night," his voice low, steady, "wasn't only discipline. It was seventeen years of restraint breaking loose. I punished you for every hour I wanted you and didn't take you. For every time I pretended I could be anything other than what I am."

My pulse stutters. The honesty in his tone slices through me sharper than any command. The truth of it vibrates in my ribs— the years between us, the weight of his hunger finally unbound.

He doesn't look away. "Now that I have you, that hunger doesn't end—it expands. You need to understand that before anything else. Things will be more intense, not less."

The words settle low in my body, molten and heavy. It should terrify me. It doesn't. It makes my skin tighten, my breath catch, and a rush of heat spreads beneath my sternum.

"Yes, Mr. Blackwell."

"This isn't a game for me." He continues, "It's not play, not some dark edge to pleasure. Control is the core of me. Command. Order. Discipline. They're how I breathe. You saw that truth last night."

He steps closer, the water cascading down his chest, tracing every plane of muscle. I want to touch him, to feel that truth beneath my palms, but I stay still—waiting, trembling, caught in the gravity between us.

"Don't mistake this for softness," he says, his voice cutting through the steam. "What you just gave me? It doesn't buy you leniency. It buys you depth."

He crowds me against the cool tile, his wet body a wall of heat against mine.

"I'm going to push you harder now. I'm going to take more. You'll hate me for it sometimes," he warns, his eyes relentless. "But you need me to be the one thing in your life that doesn't move when you hit it. You need to be able to break against me without shattering me."

He frames my face with both hands, tipping my head back so I can't look away.

"But before I take that step, I need to know one thing. We're forty-one days into a contract. The contract keeps you in my house." His thumbs graze my cheekbones, his gaze heavy. "But none of that gets me *this*. Your surrender. Your compliance. Your desire to accept my needs."

His voice drops, rougher now. "Is this real? Are you choosing this life? The discipline? The weight of my control? Because a contract can force your presence, but it can't force your will."

I look at him—really look at him. I think about the years we lost, the anger I held onto because my father kept him from me. I used to mourn that time. I used to wish we'd had those simple, easy years in high school.

But as I stand here, bruised and claimed and thoroughly unraveled, the truth hits me with jarring clarity.

"If we had been together back then," I say slowly, realizing it as I speak, "if we had been high school sweethearts... it would have been soft. It would have been normal."

I shake my head slightly. "You never would have cornered me. You never would have been in a position to force my hand, to strip everything away until I had no choice but to surrender."

I reach up, gripping his wrists. "I don't want a soft love. I don't want normal. If we'd had the easy path, we wouldn't have *this*." My voice steadies, turning fierce. "I'm glad it happened this way. I'm glad you had to force me. Because I needed to be conquered by you."

Something flares in his eyes—shock, quickly replaced by a possessive, burning dark.

"I'm choosing this. All of it."

For a heartbeat, the air between us is so charged it feels like it might snap. Then he nods once, decisive.

I step closer, eliminating the last inch of space between us, resting my forehead against his wet shoulder. The tension in my chest unspools, replaced by a strange, heavy calm.

"I'm sorry for the years I fought the idea of you," I murmur against his skin. "I'm sorry I didn't see it sooner."

His hand tangles in my wet hair, gripping tight enough to pull my head back. He forces me to look at him one last time.

"No," he says, the word final. "No more apologies. Last night was the price. The debt is paid."

Water beads on his lashes, sliding down the hard planes of his face.

"From this moment on, we don't look back," he commands. "We only build. Do you understand?"

"Yes." It's the easiest truth I've ever spoken. "I understand."

He studies me for one second longer, searing the agreement between us, then reaches past me and shuts off the water.

The hiss of the shower dies instantly. In the sudden silence, standing wet and bare in the cooling air, the atmosphere shifts. The philosophical weight of the moment evaporates, replaced by a sudden, spiking wall of heat coming off his body. His gaze drops, sweeping over me with a look that is no longer about teaching, but about devouring.

He crowds me against the wet tile, his hands planting on the wall on either side of my head, caging me in.

"I'm going to fuck you. Right now. Because what just happened in here—that confession, that surrender—it's everything I've ever wanted. I need to be inside you to verify it's real."

My heart hammers against my ribs. The demand in his eyes is absolute.

"As you wish..." I pause, the word hovering on my tongue, heavy and dangerous. I test the weight of it, the taste of it. "...Master."

His reaction is visceral. A whole-body shudder racks his massive frame, and a low, broken groan tears from his throat. Pressed against him, I feel the change instantly—his cock swelling, going rock hard and pulsing against my stomach, a physical testament to how deeply that single word strikes him.

"Don't," he grates out, though his hands tighten on the wall, betraying him. "Don't use that word. Not yet."

I blink, confused by the war I see in his face—the naked hunger for the title clashing with a fierce, sheltering restraint.

"Why not?" I whisper. "I've read your books. I've seen your handwriting in the margins. The notes you made."

I press my hands to his chest, feeling the chaotic rhythm of his heart. "Most of them are about discipline, yes. But the ones on the bottom of the stack... the ones you've read the most... they're about Master and slave dynamics. Is that what you want?"

He pulls back, gripping my chin, his expression intense and incredibly serious.

"Yes," he admits, the truth stark. "More than anything."

"Then why stop me?"

"Because it's too soon," he says firmly. "And it's too fast. That dynamic... Clara, that isn't just about authority or sex. It's about placing your entire existence into my hands without a safety net."

He runs his thumb over my lip, his eyes dark with a mixture of longing and resolve.

"It requires a level of trust that I haven't earned yet."

"You haven't earned?" I frown. "I thought the trust was my part. I trust you."

"No," he corrects, his voice dropping to a rumble. "You trust because you have to. But for me to accept that title—to truly be your Master—I have to prove I have the right to claim that space. I have to prove I can wield that authority over your life without crushing you."

He leans in close, his gaze piercing. "I won't take that title until I know I'm worthy of the weight of it. I will spend the rest of this year proving it to you. Every day. Every punishment. Every pleasure."

"And then?" I ask, my voice trembling.

"And then," he murmurs, "when the contract ends, and you ask to stay... we will see."

When you ask to stay.

The promise hangs between us, heavy and intoxicating. He intends to earn my soul, not just my body.

"Turn around."

The restraint in him snaps. He has said enough; he needs to act. The protective shelter vanishes, replaced by the predator.

"As you wish." I spin, pressing my palms against the cold tile, spreading my legs before he even tells me to. I feel him behind me, the massive, radiating heat of him, and then his hands are on my hips, fingers bruising in their grip.

There is no preparation, no gentle lead-in. He enters me in one long, aggressive stroke, filling me so completely it knocks the breath from my lungs. I cry out, the sound echoing off the glass, but he doesn't slow down.

"From now on," he growls against my ear, his hips snapping

forward with a force that jerks my body. "Every time I fuck you. Every time I discipline you."

He drives deeper, his voice turning dark and jagged.

"Every time I drag you into the Red Room and make you drown in the pain I must give you... I want you to think of the day this contract ends."

He sets a punishing pace, the slap of wet skin against wet skin sharp and rhythmic. This isn't the slow, sensuous worship I gave him earlier; this is possession. This is him stamping his mark on me from the inside out.

"I want you to ask yourself," he rasps, punctuating the words with a thrust that touches my soul, "if you still want to kneel for me."

He doesn't stop to let me answer. He drives into me, the friction scorching, his size stretching and filling me until I feel completely full of him. My mind spins, trying to hold onto a coherent thought, but the sheer physical reality of him—the heat, the sweat, the bruising grip of his hands on my hips—overrides everything.

And then, amidst the gasps and the slap of skin, a laugh bubbles up inside me.

It's a release of tension so sudden and absolute that it breaks out of me—deep and full, echoing strangely in the steam-filled shower. It sounds wild, maybe even a little unhinged given the position I'm in—bent over, possessed, breathless—but I can't stop it. The absurdity, the irony, the sheer relief of it all washes over me.

"It's crazy," I manage to get out, my voice shaking as he continues to rock into me, relentless. "If you hadn't forced me... if you hadn't made me sign that insane contract... I never would have known."

"Known what?"

I push back against him, meeting his hips, embracing the burn.

"I would have gone my whole life not knowing this part of me existed. But I'm sure. I want it. All of it. With you."

He stills for a fraction of a second, his hand splaying flat over my stomach, holding me tight against his hardness, before he resumes the rhythm—deeper now, harder, making me cry out.

"Then you wait," he commands, his voice rough against my ear, vibrating through my spine. "You don't get to give it to me today. You have to earn the right to surrender it, just as I have to earn the right to take it."

He drives into me, his body tense as a bowstring, edging closer to the finish.

"At the end of the year," he promises, the words jagged, synchronized with his thrusts. "On the last day of the contract... I will ask you to kneel. And if you still want it then... if you still look at me the way you did today... I will give it to you."

A rebellious spark flares in my chest, hot and secret. He thinks he can control the timeline. He thinks he can decide when this transition happens. But as he drives into me, filling me so completely that I can't tell where I end and he begins, I know the truth.

He can wait for the end of the year to hear the words. He can wait for the contract to expire to accept the title. But he can't stop the truth settling in my bones right now.

I know what I want, and I'm willing to kneel for him and submit to his rule.

He drives into me with a desperate, starving intensity, as if he's trying to fuse us together, to erase the years we lost with every thrust.

I squeeze my eyes shut, overwhelmed by the friction and the

fullness, my mind emptying of everything but the sensation of him. I'm not just accepting his control; I'm drowning in it, anchored by his hands on my hips and the relentless, driving proof that he is already my Master.

CHAPTER 38
DAY 45

Julian returns from a short errand, finding me in the Red Room—ropes in hand, coiled on the table, my choice evident.

"What's this? Are you curious about shibari?" The door clicks shut, and his eyes darken with hunger.

"Yes, Mr. Blackwell." The formality anchors the moment, reserved for these depths.

He doesn't smile, but the air in the room instantly grows heavier. He walks to the table, running his large hand over the coils of jute I've laid out, testing the fibers. He picks up a bundle, the red strands stark against his skin.

"Then let's satisfy that curiosity." He turns to face me, his posture shifting, settling into that terrifying, absolute stillness. "Drop the robe."

I don't hesitate. The silk slides off my shoulders and pools at my feet. I stand exposed in the cool air, my heart hammering against my ribs.

"Kneel."

I sink to the plush black rug, resting back on my heels.

"No," he corrects, his voice sharp. "If you want to play in these waters, you learn the etiquette. Spread your knees. Bow low. Forehead to the floor. Show me you understand your place."

A shiver races down my spine. This is the M/s dynamic he warned me about—the total abdication. I separate my knees and bend forward, placing my hands flat on the rug, lowering my head until my forehead touches the fibers. It is a posture of total subservience.

"Good," he murmurs above me. "Stay there."

I listen to his footsteps circling me, the heavy thud of his boots near my face. He is inspecting his property.

"Sit up."

I rise back to my heels, chest heaving.

"Offer your wrists."

I hold them out in front of me, wrists together, palms up—a beggar asking for alms. He stares at them for a long moment, the heat in his eyes intensifying. He wraps his hand around both my wrists, his grip unyielding, and pulls me slightly forward.

"The rope is not inanimate," he murmurs, looping the first coil around my wrists, binding them together in front of me before he begins to manipulate my body. "It has a grain. A temper. You have to respect it, or it will burn you."

He works with a slow, hypnotic precision. He isn't just restraining me; he is dressing me in his control. Once my wrists are secured, he pulls me up.

"Arms back."

He guides my bound hands behind me, forcing my chest out, and begins the complex weaving of the harness. He pulls the lines taut against my sternum, and I gasp, the air squeezed from my lungs in a sharp rush.

"Breathe," he instructs, his lips brushing the shell of my ear as he tightens the bind. "Don't fight the compression. Lean into it."

He weaves the pattern across my back, locking my arms into the structure, pulling my shoulder blades together until I am arched high, completely open.

"This is the *Takate Kote*," he explains, securing the final knot at the nape of my neck. "A box tie. It locks your upper body, exposing the heart."

He guides me to the full-length mirror. The sight steals the breath I have left. The red rope against my pale skin is stark, beautiful, and brutal. I look like a sculpture.

"Beautiful," he whispers, his hands running down my arms, tracing the lines of the rope. "You are art. My art."

Then, his grip tightens on my shoulders. The reverence in his touch vanishes, replaced by a dark, predatory possessiveness.

"But art is passive," he growls, turning me away from the mirror and forcing me to bend over the padded table. "And right now, I don't need a statue. I need a sacrifice."

The word hangs in the air, heavy and ancient.

"You are my captive. Trussed. Bound. Helpless to stop me. Helpless to do anything but take what I give."

He steps behind me, his hand sliding between my thighs, finding me already wet, slick with the anticipation of his use.

"Please," I whimper, the ropes biting into my skin as I try to arch into his touch.

"Begging won't help you," he says, lining himself up. "You offered yourself to the rope. Now the rope gives you to me."

He enters me in one smooth, devastating thrust.

I cry out, instinctively trying to reach for him, but the ropes hold me fast. My arms strain against the bonds, the jute digging into my wrists and shoulders, reminding me that I am not free.

I'm a vessel for his need.

He sets a relentless rhythm, his hands gripping my waist, anchoring me as he uses my body. There is no escape, no movement that isn't dictated by him. The friction of the rope against my skin mixes with the heat of him inside me, a sensory overload that drags me under.

"You belong to this," he rasps, driving deep, hitting that spot that makes my vision blur. "To me. You are mine to use."

The world narrows down to this singular point of connection. I can't speak—I can barely breathe—but inside my head, a rhythm takes hold, matching the brutal cadence of his hips.

Master.

He thrusts, and my soul answers.

Master.

He told me to wait. He told me he hadn't earned it. But as he pins me to the table, claiming every inch of me while I hang helpless in his ropes, I know he's wrong. This—this absolute surrender, this total silencing of my own will—is the only truth that matters.

Master. Master. Master.

The word loops in my mind, a frantic, blissful chant. It is a prayer. It is an acceptance. I float in the subspace he's created for me, high on the pain and the pleasure, finally understanding that this captivity is the only freedom I have ever wanted.

The days slip by like quiet tides, each one marked by some new test of control and trust.

Julian keeps his promise. He never softens; he only refines. The demands come in small, deliberate increments—rules folded into daily life, expectations layered until obedience feels as natural as breath.

Sometimes it's his tone that pushes me further. Sometimes,

it's the stillness between his words. He doesn't raise his voice; he doesn't need to. The precision of his will is enough. Each time I meet it, I learn another shade of surrender.

The Red Room becomes a place of ritual rather than punishment. The scent of leather, the glint of metal, the hush that falls the moment the door closes—all of it an unspoken agreement that this is where we unmake and rebuild each other.

The sessions blur the line between endurance and transcendence; when he works, there's nothing cruel in it, only purpose. He draws me to the edge of what I can bear, then steadies me until I find balance there.

Outside the room, the changes run deeper. His discipline follows me into every corner of the day—quiet, constant, inescapable. When I falter, the correction is swift and exacting. He never hesitates; the lesson is immediate, memorable, measured to the moment. The sharpness of it startles, but it's never cruel. It's precision—the echo of the promise he made to hold me accountable.

To claim his rightful place as my master.

I dislike the sting, always. My body resists it, even as my mind steadies under it. And yet, when it's over, the ache leaves something else behind: a calm, a strange rightness that settles low and deep. Because he was right. I need his strength to hold the line, to remind me that what we're building isn't surrender to weakness but to purpose.

The world feels sharper for it—colors brighter, sounds cleaner —because I no longer flinch from the part of myself that yields to his command. In the space where fear used to live, there's only trust. And in his eyes, when he studies me afterward, there's something that feels like pride.

"You're beginning to come into your submission." One night, his fingertips ghost over a faint mark on my wrist. "This isn't about pain. It's about precision. About knowing exactly how far you can go, and choosing to go there anyway."

"And if I fall?" I nod, breath unsteady.

"When you fall, because you will..." His smile is the same one that used to terrify me—quiet, sure. "I'll catch you. Every time."

CHAPTER 39

DAY 60

"It's been two months." The milestone is heavy but tinged with the routine we've settled into, sunlight slanting across the break-fast table, illuminating dust motes dancing in the air.

"How do you want to mark it?" He smirks as he pours coffee, the domesticity of the action at odds with the intensity always simmering beneath his skin.

"A full day free." I test the waters, though I know better.

"You'll never be free." His voice is firm but not unkind, his eyes shadowed with something that looks almost like amusement. "But how about an exchange? An afternoon to yourself—no commands, no schedule. In return, tonight you give me the Red Room."

My pulse stumbles, a spark of anticipation cutting through the calm. He's letting me choose, which somehow feels more dangerous than any order he's given. I look at him, at the hand resting on the carafe, and I make my move.

"Only if I can call you Master."

The air leaves the room instantly. Julian freezes, the carafe hovering mid-air before he slowly sets it down. The amusement vanishes, replaced by a sharp, guarded intensity.

"No," he says, his voice dropping to a warning rumble. "We discussed this. I told you—I haven't earned the weight of that word yet. Not for life. Not for real."

"Then let me pretend," I insist, leaning forward, my heart hammering against my ribs. "Let me have it for tonight."

"Clara—"

"It's the Red Room," I cut in, my voice trembling but determined. "It's a space outside of the world. It's a fantasy until we make it real. But I want to say it. I've been thinking about it for weeks. I need to hear it out loud."

He watches me, his jaw working as he fights his own desire. I can see the hunger warring with his code—the desperate need to hear that title from my lips clashing with his need to be worthy of it.

"Please," I whisper, meeting his gaze. "Please give this to me. One night..."

Silence stretches between us, thick and heavy. He studies my face, searching for any sign of hesitation, but he finds none. Slowly, dark intent bleeds into his expression. He exhales, a sound of surrendering to his own temptation.

"One night," he says, his voice rough. "Inside those walls. Nowhere else."

"Deal."

He leans across the table, his hand cupping my neck, thumb stroking my pulse point.

"Be careful what you ask for," he warns, his eyes burning into mine. "If you open that door, I won't hold back. If you call me that... I will treat you exactly like what you claim to be."

A shiver of pure thrill races down my spine. "I'm counting on it."

He nods once, the faintest smile ghosting across his mouth, and leaves me to the day.

The hours stretch wide and quiet. I ride Meteor across the pasture, wind cold against my face, sunlight flashing off his mane. The freedom feels strange—sweet, but edged with awareness. Even here, surrounded by open fields, the memory of his voice lingers, a steady tether pulling through every breath.

By the time I return to the stables, the air smells of hay and dust and distant rain. I've spent the entire afternoon thinking of Julian—how he looked this morning, the weight of his promise, the way control in his hands feels less like confinement and more like gravity.

Resistance has thinned to transparency. What remains is choice—mine, freely given. And as the sun dips low, I already know how the night will end: me, walking willingly toward the door that once terrified me.

Evening falls, and I enter the Red Room unprompted, heart pounding with choice, the door clicking shut behind me. He's there, waiting, shirt unbuttoned just enough to tease, leaning against the wall with his arms crossed.

He doesn't push off the wall. He doesn't smile. He just watches me, his gaze dragging from my eyes to my feet and back up, heavy, tactile, and completely stripped of the warmth he showed me at breakfast. The air in the room instantly depressurizes, sucked into the vacuum of his stillness.

"You came," he says, his voice a low, vibrating baritone that seems to emanate from the shadows.

"I told you I would."

"Words are easy. Presence is the only currency that matters

here." He pushes off the wall, moving toward me with a slow, predatory grace that makes the hair on my arms stand up. He stops a foot away, close enough that I can smell the sandalwood and the faint, metallic scent of his arousal, but he doesn't touch me.

"You asked for a specific reality tonight," he murmurs, looking down at me. "You asked to open a door that I have kept locked for your protection. Are you sure you want to walk through it?"

I swallow hard, my throat dry. "I'm sure."

"Then strip."

The command is flat. Bored, almost. It's not a request for a show; it's a prerequisite for his attention.

I fumble with my clothes, my fingers shaking under the weight of his stare. I discard my jeans, my shirt, my bra, until I am standing naked in the center of the room, shivering slightly in the cool air. He hasn't moved. He hasn't helped. He just watches, cataloging every inch of skin revealed as if checking an inventory list.

"Kneel."

I drop to my knees on the black rug.

"Head down. Hands behind your back. Become what you asked to be."

I bow forward, forehead touching the rough fibers of the rug, clasping my hands at the small of my back. I am a ball of white skin and vulnerability at his feet. All agency is gone. The silence stretches, agonizing and thick.

Then, I see his boots enter my field of vision. He circles me, a slow, deliberate orbit.

"In this room," he says, his voice coming from behind me now, "you are not my guest. You are not my lover. You are not even my partner."

He steps in close. I feel his hand land heavy on the back of my neck, his fingers tangling in my hair. He pulls, forcing my head up, forcing my back to arch until I am looking up at him from my knees. His face is hard, angular, stripped of all mercy.

"Tell me what you are," he commands.

My breath hitches. "I'm yours."

"That's not enough." His grip tightens, a warning pinch at my scalp. "If you want the title, you give me the submission that pays for it. What are you?"

"Your slave," I whisper, the word tasting like forbidden fruit—sweet, dark, and ruinous.

His eyes flare, pupils blowing wide to swallow the irises. "And who am I?"

"Master."

The word acts like a physical blow. He shudders, a violent tremor running through his arm and down into his hand where it grips my hair. He groans, a raw, guttural sound of restraint shattering.

"Then serve," he snarls.

He doesn't wait. He pulls me up by my hair, dragging me to the padded table, not with the careful guidance of a lover, but with the efficient handling of an owner moving property. He bends me over the edge, forcing my chest down, my hips high.

"You wanted this reality," he rasps, stepping in behind me, the heat of his body radiating against my back. "You wanted to know what it feels like when I stop holding back."

He doesn't prep me. He doesn't ask if I'm ready. He trusts that my submission is absolute. He grips my hips, his fingers digging in hard enough to bruise, and enters me in one long, reclaiming stroke.

I scream—a broken, shattered sound—as he fills me completely. It's too much, and yet, it's exactly what I begged for.

"Master," I gasp, the word tearing out of me as he begins to move.

"Yes," he growls against my ear, his voice dark and jagged. "Take it. All of it."

He isn't making love to me. He is using me. He is taking his pleasure from my body because I gave him the right to do so. The psychology of it crashes over me—the terrifying, exhilarating freedom of being an object in his hands. I don't have to think. I don't have to decide. I just have to endure. I just have to exist for him.

He sets a punishing pace, the slap of skin on skin echoing off the walls. Every thrust drives the title deeper into my psyche.

"Who owns you?" he demands, his hand sliding around to wrap around my throat, cutting off my air, narrowing my world down to the pressure of his grip and the force of his hips.

"You do," I choke out, my vision spotting. "You do, Master."

"Say it again."

"Master."

He releases my throat only to grip my hair again, pulling my head back so he can bite down on the sensitive cord of my neck, marking me.

"I told you," he pants, his control fraying, his movements becoming erratic and desperate. "I told you I would treat you like what you are."

He drives into me harder, faster, chasing his own release with a single-minded intensity that is terrifyingly attractive. I am drowning in him, in the sheer weight of his dominance. For the first time, I am not Clara, the woman fighting a contract. I am simply *his*.

When he finally breaks, it's with a roar that fills the room, his body going rigid against mine, pouring himself into me as if he's trying to fill the void of the last two months in a single moment. He collapses forward, his heavy weight pinning me to the table, his breath harsh and ragged against my skin.

For a long time, neither of us moves. The silence returns, filled with the wreckage of the wall we just smashed through. My body feels heavy, liquified, and utterly drained, but my mind is humming with a strange, dark clarity.

"Thank you, Master," I whisper into the quiet, testing the word one last time, feeling its shape in the new reality we've created.

He lifts his head, sweat dripping from his brow, his eyes dark and dilated. There is no softness in them. No post-coital gentle comedown. There is only a re-ignited fire.

"Good girl."

The praise is a growl, vibrating against my neck.

He pulls out of me, but he doesn't step away. He grips my arm, hauling me off the table before my legs have even remembered how to hold me. I stumble, gasping, but he catches me—not to steady me, but to move me.

"Up," he commands, dragging me across the room toward the St. Andrew's cross bolted to the far wall. "We aren't done. I'm not done."

"Julian—" I start, breathless.

"Master," he corrects sharply, slamming my wrists into the leather cuffs at the top of the cross. The buckles click, loud and final. He kicks my feet apart, securing my ankles until I am splayed wide, completely open, utterly helpless.

He steps back, his chest heaving, raking his eyes over me with a look of pure, unadulterated gluttony. He looks like a starving man at a banquet.

"Do you understand the difference yet?" he asks, his voice rough, pacing before me like a tiger. "In the day, I practice restraint. I pace myself. I worry about your stamina, your comfort, your limits."

He steps in close, his hand closing over my throat, thumb pressing into my windpipe just enough to make my heart stutter.

"But tonight? Tonight, I don't care if you're tired. I don't care if you're overstimulated. Tonight, I am going to indulge every dark, selfish impulse I usually keep on a leash."

He runs his other hand down my body, not gently, but with a claiming, bruising pressure. He finds a sensitive spot on my hip and digs his fingers in, watching my face twist with the sharp spike of pain. He smiles—a cruel, beautiful slash of white teeth.

"This is what you asked for," he whispers, leaning in to bite the tender skin of my inner thigh, hard enough to leave a mark that will last for days. "You wanted the Master. You wanted the sadist."

I cry out, half-sob, half-moan. "Yes."

"Good. Because I have a lot of hunger to work through."

He stands to his full height, looming over me, his presence suffocating and intoxicating. He reaches for a flogger on the wall, the leather tails heavy and black. He runs the tips over my breasts, teasing, before drawing his arm back.

"I'm going to use you until I'm empty," he promises, the threat dark and heavy with lust. "I'm going to mark you, fuck you, and break you down until you don't remember who you were before you walked through that door. And you're going to take it."

He strikes—a sharp, stinging kiss of leather against my thigh —and I scream, the sound swallowed by his mouth as he kisses me, swallowing my cry, feeding on my reaction.

For the first time, there is no safety net—only him, and the terrifying, beautiful force of his unchecked need.

The rest of the night doesn't follow the linear, careful rhythm I've grown used to. It fractures into a kaleidoscope of sensation, heat, and a terrified, soaring kind of bliss.

It begins at the cross. The air hisses, a sharp, sibilant intake of breath before the flogger lands.

I scream, the sound tearing from my throat, but he doesn't pause to soothe me. He doesn't stroke the hair from my damp face or whisper that I'm doing well. He just strikes again, harder, finding a rhythm that serves *him*.

He is painting my skin with his need, watching the welts rise with a dark, fascinated hunger. The pain is white-hot, encompassing, but the look in his eyes—that absolute, unrepentant ownership—burns hotter. I am not his partner here. I am his canvas.

When he finally cuts me down, there is no embrace. He points to the floor.

"Crawl."

I drop to my hands and knees, my body aching, and follow him to the leather chair. He sits, legs spread, one hand tangling in my hair to guide me, controlling the pace with a bruising grip. He uses my mouth, his hips snapping forward, selfish and raw. But just as his breathing hitches, just as I taste the salt of his pre-release, he stops.

"No," he growls, tangling his fingers in my hair and pulling me off him. "Not inside. I want to mark you."

He stands, towering over me. "Kneel. Look up."

I obey, kneeling between his spread boots, tilting my head back. He wraps his hand around his length, his strokes fast, aggressive, his eyes locked on mine with a terrifying intensity. He isn't making love; he is taking relief.

"Take it," he rasps.

He spills over me—hot, heavy lashes of white hitting my face, sliding down my neck, landing on my breasts. He coats me in his release, marking me like property, dirty and absolute. I squeeze my eyes shut, trembling under the humiliation and the dark, twisting heat of it.

He doesn't let me clean it off. He grabs my arm and drags me to the full-length mirror.

"Open your eyes," he commands, his voice rough. "Look."

I force my eyes open. I look destroyed. My hair is wild, my lips swollen, and his seed is streaked across my skin, vivid and undeniable against the red welts from the flogger.

"No hiding," he whispers, standing behind me, fully clothed and pristine, a dark shadow looming over my ruin. "Look at what you are. You wear my mark. You wear my mess. That is where you belong."

I stare at the reflection, at the woman who looks shattered and claimed, and I have never looked more alive.

But he doesn't let me rest. He denies me, over and over again. He brings me to the precipice of release—using his hand, the cold slide of a glass toy—and then stops. Not because I beg him to, but because he enjoys the desperation in my voice. He laughs, a low, dark sound, when I plead.

"Not yet," he whispers, biting my ear hard enough to sting. "You don't come until I give you permission. And I'm enjoying your suffering too much to end it."

He keeps me in a state of agonizing, high-wire tension for hours, until I am sobbing with need, completely unraveled.

When he finally takes me back to the bed—not the one in our room, but the narrow, firm bed in the corner of the Red Room—it is ferocious.

There is no making love.

He flips me onto my stomach and drives into me with a carnal, possessive fury. He claims me like a conqueror planting a flag, driving into me until the world dissolves into white noise. It's scary—the sheer, unchecked force of him—but it's also the safest

I've ever felt. Because in this storm, he is the only solid thing in the world.

Later—much, much later—the silence returns.

I am lying in the master suite, curled against his side. The adrenaline has crashed, leaving me feeling hollowed out and heavy. My skin stings in a dozen places, a phantom map of the night. My muscles tremble with exhaustion.

Julian is awake, his arm draped over me, his breathing finally steady. But the distance is still there, lingering like smoke. The predator has receded, but he hasn't disappeared.

"Too much?" he asks. His voice is quiet, stripped of the growl, but he doesn't sound apologetic.

I take a moment to answer, tracing the line of a bruise beginning to form on his forearm where I gripped him.

"It was... intense," I whisper. "Scary. But... good." I look up at him, my eyes searching his face in the dim light. "I'm glad we did it. I needed to know."

He looks down, his eyes serious, the protector slowly bleeding back in to replace the master, though the edge remains.

"Now, you know why we need to wait," he says softly. "That dynamic... it consumes everything. It requires a stamina you haven't built yet. And a cruelty I don't want to live in every single day." He brushes a strand of hair from my forehead, his touch gentle again. "Not yet."

I nod, resting my head back on his chest, listening to the steady beat of his heart. He's right. The fantasy was intoxicating, but the reality is a heavy coat—one I'm not strong enough to wear full-time.

"Not yet," I agree, closing my eyes. "But maybe one day."

He tightens his arm around me, pulling me closer into the warmth. "One day. Go to sleep, Clara."

"Julian?" I whisper, my voice catching in the quiet dark.

"Hmm?" He shifts slightly, his hand pausing where it rests on my hip.

"Do we have to wait?" I ask, the question feeling heavy in the space between us. "Until the end of the year? To... to go there again?"

He goes still. "You just told me it was scary."

"It was," I admit. "But I don't want to wait ten months to feel like that again. I'm not asking for it every day. I can't live in that headspace yet. But... can't we visit it? Can't the Red Room be the place where we go when we need that?"

He sighs, a deep, ragged sound that vibrates through his chest and into my back. He pulls back just enough to look at me, his expression shadowed and serious.

"Clara, tonight was... bordering on unsafe," he admits, the confession low and rough. "I had trouble restraining myself. When I had you in that chair... when I saw you in the mirror... the urge to break you completely was almost louder than the urge to protect you."

He runs a thumb over my lower lip, which is still swollen from his use.

"I didn't like how hard it was to find the brake," he says. "If we do this too often, I worry I won't be able to stop."

"I don't want you to find the brake," I tell him, the truth stark and unvarnished. "I don't want you to feel like you have to restrain yourself with me. Not in there. That's the point, isn't it? That I can take it? That I can take *you*?"

His eyes search mine, looking for fear, but finding only a dark, reflected need.

"You're okay with that?" he asks, his voice dropping to a dangerous rumble. "You're okay with me going that dark? With me using you until you're nothing but a mess on the floor?"

"Yes," I whisper. "If it's you... yes."

He stares at me for a long moment, battling his own nature, before finally exhaling—a sound of defeat and anticipation mingled together.

"God help us both," he murmurs, kissing my forehead hard. "Fine. Visits. When you can handle it. And when I can't stop myself from taking it."

"Deal," I breathe, settling back against him.

I drift off, the echo of the night still vibrating in my bones, knowing that the door is closed again—but now, we both have the key.

CHAPTER 40

DAY 75

TWO AND A HALF MONTHS IN, AND THE BOUNDARIES OF THE RANCH FEEL less like a prison and more like a shared domain. We spend the afternoon overseeing a fence repair on the north ridge. It's brutal, honest work—sun beating down on our necks, the air thick with the smell of dry grass and creosote.

For the first time, I see Julian not as the pristinely tailored billionaire, but as a man working the land. He's discarded his jacket, his sleeves rolled up to reveal forearms dusted with dirt, wielding a sledgehammer with a terrifyingly efficient grace.

"Pass me the wire," he grunts, wiping sweat from his brow with the back of his wrist.

I hand him the coil, our gloved hands brushing. "You handle that hammer like you've done this before. I thought you were strictly a boardroom predator."

"I learn quickly," he replies, securing the line. "Control is control, Clara. Whether it's a stock portfolio or a fence post." He pauses, looking out over the rolling hills. "Though I admit... I regret not doing this sooner. There's a clarity in sweat that a balance sheet doesn't give you."

"It grounds you," I agree, leaning against the hot metal of the truck bed. "My father used to say the land remembers you if you bleed on it. I used to be terrified I'd lose this place. That I'd be the one to let the memory fade."

Julian stops working. He drops the heavy hammer into the dirt with a thud that vibrates through the soles of my boots. He closes the distance between us, his presence sudden and over-whelming. The dust on his skin, the sweat dampening his shirt—it makes him look raw. Primal.

"You won't lose it," he says, his voice dropping to a growl. "And you won't fade."

The conversation snaps from philosophical to carnal in a heartbeat. The look in his eyes isn't the cold calculation of the Red Room; it's the hot, possessive heat of a mate.

"Julian—"

He doesn't let me finish. He crowds me against the truck, the metal burning hot against my back through my shirt. There is no finesse, no gentle lead-in. He grips my hips, his hands rough and dusty, and kisses me ferociously, tasting of salt and aggression.

"Mine," he growls against my mouth, his hands fumbling with my belt, tearing at the denim. "This land. This dirt. You. All mine."

He takes me right there, under the open sky, lifting me against the side of the truck. He thrusts into me deep and unrelenting, the friction sharp and desperate. It's messy, stripped of rituals and toys.

I cling to his shoulders, my nails digging into his sweat-slicked shirt, crying out as my release crashes through me, wild and uninhibited, mixing with the scent of earth and the heat of the sun.

CHAPTER 41
DAY 90

"THREE MONTHS."

We toast at breakfast, the crystal clink of orange juice glasses sounding like a bell tolling the quarter-mark of the year.

"A quarter of the way through," Julian notes, his eyes searching mine over the rim of his glass. "Does it feel like a sentence? Or a life?"

I pause, letting the question settle. "It feels like... waking up."

We spend the day celebrating with wind. We take the horses out, riding hard across the hills. I urge Meteor faster, laughing as the wind whips tears from my eyes, hearing the thunder of Julian's mount close behind me.

We collapse by a stream at dusk, the horses grazing nearby. We share a canteen of water, sitting side by side on the cool grass. But as the sun dips below the horizon, painting the sky in bruises of purple and red, the air shifts.

Julian looks at me, his hand resting heavy on my knee. "You've been settled lately. The fight is gone."

"It is," I admit, leaning into his touch. "I'm happy. I really am."

I hesitate, my heart thumping against my ribs as I voice the darker truth that's been coiling in my gut all week.

"But..." I look up at him, meeting his gaze. "I miss the other part. I miss the edge."

He goes still, his eyes narrowing slightly. "Be specific."

"I miss the fear," I whisper, the confession feeling dangerous in the quiet twilight. "I miss the absolute surrender. The way you look at me when I'm not Clara, but... *yours*. I want to go back. Tonight. I want the Master.""

He studies me for a long moment, assessing the request, looking for any sign that I'm saying it just to please him. He sees only my own desperate need.

"Then that is what you will have."

The ride back to the house is different. The laughter is gone. The silence is thick with anticipation.

Every time I glance at Julian, his profile is etched in stone, his focus entirely forward. I can feel the change in him—the protector receding, the predator surfacing.

My hands tremble on the reins, my heart hammering a frantic rhythm against my ribs. He's going to break me tonight, and the thought makes me wet.

When we enter the house, the atmosphere is suffocating. He doesn't kiss me. He doesn't ask if I'm ready. He simply points down the hallway.

"Go."

One word. A sentence.

I walk alone down the corridor, the sound of my boots echoing on the hardwood. The door to the Red Room looms at the end, a dark mouth waiting to swallow me. My stomach twists with nerves—the good, sick kind of fear that comes before a freefall.

I open the door. The scent of leather and cold air hits me, triggering a full-body shiver. I step inside, closing the door behind me. My hands shake as I strip off my riding clothes, the buttons fumbling under my clumsy fingers. I leave the pile of denim and flannel on the floor and walk to the center of the rug, naked and shivering.

I don't wait. I know what is required.

I drop to my knees. I separate them wide. I clasp my hands behind my back and lower my head until my forehead touches the rough fibers of the rug.

The wait is agonizing. Every creak of the house sounds like his footstep. I am sweating, terrified, and aching for him.

Click.

Finally, the door handle turns.

I can feel his presence like a change in barometric pressure. He walks toward me, his heavy boots stopping inches from my face. I don't dare look up.

"Welcome back," he purrs, the sound dark and jagged.

I hear the distinct sound of a zipper, the rustle of fabric.

"Up," he commands. "Greet your Master properly."

I lift my head. He is standing over me, freed from his jeans, hard and heavy and waiting. There is no softness in his face, only expectation.

"Yes, Master."

I lean forward, taking him into my mouth, squeezing my eyes shut as I sink into the deep, rhythmic service of the one who owns me.

CHAPTER 42
DAY 91

The ranch operates like clockwork now. Julian's crews have systematized everything—feeding schedules, maintenance rotations, even the placement of tools. It's more efficient than it ever was under my management, and that stings worse than his control.

"You're brooding." He finds me in the barn with Meteor.

"I'm thinking."

"About?"

"How you've made my ranch better in three months than I could in years."

"I had resources you didn't."

"You had control I didn't want to surrender." I turn to face him. "But maybe that's always been my problem. Trying to do everything alone."

Something shifts in his expression. "That's... unexpected honesty."

"Rule three, right? Complete honesty." I set down the brush. "I'm tired, Julian—Mr. Blackwell. Not just physically. Tired of fighting everything. Fighting you, fighting the truth, fighting myself."

"What truth?"

"That you know me better than I know myself."

"What brought this on?" He moves closer, careful, like I'm a spooked horse.

"Meteor." I gesture to the stallion. "You didn't have to buy him back. It wasn't part of our deal. You did it because you knew it would matter to me."

"I did."

"Why?"

"Because, despite what you think, your happiness matters to me. Breaking you was never the goal."

"Then what is?"

"Freeing you." He reaches out and strokes Meteor's neck. "From grief, from overwhelming responsibility, from the prison you built around yourself after your parents died."

"You've always been there, haven't you?" A memory surfaces. "Senior year. After my mom's funeral. You were there. In the back, trying not to be seen." I meet his eyes. "Why?"

His hand stills. "You remember?"

"I remember it all."

"You needed someone, even if you didn't know it." His voice roughens. "Your father was already sick, though nobody knew yet. You were seventeen and completely alone. I wanted to comfort you, but—"

"But our families were enemies."

"Were?" He laughs bitterly. "Your father threatened me again that day. At your mother's funeral. Said if I spoke to you, offered even condolences, he'd destroy everything I touched."

"So you waited."

"I waited. And watched. Through your father's illness, his

death, and your struggles with the ranch." He turns to face me. "Do you know how hard it was? Watching you drowning and not being able to help?"

"So you orchestrated my drowning instead?"

"I accelerated the inevitable and orchestrated your rescue." He holds my gaze, the air between us taut with something too tender to name.

The silence stretches, filled only by the soft sounds of the horses and the wind sighing through the pasture grass.

When he finally speaks, his voice is quiet, stripped of the armor he usually wears. "I have a call to take. Stay here as long as you'd like. You and Scout."

It sounds like permission, but it feels like trust.

He brushes a kiss to my forehead—unexpected, gentle—and then turns toward the house. For a moment, I watch him go, sunlight gilding his profile, the hard lines of power softened by something almost human.

Then the door closes behind him, and I'm alone with Scout, the horses, the scent of hay, and the ache of everything unsaid.

Scout trots beside me as I move down the fence line, tail wagging, nose to the ground. I trail my fingers over the wood rails, still warm from the afternoon sun. The ranch hums with quiet life —the low whicker of the horses, the distant whine of cicadas. For the first time in months, it feels like mine again.

I shouldn't feel peace in Julian's absence, but I do. And that, somehow, makes the guilt worse.

From the open study window, his voice drifts out, low, precise, commanding. The tone he uses when he's building empires. It steadies me and unsettles me in the same breath.

I wander, letting the wind carry my thoughts, until the vibration of my phone startles me. A notification flashes across the screen: Marcus.

Then another. Missed call.

I stare at it, pulse ticking faster, thumb hovering but never touching accept. I can almost hear Julian's voice in my head—obedience first, indulgence second.

By the time I pocket the phone, the sun's dipping low, painting the fields in molten gold. I turn toward the house—and freeze.

Marcus.

He's striding up the long gravel drive, dust kicking around his boots, expression hard with determination that used to charm me but now twists like a warning.

My stomach knots—not fear, exactly, but a deep, sinking dread.

Scout growls softly at my side.

I straighten, wipe my palms on my jeans, and step out onto the porch to meet him.

"Clara, we need to talk." Marcus halts, eyes scanning my face with a mix of worry and something sharper, possessive. He enters without invitation, closing the distance, his light cologne wafting up—safe, familiar, but cloying now.

"You shouldn't be here." I step back instinctively, my voice firm, but he ignores it, ascending fully so we're eye-level on the porch, his posture leaning in, crowding my space.

"I'm worried about you." He reaches out, fingers brushing my arm before closing around my elbow in a grip that's meant to reassure but feels insistent, pulling me a fraction closer. His brows furrow, frustration etching lines around his eyes as he searches my face. "This isn't you. Living with him— tucked away like some kept woman. Come on, Clara, snap out of it."

"You don't know what you're talking about." I yank my arm free, heat rising in my cheeks—not from embarrassment, but from the audacity of his judgment, the way it dismisses everything I've rebuilt here.

"Don't I?" Marcus's voice sharpens, his hands balling into fists at his sides as he steps even closer, invading my space, his body language screaming urgency. He gestures toward the house, where Julian's voice faintly carries from inside. "Everyone in town can see it. The way you defer to him—head down, following like a shadow. He's poisoned you."

"You don't know what you're talking about." My spine straightens, defiance surging as I plant my feet, meeting his gaze head-on. "You need to leave."

He recoils slightly, but only for a beat—then his expression hardens, desperation turning aggressive as he lunges forward again, grabbing both my arms this time, holding me like he can shake sense into me.

"Listen to yourself. He destroyed your father, took your ranch from you, and now he's taken you. Let me help—let me get you out. I can save you from this nightmare."

"He saved the ranch—" I twist in his grasp, pulling back harder, a flicker of empowerment blooming in my chest at the truth of it.

"To control you." Marcus's voice rises, his fingers tightening briefly before he releases me, but he doesn't back off—instead, he paces a step, running a hand through his hair, eyes wild with frustration and unspoken longing. "You're throwing your life away for that bastard. Come with me now. I won't let him—"

"Mr. Blackwell is offering what you never could." The formal title slips out unconsciously, steadying me like armor, and Marcus's eyes widen in shock, his pacing halting as he stares, hurt flashing across his face.

"Mr. Blackwell? Clara? What has he done to you?" His voice cracks, aggression giving way to pleading as he reaches for me again, but the door creaks open behind us. "We're talking about Julian."

As if summoned by his name, Julian appears in the doorway, his posture relaxed but commanding—shoulders squared, one hand in his pocket, a smirk playing at his lips as he surveys the scene like an unwelcome guest at his own table. Controlled fury simmers beneath, but he dismisses Marcus with a casual glance, voice smooth and laced with arrogance.

"Henley. You're trespassing." He steps forward leisurely, positioning himself at my side, his arm brushing mine in silent claim, eyes flicking over Marcus like he's beneath notice.

Marcus whirls, fists clenching as he squares up against Julian. "I'm checking in on a friend." His tone is defiant, but there's a tremor. Julian's presence alone diminishes him.

Julian chuckles lowly, dismissively, leaning against the doorframe as if the confrontation amuses him.

"A friend? That's rich. You're interfering with what's mine." He doesn't raise his voice, but the words cut, his gaze sliding to me possessively, thumb grazing my lower back in a subtle pull that draws me closer to his side.

Marcus steps forward aggressively, chin jutting, ignoring the dismissal. "She's not your property—"

"I'm his, Marcus." The words surprise everyone, including myself. My voice cuts through the tension as I lean into Julian's touch, the contact grounding me. "I belong to him."

Marcus looks at me like I've slapped him, his face paling, shoulders slumping before anger flares again. He shoots Julian a venomous glare, pointing accusingly.

"This isn't over." His voice is thick with unresolved fury.

"It never started." Julian's arm slides fully around my waist now, pulling me against him possessively, dismissing Marcus's threat as inconsequential vapor. "Like she said, Clara belongs to me."

Marcus hesitates, eyes darting between us, then turns on his heel, storming down the steps and across the yard, kicking up more dust in his wake.

After Marcus leaves, Julian is unusually quiet. We stand there, listening to horses shift in their stalls.

"You defended me."

"I defended our arrangement."

"You called it a choice."

"Isn't it? Isn't staying a choice I make every day?"

He turns me to face him, studies my face. "Is it?"

"Yes." The honesty hurts. "The contract says I have to stay. But..."

"But?"

"I'm not sure I'd leave if I could."

His eyes darken, a storm brewing behind the control, his hands framing my face with a grip that's firm but not bruising. But then his jaw clenches harder, the quiet fracturing into something raw.

"That arrogant bastard." A growl, his voice low and edged with venom, thumb stroking my cheek as if grounding himself against the rage. "He shows up here, on my land, thinking he can save you from me? From us? As if his safe, spineless concern could wipe away what we've built—what you've chosen."

His free hand gestures between us, possessive and fierce.

It's thrilling, this worked-up state of his—raw and wild, the intensity I crave more every day, the kind that grounds me in the chaos, makes my body hum with the promise of sensations only he can unleash.

"Show me." My hands rise to his chest, feeling the tension thrumming there like a live wire.

His eyes lock on mine—his way of checking, despite the storm in him. Inside, I'm already arching toward him—this roughness, this wild claim that makes orgasms crash harder, sensations flood deeper, leaving me breathless and centered in a way nothing else does.

A low growl rumbles from his throat, approval and hunger mixing with the fury. He spins me toward the barn, marches me over to where a sturdy overhead beam runs across the rafters—old, solid, unyielding. From a nearby hook, he grabs a length of coiled rope, the kind used for tack, his movements efficient and without hesitation.

"Hands up." A command.

I obey, lifting my arms as he loops the rope around my wrists, securing them to the beam with knots I recognize from our nights in the Red Room—precise, tight, but with enough give that I can bear my weight.

My body is stretched taut on tiptoes, the pull in my shoulders a delicious strain that heightens every nerve.

He steps back, eyes raking over me, then he moves to my shirt —yanking it up and over my head in one fluid, impatient motion, turning it into a hood, blinding me. He follows that by shoving my jeans down.

Cool air hits my bare skin, nipples pebbling, the exposure complete and vulnerable under his gaze. I step out of the fabric, kicking it aside, my body on full display—marks from past nights are faint and fading, but these next ones will be fresh, for his eyes and mine alone.

"I'm going to mark you." His voice is a dangerous promise, unbuckling his belt with deliberate slowness, the leather whispering through the loops as he folds it double. "To wipe off the stench of him—his cologne, his thoughts of saving you. You're not in need of rescue. You're for me."

The first crack of the belt lands across my ass, bare skin meeting leather in a sharp burn that jolts up my spine. I gasp, body swaying forward against the ropes. He watches the red welt bloom, eyes intent.

"Count." His free hand steadies my hip, anchoring me.

"One." The sting radiates inward, arousal twisting tight and low in my belly. I'm thankful for this, for how it centers me, and makes the world narrow to his command and my response. Another strike follows, crossing the first on my ass, the pain sharper on sensitized skin.

"Two."

Each impact is controlled—his rage channeled into precision—targeting thighs and curves where bruises will hide under my clothes, visible only in our private moments. Three, four—thudding heat building, my breath coming faster, the strain in my arms on tiptoes amplifying the fire, every nerve alight.

By five, I'm edging toward release just from the rhythm, the wild intensity triggering sensations that pulse through me, but I hold back, craving the tsunami of sensation he'll eventually allow. The welts throb now, a lattice of heat across my ass and upper thighs, each one a brand of his possession that makes my core clench tighter, my body alive in ways that scare and thrill me equally.

I think he'll stop at five. His breaths are heavier, filled with the fury that's driven him this far. Julian's possessed, the echo of Marcus's presumptuous gaze fueling him beyond control, his arm drawing back without pause.

Six lands harder, a searing line across the underside of my ass where skin meets thigh, the impact jarring my whole body forward, feet slipping in the hay as pain flares white-hot, stealing my breath in a sharp cry.

I shake it off, head dropping, but the thrill surges— this wildness, his unyielding need to claim, grounds me deeper, makes the fire spread inward like liquid gold.

Seven crosses the first welts, leather biting into already tender flesh, and the burn tips sharper, unbearable in its insistence, ripping another cry from my throat—raw, unfiltered—as tears prick my eyes. My arms tremble in the ropes, shoulders straining on tiptoe, but I don't pull away; I lean into it, the pain stripping layers of the day's tension, leaving only this electric bond between us.

Eight and nine come in quick succession, one low on my thigh, the other curving over my hip, each thud a deeper ache that radiates up my spine, my legs quivering now, knees buckling slightly as sobs build in my chest—not defeat, but release, the overwhelming intensity cracking me open.

Ten follows, the heaviest yet, a deliberate stripe across the fullest curve of my ass that makes me scream outright, body shaking violently against the beam, tears spilling hot down my cheeks as emotional floodgates break—sobbing wracks me, cathartic and fierce, all the buried weight of contracts and choices pouring out in the pain's embrace.

But I never ask him to stop. This is the wild edge I crave, the storm that leaves me remade, sensations heightened to shattering edges, thankful in the depths for how it pulls me under and lifts me higher.

He drops the belt with a clatter, stepping close, his heat enveloping me as he frees himself.

No pause—he thrusts in deep, the angle from behind filling me completely, stretching me around his thickness in one relentless drive. I cry out, the welts igniting with each movement, my body clenching instinctively.

His pace is punishing, hips slamming forward, one hand gripping my hip to steady the ropes' pull, the other sliding up my torso to capture a nipple—pinching hard, twisting to the edge of pain, the pressure building until it's a white-hot spike of sensation.

The roughness grounds me deeper; this wild fervor of his strips away the day's noise, leaving only sensation, wild and alive, my body responding with tremors that border on release.

But he doesn't let me tip over; his thrusts slow just enough to edge me, the pinch on my nipple tightening until I arch, then he releases—blood rushing back in a flood that makes me scream, the agony-pleasure so intense it bows my back, tears pricking my eyes as the orgasm hovers, denied.

"Please." The word is human and raw, no scripted surrender—just need, my toes curling in the hay, body trembling on the brink. "I can't take any more. Please let me come." I arch against him, needing more friction, more heat, and God help me, more pain.

"I mark you because I own you." A growl against my ear as he thrusts deeper, harder, his hand returning to pinch the other nipple, building the cycle anew while the first throbs. "Because you're mine—no savior, no escape. Because you need this reminder of how thoroughly you're mine—every welt, every scream, every denied peak."

His free hand slips between my thighs, fingers circling my clit, edging me higher, the welts flaring, the ropes straining as I push back, desperate. The intensity—his fury made flesh—triggers everything, sensations coiling like a spring, orgasms building to something shattering if he'll allow it.

I crave this wildness, thankful for how it makes me feel claimed, and alive,.

"Please—"

"Now."

Permission like a key, his thrusts surging as his fingers press firm on my clit.

The orgasm rips through me, fierce and unending, my body convulsing and clenching around him in waves that milk his release—hot, claiming, his groan muffled against my shoulder as he bites down lightly, another mark sealed.

He holds me through it, ropes creaking, the peak so intense from the buildup and wildness that stars burst behind my eyes, leaving me trembling, sated in a way that grounds my soul.

Slowly, he unties me, hands gentle now, rubbing my wrists and tracing the welts with care. He turns me, eyes searching mine—not anger anymore, but a fierce tenderness, thumb brushing a tear track.

"You defended me." He pulls me into his chest, the warmth of him a balm over the throb.

I pull back just enough to glance down, my fingers drifting to trace the fresh welts on my thigh—raised lines under my touch, warm and pulsing, a secret map of his fury and my surrender.

His hand covers mine gently, voice low. "Do you like my marks?"

I lean against him fully, pressing my face to his chest, fingers lingering on the skin as I nod against his shirt.

"I love that you desire me so much you must mark me." Honest and soft, the words spill out of me. "I love tracing your marks for days after, but they fade too soon. I hate when they fade."

His arms tighten around me, a low hum of satisfaction rumbling through him, the barn quiet save for our breaths syncing. And in that hush, the marks feel eternal—his desire etched into me, mine into the way I cling to him.

"I should mark you more often." A low chuckle, his hand sliding down to cup my ass gently, thumb brushing a fresh welt as if testing the idea.

"I wouldn't stop you." Tilting my head up, I meet his gaze

with a teasing smirk, my free hand trailing lightly down his chest, nails grazing just enough to spark, a playful challenge in the afterglow, emboldened by how he's unraveling me piece by piece. "But only if you promise to make them last longer next time. I might have to return the favor... bite you back, see how you like wearing my marks."

His eyes darken with amusement and fresh heat, a growl building in his throat as my words sink in. Then—his cock lengthens against my thigh, stirring hard and insistent despite the first round's toll, his body responding to my tease like fuel to flame.

"Careful what you promise." His voice is husky, one hand tangling in my hair to tilt my head back, claiming my mouth in a slow, devouring kiss that reignites the embers.

He doesn't wait long—spinning me gently. This time, there's less fury and more hunger:

He lifts one of my legs, hooking it over his hip, thrusting in deep and unhurried, the delicious friction pulls a moan from me.

His pace builds steadily, hands roaming—tracing my marks, pinching my nipples lightly to echo the earlier sting—each drive a reminder of ownership, but tender now, our bodies syncing in the quiet of the barn.

"Mine." Against my neck. He bites softly where no bruise lingers. "Come for me," and I do.

I arch into him, the second orgasm blooming slower, deeper, clenching around him as he follows with a shuddering groan, spilling hot inside me again.

We slide down to the hay together, spent and tangled, his head resting heavily on my chest as the horses nick softly nearby, their sounds a gentle underscore to our slowing breaths. The fading light filters through the barn slats in golden shafts, warming the welts on my skin, which pulse like promises—teased, renewed, ours.

Julian's fingers idly trace the curve of my hip, avoiding the tender spots but close enough that I feel the care in every light touch.

I shift slightly, my hand finding his hair, threading through the dark strands with slow, soothing strokes, the afterglow wrapping us in quiet intimacy.

I close my eyes, savoring the softness—the way he nuzzles closer, pressing a lazy kiss to the swell of my breast, not possessive now but reverent, as if mapping the territory he's claimed with something deeper than fury.

Minutes stretch, unhurried—my fingers trailing from his hair to his back, feeling the tension ebb from his muscles, while he murmurs nonsense against my skin, words too low to catch but vibrating with contentment. I trace a welt on my thigh again, the raised line a secret thrill, and he lifts his head just enough to watch, his eyes soft in the dim light.

"Beautiful." His thumb brushes mine over the mark, his touch feather-light, healing the sting without erasing the memory. Then, casually, as if commenting on the weather, he adds, "One day, I'd like to mark you permanently—something that wouldn't fade. A tattoo, maybe, or a careful cutting, just for us."

I gasp, my hand stilling on the welt, a flicker of fear tightening my chest—permanent, etched forever, binding me in ink or scar beyond the contract's end. The thought sends a chill through the warmth.

He senses it immediately, his body shifting to prop himself up on one elbow, eyes meeting mine with steady reassurance, his free hand cupping my cheek.

"Hey—only after the contract. Not now, and never forced. It would be your choice. I wouldn't take that from you."

The tension eases from my shoulders, warmth flooding back as his words sink in. I relax into the hay, my fingers resuming their trace of the mark, a small smile tugging at my lips.

"Until then." My voice is playful in the vulnerability, "you can keep marking me with your belt... or a crop. Maybe one day we could even try the cane?"

He laughs then, a low, rumbling sound that vibrates through his chest, his thumb stroking my jaw as amusement lights his eyes. "You're not ready for the cane. Not yet. That is too intense—even for you."

Doubtful. I'll endure anything for him, but it's best not to encourage him. I bite back a grin at his laughter, though the idea lingers like a forbidden thrill: bliss under his hand, the sharp kiss of rattan across my skin, his control wielding it precisely, pushing me to edges that would shatter and remake me all over again.

The talk of markings—permanent and fleeting—stirs something in him too; I feel it in the subtle shift of his body against mine, his cock lengthening once more, pressing insistent and warm against my thigh, the topic reigniting his hunger even in this soft afterglow.

Julian sits up slowly, the hay rustling beneath him, his eyes locking on mine with a loving depth that steals my breath—raw affection shining through the possessiveness, making my heart stutter.

He draws me into his lap with gentle hands on my hips, settling me astride him, our bare skin brushing in the golden light, his hardness nestling right at my core without urgency, just promise.

"Ride me." His voice is husky and tender, thumbs stroking the welts on my sides as he holds my gaze, unblinking. "As a gift—take control. Come freely on my cock, however you want. I want to watch you take pleasure from me."

Empowered, I shift in his lap, the hay prickling my knees as I rise just enough to wrap my hand around his length, feeling the heat and hardness throb under my fingers.

He's ready, slick from before, and I position myself above him, lowering slowly, savoring the stretch as he fills me inch by inch, my core clenching around him in a deep, welcoming ache that echoes the welts' throb.

A soft moan escapes me, my hands planting on his shoulders for leverage, nails digging in lightly as I find my rhythm—rolling my hips, experimental, the friction delicious against the tender marks on my thighs and ass.

Julian's hands rest on my waist, steady but not guiding, his gaze locked on mine, dark and adoring, a low groan rumbling from his chest as I lift and sink again, deeper this time, setting a pace that's mine: unhurried at first, building the pleasure in waves that coil low in my belly.

The welts press into his skin where our bodies meet, a sharp-sweet reminder that heightens everything, my breath coming faster as I grind down, circling to hit that spot inside that makes stars flicker behind my eyes.

"You're beautiful like this." His voice is rough with restraint, but he doesn't take ove. He lets me chase my pleasure, my movements growing bolder, hips snapping now, the slap of skin a quiet counterpoint to the horses' distant snorts.

I lean forward, capturing his mouth in a messy kiss, tongues tangling as I ride harder, faster, the edge rushing up, an orgasm coiling fierce and free, crashing over me in shuddering waves that clench around him, my cry muffled against his lips, my body trembling as release floods through every marked inch of me.

He follows with a guttural groan, hips bucking up to meet my final descent, spilling inside me as his hands grip tighter, holding me through the aftershocks. We stay locked, breaths mingling, his forehead to mine in the hay-scented dimness, the gift of this moment sealing the softness deeper into my bones.

Sometime later, his voice pulls me back from the haze of our joined breaths, still buried deep inside me as we linger, tangled in the hay, his fingers lazy on my back.

"I have a business trip."

I lift my head from his shoulder, a pang of reluctance twisting in my chest at the thought of separation, even brief—his presence has been woven into my days, the ranch feeling empty without his commanding weight.

"What will I do without you fucking me senseless every night? The bed's going to feel too big, too quiet."

He chuckles low, the sound vibrating through us both, his eyes crinkling with amusement and a flicker of possessive warmth as he brushes a strand of hair from my damp forehead, holding my gaze steady.

"You're coming with me."

Surprise widens my eyes, delight sparking amid the lingering ache of welts and release, my heart skips a beat as I search his face for the jest—but it's real, this inclusion in his world beyond the ranch.

"I am?"

"Did you think I'd leave you here alone? With Henley sniffing around?" His voice carries an edge. "Pack for formal events. We have dinners with investors."

"More parading me around?"

"More showing you off." He softens slightly. "Also, there's someone I want you to meet."

"Who?"

"My mother."

I freeze. "Your mother? But I thought—"

"She lives in New York. Has since the divorce." He looks

uncomfortable. "She wants to meet the woman who finally caught me."

"Caught you? You hunted me for seventeen years and forced me into a contract—"

"She doesn't know that version." He pauses. "She thinks you're my girlfriend."

"You want me to lie to your mother?"

"Would it be a lie?" He pauses, but I don't respond.

CHAPTER 43
DAY 92

Day 9

The city overwhelms after Montana's quiet, a cacophony of horns and hurried footsteps crashing against my senses. We step out of the black SUV into the shadow of Julian's high-rise building, the air thick with exhaust and the faint, metallic tang of rain on concrete.

His apartment—penthouse, really—is all glass and chrome, perched high above Central Park like a sleek predator surveying its territory. Floor-to-ceiling windows frame the sprawling green below, but the space feels sterile, cold perfection that makes me miss the ranch's worn warmth—the creak of leather saddles, the earthy scent of hay, and the way dust motes dance in sunlight slanting through barn doors.

I wander to the windows, pressing a palm against the cool glass, watching joggers blur into tiny figures far below. The city pulses with life, but up here, it's isolated, controlled—a mirror to the man who owns it.

"You hate it." His voice is low as he sets down our bags, watching me from the doorway of the bedroom.

He's shed his coat, sleeves rolled up to reveal forearms corded with quiet strength, his eyes tracking my every shift as if he can read the discomfort in my posture.

"It's not you." I turn slightly, the reflection of the park fracturing in the glass behind me.

"What's not me?" He steps closer, curiosity sharpening his gaze, no defensiveness—just that unflinching directness that always pulls truths from me.

"You're warmth underneath the control." I meet his eyes in the window's faint reflection. "This is just... control."

He moves behind me then, his arms caging me gently against the glass, hands flat on either side of my hips, his chest brushing my back in a way that sends a shiver through the chill of the pane. His breath warms my ear, voice a murmur laced with something deeper, almost vulnerable.

That night, he keeps me close. Not restrained. Not commanded. Just held.

We lie tangled in the quiet, the city lights flickering through the glass, his fingers idly tracing the inside of my wrist like he's memorizing the beat of my pulse. There's no dominance here— only gravity, the pull that keeps drawing me back, no matter how far I try to drift.

"This is where I learned." His voice is low, almost contemplative. "The things I needed to know to make you mine. I was cold and unyielding, everything shaped to my will. But you're remaking me, softening the edges I didn't know were there, showing me how to be warm beneath the control."

His words settle deep, heavy, and quiet. I don't trust myself to speak, so I just lean into him, breathing in the faint scent of cedar and smoke.

We drift somewhere between sleep and stillness, our bodies fitting together like a key and a lock. Before the quiet can settle completely, he speaks again, his tone more deliberate.

"My mother will be here in the morning."

That pulls me fully awake.

"Your mother?"

"She's... curious. I've never told her about my particular lifestyle choices, but she's a perceptive woman. You should know that before she arrives."

Something flutters low in my stomach. "So what do I tell her?"

"The truth," he brushes a thumb along my jaw. "Or enough of it to sound believable. She'll look for cracks—she always does—but don't let her see more than you want her to."

"She sounds formidable."

He studies me for a moment longer, then smiles faintly. "She'll like you. She likes strong women."

When I don't answer, he adds softly, "Sleep, Clara. Tomorrow will be... interesting."

His arm tightens around me, drawing me close again, and this time when my eyes close, it's not fear that keeps me awake—it's the awareness that even Julian Blackwell can sound almost human when he talks about his mother.

CHAPTER 44

DAY 93

Julian's mother is dressed in flowing linens and bold jewelry, nothing like the polished society matron I **expected**.

Instead, she hugs Julian fiercely, pulling him down to her level despite his height, and **kisses** his cheek, leaving a faint lipstick mark, which he doesn't bother wiping away.

"You're Clara." It's not a question, her voice rich and accented with the faint lilt of old East Coast money. She turns to me with arms outstretched. "He's talked about you for years."

"Mom—" Julian's **voice carries a hint of exasperation**, though his hand lingers on her shoulder, protective in its casual firmness.

"What? It's true." She waves him off, taking my hands in hers and **studies** me with an intensity that's appraising but kind. "Every Christmas, every birthday, I heard about Clara Hayes. The girl from the ranch next door, the one who could outride him, outstubborn him. You're prettier than he said. Stronger, too."

Her grip tightens briefly, a subtle squeeze that conveys

approval, **her gaze moving** over me as if cataloging the confidence in my stance, the way I don't pull away from Julian's orbit.

"Thank you?" **A** smile **tugs** at my lips despite the flush creeping up my neck. "It's nice to meet you, Mrs. Blackwell."

"Don't thank me yet." She pulls me aside while Julian's phone buzzes, drawing him toward the kitchen for a call. His posture straightens instinctively, that dominant edge sharpening as he nods to her and steps away. "And call me Evelyn. Mrs. Blackwell makes me feel a thousand years old. Now, tell me everything about you."

She links her arm through mine, leading me to the sleek leather couch overlooking the park. She settles in with a sigh, her body language open, inviting.

Still, there's a subtle undercurrent: the way **she watches** the faint tension in Julian's shoulders as he speaks lowly into the phone, or how she notes the possessive brush of his hand against my lower back before he leaves us.

She knows her son—the unyielding set of his jaw, the quiet command that bends rooms to his will—and there's pride in it, threaded with an unspoken awareness of the deeper layers, the control that likely extends into shadows she doesn't name but senses, like the faint scars on a favorite painting.

"Has he told you about the notebooks?" she asks, voice dropping to a conspiratorial whisper, though her eyes glimmer with mischief rather than malice.

"What notebooks?" **I** lean in before I can stop myself. The question feels like touching a bruise—dangerous, irresistible.

Her smile widens, knowing and unhurried. "Ah. Then you haven't found them yet." She gives a soft, indulgent laugh, the kind only a mother can pull off. "My son has always been... *intense.* Even as a boy, he needed to order the world somehow. Those notebooks were his way of doing it. Thoughts, plans, ideas

—things that mattered only to him." She pats my hand, a gesture of fond amusement. "If you come across them, don't read too much into what you find. Some brilliance looks like madness when written down too young."

I force a polite smile, but her words spark heat low in my stomach.

I found them— bound in worn leather, pages filled with fevered script. Fantasies. Possession. Desire inked in meticulous, desperate lines—an unfiltered glimpse into a teenage mind already obsessed with control and me.

Notebooks that blurred love and domination long before either of us had the language for it.

"I'll keep that in mind." **A flush creeps up my neck. I force my voice steady.**

She watches me a beat too long, eyes soft but sharp, as if she can see every thought I don't speak. Then she smiles again, easy and warm.

"Julian's never done well with half-measures. Neither have you, I think."

I manage a faint laugh, but my **pulse hammers**. Because she's right—and because those notebooks prove what's always been inevitable.

She laughs, **though something hollow threads through it**, her fingers twisting a ring on her thumb—a simple silver band etched with abstract swirls.

"He kept journals about you. Starting freshman year. Every interaction, every observation, scribbled in those black leather books he hid under his bed. His father found them once, said it was unhealthy—obsessive, even."

Her tone softens, defensive on his behalf, her love for Julian evident in the way her eyes mist slightly. "Julian's always been intense. When he fixates on something—or someone—it becomes his world. He doesn't bend; he shapes everything around it. It's what makes him brilliant, what built his empire."

She pauses, **glancing toward** him again, where he's ended the call and stands by the window, arms crossed, exuding that effortless dominance that fills the space without a word.

There's a subtle tell in her smile—the way it deepens with quiet pride, as if she knows the intensity runs deeper, into private realms of power and surrender, the kind of strength that commands not just boardrooms but bedrooms, though she'd never voice it aloud. It's there in the knowing tilt of her head, the acceptance of her son's unapologetic nature.

"It sounds obsessive," I admit, though the words feel less certain now, glancing at Julian and seeing the boy who waited, who planned, beneath the man.

"Is it?" Evelyn tilts her head, studying me with those sharp eyes. "Or was it a boy who knew what he wanted and was willing to wait for it? Clara, you have no idea how long he's carried this torch. He was so alone after his father... well, after everything. But now?"

Her face lights up, joy blooming genuine and bright as she squeezes my hand again. "He finally found someone who sees him, challenges him. I'm so happy for him—for you both."

Before I can respond, Julian reenters the room, his presence drawing her attention like gravity.

Dinner that night is a blur of elegant restraint at a rooftop restaurant—silverware clinking, city lights twinkling below. But I feel Evelyn's eyes on us.

She watches the way Julian orders for me without asking, the way his hand rests on the nape of my neck—heavy and claiming —while we drink our wine. She sees the ownership. And she doesn't look away.

Instead, she corners me the next morning over coffee in the apartment's gleaming kitchen.

CHAPTER 45
DAY 94

The next morning, the apartment is quiet. Julian has gone for his run, leaving the space filled with the smell of brewing coffee and the morning sun.

I walk into the kitchen, rubbing sleep from my eyes, only to find Evelyn already there. She's perched on a barstool, nursing a cup of tea, looking perfectly put together in a silk robe.

"Good morning, Clara."

"Morning, Evelyn." I move to the coffee machine, feeling exposed in just my oversized shirt—Julian's shirt.

"Sit with me," she says. It's not a command like Julian's, but it has the same underlying steel.

I pour a cup and sit. She studies me over the rim of her mug, her expression thoughtful.

"I saw the way he touched you last night," she says, cutting straight through the pleasantries. "At dinner."

"Oh?" My grip tightens on the ceramic mug.

"He doesn't touch you like a girlfriend," she observes quietly.

"He touches you like an anchor. Like if he lets go, he might float away—or worse, tear the world apart."

She sets her cup down.

"My son is a man of extremes. He always has been. He requires... a great deal of gravity to keep him centered. I used to worry that no woman would be able to withstand the weight of his attention. That his need for control would crush anyone who got too close."

She reaches across the island, covering my hand with hers. Her skin is cool, her rings clicking against the granite.

"But you aren't crushed, are you?"

I look at her, seeing the resemblance in the eyes—the intelligence, the perception. She knows. She might not know about the contract, or the Red Room, or the title I whisper in the dark, but she knows the dynamic.

She knows I serve him.

"No," I answer, my voice clear and certain. "I'm not crushed. I'm exactly where I want to be."

Evelyn searches my face, looking for a lie, but finding only the truth. She lets out a breath she seems to have been holding for years.

"Good," she whispers. "Because he won't let you go. You know that, don't you? Now that he has you... he will never let you go."

"I know," I say, and for the first time, I admit the darkest part of it to another soul. "I'm counting on it."

A slow smile spreads across her face—not the polite society smile, but something fiercer. A mother realizing her wolf has found a mate who can run with him.

"Then I have no worries," she says, picking up her tea again as the front door unlocks and Julian walks in, sweating and breathing hard from the street.

He stops, looking between the two of us—his mother and his

submissive, sitting in the sunlight. His eyes narrow slightly, sensing the shift in the air, the silent accord we've reached.

"Everything alright?" he asks, wiping his face with a towel.

"Perfect, darling," she says. "Just getting to know the family."

He lingers for a moment, his gaze shifting between us with a predator's wariness, sensing the invisible thread that has just been tied between his mother and his property. He crosses the kitchen, the scent of fresh sweat and cold air clinging to him. He stops behind my stool, his hand coming to rest on the nape of my neck, his thumb pressing into the soft skin there—a habitual check of his ownership.

"Don't tell her everything, Mom," he warns, though his voice is low and lacks actual bite. "She has enough ammunition against me as it is."

"I'm only filling in the blanks, Julian." Evelyn smiles innocently over her tea. "Go shower. You smell like the Hudson River."

He grunts, leans down to press a hard, brief kiss to my temple —a silent command to stay—and disappears down the hall.

When he re-emerges, the runner is gone, replaced by the Titan.

Julian's mother waves him off with a flick of her wrist. "Go conquer the world, darling. Clara and I need girl time."

He hesitates—a rare thing for him—his hand pausing mid-button. His gaze shifts to me, one brow arching in silent question. I nod, even as something uneasy curls low in my stomach.

"Be good," he murmurs, low enough for only me to hear. His fingers brush my waist—a fleeting touch that's both promise and warning. Then he's gone, the door closing behind him with the finality of a gavel.

"He's used to getting the last word. I've been trying to cure him of that for thirty years." Evelyn Blackwell turns to me with a smile that's all warmth and mischief.

Brunch is her idea—a sunlit café tucked on a quiet street in the Village, far removed from the steel-and-glass world Julian commands. The place smells of coffee, citrus, and fresh flowers. She orders mimosas before I can answer, settling into the wrought-iron chair with an ease her son never quite manages.

"Now," she says, eyes crinkling as she stirs her drink, "tell me everything. And not the polite version—the real one. How did my impossible son finally win you over?"

I trace the rim of my glass, the bubbles rising like secrets I don't dare voice. "It's... complicated. The ranch. My father's debts. It started with control, not choice."

Her expression doesn't change, but her eyes—sharp and intelligent—soften with something like understanding. She takes a slow sip, hums thoughtfully.

"Control," she echoes. "Yes. That sounds like Julian."

I look up. "You're not surprised?"

"Oh, sweetheart." Her smile is rueful, almost tender. "Julian came into the world trying to control it. Even as a boy, he needed things his way. When the other children played pirates, he built an armada. When they drew castles, he drafted city-states—with tax systems." She laughs softly, shaking her head. "His father adored that about him. I... worried."

"Worried?"

"That he mistook control for safety." She sets her glass down, fingers lacing delicately. "When he feels too much, he tightens his grip. On work. On people. On himself."

There's affection in her voice, but also a shadow.

"He's built empires on that instinct," she continues, pride creeping back in. "Empires rise and fall, but Blackwells endure. And now, with you..." Her tone changes, softens, and she reaches across the table, covering my hand. "He's lighter. I see it. You've given him something he's never allowed himself—someone to care for. To protect."

Her thumb strokes my knuckles absently, but her gaze holds mine, searching. "Does he protect you?"

The question is gentle—too gentle. My breath catches.

"I—yes," I manage, forcing a smile. "He does."

"I'm glad." She leans back, the tension dissolving, though her eyes still gleam with quiet knowing. "Just remember, protecting and controlling aren't the same thing. Men like Julian sometimes forget the difference. As his mother, I hoped one day he'd find someone who could balance him. Someone strong enough not to be swept under the current."

"I'm trying," I say quietly.

Her eyes soften again, a mother's warmth wrapped in shrewd awareness. "I know you are. Take care of him. And let him take care of you. But make sure you're both choosing it. That's the difference between devotion and captivity."

When she hugs me goodbye outside the café, she smells of paint, citrus, and faint sadness.

And for the first time, I wonder if Julian's mother isn't just trying to understand me, but to make sure I survive her son.

Back at the penthouse, the city hums beneath us, lights glinting off glass and steel, stretching toward infinity. The living room is quiet, painted in gold with the last spill of sunset, when the elevator doors whisper open behind me.

I don't turn. I don't have to. The atmosphere shifts—charged, heavier, threaded with something distinctly him.

Julian crosses the space, the muted click of his shoes on the marble the only warning before his presence wraps around me. He smells of rain and power and faint cologne, the kind that lingers on skin and memory.

He doesn't say a word at first. His hand finds my waist, warm and deliberate, fingertips grazing the curve of my hip before settling there like a claim. The simple touch unravels something inside me.

Then his other arm slides around, drawing me back until I feel the solid wall of his chest against my spine. His breath fans against the side of my throat, slow and heavy, each exhale tasting of whiskey and exhaustion.

"My mother monopolized you all day," he murmurs finally, his voice rougher than usual, low and intimate. "Now, it's my turn."

He doesn't kiss me right away. Instead, his hand drifts up, over my ribs, flattening beneath my breasts, feeling the way I breathe. His lips brush the shell of my ear, a slow drag of heat that leaves me trembling.

"I don't want to talk about work," he says, the words half a confession, half command. "I want this."

He turns me then, his hands firm but reverent, and when our eyes meet, the control in him fractures for just a heartbeat. There's hunger, yes—but also something softer, something unguarded.

He cups my jaw and kisses me—not possessively, not to conquer, but like a man starved for something only I can give.

And for the first time since he walked into my life, I let him take without resistance. Because right now, in this moment between skyline and shadow, I need it too.

His fingers work the buttons of my blouse slowly, one by one, exposing skin inch by inch to the cool air and his gaze—tender in the unhurried reveal, yet dominant in the way he controls the pace, denying me the rush even as anticipation coils tight in my belly.

The fabric slips from my shoulders, pooling at my feet, and he unzips my skirt next, letting it fall with a whisper, his knuckles grazing the curve of my hips.

I press my palms to the glass for balance, the chill seeping into my skin as he traces lower, fingers ghosting over the faint lines on my thighs and ass—the welts from the barn, faded now to pale pink reminders under the city's glow.

His touch reignites the memory: the sharp crack of leather, the cathartic burn, the way it stripped me bare and rebuilt me in his hands.

"These," he says softly, thumb pressing lightly on one, drawing a gasp from me as heat flickers to life anew, "still mark you as mine. Even here, in my world."

His free hand slides between my thighs, finding me slick, circling with deliberate slowness that makes my breath hitch, fogging the pane in uneven bursts.

His words pull a soft moan from my throat, vulnerability mixing with desire.

He doesn't spin me; instead, he nudges my legs wider with his knee, his body aligning behind mine—solid, commanding—as he frees himself from his pants, the heat of him brushes my entrance.

My hands splay against the glass, bracing as he thrusts in deep, filling me completely, the stretch eliciting a sharp gasp that clouds the window further.

The position exposes me to the city's indifferent gaze, my breasts brushing the cold pane with each roll of his hips, but it's his control that anchors me—his hands gripping my hips firmly, setting a deliberate rhythm: slow, powerful drives that build the tension like he's reshaping me anew.

I reach back with one hand, fingers digging into his thigh for purchase, nails scraping lightly as the friction ignites every nerve, the welts tingling under his occasional brush.

Whispers of "mine" are breathed against my neck between

nips of teeth that echo the barn's intensity without the pain—possessive, tender, setting my world straight in this blend of surrender and command.

"Mine to have, mine to take." His pace quickens just enough to coil the pleasure tighter, my gasps blending with the distant hum of traffic far below. "Mine to own. Come for me. Come for the one who owns you."

Release builds in slow, shattering waves, my body arching, clenching around him as it crashes over me—tremors rippling through, my cry fogging the glass in a final, hazy bloom before he follows with a low groan, spilling hot inside me, hips grinding deep through the aftershocks.

We stay there a moment, breaths ragged, his forehead pressing to my shoulder as he eases out, hands turning gentle on my waist—rubbing soothing circles over the faded marks.

Then, without a word, he gathers me in his arms and carries me to the bedroom. The city's glow filters through sheer curtains like a soft veil.

The bed is vast and welcoming, sheets cool against my heated skin as he lays me down, stripping off the rest of his clothes before joining me, his body covering mine in a protective drape.

Tonight, his hunger isn't sated. Instead, he's ravenous. I feel it in the insistent press of him against my thigh, the way his eyes darken with that deeper intent.

"I want all of you," he murmurs, his voice a low, seductive rumble against my ear, laced with dominant intent that brooks no refusal—final, possessive, as his hand tightens on my hip. "Tonight, I'm taking your ass again—deep, slow, until you're clenching around me and begging for more, because this belongs to me too."

He rolls us so we're both on our sides, him curving against my back in a close spooning embrace—intimate, enveloping, his chest to my spine, one arm banded around my waist to hold me steady while his free hand lifts my top leg slightly, bending my knee for access.

The position feels protective yet exposing, his hardness pressing insistent against me, a solid anchor as vulnerability stirs deeper, the command sealing my surrender before it even begins.

My body tenses instinctively, muscles clenching as his fingers trail down between us, slicking himself with the remnants of our release before circling my entrance there. He pauses at the resistance, his touch light but insistent, and his lips brush my neck in a warm counterpoint to the cool sheets.

"You're still uncomfortable with this, aren't you?" he murmurs, the words a soothing growl that acknowledges my tension without yielding ground, his free hand stroking my thigh to ease the knot. "But you won't refuse me, will you? You'll take it because you crave the obedience, the way surrendering to my dominance sets you free—because deep down, you need me to take this as much as I need to claim you."

"Yes, Mr. Blackwell," I whisper, the formal title slipping out like an anchor in the storm of my nerves, my voice breathy and edged with truth, affirming the dynamic even as I hate how he unerringly reads my hidden fears and desires.

He hums his approval, a low vibration against my back that sends a shiver through me, his fingers resuming their gentle circles with renewed tenderness. He presses a lingering kiss to my shoulder, dominance tempered with care in the quiet rumble.

"Like last time, I'll be gentle, and I'll guide you through every inch until the burn turns to pleasure. Come as often as you like. Thank you for the gift of your surrender; it's mine to cherish."

The admission unravels something in me—the truth of it loosening my muscles just enough—as he resumes teasing, gently applying pressure that sparks a mix of apprehension and anticipation.

I flinch, discomfort flickering as he presses a finger in, slow and probing, the stretch unfamiliar and tight despite the preparation.

"Shh," he soothes, voice low and reassuring, his free hand cupping my face, thumb stroking my cheek.

I don't have the choice to pull away; I must allow it, surrender to the sensations he's drawing out, and in that lack of option, freedom blooms—permission to feel without overthinking, to let him guide me through.

"Breathe with me. Relax into it. You've done this for me before—you can again. It's just us."

I exhale shakily as he adds a second finger, scissoring carefully, the initial burn easing into a strange, building pressure that mingles with arousal when his other hand slips between us, circling my clit in firm, rhythmic strokes.

Discomfort lingers at the edges, a tight ache as he withdraws his fingers and positions himself, the head of his cock nudging insistently—slow, so slow, inching in with murmured encouragements.

"Good girl, that's it—open for me. Feel how tight you are, how perfect." The fullness borders on overwhelming, drawing a whimper from me, but his words ground me, his pace unhurried, letting my body adjust as he rocks shallowly, pleasure sparking where pain fades.

It shifts then—the discomfort transforming under his touch, the dual sensations coiling as he thrusts deeper, his fingers never ceasing their work on my clit.

"Let go," he whispers, lips brushing my forehead, vulnerability in the raw need of his voice. "Take what I give you—come for me like this."

The command releases me fully, my orgasm building from that forbidden place, shattering in waves that clench around him impossibly tight, pulling his own release from him in a shuddering groan, hot and claiming.

He holds me through it all, unmoving after, his arms a secure cage as our breaths sync in the quiet. The day's revelations lace the intimacy even deeper now—his intensity, born of notebooks and waiting, poured into this total surrender.

"Evelyn's words... they stirred old doubts," he admits after a long silence, voice rough with the afterglow, fingers tracing idle patterns on my back. "That I shaped you, forced this. But you're choosing me—here, now, giving yourself like this—it silences my doubts."

His hold tightens, vulnerability raw in the quiet, a crack in the dominant facade that makes me press closer, my choice sealing the bond deeper than any mark.

I shift slightly in his embrace, turning my face toward his chest, my voice a soft murmur against his skin, laced with the weight of our shared transformation.

"You're changing me... Julian—" I catch myself mid-word, the intimacy of his given name feeling too presumptuous in this moment of raw exposure, and I correct with a breathless flush. "Mr. Blackwell, you make me crave the darkness you bring, needing your commands like I need air to breathe. Don't ever stop forcing me, commanding me... in that, you were right from the beginning. At first, I hated it, the way you stripped away my control, but now I can't imagine living any other way."

His breath catches sharply, a low hum of satisfaction rumbling in his chest as he tilts my chin up with gentle fingers, his eyes locking onto mine in the dim light—dark with possession, softened by the raw honesty between us, but now flickering with that familiar authoritative glint.

"That's why I'm going to punish you for using my name instead of my title," he says, his voice a gravelly murmur of intent, laced with affection rather than anger, his thumb brushing my lower lip in a possessive stroke. "Because you need to know I will never stray from disciplining you—it's the structure that binds us, the reminder of who we are."

He pauses, searching my eyes with a tenderness that belies the words, his free hand cupping my cheek.

"Do you want to try the cane for this one?" he asks lovingly, the question soft but deliberate, his gaze steady. "I've withheld it until now because it's extreme—the sting is sharp, the marks it leaves will last far longer than the belt—but if you're ready, it will etch this lesson deeper, a visible claim for days to come."

"Yes, please," I whisper, the words tumbling out with a mix of trepidation and trust, my pulse quickening at the vulnerability of the choice, yet feeling the rightness of it in my bones—the next step in our remaking.

He nods, pride warming his expression as he shifts us both from the tangled sheets, guiding me with firm but careful hands.

"Good girl," he murmurs, helping me to my feet before positioning me to kneel on the floor at the edge of the bed, my forearms resting on the mattress for support, back arched slightly to present myself—exposed, obedient, the cool air raising goosebumps on my skin.

He retrieves a cane from a discreet drawer in the nightstand, a slender rod of polished rattan that whistles faintly as he tests it with a swish. The sound alone sends a shiver through me. Standing behind me, one hand settles warmly on the small of my back, anchoring me as the other draws the cane lightly across my skin, building the anticipation without true contact.

The first strike lands with a sharp crack—precise, controlled, blooming into a line of fire that far eclipses the belt's thudding ache, the pain a blinding, obliterating force that steals my breath, my body jerking forward as I cry out, a raw, keening sound that echoes in the room.

"Oh my God, it's too much. Stop—please. I can't—" The words break free in a desperate plea, my fingers twisting in the sheets as fresh tears spill down my cheeks, the intensity overwhelming, my mind fracturing under the assault.

"I won't stop," he says firmly, his voice steady and unyielding, though threaded with that same loving resolve, his anchoring hand pressing firmer to hold me in place. "You chose the cane, and I will follow through. Trust me to guide you; breathe for me now." His tone leaves no room for negotiation, a reminder of the boundaries we've set and the discipline that binds us.

The second strike follows after a measured pause, the cane whistling through the air before it bites again. The pain explodes anew—sharper, deeper, a relentless blaze that has me crying out once more, my body convulsing as sobs wrack me, the world narrowing to the throbbing welt it leaves behind.

He soothes me then, his free hand gliding over the inflamed skin in slow, circular rubs, the touch gentle and grounding, murmuring softly against my ear,

"That's it, my brave girl—feel my hand, let it center you. You're doing so well."

I nod shakily into the mattress, tears soaking the fabric, my breath coming in ragged hitches, but his words pull me back from the edge, the care in his voice a lifeline amid the storm.

"Now the next three in quick succession," he warns, his hand resuming its warm weight on my back, preparation in his tone. "It will hurt, but not as much as drawing it out—brace yourself."

He waits a beat, letting me steady.

"Breathe—deep and even."

I draw in a shuddering inhale, and then the strikes come in

rapid fire: three swift cracks that layer the agony into a crescendo, each one a blinding lash that rips cries from my throat, the pain merging into an all-consuming fire that leaves me limp and weeping, my skin a canvas of raised, pulsing stripes.

His voice weaves through it all, a steady murmur of praise and command—"Breathe through it; you're taking this so beautifully for me"—ensuring I feel held even in the discipline.

By the end, my skin is striped with raised, tender lines that throb in rhythm with my heartbeat, the ache a profound reminder of his authority, tears streaming freely from the intensity but mingled with a deep, cathartic release.

He sets the cane aside then, drawing me into his arms, inspecting the marks with featherlight touches before pulling me back onto the bed.

"I won't ever stop," he promises, voice a gravelly vow that sends a shiver through me, his thumb brushing my lower lip in a tender claim. "You'll always need my discipline, and I'll always give it—because you're mine, and this need we share... It's the truest thing we've built."

He seals the words with a deep, lingering kiss, the vulnerability in his admission weaving tighter into the dominance that defines us, the fresh marks a secret bond pressing between us.

We stay tangled like that until dawn, the night stretching into a haze of gentle intimacy where he takes me several times—slow, reverent, his touches mindful of my stripes and welts, positioning me carefully to avoid pressure, each union a soothing balm that reaffirms the trust we've forged. His whispers of possession and praise lull me into exhausted peace as the city awakens beneath us.

But home calls—the ranch, the horses, the wild expanse that grounds us both—and by midday, we're airborne again, the jet slicing through clouds back toward the life we've built.

When we land, Julian's hand rests possessively at the small of my back, guiding me toward the waiting car, his presence a steady anchor amid the shift from urban intimacy to rugged reality.

I feel the pull of home settling deeper,

Evelyn's revelations fade into the rearview as the ranch comes into view—its sprawling fields, the barn where marks were made and remade. I can't help but trace the new marks, marks made with love and discipline.

Julian glances over from the driver's seat, his sharp gaze catching the motion immediately, one eyebrow arching in quiet curiosity as he navigates the winding road.

"Tracing them already?" he asks, voice low and even, not accusatory but inviting, his free hand reaching to squeeze my thigh briefly before returning to the wheel.

I flush, my hand stilling as if caught in something forbidden, the words hesitant on my tongue—I'm still processing the raw intensity, the way it shattered and rebuilt me in turns, and admitting my thoughts feels like exposing another layer.

My gaze drops to my lap. I twist my fingers together. "They're... intense. I'll avoid the cane at all costs next time. It hurt so much more than I thought—but... I'll wear the reminder proudly. For you." The confession comes out in a near-whisper, truthful but tentative, like testing the waters of this deeper honesty between us.

He nods, a faint smile tugging at his lips, appreciation warming his eyes as the vehicle rumbles over a gravel patch. "What do you think of them, then? The welts—be honest."

I hesitate again, biting my lip, the processing still fresh, words tumbling out haltingly. "They're... beautiful, in a way? A mark of trust. But God, they're severe—I can feel every one." My voice trails off, unsure, waiting for his lead as always.

"I mean to keep you constantly marked by me." His chuckle is soft and reassuring as he pulls off onto a scenic overlook. He turns to face me.

"Does this mean you'll use the cane for punishments now?" My gaze lifts to meet his— a flicker of uncertainty there despite the budding comfort in voicing it.

"No." His tone carries that affectionate edge as he reaches to tilt my chin, studying me gently. "It's too severe for you. Although I admit that looking at those welts will drive me crazy until they fade. I won't be able to keep my hands off you. The temptation to mark you like that more often... It's too much."

A small, shy smile breaks through my hesitation, the tension easing as I lean into his touch. "When have you ever kept your hands off me?" The words come out light—teasing in their truth, the dynamic feeling more settled, more ours to discuss openly.

He laughs then—a rare, genuine rumble that fills the cab, his eyes crinkling at the corners as he brushes his thumb over my cheek.

"Fair point." He starts the truck again, but keeps his gaze lingering on me. "The stripes do something to me. It's primal and dark. That's why I'll stick to the belt. The cane... it'll come out only for something that truly tests boundaries. But this? Us talking about it like this—it's good. It makes us stronger."

CHAPTER 46
DAY 120

The coffee tray is warm in my hands, the familiar weight of our morning ritual. Four months in, and I've learned to anticipate Julian's needs before he voices them—black coffee at precisely the right temperature, the way his shoulders ease when I set it beside him without being asked.

I've been happy. It hits me as I pad down the hallway in bare feet, one of his shirts hanging loose on my frame.

Actually happy.

Not the brittle contentment of survival, but something deeper. Something that feels like belonging.

At least he stopped making me drink that orange juice. I complained about it so many times—too acidic, too bitter—and finally, he listened.

Julian does listen, sometimes, in his own way. It's one of the things that makes this bearable. More than bearable, if I'm honest.

His voice carries through his cracked office door, the blue glow of his laptop screen visible. A video call.

"—results are extraordinary, Nathan. Beyond what we theorized. Four months, and her acceptance of the dynamic is seamless."

"The members will be thrilled." The other voice sounds equally pleased. "This is exactly the vision. No more failed dynamics, no more resistance. Just perfect harmony."

"Perfect harmony undersells it." Papers rustle. "She anticipates my needs, seeks my approval, and submits with genuine eagerness. The members are going to want this immediately."

Members? Want what?

Why are they discussing me like... like a product demonstration?

"They're already asking." Nathan chuckles. "They want to know when the protocol will be available. You've created the holy grail here. A way to guarantee a perfect submissive."

My hands tremble. Protocol? Perfect submissive? Guarantee?

"The key is the delivery system." Pride laces Julian's voice. "Daily oxytocin microdosing through the morning orange juice—completely masked by the citrus. She complained about it constantly, but drank it because I made it a rule."

The orange juice?

Oh God. I drank the orange juice every morning. Was he putting something in it?

"Brilliant. Using the power dynamic itself to ensure compliance with the dosing. And the supplementary doses?"

"Champagne at social events—" Julian says, "the Empathine in her water during Red Room sessions. She thinks the euphoria is from the scenes themselves, has no idea it's chemically enhanced."

The champagne?

That first gala when everything felt so warm, so right. The water he always insisted I drink during scenes. It's what?

Drugged?

I don't believe it. I can't. Yet they're talking about exactly that.

"The Bondix component is the real innovation," Nathan adds enthusiastically. "Converting pain to pleasure at the neurological level during states of arousal—that's what ensures they crave discipline, not just tolerate it."

What?

Is that why the punishments started feeling like release? Why I began craving the belt, the commands? It wasn't me growing into the dynamic—it was chemicals rewiring my brain?

"It worked better than we hoped." Julian agrees. "Sometimes too well."

"Too well?" Nathan sounds confused. "How can it work too well?"

"Yesterday, she knelt beside my chair for an hour. Unprompted. The perfect picture of submission." Julian's voice carries a mix of satisfaction and something else—uncertainty? "This week alone, she initiated sex five times. Came to me in the shower, in my office, woke me at three AM because she needed— her words—needed to feel me inside her."

Five times? Was that really me? I remember the shower, the desperate hunger I couldn't explain...

"That's fantastic," Nathan sounds enthusiastic.

"She's asked for the Red Room. Begged. Said she needed the intensity, the way pain grounds her." A pause, papers shuffling. "She said she thinks better when restrained."

The rope. I remember the peace that washed over me when he tied those knots. I thought I was discovering myself, but it was just... chemicals making me crave it?

"The protocol is working perfectly then," Nathan says.

"Too perfectly. The dynamic is everything I wanted it to be, but watching her transform this completely, knowing what's driving it..." Another pause. "It's almost too easy."

Nathan laughs. "Too easy? That's the point. To remove the struggle, the resistance. To fast-track what might take years naturally."

"I know. And it's working. The Club members will be ecstatic." The chair creaks. "We need to discuss implementation guidelines, though. When we roll this out, we have to ensure members understand the boundaries."

"Boundaries?" Nathan laughs, genuinely amused. "Julian, we're drugging women. I'd say we've already tap-danced all over those boundaries."

"We're enhancing what they've already consented to." Julian's tone sharpens with conviction, though there's an edge of defensiveness. "The contracts specify acceptance of all methods deemed necessary. That language covers this."

"Covers it legally, maybe. But ethically? We both know we're threading the needle here."

"The edge is where real power exists." Julian's voice drops, intense. "Yes, we're skirting the line. But we're not crossing it. These women sign contracts and agree to a total power exchange."

"We're talking about neurochemical manipulation."

"Every dominant manipulates neurochemistry—through commands, scenes, and conditioning. We're just more efficient about it." A pause. "Look, I know what we're doing exists in a gray area. But it's still on the right side of that line. Barely, perhaps, but still there."

Gray area. Right side of the line. He knows what he's doing is wrong, but he's convinced himself it's justified.

"That's a dangerous philosophy, even for us."

"The entire lifestyle is dangerous, Nathan. That's what makes it powerful."

He actually believes this. He thinks drugging me is the same as using ropes or a paddle.

"The drugs are just another aspect of that care."

Care? He calls secretly drugging me...CARE?

"Speaking of which," Nathan continues, "When do you want to present to the members?"

"Soon. I want more data first." Julian's voice shifts, thoughtful. "I started withdrawing her last week."

"Withdrawal?" Shocked silence. "Without telling me?"

"I stopped the morning doses seven days ago. Told her I was listening to her complaints about the orange juice." A slight chuckle, but it sounds forced. "She was so pleased I finally 'heard' her."

Last week. When I thought he was being considerate. When I was grateful he listened. It was part of his experiment?

"Julian, you can't just—we agreed on the full year protocol."

"I know what we agreed to." Julian's voice carries something I've never heard from him—uncertainty, maybe even guilt. "Why keep drugging her when we've achieved the desired outcome?"

"Because that's the protocol. Twelve months ensures permanence—"

"Does it? Or does it create unnecessary dependency?" Papers rustle. "I watch her take that water during scenes, trusting me completely, and I think... she doesn't need it anymore. The drugs did their job. She's mine. Continuing feels..."

"Feels what?" Nathan presses.

"Wrong." The word comes out quietly. "Not the outcome—I don't regret that. But maintaining the drugs when she's already compliant?"

"You're getting soft."

"I'm being practical. The point was to create perfect submission, not chemical addiction. We've achieved the first. Why risk the second?"

"Because we need the data. The full year shows us long-term effects, tolerance buildup, and whether the neural pathways remain stable—"

"She's not data." Julian's voice hardens. "She's—"

"She's your obsession, Julian. The girl you've wanted since high school. And now she's yours."

A long pause. "She's the proof of concept. And the concept is proven. Four months of enhancement got us here. Let's see if it holds without chemical support."

"You're gambling everything on your feelings."

"I'm testing whether our protocol creates lasting change or chemical dependency. That's valuable data."

Valuable data. Even his guilt is wrapped in scientific justification.

"The point is to see if what we've built survives without it." A contemplative note enters Julian's voice. "If she maintains the dynamic after withdrawal..."

"That's an enormous risk. The rebound effects—"

"Would tell us if the bonding is genuine or chemical dependency. Critical data for the Club members."

I'm data. Critical data for his club of dominants.

"This is about more than research, isn't it?" Nathan's tone turns suspicious. "This is about Clara. Your high school obsession."

"This is about perfecting the protocol." Julian deflects. "If she maintains submission after withdrawal, we know the conditioning holds. If she doesn't..."

"If she doesn't, you've ruined four months of perfect work. A risk."

"Or I've proven the drugs are a crutch, not a solution. A year may be too long, and I want to be sensitive about the use of these drugs."

"Julian, you're overthinking this. The drugs work. She's happy, you're happy, the dynamic is flawless. Why sabotage it?”

"I'm not sabotaging. I'm testing." A pause. "I want her off the drugs to see what remains."

Complete cessation. He stopped drugging me to see if I would remain obedient. Like I'm a lab rat.

"You're going to regret this. When she crashes, when the conditioning breaks—"

"Then we'll know the protocol needs the full year. It's better to find out now than after the members have implemented it."

"Or you'll destroy something perfect because you grew a conscience."

"I founded the Obsidian Club to give men like us the tools to perfect their dominance, not abuse it. Ethical power dynamics. If those tools only work with constant chemical support, they're not perfect, or ethical."

Nathan sighs heavily. "Fine. But when this goes wrong—"

"It won't. Either she maintains the dynamic, and we've proven the protocol creates lasting change, or she doesn't, and we refine the formula."

"And what about Clara? What happens to her if the withdrawal breaks the conditioning?"

"She's mine either way. The contract ensures that."

The contract. He keeps falling back on that contract like it justifies everything.

"Cold, even for you."

"Practical. That's why the contracts exist—to maintain control regardless of the variables."

"Sometimes I forget how ruthless you can be."

"I prefer obsessed.'" Julian chuckles darkly. "The members are counting on us to deliver. One way or another, we will."

Obsessed. He admits it. This whole thing—the contract, the drugs, our entire relationship—it's all his obsession manifested.

"Even if it means sacrificing your perfect submissive?"

"She won't be sacrificed. She'll be studied. There's a difference."

Studied. I'm being studied.

"Does she know she's a study?"

"Of course not, but she knows she's mine. That's all that matters." Another pause. "I need to go. She'll be here soon."

"Julian... be careful. If she ever finds out—"

"She has no reason to suspect anything. As far as she knows, her submission is entirely natural."

Natural?

I thought I was growing into this—that my body's responses were real. That when I came to him willingly, initiated intimacy, begged for the Red Room—that was my choice. My desire. My need.

But it's not.

Every morning, swallowing that bitter orange juice while he watched. Every glass of champagne he handed me with that small smile. Every sip of water in the Red Room when I was already vulnerable, already open. He was drugging me. Reshaping my brain.

Making me need him.

The night I came to him in the library, kneeling without being asked—I was so proud of myself for taking that step. The morning

I woke him with my mouth, desperate to please—I thought that hunger was mine. Every time I begged him to take me harder, hurt me more, control me completely—

Chemicals. It was all chemicals.

My hands shake. The tray rattles. Four months. Every kiss. Every submission. Every orgasm. Every moment I thought I was falling—

Oh God. I thought I was falling in love with him.

My vision blurs. He created a drug to make women perfect submissives. Tested it on me. The girl he's been obsessed with since high school. And I—I *thanked* him.

The tray crashes from my numb fingers.

Porcelain explodes across hardwood. Coffee spreads in dark rivers. The sound rips through the quiet like a scream.

The door flies open. Julian's eyes lock on mine, and his face transforms—confusion, then understanding, then something I've never seen before: fear.

He pales, jaw slackening as he takes in the scene—me standing in the hallway, trembling with rage, coffee and shattered porcelain at my feet like the ruins of everything we built.

"Clara—"

"You drugged me." The words rip from my throat, raw and fractured. My whole body shakes—not the trembling of submission I've grown used to, but violent tremors of betrayal so deep it feels like drowning. "You've been drugging me. Every day. Every morning."

His laptop is still open behind him, Nathan's face frozen on the screen. Julian moves to close it, and that small motion—trying to hide evidence even now—ignites something feral in me.

"Don't!" The scream surprises us both. I've never screamed at him. Never raised my voice like this. "Don't you dare try to hide it now!"

He ends the call. His mask already sliding back into place, but I saw it—that flash of a man caught, exposed, guilty.

"Let me explain—"

"Explain?" The word tastes like acid. My legs shake so badly I have to grip the doorframe. "Explain how you poisoned me? How you stole my mind? How you made me—" My voice cracks, tears burning hot down my cheeks. "How you made me think I wanted this?"

His jaw tightens. He straightens, and I watch him rebuild himself—the dominant replacing the guilty man, authority replacing vulnerability. "Clara, the drugs don't—"

"Stop." The word comes out half-sob, half-snarl. "Just stop. I heard everything. Every vile word. Your perfect submissive. Your test case. Your proof of concept."

I stumble backward as a tsunami of rage and grief crashes through me.

"The orange juice." My voice breaks. "Every morning for months, you made me drink it. Watched me drink it. And last week, when you stopped—I was grateful. But you were just... testing if your conditioning would hold?"

"Clara, please, just let me—"

"Create submission from nothing?" I'm backing away, trembling. "I heard you. You created the perfect submissive. Four months of data for your Club members."

"You're everything to me—"

"No, I'm your test subject. Someone to perfect your protocol for other rich assholes who want guaranteed obedience."

"That's not what this is." His voice cracks with desperation. "Clara, you have to understand—"

I slide down the wall, sitting in the spreading coffee. "I was happy. This morning, I was actually happy. But it's not real, is it? It's your drugs."

He moves closer, careful, controlled. "The drugs enhanced what is already there—"

"Enhanced?" You rewired my brain without my consent. Made obedience feel like breathing. Made me crave discipline." Tears stream down my face. "Every time I knelt for you, every time I anticipated your needs, it was your chemicals, not me."

"No, Clara, listen to me—the desire was yours, it was always yours—"

The full horror crashes over me in waves. "Oh God. Oh God, the Red Room. I begged. I actually begged." My voice rises, hysterical. "I asked for the cane. I asked you to mark me with it. Said I wanted to wear your marks, that they made me feel owned—"

"Because that's who you are." He's on his knees now, reaching for me but not touching. "The drugs didn't create that need, they just—"

My hands go to my stomach, frantic as if I could scrub the drugs from my system, claw them out through my skin. The motion is involuntary, desperate—my body trying to expel months of poison that's already seeped into every cell, every neural pathway.

"Clara, stop, you're going to hurt yourself—"

They're under my skin. In my blood. His chemicals. His control.

I press my palms against my eyes, trying to block out the memories. "I treasured those bruises. Traced them in the mirror. Felt proud when they lasted longer. And you—you knew. You knew it was the drugs making me crave pain, making me desperate for your control."

"It wasn't the drugs." His voice is raw now, desperate. "The real you always showed through—"

A broken laugh escapes as I dig my fingers into my abdomen,

the pressure doing nothing to ease the sick violation churning inside me.

"God, you must have been laughing at me. Your perfect little pet, performing exactly as designed. Begging for more intensity, more pain, more dominance. Following the script your chemicals wrote in my brain."

"I never laughed. Never. Every moment was—Clara, please look at me—"

I look at him through blurred vision. "Did you celebrate each time? When I crawled to you? When I thanked you for punishing me? When I—" My voice cracks completely. "When I told you I couldn't imagine life without your control? Was that a triumph? Proof your formula worked?"

"It was proof that we're meant for this." He's losing control now, his perfect composure cracking. "What we have is real—"

"I thought I was discovering myself. Growing. Learning what I needed. But it was just... You, and whoever Nathan is, designing the perfect drug to turn me into what you wanted. Your obsession is cruel, Julian. Cruel."

"The foundation was always you—the fire, the defiance, the strength—that's all you—"

"How would I know? You've been drugging me since day one. That champagne at the gala—our first time together—you drugged me before the first time we had sex."

His jaw tightens, then his expression shifts to something almost righteous. "The champagne was a mercy."

"A mercy?" The word comes out strangled.

"You were terrified. Fighting yourself. Fighting what you wanted." His voice takes on that tone of absolute conviction. "I could see it in your eyes—you wanted to surrender but couldn't let yourself. The champagne made that decision easier. Allowed you to let go of the fear and embrace what your body was already telling you."

"You call drugging me without my knowledge a mercy?" My stomach churns harder, hands pressing deeper into my abdomen.

"I call it giving you permission to stop fighting yourself. The drugs didn't make you want me—you already did. They just quieted the voices telling you not to."

"Those voices were mine. My choice. My consent to give or withhold."

"You already consented. The contract—"

"The contract says I submit to you, not to being a pharmaceutical experiment." I stare at him through tears. "You founded a club to teach men dominance? And I'm your proof that drugs can perfect it? I've been so stupid."

"The Club teaches the psychology, safety, and the art of dominance. The drugs are just—"

"The drugs are everything. They're why I stopped fighting. Why I started craving your control. Why I thought I was falling in —" I stop, unable to finish the sentence.

"Falling in love with me?" He finishes quietly.

"Don't." The word comes out broken. "You don't get to say that, and don't you dare make this about love when it's about your cruel obsession."

He stands, commanding even now. "Get up."

"No."

"Clara—"

"I said no." The defiance feels like finding myself again, even as something in me pulls toward obedience.

"You can't refuse me." His voice sharpens, shifting to that tone of absolute authority. "You have one hour. Clean yourself up. Then present yourself in the Red Room."

"For what?"

"For eavesdropping. For defying me just now. For your punishment."

"You're going to punish me for discovering you've been drugging me? That's absurd."

"I'm going to punish you for eavesdropping and disobedience. The contract is still in effect." His voice is ice. "One hour. Be kneeling in position, or the contract is void, and you lose everything."

"You can't be serious—"

"You know how serious I am. You have one hour."

He steps over the shattered porcelain, returning to his office. At the door, he pauses. "For what it's worth, I stopped the drugs last week to see what was real. In another week, you'll be completely clean. Then we'll both know what survives—the real connection or the chemistry."

The door closes.

I sit in the ruins of our morning, feeling the pull he talked about—that insidious need to obey, to present myself as commanded.

Is it the drugs still in my system? Is it four months of conditioning? Or worst of all—is it actually me?

The most terrifying part isn't that he drugged me.

It's that even knowing what he's done, part of me is already planning to be in the Red Room in an hour.

I sit in the ruins of our morning and feel the true weight of the contract. Four months done. Eight months remaining. The ranch versus my sanity. My father's legacy versus my body's autonomy.

I can't afford to break the contract.

Fresh tears come— different now—not hot rage but cold grief. The kind that comes with accepting something unbearable because the alternative is worse.

I breathe deep. Move. Mop coffee from the floor. I clean

mechanically, the way I've learned to move through this house—anticipating his needs and preventing his displeasure.

Even now, knowing what he's done, my body follows the patterns he's trained into me.

The walk to the Red Room feels like a funeral procession. Each step echoes—bare feet on marble, then hardwood, then the thick carpet of the hallway that muffles sound.

The red door looms, and I think absurdly of Bluebeard's chamber, of women who opened doors they shouldn't and paid the ultimate price.

Except I'm not being punished for curiosity. I'm being punished for discovering the truth.

I kneel in position—knees spread, hands behind my back, head bowed. The posture comes automatically, muscle memory that might be mine or might be chemistry. I'll never know now.

The door opens exactly one hour after he gave the command. Julian is nothing if not precise.

"Look at me."

He's changed clothes—black pants, black shirt, the uniform of discipline. His face shows no remorse, no uncertainty. The man who felt guilty talking to Nathan is gone, replaced by the dominant who owns me for eight more months.

"You eavesdropped."

"I brought you coffee." My voice is flat.

Dead.

"You stood outside my door, listening to a private conversation."

"And discovered you've been drugging me."

"You discovered the mechanism behind our dynamic." He circles me slowly. "Nothing more, nothing less."

"You violated—"

"I enhanced. Accelerated. Removed barriers." He stops in front of me. "I'm not sorry. I won't pretend to be. The drugs were a tool, like any other, to achieve what we have."

"What we *had*. Past tense."

"What we *have*. Present tense. For eight more months." He selects a paddle from the wall—heavy leather, unforgiving. "You defied me in the hallway. Refused a direct command. There are consequences."

"Just do it." The words come out lifeless.

"No." He sets the paddle down and pulls a chair to face me. "First, we talk. You need to understand something."

"What could you possibly—"

"Listen." The command cuts through my numbness. "The drugs are already leaving your system. In another week, they'll be completely gone. What happens then will tell us the truth."

"The truth is you're a monster who—"

"The truth is you're angry. You feel betrayed and hurt. All justified. But you're also still here. Still kneeling. Still responding to my commands."

"Because of the contract. The ranch—"

"Because part of you, beneath the rage, still craves this." He leans forward. "The drugs didn't create that craving. They revealed it. Amplified it. But the seed was always there."

"You don't know that."

"I do. The drugs can't create submission in a vacuum. There has to be a seed. And in a week, when you're completely clean, we'll both know." He stands, picks up the paddle again. "But right now, you're mine. And defiance has consequences. Stand. Hands on the wall."

I move mechanically, assuming the position I've taken dozens of times. But this time, everything is different. When the first strike lands, I feel it; the sharp impact, the spreading heat. But it's distant, like watching someone else's pain.

"Count." A command.

"One." The word is hollow.

The second strike falls. My body responds—skin heating, nerves firing—but my mind floats somewhere else, disconnected. This is what he's done to me. Made my body a traitor that warms to his touch even as my soul recoils.

"Two."

By ten, tears stream down my face. Not from pain—I've taken worse with joy—but from the betrayal of my own responses. Even now, even knowing what he's done, my body softens, prepares, and *wants*.

"That's enough." He sets the paddle aside and moves behind me. "You took that without fighting. Without begging. Without anything."

"There's nothing left to give."

"There's everything left to discover." But his voice carries less certainty than before.

He doesn't touch me otherwise. No aftercare, no intimacy. Just a quiet command: "Go shower. Dinner is at seven."

The week that follows is a study in emotional permafrost.

I move through the house like a ghost, performing my duties with detachment. I bring his coffee—regular coffee now, no orange juice in sight. I kneel when commanded. I follow every rule.

But I don't smile. Don't initiate. Don't seek his touch.

When he takes me—and he does, because the contract gives him that right—my body responds because four months of conditioning doesn't suddenly stop. But when the pleasure builds, when my treacherous flesh races toward climax, I bite my lip rather than beg.

"Ask for permission." The command comes on the third night, his fingers skilled and relentless between my thighs.

I remain silent, even as my body shakes with the need to release.

"Ask."

"No."

"No?"

"Unless that's a command, Mr. Blackwell." My voice is steady despite my body's trembling. "Are you commanding me to beg for release?"

His jaw tightens, frustration flashing across his face. For a moment, his fingers resume their torment, pushing me closer to the edge—then he withdraws completely, leaving me gasping.

"You know the rules," he says, voice clipped with barely controlled anger. "No orgasm without permission. And permission must be requested."

"Then I won't come." The words scrape my throat raw.

"Fine." He pulls away entirely, his own breathing harsh. "Suffer for your pride, then."

I turn away and pretend to sleep while my body throbs with unfulfilled need. His frustration radiates beside me—the dominant who is losing control of his submissive.

By the fifth day, his frustration is visible. He finds me in the library, staring at but not reading one of his books on power exchange.

"This isn't sustainable." Flat. Final.

"I don't care. You have me for eight more months, Mr. Blackwell; better take advantage of me while you can, because I'm leaving once the contract is over."

"You're punishing yourself more than me."

"I'm surviving."

"You're withering." He sits across from me. "You don't eat unless I command it. Don't speak unless questioned. You're becoming a shell."

"I'm becoming what you made me. A perfectly empty submissive."

"That's not what I want—"

"But it's what you created." I finally look at him. "Your drugs, your conditioning, your control. This is the logical endpoint."

"The drugs are almost gone. Two more days, and you'll be completely clean."

"And then what? I suddenly forgive you? Fall back into your arms? Kneel at your feet and beg for your cock? Race to the Red Room to—"

"Stop." The command lands hard. "In two days, we'll see if you still crave my dominance."

The question terrifies me because I do crave it.

Crave him.

My body aches for his touch, his commands, and the security of surrender. I can't tell if it's the drugs' lingering effects, the conditioning, or something deeper and more shameful—that maybe he's right about what I've always needed.

"I hate you," I whisper it, but even I hear the uncertainty in it.

"No," he says softly. "You hate that you might not hate me. That's worse. Knowing that even with this betrayal between us, part of you still wants to kneel."

He's right. That's the cruelest truth of all.

When he stands to leave, I speak without planning to: "Why didn't the drugs make me happy about discovering them? If they're supposed to make me perfectly submissive, why do I feel this rage?"

He pauses at the door. "The drugs enhance natural responses; they don't replace them. Your anger is real. My betrayal is real. Your rage is real." He turns to face me. "But so is your submission. The drugs just helped you access it."

"That's convenient logic."

"That's the truth."

He leaves me alone with that, and I wrap my arms around myself, trying to hold together the pieces of who I was, who I've become, and who I might be when the chemicals leave my system.

The terrifying part is not knowing if I'll be free—or if I'll discover that the cage was always inside me, and Julian just found the key.

CHAPTER 47
DAY 121

The vial sits on the breakfast table between us like poison.

Clear liquid. Innocent-looking.

A tapering dose spread over seven days to prevent the crash from being too severe. As if there's a gentle way to discover you've been chemically manipulated for months.

"Open." It's a command, not a request.

I stare at it. At him. The morning light cuts through the windows of my family's home, turning everything sharp and clinical. We're at the ranch. Julian is overseeing more improvements to *my* land.

No matter what it takes, or what I have to endure, this is *my* home, *my* land, and he will surrender it to me at the end of this horrible disaster.

He looks tired—shadows under his eyes, jaw tighter than usual—but his gaze is steady.

Waiting.

"You think this fixes it?" My voice sounds strange. Hollow. "After what you did?"

His jaw flexes, but he doesn't push. Doesn't command. That alone tells me how badly he knows he fucked up.

"It doesn't fix anything. It prevents the crash—the anxiety, the fog, the symptoms that could break you worse than the truth already has. At least, that's what Nathan says." He slides the vial closer. "Swallow it. Or spit it out. Your choice."

"My choice?" The words taste like ash.

My hand trembles as I take it. The glass is cool against my palm, solid and real. I tip it back. Bitter on my tongue, coating my throat like regret. I swallow and set the empty vial down.

Something darkens in his expression as he tracks the flush creeping up my neck. He reaches across the table, brushing his thumb over my lower lip with a tenderness that makes my chest ache.

"Clara—"

"Don't." I pull back. "Just... don't."

The breakfast sits uneaten between us. Scout whines softly from his spot by the door, sensing the tension. Julian's hand falls back to the table.

"The anxiety will be mild today." A long silence, then a clinical explanation, like it's safer ground. "Tomorrow might be worse. By day three, you'll feel the worst of it—irritability, emotional volatility. Then it levels out."

"I thought you stopped it a week ago? Or was that a lie, too?"

"Clara—"

"Why do I still have to take it?"

"Nathan's concerned about withdrawal. Says it's safer this way." He doesn't flinch.

"I need air." I push back from the table, chair scraping.

"Clara—"

"I said I need air."

I'm halfway to the door before his voice stops me. Not a command. A question.

"Will you come back?"

I turn. He's still sitting there, one hand on the table, the other fallen to his lap. He looks... small isn't the right word. Julian Blackwell doesn't do small. But diminished, maybe. Like something vital has been carved out of him.

Good. I want him to hurt.

"Of course I'll come back." My throat tightens around the words. "You own me, remember? For a year. Eight more months." My words are sharp enough to cut. "But I need air."

He rises, slow and deliberate. "If that's what you need, I'll give it to you."

I let out a shaky laugh. "You'll *give* it to me? I hate you." My gaze locks on his, aching and defiant. "Even my need for space has to be granted by you." I shake my head, something between disbelief and grief cracking through.

He flinches, barely, like I landed a blow. "I'm trying to figure out how to hold onto you without breaking you."

My breath stutters. "You already broke me. You made me need you. Made me crave... all of it. How am I supposed to know what's real?"

He stays where he is, shoulders bowed beneath the weight of his own silence. "I don't know." The words come slowly. "I don't have an answer for that."

"Then we have nothing to talk about."

I leave, and the door closes with a soft click that feels louder than if I'd slammed it.

Outside, the ranch spreads before me—endless sky, the barn where he's marked me a hundred different ways. My mother's garden blooms in the distance, roses he restored for me. Evidence of his obsession is everywhere I look.

Is any of it real?

The question repeats on an endless loop.

Scout finds me by the fence, pressing his warm body against my legs. I bury my fingers in his fur, anchoring myself to something simple and true.

Dogs don't lie. Don't manipulate. They love without conditions.

"At least you're honest."

He licks my hand and gives a happy yip. I love dogs and their unconditional love.

The day passes in a haze. I avoid the house, spending hours in the barn with Meteor, in the garden, anywhere Julian isn't. He doesn't follow. Doesn't summon. When I finally return at dusk, he's in my father's study, the door half-open. He's bent over papers, hand pressed to his forehead like he's warding off pain.

Good. Some vicious part of me wants him to hurt.

But another part—a quieter, more treacherous part of me—wants to go to him. Wants to curl into his lap and pretend none of this happened. Wants him to wrap his arms around me and make the world simple again. Part of me wants him to take his belt to my ass, then bend me over the desk and fuck me senseless.

And that feels like a steel band constricting my chest. That I want him like that, need what only he can give.

Drug, I remind myself. *That's the drug talking.*

Dinner is silent. We eat across from each other, the table an ocean between us. He pours wine—I stare at it suspiciously until he takes a drink from my glass first, proving it's clean. The gesture is both reassuring and damning.

That I need proof.

That he understands why.

"I should have told you from the beginning."

"You never should have done it in the first place."

"I was afraid."

"Of what?" I look up, searching his face. "That I'd say no? That I wouldn't fall into your perfect fantasy?"

"That I'd lose you before you had a chance to see what we could become." His voice is raw. "I've wanted you for seventeen years. Seventeen years of watching, waiting, planning. When I finally had you, I—" He stops. Starts again. "I thought the chemicals would... speed up the inevitable."

"You took away my choice."

"I know."

"You violated my consent."

"I had the contract." His voice hardens, shifts from desperate to certain. "The contract you signed gave me complete control. 'Complete obedience in all matters.' 'Submit to my will.' 'Be used however I see fit, whenever I desire.' Those were the terms you agreed to."

He stands slowly, the CEO returning, the dominant reasserting himself. "The contract specified total power exchange. You agreed to let me make every decision, control every aspect. The drugs fall under that authority."

"That's not—"

"It's what you signed." His eyes bore into mine. "The contract is the foundation of everything between us. The power dynamic, the commands, the sex, the discipline—all of it stems from that document. You gave me permission to own you completely for one year. To shape you, train you, use whatever methods I deemed necessary."

"I didn't know about the drugs—"

"You didn't need to know my methods. You agreed to submit to my will, follow my rules, and obey my commands. The contract gave me the right to decide how to achieve your submission." He moves closer, voice dropping. "And it worked. We built something extraordinary on that foundation. Something that goes beyond paper and signatures."

"Built on lies—"

"Built on the power exchange you agreed to. The contract made you mine. The drugs just helped you stop fighting what you already wanted."

"Fine." The word comes out bitter, defeated. "You're right. I signed the contract. I agreed to complete obedience, to submit to your will, to be used however you saw fit. But there's a fine line between consenting to dominance and discovering you've been drugged without your knowledge. And you know it."

His jaw tightens. "Clara—"

"You know it was wrong." My voice is steady now, cold. "You can hide behind the contract's language all you want, but we both know there's a difference between agreeing to submission and agreeing to be drugged. I thought I was consenting to commands, rules, and sexual control. Not... not having my brain chemistry rewritten."

"The contract—"

"Stop saying that. The contract gave you power, not the right to violate me like this." I wrap my arms around myself. "I feel violated. Do you understand? Every response I've had, every moment of surrender, every time I thought I was discovering something about myself—it's all tainted. I don't know what's me and what's your chemical manipulation."

He's quiet for a moment, and when he speaks, his voice is lower. "I know."

"Do you? Because you keep justifying it—"

"I know it was a violation." The admission seems to cost him something. "I know the line I crossed, even if the contract covered it. I know the difference between earning submission and manufacturing it."

"Then why—"

"Because I'm selfish." His eyes meet mine, unflinching. "Because I wanted you so desperately that I convinced myself the ends justified the means. That once you experienced true submission, you'd understand. That the contract gave me the right to use any tool necessary. I'd already stopped the drugs. I wanted to see if our dynamic continued without them."

"And how did that work out for you?"

"Now it's poisoned by how I achieved it." His voice is raw. "Is that what you want to hear? That I know I violated your trust even while staying within the contract's bounds? That I chose the letter of our agreement over its spirit?"

"I want to know if you regret it."

A long pause. "I regret hurting you. I regret the betrayal you're feeling. But I don't regret the results. I don't regret what we've become, even knowing how we got here."

The honesty of it—the lack of pretty lies or false apologies—somehow makes it worse.

"Are you sorry?"

"I'm—" He stops, and something shifts in his expression. Honesty, stark and brutal. "I'm sorry you found out. I'm sorry I hurt you. But am I sorry I did it?" His jaw tightens. "I'm not."

"How can you stand there and say you're not sorry?"

"Because we got here, didn't we? To this place where you crave what I give you. Would we have gotten here without it? Maybe. Maybe not."

The truth of it hangs between us. At least he's not pretending.

"I can't—" My throat closes. "I need to be alone."

"As you wish." Julian stands. Pauses at the door. "Will you sleep in our bed tonight?"

Our bed. Like it's shared. Like anything here is shared and not his kingdom where he allows me space to exist.

"Do I have a choice?"

"Yes."

I sit in the empty dining room until the food goes cold. Until the wine glass sweats in my hand. Until the silence becomes unbearable and I have to move or scream.

The bedroom door is open when I reach it. The bed is turned down, one side clearly his—the book he's been reading on the nightstand, his watch, his phone. The other side is mine by permission, not right.

I stand in the doorway, warring with myself.

Then his voice from inside, quiet: "You don't have to sleep with me."

He's standing by the window, staring out at the dark ranch. He's stripped to his undershirt and pants, casual in a way he rarely allows. Vulnerable. Or as close as Julian Blackwell gets.

"I don't know what I want." The admission scrapes raw in my throat.

"Then lie down. Sleep. Everything else can wait."

It should be that simple. It's not. Because when I climb into bed—his bed, the bed where he's taken me apart a thousand ways —my body recognizes the space. The sheets smell like him. Like us. And that traitorous heat blooms again.

He notices when he slides in beside me, maintaining distance. "Clara—"

"Don't." I close my eyes. "Don't say anything. Don't touch me. Be quiet. Please..."

Silence falls. The kind that presses against my skin, suffocating.

Minutes pass. Ten, twenty. I count them, unable to sleep.

Then: "I'm hard." His voice cuts through the dark, raw and honest. "I've been hard since dinner. Since you walked into this room. My body doesn't care that you're angry, that we're broken. It wants you anyway."

My breath catches. "My body doesn't care that I'm mad at you." I roll to face him. His eyes shine in the darkness, storm-gray and desperate. "I don't know what's real anymore."

"Then find out." He doesn't move. Doesn't reach for me. "Test it. Take what you need and see if it feels true or false."

It's permission. An offering. And God help me, I'm crawling across the space between us before I can stop myself, straddling him, feeling his hardness press against me.

"This is insane." The words escape on a shaky exhale as I sink down onto him, the slow, deliberate slide stealing both our breaths, his body filling me completely in the dim glow of the bedside lamp.

"Probably." His voice is rough. His hands settle on my hips—not guiding, but steady. As if he's bracing himself against the edge we're both teetering on.

The sheets tangle around my knees, the bed is a rumpled mess beneath us, and for a moment, everything feels right. I can't shake the pull of him, the way my hips roll tentatively to take more, chasing that forbidden spark even as doubt coils tight in my chest.

His eyes meet mine in the low light, dark and stormy, holding a flicker of uncertainty.

The fullness of him stretches me with that deep, aching fit that makes my nerves hum. My hips roll instinctively to find a rhythm, pleasure blooming in waves that coil low in my belly, my hands bracing on his chest to feel the steady thud of his heart under my palms.

I lift and lower experimentally, the friction sending sparks up my spine, my breath coming shallow as the heat builds—but even in this, doubt creeps in, sharp and unbidden, making me falter.

"Clara—" He grips my hips, steadying me, fingers digging in enough to ground me, but not enough to take over.

"Is this me?" I gasp, my voice fracturing as I lift and sink again, the pleasure coiling tighter, hotter, my nails digging in as I chase the edge. "Or is this what you made me?"

"Fuck, Clara, it's you. I know it." His voice breaks raw against my ear, and his hands tighten on my hips as if the admission costs him everything.

"How can you be so sure?"

The man who orchestrated my fall now unravels under the question, his breath ragged as I rock above him. The words hang heavy, a confession torn from him in this moment of doubt, his fingers flexing against my skin like he's anchoring himself to me as much as I'm holding on to him.

The honesty breaks something in me, a dam cracking open as I lean down, capturing his mouth in a kiss that's more bite than tenderness—teeth grazing his lower lip, tongue demanding truth from him.

I chase a peak that hovers out of reach, my hips snapping, the pleasure coiling tight and low in my belly, but it's not enough. I can't reach the peak.

He grips my hips suddenly, firm and unyielding, flipping our positions in one fluid, powerful surge that leaves me gasping. The world tilts as he rolls us, pinning me beneath him on the rumpled sheets, my back arching against the mattress as he thrusts deep.

The shift steals my breath, the sudden loss of control sending a thrill of fear-laced heat flooding through me. My legs wrap instinctively around his hips as he drives in, deep and claiming, the angle hitting every sensitive spot.

He takes my wrists and stretches them overhead in an iron hold. He sets a rhythm that's all his now—slow at first, deliberate, each drive reclaiming what I thought was mine for the moment.

His eyes lock onto mine, his gaze dark and intense, sharpening into something dominant, unyielding.

"No matter what you think, this is real." His voice is rough with the edge of command as he pins my wrists. He cups the back of my knee, hitching my leg higher around his waist, opening me wider as he drives in with measured surges—each one a reminder of the dynamic flipping back to what it is between us.

He takes control, not in punishment but in raw, inevitable truth, his mouth claiming my neck with nips that mark. His controlled rhythm builds the fire coiling tight inside me.

I writhe beneath him, wrists straining against his grip, the sheets twisting around us as the friction ignites every nerve in my body. The shift from my lead to his dominance strips away my doubt.

This is real— the heat of him burying deep, the way he breaks only to rebuild, his control wrapping around me like the arms I both fear and crave.

Tears prick my eyes from the intensity of it all, my hips bucking up to meet his, chasing the peak that's his to give, my vulnerability raw and electric in this bed where we've shared everything from fury to tenderness.

"Come for me," he commands.

His thumb finds my clit, circling with punishing precision that sends pleasure ripping through me like wildfire. My cry echoes off the bedroom walls as I shatter around him, waves of blinding ecstasy pulsing hot and unrelenting through me.

He follows seconds later, groaning my name like a prayer, spilling deep inside me with a shudder.

He doesn't pull away immediately, collapsing over me in a tangle of limbs and ragged breaths.

"No more drugs." The murmur comes against my lips, his

voice rough but tender, his thumb tracing my jaw as if sealing the moment. "We figure it out together, but you're still mine. Always."

I burst into tears.

"Clara? What's wrong?"

"I came." The sob wrenches out against his chest. "I came so hard. Just like always. My body responded exactly the same. So how do I know?" I pull back to look at him, tears streaming down my cheeks. "How do I know if it's real or if you programmed me to respond like this?"

He has no answer. Just pulls me against him, one hand stroking my hair while I cry.

"I'm sorry." He whispers it over and over. "I'm so sorry."

But sorry doesn't undo what's been done.

We lie there in the wreckage, neither of us sleeping, both of us broken in different ways.

Outside, the ranch sleeps under starlight. Inside, we're just two people who might have loved each other if our foundation hadn't been built on lies.

CHAPTER 48

DAY 122

The Red Room door stands open like a mouth waiting to swallow me. Two days since the first vial. Two days of this gray fog settling over everything—not quite anxiety, just a flatness, like someone turned down the volume on the world.

Colors are duller.

Sounds are muted.

Even my anger feels distant, observed rather than felt.

Julian stands in the doorway, one hand on the frame, watching me with an expression I can't quite read. His presence still commands the space, but there's something different in his eyes—not hesitation, exactly, more like a careful assessment.

"We're still doing this?" My voice comes out smaller than intended. "After everything? After what you told me?"

"You need it." Simple. Certain. No apology in his tone.

"How can you say that? You drugged me to make me need—"

"No." He steps into the room, closing the distance between us with that familiar predatory intent. "The drugs enhanced things, yes. Made you more receptive. But look at yourself. You're standing at the threshold of the Red Room, body already responding to being here. That's not the drugs. That's you."

"That's conditioning. Training. You broke me—"

"I revealed you." He cups my jaw, thumb stroking along my cheekbone. "Two days without the supplements, and you're here because I command it. Because your body knows what it needs. Structure. Dominance. The freedom that comes from surrendering control."

I want to argue, but my skin is already heating under his touch, that familiar ache building despite the fog in my head. "This is wrong. We both know it's wrong."

"What's wrong is denying what you need because you're angry about how you discovered it." He moves behind me, settling his hands on my shoulders. "You think the drugs created this need? You were reading those books on your own. Coming to the Red Room voluntarily before you knew. Your body's been honest even when your mind wasn't ready to be."

"So what—we just continue like nothing's changed?"

"No." His voice drops to that commanding register that still makes my knees weak. "We continue because you need this structure while your body adjusts. You need the endorphins from pain, the grounding from submission, the release from giving up control. The withdrawal is making everything feel flat, disconnected. This room, what we do here—it'll help."

"You mean it'll keep me dependent on you."

He tightens his grip on my shoulders. "You're already dependent on me. Have been for months. The only question is whether we acknowledge it and work with it, or pretend otherwise and watch you fall apart."

The truth of it sits heavy in my chest. Because he's right—I am here. I did come to this room knowing what would happen. Even through the gray fog of withdrawal, my body remembers and craves the familiar patterns.

"I hate you for this," I whisper.

"I know." He turns me to face him, and his eyes are dark with certainty. "But you need me more than you hate me. And I'm going to give you what you need, even if you can't ask for it."

"That's not—"

"Strip." The command cuts through my protest, and my hands move before my mind catches up. "This is what you need. Let me give it to you."

It's true. For months, the Red Room has embodied rituals of dominance and submission, pain and pleasure woven so tightly together that I can't separate them. My body knows the pattern.

Expects it.

Craves it.

Or was trained to expect it.

"Whatever you want, Mr. Blackwell." I turn to him. "Isn't that right? I do whatever you want. It's in the contract I signed."

Something flickers across his face—pain, maybe, or recognition. But he moves toward me, finding the hem of my shirt.

"Arms up." It's not a request.

I'm standing naked in the red glow, goosebumps rising despite the warm air. He looks over me—cataloging, assessing. Looking for something he doesn't find.

He moves to the wall of equipment and selects soft rope. Red silk. My favorite, though I never told him that.

Stop. Focus. Be here.

The rope whispers around my wrists, his fingers deft and sure. He's tied me a hundred times, maybe more. Knows exactly how tight to make it—secure but not cutting, restrictive but not damaging. The knots are beautiful, efficient. Works of art on my skin.

He guides my arms up and secures them to the overhead ring. My body stretches. The position is vulnerable, exposing. It should evoke a response—fear, arousal, or surrender.

I feel nothing.

"Good?" He steps back.

"Fine, Mr. Blackwell." My tone is flippant, and I don't care. This used to feel different. I used to be excited. Now, I'm at a loss. Part of me is missing.

He circles me slowly. One hand trails down my spine, testing my reaction. My skin registers the touch—warm, slightly callused, familiar. No shiver follows.

"You're not with me," he observes.

"I'm right here. Tied up. Waiting for whatever you want to do to me. Isn't that what you want?"

"Not like this." He stops in front of me, tipping my chin up with one finger, searching my eyes. "Clara, where are you?"

"I don't know." The truth slips out. "I'm trying. I'm trying to be present and feel this, but it's like I'm watching from outside my body. Like I'm performing instead of being me."

He drops his hand. Steps back. The distance between us yawns open.

"Maybe I was never really here." I close my eyes. "What if I never wanted this, and you just... forced me—"

"No." His voice is sharp. Definitive. "No. The drugs didn't create desire. They lowered your inhibitions and made you more open to exploring things you were already curious about. But the core of it, the wanting—that was always yours."

"You can't know that."

"I do know it. I saw it in you seventeen years ago. I saw it the week leading up to the gala, before the drugs. You wanted me then. You just didn't allow yourself to want me."

"That was attraction. Physical attraction. Not—" I gesture around the room. "Not this."

"Wasn't it?" He's closer now, voice dropping. "You've always been drawn to this. The drugs didn't put that in you. They just made it easier for you to admit it."

"You're lying." I want to scream. Want to call him a liar, a manipulator, a monster. But a small voice in the back of my mind whispers: *What if he's right?*

"We're not doing this tonight." He moves to the knots, working them loose with the same efficiency with which he tied them.

"Why?"

"Because your mind isn't present."

The rope falls away. My arms drop, heavy and aching.

He reaches for me, then stops himself. His hand hovers in the air between us—wanting to touch, afraid to.

"I don't want to lose you."

"You might have already." The words hang heavy. "You lost me the moment you gave that first dose."

"I'll spend the rest of my life making this right."

"What if you can't?" My voice breaks. "What if there's no making it right? What if we're just... broken now?"

We stand there in the Red Room, two people who've shared the most intimate acts imaginable, and we're strangers. The rope lies coiled on the floor between us like a dead snake.

"I don't want you to be alone with this."

"I'm alone with it whether I'm in this room or not." But I don't move toward the door. Don't leave. Because despite everything, despite the numbness and confusion and hurt, some part of me doesn't want to leave him.

We end up sitting on the floor, backs against the wall, carefully not touching. The silence stretches, but it's different than before. Less angry. More lost.

"Tell me about the drugs." The words come out flat. "Not how you justified them. How they work."

He's quiet for a long moment. Then he takes a breath and speaks. "They're called empathy enhancers. Originally developed for PTSD treatment. They increase oxytocin production, lower cortisol, and enhance emotional bonding."

"How did you get them?"

"Money buys a lot of things. Including experimental pharmaceuticals from research labs that don't ask questions." His voice is flat, clinical. "Nathan created them."

"The one on the phone that day?"

"Yes." He runs a hand through his hair, a rare gesture of agitation. "In my mind, I was removing obstacles. Breaking down walls that shouldn't have been there in the first place."

"Those walls were my consent."

"At the time—" He stops. Starts again. "I waited so long. Wanted you so desperately. And you were finally mine. I could see you building those walls higher every day. The fear, the resistance."

"So you drugged me."

"I drugged you." No excuses this time. He's owning the brutal truth.

I draw my knees up to my chest, wrapping my arms around them. "What are the side effects? The long-term ones?"

"The research is limited. But the tapering protocol should prevent most issues. Some people report increased anxiety for a few weeks after stopping. Difficulty regulating emotions. Insomnia."

"Anything permanent?"

His pause is too long. "There's a small possibility of... imprinting. The enhanced bonding experiences during drug use can create very strong neural pathways. Even after the drug is gone, those pathways remain."

"Meaning?"

"Meaning your brain might have associated me so strongly with pleasure and safety that the response persists. Like classical conditioning, but with orgasms instead of bells."

I laugh. It comes out harsh and bitter. "So even if the drug is gone, the programming might not be."

"It's not that simple—"

"Isn't it?" I turn to look at him. "You conditioned me to respond to you. To crave your dominance. To come on command. And now you're telling me that even without the drug, those pathways might persist? How am I supposed to know what's real?"

"Pathways aren't destiny. They're tendencies. You can choose to follow them or not."

"Can I? Or will I always feel that pull? That need?" I shake my head. "I don't know who I am anymore. When I look at myself, I see someone who begs to be hurt. Who gets wet from being commanded. Who needs submission like air. Is that me? Or is that your creation?"

"It's both." He reaches toward me, then pulls back. "The drugs just made it easier for you to explore these things, but the capacity for it was always in you. You can't drug someone into having a submissive nature. You can only help them access what's already there."

"You sound very certain about that."

"I've done a lot of research."

"Before or after you decided to experiment on me?"

"You weren't an experiment." His jaw clenches. "I've been studying the psychology of dominance and submission since college. Went to workshops, read everything I could find, and even worked with a mentor to learn proper technique. I learned how to do this right."

"Except for the part where you forgot to get my consent."

"I had consent." He looks away.

"The contract?"

"Yes."

"Keep holding onto that, but you know it was wrong."

We sit in that truth for a while. The Red Room feels different now—not arousing or frightening, just sad. A beautiful space built on a rotten foundation.

"I can't do this anymore." The admission scrapes out of me. "I can't be here. Play these roles. It all feels fake, like I don't know my lines anymore."

"Okay."

"Just like that? Okay?"

"What else can I say?" He looks at me, and his eyes are hollowed out. "I spent seventeen years building toward this. Toward us. And I destroyed it in the first four months. So yes, okay. Whatever you need. Whatever you can give. I'll take it."

"Even if it's nothing?"

"Even if it's nothing."

I push to my feet, joints stiff from sitting on the floor. He rises too, fluid and controlled as always. We face each other in the center of the room.

"I need time." My voice sounds foreign to me. "Space to figure out who I am without the chemicals. Without the constant—" I gesture vaguely. "Without you and all of this."

"How much time?"

"I don't know. Days? Weeks? I don't know." I can't say forever. Can't even think it.

He nods slowly. "The tapering continues for five more days. I have to monitor you during that time. After that, you can have space. Maybe then things will be clearer."

We walk to the door together. He opens it, gestures for me to go first. Always the gentleman, even in ruin.

At the threshold, I turn back. "Julian?"

"Yes?"

"Do you love me?" The question surprises us both. "Without the drugs, without the sex, without any of it—do you actually love me? Or do you just love the idea of me? The fantasy you've been building for seventeen years?"

He's quiet for so long I think he won't answer. Then: "I love you more than I can say, but maybe I also fell in love with my obsession." His voice drops to a whisper. "And maybe that's the worst thing I've done."

I leave him standing in the doorway of the Red Room, a king in an empty kingdom, and walk down the hall alone.

CHAPTER 49
DAY 124

The study door is open when I find him. Julian sits behind his massive desk, laptop open, phone to his ear. He's deep in some business negotiation, voice sharp and commanding. The executive mask is firmly in place.

I watch him for a moment from the doorway. This is Julian Blackwell, the businessman—ruthless, brilliant, completely in control. He built an empire through sheer force of will. Conquered markets the way he conquered me.

Stop thinking like that.

He sees me, holds up a finger. "I don't care about their timeline. Either they meet our terms by Friday, or we walk. Yes. Friday." He ends the call and sets the phone down. "Clara? Is everything okay?"

"I need to try something."

His expression shifts—surprise, then wariness. "Try what?"

Instead of answering, I walk into the room and approach him like I have so many times before. Times when serving him and pleasing him brought me joy.

He tracks my movement, understanding dawning.

"Clara, you don't have to—"

"I need to know." I move around the desk, my heart pounding. "I need to know if I want it, or if it's just conditioning."

"This isn't how—"

"Please." I drop to my knees beside his chair. "Let me do this. Let me initiate. No commands, no coercion. Just... let me see if I want this when it's my choice."

He goes very still. "Are you sure?"

"No. But I'm doing it anyway."

My hands shake as I reach for his belt. He doesn't stop me, but he doesn't help either. He watches with those storm-gray eyes as I work the buckle open and lower his zipper. He's not hard yet—keeping his arousal at bay.

I free him from his pants and wrap my fingers around him. Familiar weight, familiar heat. My body remembers this. Has done this dozens of times.

But did I want it? Or was I chemically coerced to want it?

"Clara—" His voice is strangled. "You don't have to prove anything."

"I'm not proving anything. I'm figuring something out." I lean forward, lips parting.

"Wait." He catches my chin, tilting my face up. "Look at me."

I do. His eyes are dark, conflicted. "If you do this, and it feels wrong, you stop. Immediately. Promise me."

"I promise."

"And this isn't—you don't owe me this. Or anything. You understand that?"

"I know." My throat is tight. "But I need to know. I need to know if this pull is real or... not."

"Okay~~, then~~... proceed."

I take him in my mouth.

Familiar taste. Familiar weight on my tongue. I work him slowly, using the techniques I've learned over months—the swirl of tongue, the hollow of cheeks, the pressure and suction that makes him groan.

He hardens in my mouth. He finds my hair, not forcing, just holding. Grounding us both.

I focus on the sensations. The stretch of my jaw. The salt on my tongue. The sound of his breathing turning rough and aroused. Physical facts I can catalog and assess.

And underneath it all: Do I want this?

His cock slides deeper. I relax my throat, taking him further. He curses softly, hips jerking despite his effort to stay still.

"Clara. God, Clara—"

The arousal between my thighs is unmistakable. I'm wet. Getting wetter. My body is responding exactly as it always has.

But is it me?

I pull back slightly, tongue circling his tip. He tightens his grip in my hair. Not painful—connection between us.

"You don't have to finish—" he starts.

"I want to..." What? Serve him? Pleasure him? What I want is unclear, but this feels...right.

I take him deep again, faster now, wrapping my hand around the base to stroke in rhythm with my mouth. Chasing his pleasure with intensity. Wanting to give him this. Wanting—

Wanting to prove I can still have an impact on him? Wanting to have power? Wanting because I genuinely need to give him pleasure? Or wanting this because I'm conditioned to want it?

The questions swirl, making me dizzy.

He's close. It's there in the way his thighs tense, the way his breathing stutters. I hollow my cheeks, sucking harder, and—

Tears stream down my face, dripping onto his pants, and

suddenly I'm sobbing around his cock, pulling back, gasping for air while my whole body shakes.

"Stop. Stop, we're stopping—" He's pulling me up, out of position, dragging me into his lap. "Breathe, Clara. Just breathe—"

"I can't tell." The words break between sobs. "I can't tell if I want this or if you programmed me to want it. I got wet. I got wet doing that. My body responded like it always does. So how do I know? How do I know if it's real?"

He holds me while I fall apart, one arm banded around my waist, the other hand cradling my head against his chest. His heart pounds beneath my ear—rapid, uneven. He's as wrecked as I am.

"I don't know," he whispers. "Christ, Clara, I don't know."

"You ruined me." I clutch his shirt, fisting the fabric. "Even if you didn't mean to. Even if you thought you were helping. You ruined me. Because now I'll never know if what I feel is real or if it's just echoes of what you made me feel."

"I know. I know, and I—" His voice breaks. "I would take it back. All of it. If I could go back to the night of the gala and make a different choice, I would, even if it meant losing you. Because this —breaking you like this—is worse than never having you at all."

We sit there in his office chair, tangled together.

"I'm sorry." Over and over. "I'm so fucking sorry."

"Sorry doesn't fix it."

"I know."

"Sorry doesn't give me back my certainty."

"I know."

"Sorry doesn't—" My voice fails, and I pull back, looking at him through tear-blurred eyes. Something desperate and hollow claws at my chest. "Fuck me."

"What?" His eyes widen.

"Please." My hands tremble. "I need—I need to feel something. Anything."

He catches my wrists gently. "You're in withdrawal, you're emotional—"

"No." I shake my head, tears still falling. "No, I'm not sure. But I need to feel you. I need to feel something real, even if everything else is a lie. Please, make me feel something."

He searches my face for a long moment, conflict in his eyes. Then something resolves there—not quite his usual dominance, but a desperate need that matches mine.

A growl escapes him, and he's on me in an instant.

"On your feet. Turn around." He grabs my waist, turning me around and bending me over his desk with a force that knocks the breath out of me. Cool wood presses against my cheek, contrasting with the heat of his body behind me.

He enters me with one hard, claiming thrust. A gasp escapes me, hands gripping the edges of the desk, my body struggling to accommodate him. He doesn't wait, doesn't give me time to adjust. Instead, he sets a punishing pace, each thrust powerful and demanding, claiming me in the most primal way.

He pushes between my shoulder blades, holding me firmly in place. Teeth graze my shoulder, a primal marking that sends a shiver down my spine. He grips my hip with his free hand, his fingers digging into my flesh, holding me steady as he pounds into me. The desk groans beneath us with each powerful thrust.

Suddenly, he pulls out, only to flip me onto my back. He grabs my thighs, pushing them up and apart, opening me wide as he slams back into me. He returns his hand to my throat, his grip tighter this time, eyes locked onto mine, fierce and possessive.

He's coiled with tension, every muscle taut as he drives into me, hips pistoning with a relentless rhythm. His lips curl in a snarl, exposing clenched teeth. A brutal, animalistic need etched onto his face.

He tightens his grip, pressing firmly into my skin. My hands fly to his, trying to pry his fingers loose, but he's unyielding. Panic surges, heart pounding, body aching for release.

He leans down, his breath hot against my ear. "This is what you're running from," he rasps, voice low and harsh. "It's not the drugs. It's this. It's needing me to fuck you until you can't think straight. It's needing me to obliterate every doubt in your mind."

His fingers tighten further, restricting my airflow, making me lightheaded. His thrusts become harder, more insistent, the hand on my throat a constant reminder of his dominance.

"Come for me." A low, guttural command.

My body responds instantly, orgasm ripping through me with a force that leaves me gasping. He tightens his grip briefly as he follows, body tensing as he finds his own release, a primal, guttural growl escaping him.

We lie there, panting and spent, his body covering mine. The room is filled with the sound of our ragged breaths and the scent of sex.

Questions linger, but in this moment, there is only us, bound by the most basic, carnal desire. He stares down at me, fierce and possessive, a silent promise that this isn't over.

That we're not over.

We stay like that until my tears dry up. Until we're both empty, wrung out. His softened cock slips free—a reminder of where this started, how it ended.

Incomplete. Broken.

"Tell me what you need. I'll do anything." He pulls back enough to look at me. His eyes are red-rimmed, devastated.

"I need to know who I am. Without the drugs. Without you in

my head." I touch his face, thumb tracing his jaw. "I need time to figure out if Clara Hayes wants to kneel for Julian Blackwell."

"The tapering ends in three days." He's quiet, like it costs him. "After that, you'll be free of the drugs."

"I need more than that."

"What do you need?"

"Space. No commands, no rules, no expectations. Just... let me exist without your control while the drugs leave my system."

His jaw works; the dominant in him clearly warring with the man who knows he crossed a line.

"You'll finish the withdrawal protocol." He's firm and unyielding. "Three more days of tapering doses. I won't compromise on that—stopping cold could be dangerous, and I won't risk your health."

"I don't want any more—"

"The doses get smaller each day. It's the safest way." His voice brooks no argument on this point. "During those three days, you'll stay here—that's non-negotiable. But I won't make demands. No commands, no rules, no punishments. You can do what you want within the house."

"And after the three days?"

"After you're clear, you can have more space. You can leave during the day—go to the ranch, go wherever you need to go. But you sleep here. In my bed. Every night."

"But—"

"That's not negotiable." His arms tighten around me. "The contract specifies you reside in my home and sleep in my bed. I'll give you space during the day, won't touch you unless you initiate, won't command you at all. But every night, you come home. You sleep with me."

"That's not really space—"

"It's all the space I can give." His voice cracks slightly. "Those are my terms."

I study his face—the desperation beneath the control, the genuine fear of losing me entirely.

"So three days of withdrawal here, then freedom during the days but nights in your bed?"

"Yes."

"For how long?"

"Until you decide what you want. What's real. However, the contract still has eight months remaining. This suspension of terms is me trying to... to give you what you need while keeping you safe."

I consider this. It's more than I expected, less than I want.

"Fine. Three days of tapering doses. Then your version of space."

We seal this new arrangement not with a kiss but with exhausted silence, both of us knowing these next days will determine everything.

"I love you." His words fall between us like stones. "I know you don't believe me. I know you think it's just an obsession. But I love you."

"I know." I leave him in his office, looking more lost than I've ever seen him.

The next three days blur together. We move around each other like ghosts—occupying the same spaces but never quite connecting. He continues giving me the vials. I continue taking them. The doses decrease each day, and the crashes become milder.

CHAPTER 50
DAY 125

I avoid him entirely. The house, usually a place of shared existence, has become a minefield of silence. I lock myself in the guest bedroom, then migrate to the library, the sunroom, the kitchen—anywhere he isn't.

His footsteps sound through the house—heavy, deliberate. They are careful, I realize. He is giving me a warning, broadcasting his location so I can escape before we meet. It's a courtesy that hurts more than a confrontation would. It implies a gap so wide it requires navigation.

When his office door closes for a conference call, I slip into the kitchen for water, for the apple I can barely stomach. At seven, I find dinner waiting for me on the island. A simple pasta dish, still warm, covered in foil. Beside it, a note in his jagged, confident handwriting:

You need to eat. Please.

The "Please" is underlined. A crack in the armor.

He's already eaten, his plate rinsed and sitting in the sink. I eat alone, standing at the counter, every bite mechanical and tasteless, swallowing around the lump in my throat.

At ten PM, I can't delay any longer. His concessions were clear during the argument—I get my space, but I sleep in his bed. That was the line he drew in the sand. *You sleep where you belong.*

I stand outside the master bedroom for five minutes, staring at the wood grain, my hand hovering over the handle. My heart is hammering a frantic, unhappy rhythm. Entering that room feels like walking into a pressure chamber.

I push the door open.

He's already there, propped up against the headboard, reading on his tablet. He's wearing dark sleep pants and nothing else, his chest broad and golden in the lamp light. He doesn't look up when I come in—he doesn't even blink—but I see the change. Tension ripples through his shoulders, turning the muscles to stone, and his grip on the tablet tightens until his knuckles turn white.

He is ignoring me. Because if he looks at me, he might break the truce.

I walk to the bathroom in silence, the air thick enough to choke on. I wash my face, brushing my teeth with aggressive thoroughness just to delay the inevitable. Then, deliberately, I open the drawer where I moved some clothes.

Underwear.

Cotton, plain, functional. A barrier I haven't worn to bed in four months. Usually, I sleep skin-to-skin with him, wrapped in his heat. Putting these on feels like an act of war. The fabric feels foreign against my skin, binding and rough. It feels wrong. It feels like a cage.

Tonight, every layer is armor against the night. Against him. And mostly, against my own wanting.

I walk back into the bedroom. I don't look at him, but I can feel his attention shift to me, heavy and tactile, tracking my movement across the room. I pull back the duvet on my side—the far side—and slide in.

I stay on the very edge of the mattress, back turned to him, body rigid.

He turns off the light without a word. The room plunges into darkness, leaving only the faint moonlight filtering through the curtains.

In the darkness, every sound amplifies. The silence isn't empty; it's screaming. I hear the intake of his breath. The whisper of the sheets when he shifts. The faint, rhythmic ticking of the clock that usually gets drowned out by our breathing.

The space between us—maybe only six inches—crackles. It feels like a magnetic field I'm fighting to stay out of.

My body aches for him. It's a physical withdrawal, a phantom limb sensation. My skin prickles, missing the weight of his arm across my waist, the solid warmth of his chest against my back. I miss the way he subconsciously pulls me against him in sleep, tangling his legs with mine like he couldn't bear any distance between us.

Now, the bed feels massive. Cold.

My skin feels too tight, too sensitive, and hyper-aware of the heat radiating from him just inches away. I squeeze my eyes shut, my hand clutching the pillowcase. I want to roll over. It would be so easy. Just one turn, one touch, and the ice would shatter. I know he's waiting for it. I know if I reached out, he would pull me in and never let go.

But I don't. I curl into myself, knees to chest, fighting the urge to seek the comfort I'm denying myself. This is what I asked for— space. This is the autonomy I fought for today.

But lying here, inches from him but untouchable, feels like a special kind of torture.

I hear him exhale—a long, frustrated sound in the dark. He shifts, turning his back to me, mirroring my rejection.

Neither of us sleeps for a very long time.

CHAPTER 51
DAY 126

THE SILENCE IN THE KITCHEN IS BRITTLE, READY TO SNAP AT THE slightest movement. Julian is sitting at the head of the table, his coffee steaming in the morning light, dark circles bruising the skin beneath his eyes. He looks like he hasn't slept, which makes two of us.

He tries to bridge the gap. He sets his mug down, the ceramic clinking sharply against the granite.

"Clara, we should—"

He doesn't get to finish. The sound of his voice, calm and reasoning, scrapes against my frayed nerves. I stand abruptly, my chair screeching against the floor. I leave my coffee untouched, the steam still rising, and turn my back on him.

"I can't," I mutter, fleeing the room before he can command me to stop. I escape to the guest room, the sanctuary that feels more like a cell, and close the door, leaning against it as my heart hammers a frantic rhythm.

By afternoon, the four walls of the guest room are closing in. I'm desperate for distraction, for anything to drown out the noise in my head. I slip out into the hallway, moving silently toward the library. It's usually empty at this hour; Julian should be in his office, buried in calls.

I push the heavy double doors open, expecting solitude.

But he's there.

He is sitting in the wingback leather chair by the window, a book in hand, bathed in the afternoon sun. We both freeze. It's a moment of suspended animation—the air instantly sucked out of the room.

"I didn't know—" I start, my hand gripping the doorknob, ready to bolt.

"It's fine." He lowers the book but doesn't close it. His voice is tight, controlled. "You can—" He gestures vaguely to the shelves, cutting himself off. *You can stay. You can look. You can be here.*

I should leave. Every instinct screams at me to run back to safety. Instead, I step inside, drawn by the perverse need to be near him even if I can't have him. I move to the fiction section, hyper-aware of every step I take on the Persian rug.

He returns to his book, lifting it to block his face. But his stillness is performed. No pages turn. His breathing is too controlled, too quiet. He isn't reading; he is listening to me breathe.

My fingers trail along the leather spines, not reading the titles, just needing something to do with my hands. They're trembling —a fine, persistent shake. It's the withdrawal, the drugs leaving my system, leaving me raw and exposed. But it's also him.

The silence presses down, thick with everything unsaid. It's heavy with the memory of his hands on me. It's heavy with the effort it takes not to cross the six feet between us and collapse at his feet.

I pull a book from the shelf—I don't even look at which one— but my grip fails. My shaking fingers betray me.

Thud.

The book hits the floor, the sound exploding like a gunshot in the quiet room.

We both react on instinct. I drop to a crouch to retrieve it just as he lunges forward from his chair.

We reach for the book at the same time.

His hand lands on the cover. My hand lands on his.

The contact is electric. A shockwave of heat travels up my arm, seizing my chest. For a fraction of a second, neither of us moves. I stare at his hand—large, familiar, capable of so much violence and so much care. I want to thread my fingers through his. I want to climb into his lap and weep.

Then, he pulls back like he's been burned.

He snatches his hand away, retreating to the safety of his chair, his jaw clenched so hard a muscle ticks in his cheek. He refuses to look at me. He is respecting the boundary I set, and it feels like a slap in the face.

I grab the book, clutching it to my chest like a shield, and scramble to my feet. I don't look back as I hurry out of the room.

That night, the distance in the bed feels vast. An ocean of cold sheets.

He faces away from me this time. No tablet. No pretense of reading. Just a wall of back muscle and silence.

I lay on my side, staring at the dark window. The cotton underwear I'm wearing again—utilitarian, unappealing—digs into my hip. It feels like a flag of surrender. Not a surrender to him, but a surrender to this unbearable space I demanded.

I wanted safety. I wanted autonomy. But lying here, shivering in the sterile cotton, listening to the man I love breathe in the dark, I realize that safety is cold. And I am freezing.

CHAPTER 52

DAY 127

Today is the last vial. Julian brings it to me in the morning, and we both stare at it like it's an ending and a beginning at once.

"Last one." He sets the vial on the breakfast table quietly.

I pick it up and study the clear liquid. Seven days ago, this was poison. Violation. Now it's just... liquid. The means to an end.

"And after this?"

"No more chemicals. Just you."

Just me. Whoever that is.

I tip it back, swallow. The bitter taste is familiar now. Comforting in its way. I set the empty vial down with a soft clink.

Julian watches me, waiting for... what? A transformation? An absolution? A sign that everything will be okay?

"How do you feel?" The question comes careful and measured.

"Tired." It's true. The emotional exhaustion weighs heavier than any physical fatigue I've ever known. "Empty."

"That should improve. Over the next few days, your system will stabilize—"

"I don't want a medical report." My voice is flat. "I want to know what happens now. After today."

He's quiet for a long moment, fingers curved around his coffee cup like it's the only thing keeping him anchored. "That depends on you."

"On me?"

He sets the cup down, the soft click loud in the silence. "I can apologize a thousand times, and it won't undo what I did. So the only thing I can do is... give you the space you asked for. Let you figure out who you are without me." He pauses, meeting my gaze. "But the contract remains in place. You sleep with me or void the contract. I will hold you to that."

"How noble."

He moves closer, stopping just outside my personal space. Not crowding, but present. "While you're figuring it out, can I ask one thing?"

"What?"

"Don't shut me out completely." He holds out his hands, as if we're striking a bargain, which I suppose we are.

I stare at his hands for a long moment. Taking them feels like accepting something. A new beginning. Or a new end.

I take his hands.

His fingers close around mine—warm, steady. Not possessive. Just... there. Then he pulls gently, drawing me into him. Not sexual, not demanding—just pulling me against his chest, wrap-ping his arms around me in a hug that feels like shelter and goodbye all at once.

"I'm going to miss this," he says quietly, against my hair. "I'll honor your need for space, but God, I'm going to miss holding you. Touching you without you flinching. Being able to just..." His arms tighten slightly. "Just be like this with you."

I let myself lean into him for a moment, memorizing the cedar and smoke scent, the solid warmth of his chest, the way my body fits against his, as if it was designed for this exact space.

"Me too."

We stand there, holding each other in the wreckage of trust, both knowing that when he lets go, it might be for the last time. He cradles the back of my head, thumb stroking once through my hair—a gesture so tender it breaks something in me.

"Thank you," he says quietly.

"For what?"

"For the chance to prove this is real."

"Don't thank me. This might be the beginning of us destroying each other all over again."

He pulls back enough to look at me, hands framing my face. "Or it might be the beginning of rebuilding what we had."

"You're an optimist."

"I'm obsessed and desperate, and despite what you feel, I'm right about what we can be together. I'm not giving that up, but I will give you the space you need to decide if you agree with me."

We stand there, neither of us sure what comes next.

"So what will you do today?" He breaks the silence first.

"I want..." I trail off. What do I want? "I want to ride Meteor. Out to the far pasture."

"Okay." He nods, releasing my hand. "I'd like for you to be back by dinner. Maybe we'll watch something mindless on TV. Pretend we're normal people for a few hours."

"I have one other request."

"What?"

"I'd like to call you Julian. Mr. Blackwell feels..." I search for the words.

"We'll put Mr. Blackwell on the back burner and be just Julian and Clara. Figure out what we are, together."

"Thank you."

I rise on tiptoe to kiss his cheek—a simple, grateful gesture. But my lips against his skin feel wrong and incomplete. We don't do chaste pecks. We do consuming kisses that leave bruises, that claim and devour. This light touch feels like trying to breathe underwater. It's unnatural and impossible.

His hands flex at his sides, and I know he feels it too—this wrongness of platonic affection between us. We're either everything or nothing. Fire or ice. This lukewarm middle ground doesn't fit the shape of what we are.

I pull back quickly, see the struggle in his eyes. He wants to grab me, crush his mouth to mine, show me exactly why a kiss on the cheek will never be enough. But he doesn't. He lets me step away.

"Clara—" His voice is rough.

"I know. This isn't who we are. But for now, it's what I need."

I leave him and go to change for riding. As I pull on jeans and boots, I catch my reflection in the mirror. Same face, same body. But something's different. There's a subtle shift in my eyes, maybe, or a loosening in the set of my jaw.

I look like someone waking up from a long dream. Not sure if she's relieved or terrified to find herself back in reality.

CHAPTER 53
DAY 128

The ride is exactly what I need. Meteor moves beneath me, powerful and uncomplicated. Animals don't lie. Don't manipulate. They just are.

I let him run, feeling the wind tear through my hair, the sun on my face. Out here, I'm just Clara. Not Julian's submissive, not his creation. Just a woman on a horse, racing across open land.

When I return from my ride with Meteor, Julian's truck is in my driveway. He's sitting on my porch—my father's porch—looking absurdly out of place in his expensive clothes against the weathered wood.

"Good ride?" he calls.

"Yeah. Really good."

"Lunch is ready," he says, gesturing to the spread on the old porch table. Simple sandwiches, fruit, and water. Nothing elaborate. "Figured you'd be hungry after riding."

"You didn't have to—"

"I wanted to." He pauses, studying me. "How was it? Being back at the ranch?"

"Good. Free. Like I could breathe again." I sit down, realize I'm starving.

"You look good. More color."

We eat in relative quiet, the ranch spreading out before us—the improvements he made are subtle but everywhere. New fencing. The irrigation system. Mom's garden is blooming.

"I've been thinking," he says eventually. "If you're going to spend your days here, at the ranch..."

"Yeah?"

"Then I want to spend our nights here too." He sets down his water. "The contract says you have to sleep in my bed. It doesn't specify which residence my bed is in."

"You want to sleep here?"

"I want to sleep where you're comfortable. Where you feel most like yourself." He looks at the house. "If that's here, then this is where we'll be at night."

The thoughtfulness of it catches me off guard. Then I process what he's really saying.

"Wait. You're... you're moving into my house?"

"I'm honoring our agreement. You sleep in my bed every night." His expression is perfectly innocent. "I'm simply relocating my bed."

"That's not—Julian, I came here for space. The whole point was I'd have my days at the ranch and then return to your house at night."

"And now you can have your days and nights at the ranch. More convenient for you, really."

"But you'll be here."

"I'll set up an office in your father's office. You'll barely notice me."

I stare at him, caught between indignation and something

dangerously close to amusement. "You're supposed to be giving me space."

"I am giving you space. All day."

"But you're literally moving into my home."

"I'm simply interpreting the contract in a way that makes you most comfortable." He takes a bite of his sandwich, casual as anything.

"By invading my space?"

"By ensuring you can stay where you feel most yourself while still honoring our agreement. Or, did you not hear that part?"

The manipulation is so transparent, so classically Julian—finding the loophole that lets him maintain control while technically following the rules. He's giving me what I asked for while taking what he needs.

"No, I heard you." I shake my head. "You're impossible, you know that," but there's no real heat in it.

"I'm adaptive." A small smile plays at his lips. "Is that a yes to the office space?"

"Like you'd take no for an answer."

"I absolutely would. Your house, your rules." He pauses. "But the contract is very clear about sleeping arrangements."

Despite everything, my lips twitch.

"Fine. You can use Dad's old study."

"Thank you."

We eat in silence for a moment, then I can't help adding: "You realize you just manipulated your way into moving in with me while making it seem like you're doing me a favor?"

"I have no idea what you're talking about." But his eyes glint with satisfaction. "I'm simply being accommodating."

"You're being you—controlling."

"Is that a bad thing?"

I should say yes. Should be angry at this maneuver. Instead, I find myself oddly charmed by his scheming—so determined to stay close while pretending to give me distance.

"Just... don't rearrange my entire house."

"Wouldn't dream of it." He looks at the porch steps. "Though these could use reinforcement."

"Julian."

"What? It's a safety issue." He suddenly stands and dusts off his pants. "I have business calls all afternoon. Very important. Tokyo investors, merger details—so try not to bother me. You understand, of course." He's already heading toward the house. "I'll need complete quiet in the study. No interruptions."

I stare at him. "No interruptions. In my house. Where you invited yourself to live."

"I'll be locked in the study for hours. You won't even know I'm there."

"In MY house."

"Exactly." His smirk is pure satisfaction. "I'll probably need to install a better internet connection, though. Maybe a dedicated line for video calls. But don't worry—I'll handle all that without bothering you."

"Julian—"

"Oh, and I'll need the WiFi password. And probably a better desk chair. That one looks terrible for posture. But after that, complete space. Total privacy for you." He disappears inside MY house, already pulling out his phone. "I need to overnight some office supplies to a new address..."

I sit on my porch, mouth open. He's colonized my space and somehow made it seem like he's the one being inconvenienced.

The worst part? There's something endearing about his complete inability actually to give me space, even when he's trying, or pretending to try.

From inside, his voice drifts out: "Clara? Does this house have a printer? Never mind, I'll have one delivered."

In MY house. I shake my head and smile.

The afternoon passes quietly. I curl up with a book—some thriller I grabbed randomly. Julian's voice drifts from the study, muffled discussions of market shares and acquisitions. Normal CEO things.

It's surreal. This domesticity. This careful distance between us.

Dinner is equally simple—pasta he makes while I set the table. We eat on the back porch, watching the sun set behind the mountains. He tells me about his day, the deals he's working on. I tell him about a foal being born at a neighboring ranch.

Like normal people.

Like we're not carrying the weight of everything that's happened between us.

As darkness falls, we move to the living room. He turns on the TV and scrolls through the options.

"What do you want to watch?"

"Something mindless."

He settles on some action movie—explosions, car chases, no emotional depth required. We sit on opposite ends of the long couch, a gulf of leather between us.

Halfway through, I realize I'm not watching the movie. I'm watching him. The way the TV light plays across his face. The rare moments when he almost smiles at some ridiculous stunt. The way his hand rests on his thigh, fingers occasionally tapping to some internal rhythm.

He catches me looking. "What?"

"Nothing. Just... trying to figure you out."

"Any luck?"

"Not yet."

"Let me know if you do. I've been trying to figure myself out for thirty-five years."

Despite everything, I smile at that.

When the movie ends, we sit in the sudden silence, not sure how to end the evening. Shaking hands seems ridiculous. Hugging feels impossible. Kissing is out of the question.

"The bathroom's small," I warn as bedtime approaches. "Not like yours."

"I'll manage."

We take turns—me first, changing into sleep clothes in the bathroom where I once played with bath toys. Cotton underwear, an old T-shirt, and shorts. Armor that feels increasingly pointless.

When I emerge, he's looking at the family photos lining the hallway. Me at seven with missing teeth. Mom in her garden. Dad young and proud with his first horse.

"You were adorable," he says softly.

"I was a mess."

"An adorable mess." He disappears into the bathroom.

I get into bed—my bed, the same full-size I've had since high school. It seems impossibly small for two adults, especially when one is Julian's size.

He comes out in sleep pants, hesitates at the doorway. "This feels..."

"Weird?"

"Intimate. Different intimate." He approaches the bed like it might bite. "Your childhood room."

"The trophies are embarrassing." I gesture to my 4-H ribbons, the barrel racing awards.

"They're you." He slides into bed, and we immediately bump into each other. There's no space here, no way to maintain distance.

"Sorry," I mutter, trying to press against the wall.

"It's fine." But his voice is strained. In his king-size bed, we could pretend at separation. Here, every breath brings us closer. His warmth radiates across the inches between us.

And that's when I realize exactly how diabolical Julian is.

This wasn't about my comfort or letting me be where I feel most myself. This is pure strategy. In his mansion, his California king gave us oceans of space—I could hug one edge while he stayed on the other, two bodies that never had to touch.

We could maintain the fiction of distance.

But here? My full-size mattress barely fits one adult, let alone two. There's nowhere to retreat. Every shift brings contact—his shoulder, his hip, his leg brushing mine. The bed forces us together even as we're trying to stay apart.

"You planned this," I whisper into the dark.

A pause. "I don't know what you mean."

"My bed. You knew it was smaller."

"Your comfort is my priority—"

"You're impossible." I turn slightly and feel his breath on my face. We're so close. "You looked at this room earlier. Saw the bed. Did the math. You knew exactly what you were doing when you suggested sleeping here."

Silence. Then, quietly: "Would you have preferred I let you drive back and forth? Risk you being too tired one night and not coming back?"

"So you manufactured forced proximity instead?"

"I honored our contract while ensuring you stayed close." His voice carries that particular tone—part confession, part satisfaction. "The size of the bed is merely... fortunate."

"Fortunate. Right." I should be angry. Should kick him out to the couch. Instead, I'm fighting not to laugh at the sheer audacity. "You're literally incapable of giving me space, aren't you?"

"I'm giving you emotional space. Physical space was never specified."

"You're impossible."

"So you've said." He shifts slightly, and his thigh presses against mine. Neither of us moves away. "Is it working?"

"Is what working?"

"The bed. The proximity. Making you remember what it feels like when we're not fighting the inevitable."

My breath catches. Because yes, damn him, it's working. Every point of contact burns through the cotton barriers I've put between us. My body remembers his perfectly, even as my mind tries to maintain distance.

"Go to sleep, Julian."

"Can't. Bed's too small. You're too close."

"Whose fault is that?"

I feel rather than see his smile in the dark. "Mine. Entirely, and deliberately mine."

We lie in the dark, hyperaware of each other. The house creaks differently than his modern mansion—old wood settling, the wind whistling through the original windows. His breathing seems louder here. More present. More real.

"Clara?"

"Yeah?"

"Thank you for letting me into your space."

I don't answer, but my hand moves slightly, just enough that my pinky brushes his. Neither of us pulls away.

Despite everything, I almost smile at our movie night awkwardness and this strange new dance we're learning—how to be together while apart, how to share space without sharing ourselves.

When the darkness gets too heavy, I whisper: "Goodnight, Julian."

"Goodnight, Clara."

But I lie awake anyway, listening to him breathe in my childhood bed, wondering if this is what freedom feels like. And if it is, why does it hurt so much?

CHAPTER 54
DAY 129

The aroma of coffee wakes me. Julian's up, following old patterns even though everything's changed.

I pull on clothes and pad down the hall. He's in the kitchen, spatula in hand, pushing scrambled eggs around a pan. **Hair** wet from a shower, shirt unbuttoned at the collar. Casual in a way he rarely allows.

He sees me. "Morning. Coffee's ready. Eggs will be done in a minute."

"Thanks."

I pour coffee—black, bitter, exactly what I need. No orange juice on the table. Just water, coffee, plain options. No more chemicals hiding in plain sight.

"Sleep okay?" **He** plates the eggs.

"Not really. You?"

"Not at all. I was hard all night." He says it casually, like he's commenting on the weather. Sets a plate in front of me, takes his own to the opposite side. "Your bed's too small. You kept pressing your ass against my cock."

I nearly choke on my coffee. "Julian—"

"What? You asked." He takes a bite of eggs, eyes steady on mine. "Complete honesty, remember? That's still a rule, even if the others are suspended."

"You can't just say things like that."

"Why not? It's true. You were warm and soft and right there, and I couldn't touch you. Do you know what that does to a man who's used to taking you whenever he wants?"

Heat floods my face, my body. Because I do know.

Before this strange truce, he would have rolled me onto my stomach in the middle of the night, pushed inside me while I was still half-asleep. Or pulled me to the edge of the bed and fucked my mouth until I was fully awake and desperate. Or carried me to the kitchen counter, the shower, the porch—anywhere the need struck him.

"That's not—we're not doing that now."

"I'm aware." He stands, brings the coffee pot over to refill my cup. Leans down close enough that I smell his skin. "Doesn't stop my body from remembering. Doesn't stop me from being hard right now, watching you in my shirt at your kitchen table."

I look down. I am wearing his shirt—grabbed it without thinking this morning.

"It's just a shirt."

"It's my shirt on your body in the house where you grew up." His voice drops. "Do you know how many times teenage me fantasized about exactly this? You in my clothes, eating breakfast I made you, looking freshly fucked even though I haven't touched you in days?"

"Stop."

"Why? Does it bother you?" He returns to his seat, but his eyes never leave mine. "Or does it remind you that your body's probably as frustrated as mine?"

My body's been wound tight, aching, trained to need his permission, and now abandoned without it.

"Fuck you."

"I wish you would." He stands and takes his plate to the sink. "But you asked for space. So instead, I'll be in your father's study, doing business calls, thinking about all the ways I'm not fucking you on every surface of this house." He stops. Starts again. "This is strange for both of us. All our old patterns, the structure we built —it's gone now. We're just... improvising."

"Is that hard for you? Not being in control?"

"Yes." His jaw tightens. "Every instinct I have is screaming to fix this, to take charge, to command you into feeling better. But I can't. I won't."

"Good."

"Is it?" He looks at me directly. "Because I'm not sure either of us knows how to do this. Be together without the dynamic."

"Then maybe we can't."

"Or maybe we learn how to find our way back."

I push eggs around my plate. "You said no expectations. No commands. But dominance isn't just commands. It's in how you move, how you speak, how you exist. Can you really turn that off?"

"I've never tried." His voice is quiet. "But I'm trying now. For you."

"Don't do it for me. Do it because it's right."

"Both can be true."

We finish breakfast in heavy silence. When I stand to take my plate, he's already up, reaching for it.

"I can do my own dishes," I say.

"I know. But I'm already up." He takes it to the sink. Not commanding, just... doing.

It's a small thing. Insignificant, really. But it highlights the shift—he's not ordering me around, not structuring my every move. We're just two people sharing space.

I should be relieved.

I'm not.

"I'm going to work with Meteor. Maybe ride out to the north pasture."

"Sounds good. Want company?"

The offer surprises me. "I thought you had work."

"I do. But it can wait. If you want me there."

"I..." Do I? "No. Thank you, but no. I need time alone."

"Okay." If he's hurt, he hides it. "I'll be in my study if you need anything." He pauses at the doorway. "By the way, the kitchen table seems sturdy enough. For future reference."

"Julian!"

But he's already gone, leaving me wet and aching and furious at my own body's response. The worst part is he's right—I've tried touching myself, tried finding relief, but my body won't cooperate. Won't come without his voice, his permission, his command.

Breathing is easier once I'm away from the house. From him. The morning is clear and bright, perfect Montana weather. Meteor nickers when he sees me, pushing his nose into my palm.

"At least you're simple," I murmur, stroking his neck. "No hidden agendas. No chemical manipulation. Just hungry and wanting attention."

I saddle him up and ride out, letting the rhythm of his gait settle my thoughts. Out here, things make sense. Horses respond to clear communication and firm guidance. No games, no questions about what's real.

I ride for hours, until my thighs ache and the sun's high overhead. When I return, the ranch feels different. Lighter. This place is mine—or will be again, once the contract ends. My legacy, my responsibility.

The thought steadies me.

Back at the house late afternoon, I find Julian in my dad's study. The door's open—he's on a video call, gesturing at his screen. I catch a glimpse of his face: focused, intense, and completely in his element. This is his domain, where he's unquestionably powerful.

I keep walking, not wanting to interrupt. Not wanting to eavesdrop, but his voice carries:

"—not interested in excuses. The deadline was clear. Either deliver or we find another vendor."

Sharp. Uncompromising. The Julian Blackwell who built an empire.

My body reacts immediately—nipples tightening, pulse quickening, that familiar clench low in my belly. The reaction is so sudden and intense that it stops me mid-step. My hand flies to the wall for support as heat floods through me, cutting through the gray fog like lightning.

Fuck.

It's sexy.

More than sexy—it's magnetic.

That command, that absolute certainty in his voice. The way he doesn't ask but states what will happen. My thighs press together involuntarily, seeking friction that won't be enough.

This isn't the drugs. Can't be. Two days clean, and my body still responds to his dominance like a trained animal. Like I've been conditioned to get wet at the sound of his voice.

I lean against the wall, breathing hard, hating myself for the dampness already gathering between my legs. Hating him more for making me this way.

But mostly hating how much I miss it—miss him ordering me

to my knees with that same uncompromising tone. Miss the simplicity of obedience, the freedom of surrendering all choice to someone who wields power like breathing.

"The contract is non-negotiable," he continues inside, and I have to bite my lip to suppress a whimper. "You knew the terms when you signed."

God. The parallels aren't lost on me.

I miss being commanded. Miss being his. Not the drugged compliance, but the raw, electric feeling of submitting to someone powerful enough to take my submission and shape it into something beautiful and terrible at the same time.

The realization terrifies me more than any withdrawal symptom could.

Is this real? Or is it conditioning?

I grab a book at random and curl into the reading chair, but the words blur. My mind's elsewhere—on the man down the hall, on the way authority drapes him like a second skin.

I'm wet and aching.

I press my thighs together, trying to will the arousal away. It doesn't work. If anything, acknowledging it makes it worse. My nipples are tight against my shirt. My core throbs with need.

This can't be happening. I'm supposed to be figuring out what's real. Not getting turned on by his goddamn business calls.

But I am. My body doesn't care about my confusion, my hurt, my need to understand. It just knows what it wants.

Him.

I force myself to read until the feeling passes. Or doesn't pass so much as becomes bearable. By the time Julian's call has ended. He's in the kitchen.

"You're back," he observes. "Good ride?"

"Yeah. Good ride."

The words come out strained. Because what I really mean is

that I wish he'd been riding me instead. Wish he'd bent me over Meteor's stall with the crop in his hand, making me count each strike before he—

No. Stop.

I can't let myself think about that. About the crop he bought specifically for me, the one with the leather tip that leaves perfect heart-shaped marks. About how he'd trace each welt with his tongue before fucking me so hard I'd feel it for days. About how I'd beg for more, *harder, please Mr. Blackwell, please mark me as yours—*

"Clara?" His voice cuts through my spiraling thoughts. "You okay?"

"Fine." I grab a glass of water and drink it too fast. "Just tired from the ride."

But my body betrays me—flushed cheeks, dilated pupils, the way I can't quite meet his eyes. He knows. Reading my body is second nature to him.

"If you need anything—" he starts.

"I don't." Too sharp. Too fast. Too desperate.

I flee before he can respond, before I do something stupid like drop to my knees and beg him to take control again. To make the decisions. To tell me when to come, how to breathe, how to exist.

The worst part is, I don't know if that need is mine or something he built into me.

And I'm terrified to find out it's me.

Later that night, he chops vegetables with the same precision he applies to everything. Efficient, controlled. Even his cooking is dominant—ingredients submitting to his knife.

Stop it. Stop sexualizing everything he does.

"Need help?" I offer.

"If you want. Or you can relax. Either way."

I grab a cutting board and start on the salad. We work side by side, not talking much. His arm occasionally brushes mine—casual contact that sends electricity through me each time.

He notices. "Clara—"

"Don't."

"I'm not—I just want to make sure you're okay."

"I'm fine."

"You're aroused."

Heat floods my face.

He stops himself. "I'm sorry. I shouldn't have said that. It's not my place to observe anymore."

"But you did."

"Old habits." He goes back to chopping. "Dominants learn to read body language. It's automatic. I can try to stop, but—"

"It's who you are."

"Yes." He sets down the knife. "I meant what I said. No commands, no expectations. But I can't stop being who I am. The way I see the world, the way I read people—that's not something I can turn off."

"I know." I set down my own knife. "And I'm not asking you to. Just... don't act on it. Don't comment on it. Let me figure out my own body without your analysis."

"Okay." He picks up the knife again. "I'll try."

We finish making dinner in charged silence. Every movement feels weighted, observed. When his hand brushes mine, reaching for the same utensil, we both freeze. The contact lingers a heartbeat too long.

"Sorry," he murmurs, pulling back.

"It's fine."

But it's not fine. The tension is unbearable—this careful distance while our bodies remember everything we've been to each other.

Dinner is torture. We eat on the porch again, watching the

sunset. Beautiful scenery, good food, and underneath it all, a current of want neither of us is supposed to acknowledge.

"Tell me about today," he says. "Where you rode. What you saw."

So I do. Describe the north pasture, the deer I spotted, and the way the light hit the mountains. Safe topics. Neutral ground.

He listens intently, asking questions and showing genuine interest. This is different than before—not a dominant gathering information about his submissive, but a man trying to know a woman.

"You love it out there," he observes. "The ranch. The land. I can hear it in your voice."

"I always have. Even when things were falling apart, when I couldn't pay the bills or fix the equipment—I loved it."

"You'll have it back. Fully. When the contract ends." He takes a drink of water. "What will you do? When it's yours again?"

"Rebuild. The way I should have from the start, instead of—" I stop.

"Instead of getting tangled up with me."

"Yeah."

"Do you regret it? All of it?"

I consider the question seriously. "I regret how we started. The drugs, the manipulation. But the rest?" I shake my head. "I don't know. Some of it was... good. Really good. I just don't know how much was real."

"Maybe that's something we can figure out."

"Maybe."

After dinner, he cleans up while I shower. The hot water feels good on trail-worn muscles. I stand under the spray, letting it wash away the day's tension.

When I emerge, the TV is on. Another movie night, apparently. Our new routine.

I find him on the couch, in the same position as last night. He's changed into sleep pants and a T-shirt—casual and comfortable. Almost approachable.

"Mind if I join?" I ask.

"Please." He gestures to the other end.

I settle in, tucking my feet under me. We watch some comedy that neither of us is really into. The laugh track fills the silence between us.

Halfway through, I realize I'm exhausted. Bone-deep tired in a way I haven't been since—

Since the drugs stopped.

"I'm fading," I admit. "Think I'll head to bed."

"Okay." He reaches for the remote, muting the TV. "Clara?"

"Yes?

"Thank you."

"For what?"

"For trying. For giving us a chance to figure this out."

"I haven't decided anything."

"I know. But you're here tonight. That's something."

I leave him there and make my way to my room. As I'm changing for bed, I hear him moving around. Shower running in the bathroom. Normal night sounds.

But nothing feels normal.

I climb into bed, expecting another sleepless night. Instead, exhaustion pulls me under almost immediately. Deep, dreamless sleep that swallows me whole.

I don't hear him pause outside my door again. Don't know that he stands there listening to me breathe, making sure I'm really asleep before he climbs into bed beside me.

CHAPTER 55
DAY 130

Morning comes too fast. I wake to silence—no coffee brewing, no breakfast cooking. For a moment, panic flutters. Then I remember: no expectations. He's not responsible for me anymore.

I make my own coffee, scramble my own eggs. The kitchen feels empty without him, but there's a freedom in it too. My choices, my pace.

He appears as I'm finishing. Dressed for business—sharp suit, expensive watch. CEO armor fully in place.

"Morning." He moves to the coffee pot. "Sleep better?"

"Actually, yes. You?"

"Some." He pours coffee and leans against the counter. "I have meetings in town today. Might not be back until evening. Will you be okay without me?"

He stands there, maintaining that careful distance between us, and I remember how this scene would have played out just a week ago.

He would have caged me against the counter already, suit be damned. Lifted me onto it, shoved my nightgown up, and fucked me until I screamed. His appetite for me was all-consuming—taking me between meetings, during phone calls, whenever the urge struck.

Now he grips his coffee mug with both hands, knuckles white with restraint.

Where is all that hunger going? That relentless need that had him inside me multiple times a day? He's always been a man of enormous appetites—for power, for control, for me. Those needs don't disappear.

"You're staring." His voice is quiet.

"You're keeping your distance."

"You need space to think clearly. I'm giving you space."

"Since when has what I need stopped you from taking what you want?"

The words hang between us, sharp and accusatory. For a moment, I see it—the predator barely leashed, the hunger that still burns beneath his careful control.

"Since I realized I was destroying the thing I wanted most." His voice is rough. "My appetite for you hasn't changed. I'm just choosing not to feed it at your expense."

"So what do you do instead? How does Julian Blackwell handle denial?"

He sets down his mug with deliberate control, and something shifts in his expression—a wry honesty replacing the careful mask.

"You want the truth?"

"Yes." Although I already know it's a mistake to ask.

"I masturbate. A lot." He says it matter-of-factly, but there's dark humor in his eyes. "Six times yesterday. Twice already this morning. My cock is actually getting chafed, which hasn't happened since I was fifteen."

I nearly choke on air. "Julian—"

"You asked." He leans against the counter, studying me. "Every time I look at you, every time I smell your skin, every time you make those little sounds in your sleep—I have to leave the room and handle it myself. Because the alternative is breaking my promise and fucking you against the nearest surface."

"That's..."

"Pathetic? Desperate?" He shrugs. "Add it to the list of things I've become since you found out about the drugs. Desperate, pathetic, and apparently left-handed now since my right hand needed a break."

Despite everything, my lips twitch. "You're being crude."

"I'm being honest. You wanted to know how I'm handling denial? Badly. With lotion and determination and an embarrassing amount of tissue." His voice drops. "Sometimes I use your panties. The ones you leave in the hamper."

Heat floods my face. "That's—"

"Violation of your privacy? Probably. But it's that or violate our agreement, and the panties seemed like the lesser evil." He pushes off from the counter. "Does that answer your question about how I'm managing my hunger?"

It does. And somehow his crude honesty, the almost teenage desperation of it, makes him seem more human than he has in days. Not the controlled dominant, or the master manipulator. Just a man jerking off like a frustrated teenager because he can't have what he wants.

Because even through my anger, even through the withdrawal fog, the cost of his restraint is visible. The rigid set of his shoulders. The way his hands flex like they're aching to grab, to possess, to claim.

He's starving himself of me. And some broken part of me wonders if that's its own kind of cruelty—to both of us.

"Will you be okay while I'm at work?"

"I'm not a child."

"I know. But I'm trying to be considerate, and I don't have a map for this. So I'm asking: will you be okay?" His eyes narrow slightly, and when he speaks again, his voice drops to that commanding register that once ruled my every breath. "I asked you a question. I'd appreciate it if you answered it."

The shift is instant—my spine straightening, pulse jumping, that automatic response hardwired into my nervous system. My thighs clench involuntarily, and I hate how my body betrays me, how quickly I want to comply.

"I—yes. I'll be fine." The words come out breathless, submissive despite my best efforts.

Something flickers in his eyes—recognition, maybe satisfaction—before he deliberately softens his tone again. "Good. Call if you need anything."

But the damage is done. That brief flash of dominance has lit up pathways in my brain that days of withdrawal haven't dimmed. My body remembers that voice, craves it, even as my mind screams in protest.

What does it mean that I still respond like this? That, even knowing what he did, knowing about the drugs, my body turns liquid at his command?

Is that real desire?

He gathers his things, and his hands shake slightly as he checks his phone. He felt it too—that electric moment when we fell back into our roles. Commander and commanded.

"Julian?"

He pauses at the door.

"Your restraint... does it hurt?"

His knuckles go white on the doorframe. "Every second."

His honesty deflates my defensiveness.

"I'll text when I'm heading back." He heads for the door. At the threshold, he pauses. "Clara?"

"Yeah?"

"If you need anything—anything at all—call me. I'll answer. Whatever meeting I'm in, whatever I'm doing, I'll answer."

"Okay."

Then he's gone, leaving me alone with coffee growing cold and the echo of his commanding voice still thrumming through my veins.

The house settles into silence.

I spend the morning listless. I wander through the house until I come to my father's study—Julian's commandeered space.

Everything is obsessively organized.

I shouldn't snoop. It's his private space.

But I'm drawn to a stack of books on the side of the desk. Not business books—personal ones. Psychology texts, books on dominance and submission, memoirs from BDSM practitioners.

And there, on the bottom, a series of black leather notebooks.

My heart pounds as I pull one out. It's old, worn. The spine cracks as I open it.

September 15, Clara Hayes wore a yellow sundress to school today. She laughed at something her friend said, and the sound made my chest ache. I know she'll never look at me that way—like I'm someone worth laughing with instead of someone to fear. But I can wait. I'm good at waiting.

I flip ahead, hands shaking.

October 3, Found out she likes horses. Spent two hours researching equestrian programs at every college she might attend. If I can't be with her now, maybe I can engineer situations where we end up in the same place later. Pathetic? Probably. But I don't care.

November 12, She wore her hair down today. I've been keeping track—she only does that on Wednesdays and Fridays. Filed that infor-

mation away with everything else. The way she bites her lip when thinking. How she twirls her pen during tests. Small details nobody else notices. But I notice. I notice everything.

Page after page. Year after year. His obsession is meticulously documented.

And then, later volumes. After high school.

July 18, Attended my first BDSM workshop today. The instructor talked about dominance as service—using power to give someone what they need. I kept thinking about Clara. About how she carries everything alone. How she never asks for help. How she'd probably fight submission tooth and nail...and how perfect it would be when she finally stopped fighting.

March 23, Met with Nathan about the empathy enhancers. He asked if I was sure. I said yes. The moral implications are clear—this is a violation, manipulation, everything I claim to despise. But I don't care. When I finally have Clara where I want her, I won't leave it to chance. I'll make her feel what she should have let herself feel seventeen years ago.

I drop the notebook like it's burned me.

This isn't just obsession. This is premeditation. Years of planning, studying, preparing to take over my life so completely that there'd be no escape.

And the worst part?

Reading his raw honesty, his desperate need—some part of me is moved by it. Some traitorous part of me thinks: *He wanted me that much. Waited that long. Changed himself to be what I needed.*

No. Stop. That's the conditioning talking.

His truck pulls up.

He's home.

I shove the notebook back under the stack, trying to make it look undisturbed. Race from the study to the living room, grabbing a magazine to look casual.

He comes through the door, loosening his tie. "Hey. How was your day?"

"Fine. Good. Productive." The words tumble out too fast.

His eyes narrow slightly. "You okay?"

"Yeah. Why?"

"You seem..." He studies me. "Flustered."

"Just been reading. Boring stuff. How were your meetings?"

"Successful." He pulls off his tie and drapes it over the back of a chair. "I'm going to change. Then maybe we can order takeout? I don't feel like cooking."

"Sure. Sounds good."

He heads upstairs. I sit frozen, heart pounding.

He waited seventeen years. Documented everything. Planned it all.

Part of me is horrified. Another part—that traitorous, conditioned part—whispers: *Someone wanted you that much. Loved you that much.*

That wasn't love. That was obsession.

Is there a difference?

When he comes back down—jeans and a soft shirt, casual and dangerous—I'm still tangled in the question.

"Thai okay?" He scrolls on his phone. "Or we could do Italian. Your choice."

"Thai's fine."

He places the order, then settles on the couch. I take my usual spot at the opposite end. The magazine lies forgotten between us.

"Clara." His voice is soft. "You were in my study."

My blood runs cold. "How—"

"I always know. The air smells different. Papers shifted slightly." He doesn't sound angry. Just... observant. "Did you find what you were looking for?"

"I don't know what you mean."

"The notebooks." Not a question. "You found them."

I could lie. Should lie. But Rule Three echoes in my head—complete honesty. Even now, even broken, I can't shake his rules.

"Yes."

He nods slowly. "Which volumes?"

"The early ones. High school. Some later ones about... the preparation."

"Ah." He leans back and stares at the ceiling. "So now you know the full depth of it. The obsession. The planning. How completely I designed this."

"Why keep them? Why document it all?"

"Because I needed to believe it would happen someday. The notebooks were proof I was serious, that this wasn't just teenage fantasy." He looks at me. "And maybe because part of me knew I'd have to answer for it eventually. That you'd find them and see exactly what you were dealing with."

"You're insane."

"Probably. Although I prefer *obsessed*." No argument. "I'm eternally obsessed with you. It's pathologic." He sits forward, elbows on his knees. "Read them all if you want. I won't stop you. Maybe it'll help you understand."

"Understand what? How deeply disturbed you are?"

"How deeply I love you." His voice is quiet. "Even if that love is twisted. Even if it destroyed us. It's still real. Obsessive and wrong and built on violation—but real."

"That's not love."

"Isn't it?" He meets the challenge head-on. "What is love, then? Wanting someone's happiness? I wanted that. Wanting to protect them? I've done that. Wanting to possess them so completely they're burned into your DNA?" He shrugs. "Maybe that part isn't the traditional definition. But it's how I feel."

I want to yell. Want to call him every name I can think of. But I'm exhausted. Wrung out.

"The doorbell's going to ring in about ten minutes." He checks his phone. "Food delivery. We can eat and pretend this conversation didn't happen. Or we can talk about it more. Your call."

"I don't know what to say."

"Then say nothing. We'll eat. Watch something mindless. Continue our careful dance around each other."

"Is that what we're doing? Dancing?"

"What else would you call it?" He looks at me directly. "We're circling. Neither of us is willing to walk away. Both of us are trying to figure out if there's anything beneath the wreckage."

The doorbell rings. He gets up to answer it, comes back with bags of Thai food. We eat at the dining room table, mostly silent. The food is good. None of it tastes like anything.

"I have a business dinner tomorrow night." He sets down his fork. "I'd like for you to come, but no pressure."

"With who?"

"Potential investors. The agricultural development project." He takes a drink of water. "You'd be an asset. They respect practical knowledge, and you know ranching better than anyone I could bring."

"You want me there for business."

"I want you there because I enjoy your company. The business angle is secondary."

I push rice around my plate. "Let me think about it."

"Okay."

After dinner, he cleans up. I retreat to my cozy chair to read. Can't stop thinking about those notebooks. About seventeen years of waiting.

Around ten, he appears in the doorway. "I'm heading to bed. Just wanted to say goodnight."

"Goodnight."

He hesitates. "Clara? Those notebooks don't justify what I did. Nothing justifies it. But they're honest. Probably the most honest thing about me. If you want to understand who I really am, read all of them."

"And if what I see there terrifies me?"

"Then at least you'll know why you should run."

He leaves. I stay up until well past midnight reading, then drag myself to bed where Julian is already lying on his side, taking up more than half the narrow space.

I slide in behind him, and immediately our bodies connect— my breasts against his back, my thighs against his ass. There's nowhere else to go in this bed he strategically chose.

The notebooks are still swirling in my mind—seventeen years of meticulous planning, obsessive desire, careful study of dominance and submission. Not just to have me, but to master the art of owning someone completely.

He doesn't move, but his breathing changes. He's awake.

"Can't sleep?" I whisper against his shoulder blade.

"Difficult when you're pressed against me like that."

I should pull back, except there's nowhere to go. And after reading his notebooks—seeing the boy who channeled teenage rage into empire-building, who studied rope work and impact play with academic precision, who wrote my name ten thousand times in the margins while planning his future—I understand him differently.

"The notebooks." My voice is quiet. "You really spent seventeen years preparing for me."

"Yes."

"Learning about dominance, control, and power exchange. All for the possibility of having me."

His body tenses. "Yes."

"That's insane."

"I know."

"And romantic. In a deeply fucked up way."

He turns slightly, enough that I can see his profile in the darkness. "Clara—"

"I'm not forgiving the drugs." The words come quickly. "But I'm starting to understand you weren't just some predator who wanted to own something. You were a man who wanted me specifically, who built his entire life around the possibility of us."

"Does that make it better or worse?"

"I don't know." My body is responding to his warmth, his scent, the solid presence of him. After days of distance, being pressed against him feels like coming home and drowning at the same time.

"I miss it." The words are barely audible. "Miss what we had. The structure, the commands, the way you made everything simple. I hate that I miss it, but I do."

His hand finds mine in the darkness, fingers interlacing. "It's still here. We're still here."

"But it's poisoned now. I don't know what's real—"

"This is real." He presses my hand to his chest where his heart pounds. "This bed, too small for us both. The way you fit against me perfectly, even when you're angry. The fact that we're both awake at 2 AM because being this close without touching is killing us."

I press my forehead against his back, breathing him in. The notebooks showed me something I hadn't understood—he's not just dominant.

He's dominantly devoted.

Every controlling tendency, every possessive instinct, all of it focused entirely on me.

"I don't know how to forgive you." A whisper.

"I'm not asking you to. Just... don't run. Stay here, pressed against me in this ridiculous bed, and give us time to figure out what's real."

I fall asleep like that, curved around him, and dream of leather and roses, of contracts and chemically-enhanced kisses, of a boy who loved me so obsessively he became a man capable of destroying us both.

The question that haunts me as sleep takes over: Can I love someone who destroyed me to save me from myself?

CHAPTER 56
DAY 131

Morning tension cracks like ice over deep water.

I'm making coffee when Julian appears, already dressed for work. We move around each other carefully—practiced avoidance, polite distance. But something's different today.

Something's sharp in the air.

"Sleep well?"

"No."

"Me neither." He pours his coffee and leans against the counter. "About tonight. The dinner. Have you decided?"

"I'm not going."

The words drop like stones. His hand stills on the coffee mug, knuckles flexing once. The pause stretches—one heartbeat, two— while he visibly processes my refusal. His shoulders tighten beneath the expensive suit jacket, a muscle jumping in his jaw as he sets the mug down with excessive care.

"Okay." The word comes out controlled, but I catch the micro- expressions—the way his eyes go dark, the slight flare of his nostrils, the deliberate breath he takes before looking away.

"Okay? That's it?"

He turns to face the window, hands braced on the counter's edge, fingers splayed wide like he's trying to ground himself.

"What do you want me to say?" His voice has an edge now, carefully modulated but sharp underneath. "You made a decision. I'm respecting it."

"You're pissed."

A harsh exhale. His head drops forward slightly, tendons standing out in his neck from the effort of restraint. When he turns back to me, his expression is schooled, but his eyes burn with something raw.

"I'm disappointed. There's a difference."

"No, you're pissed that I'm not playing along." I step closer, driven by some need to provoke, to crack that careful control. "That I'm not being your perfect accessory—"

"That's not fair." The words come out low, dangerous. His hands grip the counter behind him hard enough to whiten his knuckles, like he's physically holding himself in place.

"None of this is fair." The words explode out of me. "You drugged me. You took away my choice, my agency, my ability to know my own mind. And now you're disappointed that I don't want to go to your business dinner?"

"I just thought—"

"What? That we could pretend? That I'd smile and play the supportive partner while inside I'm dying from not knowing what's real?"

He turns with deliberate calm. "You're right. I apologize. The dinner was a bad idea."

"Stop doing that."

"Doing what?"

"Being so fucking reasonable. So controlled." I'm shaking now, weeks of suppressed rage bubbling up. "Get angry. Yell.

Show me something real instead of this careful, calculated performance."

"You want real?" His control fractures—just a crack, but it's there. "Fine. I'm furious. At myself, at the situation, at my own stupidity. I had you. I had everything I wanted. And I destroyed it because I couldn't trust it to happen naturally." He takes a step closer. "Is that real enough for you?"

"Keep going."

"I wake up every morning terrified you'll be gone. That you'll walk out and I'll never see you again. I sit in business meetings thinking about you. Come home hoping you'll be here. I'm a fucking mess, but I'm trying to hold it together because falling apart doesn't help either of us."

"Maybe it would help me. Maybe I need to see you break a little instead of watching you control everything, including your own emotional devastation."

"You want me to break?" A bitter laugh. "I've been breaking since the day you found out. Every day, watching you pull further away. Every night, sleeping next to you, feeling like you're on another planet. I'm breaking. I'm just doing it quietly because I don't know how else to do it."

"Show me." I move closer, invading his space. "Stop controlling it. Stop managing everything. Just... react."

"If I do that—if I stop controlling it—" His voice drops dangerously. "You won't like what happens."

"Try me."

"Clara—"

"What? Are you afraid you'll command me? That your dominance will slip out?" I'm pushing deliberately now, my heart hammering as I stand across from him in the quiet kitchen, the morning light slanting through the window like a fragile truce we both know is fraying at the edges.

We've been in this uneasy peace for days now, his commands silenced as I process the betrayal: the way he shaped my haze, not to trap me, but to guide me toward him, blurring lines until surrender felt like a choice. But I need more—need to see if this truce is real, or just another layer of his control.

"Go ahead. Order me around. Tell me what to do. Show me who you really are when you're not performing."

Julian's eyes narrow, the storm-gray darkening to something sharper, more primal, as his hands flex at his sides. For a heartbeat, he's still—too still, like the gathering hush before thunder— and it cracks open, the fracture I've been waiting for, the one that peels back the careful restraint he's worn these past days.

"Stop."

The word is low, a warning rumble that vibrates through the space between us, but I don't. Can't.

"Why? Does it bother you? Having me challenge you? Does it make you want to put me in my place?"

I lean in closer, pulse racing with the thrill of it, fear coiling low in my belly even as a treacherous heat stirs—needing this glimpse beyond the careful man who's given me room to breathe, to question, to almost forgive the haze he'd woven around me.

Beneath his restraint, a storm rages: every cell in him screaming to shatter the distance, to bend me over this counter and reclaim what's his with the bite of his belt, the unrelenting thrust until I gasp "Mr. Blackwell" like a prayer, tears streaking my face as I yield.

He wants to punish this defiance, to mark me with welts that throb for days, fucking me until the betrayal fades and I'm his again—body and soul—because that's the fire that defines us, the obsession that turns his love savage.

"You're playing with fire." His voice is gravel over silk, rough- ened by the effort of holding back, and the fracture widens—the way his fingers curl as if imagining the leather of his belt between them, the controlled fury flickering in his eyes like lightning forking the sky.

But he doesn't move, doesn't close the gap, his body rigid as a bowstring drawn tight, every muscle coiled with the overwhelming urge to dominate, to punish me for daring to test him.

"Good."

"You don't understand—"

"Then make me understand." I step closer, my voice steady despite the tremor in my chest, the tension crackling between us —the way his breath hitches, his hands flexing harder, knuckles white as bone. "Stop hiding behind careful words and controlled expressions. Be honest for once, without filtering it through what you think I need to hear."

My words land like a spark on tinder, and he breaks—not shatters, not unleashes, but breaks, his control splintering in the quiet kitchen like glass under pressure. His eyes blaze, dark and unyielding, the obsession surging to the surface in the raw clench of his jaw, the way his chest rises and falls too fast, every cell in him screaming for it.

"Fine." His voice drops to that register I know too well—the one that used to make me wet instantly. "You want honesty? Here it is. Every cell in my body is screaming to bend you over this counter. To remind you exactly who you belong to. To fuck you until you remember what we are to each other."

Heat floods through me—immediate, undeniable. My body responding exactly as it always has.

The heat of him is dizzying, my own pulse thundering in echo of his—fear flickering at the edge of what he could do, but trust blooming deeper, warmer, in the way he stops himself.

That restraint is a gift more profound than any command.

"Julian." The name is soft on my lips, not a provocation this time, but an anchor, my hand lifting tentatively to brush his cheek, feeling the tremor there like it's mine to soothe.

He exhales sharply, the sound ragged as his eyes close for a beat, his forehead dropping to rest against mine, the cage of his arms softening just enough to hold without trapping. His voice, when it comes, is rough but steady, the fracture mending in real time.

"I want to—God, I want to punish you for pushing like this, to mark you until you call me Mr. Blackwell and yield like you were made to. But not like this."

His thumb grazes my jaw, a touch that's almost tender now, the storm ebbing into something quieter, more vulnerable—the man behind the obsession surfacing, raw and real.

"You've seen what I did with the haze, the control I took. I won't cross that line again—not until you ask for it, clear and willing. Even if it kills me to hold back."

The words settle between us, heavy with the weight of his restraint, and I feel it then—the shift, the way his breaking isn't destruction but proof, his obsession a fire he banks for me.

"I believe you." I lean into him just enough to feel his heartbeat steady against my chest, the truce holding, fragile but unbroken.

"There it is." He watches my pupils dilate. "Your body knows. Even if your mind won't admit it. You want this. Want me. Still."

"That's the conditioning—"

"Is it?" He takes another step closer. "Tell me, when you saw me yesterday in my study, heard me commanding others—did you get wet?"

My silence is answer enough.

"I could smell it. Could see it in how you moved. Your body responding to my dominance even when it wasn't directed at you." Another step. "That's not conditioning. That's attraction."

"You don't know that."

"Don't I?" He's close enough now that I feel his heat. "Your pulse is racing. Breathing's shallow. Nipples hard under that shirt." His eyes travel over me with clinical precision. "Every physical indicator says you want me. Right now. Despite everything."

"Physical response doesn't mean—"

"Doesn't mean what? That you want it? Or that you need it?" He doesn't touch me, but might as well. His presence alone overwhelms. "You said you wanted to know if your responses are real or programmed. Here's a test: Tell me to stop. Tell me to back off. If you can say it and mean it, I will."

I open my mouth. No words come.

"Can't do it, can you?" His voice softens slightly. "Because some part of you—maybe the part the drugs revealed, maybe the part that was always there—needs this. Needs me to dominate. Needs the structure of power and control."

"I hate you."

"You hate that I'm right." He does touch me then—one finger under my chin, tilting my face up. "You hate that your body knows what your mind won't accept. That we could be good again if you'd stop fighting it."

I slap his hand away.

"There she is." A sharp, knowing smile. "There's the fire. The fight. That's real. More real than the careful politeness we've been dancing around."

"You're an asshole."

"I'm honest. You asked for honest."

"I asked you to break, not dominate me."

"For me, they're the same thing." He steps back, giving me space. "My control is how I hold myself together."

I'm shaking. From anger, from arousal, from confusion. "This is exactly why I can't trust anything. Because you're right—my body responds. But I don't know if it's real or if you trained me like Pavlov's fucking dog."

"Then test it. Without me."

"What?"

"Touch yourself. Tonight, alone in your room. See if the arousal is about me specifically or about submission in general. If you get off thinking about being dominated, period, then maybe it's just who you are. If you can only get off thinking about me dominating you—" He shrugs. "Then we know you still want me."

The suggestion is clinical. And somehow more intimate than anything we've done.

"You want me to masturbate as an experiment."

"I want you to have information. Knowledge is power. Find out if this pull you feel is about submission itself or about submission specifically to me."

I stare at him. "You're serious."

"Completely."

"And if I can get off thinking about other men?"

"Then you're free. Your submission exists independent of me." His voice remains steady, but something flickers in his eyes. "And maybe you can find someone who didn't poison it from the start."

"And if I can't?"

"Then we have different information to work with."

I should be furious at the suggestion. Instead, I'm considering it. Because he's right—it would provide data. Clarity.

"I can't do this. I can't be here with you." I grab my jacket and leave. Outside, the cold air hits my face like a wake-up call. My pulse is still racing, thighs still slick. My body is humming with frustrated arousal.

Damn him. Damn him for being right.

I spend my day as far from the house as possible doing honest, hard labor. By the time I return at dusk, I'm calmer. More centered.

Julian's gone—at his dinner with investors—leaving me to fend for myself.

I make chicken. Nothing fancy.

After dinner, I stand under the shower for a long time, letting the hot water work through tired muscles.

When I emerge, wrapped in a towel, I catch my reflection. Flushed cheeks. Hard nipples. The evidence of arousal I can't shake.

Julian's words echo: *Test it. Without me.*

I close the blinds. Lie down on the bed, one hand trailing down my body.

Not about him. Think about something else. Someone else.

I try to conjure a generic fantasy. Anonymous dominant. Could be anyone. Commanding voice, firm hands. The scenario plays in my mind—being told to kneel, to submit, to yield.

My hand slides lower. I'm wet—have been since this morning's confrontation. I circle my clit, building the sensation.

Any dom. Not Julian. Just someone in control.

But as arousal builds, the fantasy solidifies. Dark hair. Storm-gray eyes. That particular timbre of voice that makes my spine straighten automatically.

No. Stop. Think of someone else.

I try. I try so hard. But every fantasy path leads back to him. His hands on my wrists. His cock in my mouth. His voice commanding my pleasure.

I come hard, back arching, his name on my lips.

Afterward, I lie there staring at the ceiling, tears sliding down my temples.

Because I have my answer.

It's him.

Specifically him. The drugs might have accelerated it, but they imprinted me on Julian Blackwell so completely that I can't separate submission from him.

I'm his.

Even when I don't want to be.

Even when I can't trust it.

I curl on my side, pulling my knees to my chest, and cry.

CHAPTER 57
DAY 132

Breakfast is a performance. A high-stakes piece of theater titled Everything is Normal.

We sit across from each other at the sun-drenched table—coffee steaming, toast cooling, and the Wall Street Journal spread out as a shield between us. The sunlight streams through the bay windows, illuminating the dust motes and painting everything in a false, aggressive cheerfulness that makes my head ache. We are suffocating in the light.

"Sleep okay?" He doesn't look up from the markets section. His voice is level, polite. The voice of a stranger.

"Fine."

It's a lie. A flat, brittle lie. I spent half the night staring at the ceiling, reliving the humiliating revelation from yesterday—that my body is so wired to his touch, so conditioned by the last four months, that I can only find release by thinking of him. By thinking of the things he did to me that I'm supposed to hate.

"Good." He turns a page with a sharp snap. He doesn't ask

follow-up questions. We've learned this dance—stay on the surface. Don't dig. If you dig, you hit the landmines.

I butter my toast. The knife scrapes loudly against the crust, the sound violent in the hush. Scout whines from his bed by the back door, his ears flattened. He senses the tension radiating off us, the static charge of two storms colliding but refusing to rain.

Julian's hand reaches for the silver coffee pot. Mine does too.

We freeze.

Our fingers are inches apart. The air between us instantly charges, snapping tight with that old, terrifying electricity. It's still there. Undeniable. Magnetic. Even now, with a canyon of lies and hurt between us, my skin reaches for his.

He withdraws his hand first, pulling back as if he's touched a hot stove. "Sorry."

"It's fine."

Neither of us moves. The coffee pot sits between us, a demilitarized zone.

"You should—"

"No, you—"

We stop, cutting ourselves off. This is exhausting. The politeness is more draining than the screaming matches ever were.

"I have calls this morning." He finally stands, abandoning the coffee. He takes his plate to the sink, rinsing it with the same sharp, efficient precision he applies to everything—fences, stocks, me. "I'll be in my study."

"Okay."

He pauses at the door, his hand gripping the frame. I see the muscles in his back tense. He wants to say something. Maybe about last night. Maybe about the elephant crushing the air out of the room. But he just nods once, a sharp jerk of his chin, and leaves.

I sit at the table alone until the coffee goes cold, a bitter film forming on the surface.

Every moment like this—these careful, weighted interactions—reminds me that we're broken. That whatever we were before the truth came out is gone, replaced by this awkward choreography of avoidance.

The dissonance is becoming unbearable.

My body is a traitor. It still responds to him. This morning, when his hand brushed near mine, my pulse jumped a frantic stutter-step. When he walked past me and his scent—cedar, smoke, and expensive soap—drifted across the table, I got wet.

It's a physiological betrayal. Reactions I can't control, can't trust, can't separate from what the drugs did to my neurochemistry. But the terrifying part isn't the drugs. It's the target. It's him specifically. Only him. Forever him.

The thought makes me want to scream.

I spend the day riding, pushing Meteor hard toward the ridge line. I want the wind to scour me clean. I want the burn in my thighs and the ache in my arms to drown out the noise in my head. But even the gallop can't settle me. I'm restless, anxious, trapped in my own skin.

When I return that evening, the house smells of garlic and curing meat. Julian is making dinner.

I wash up and join him. We cook side by side—him at the stove, me chopping parsley at the island. We move around each other like dancers who have forgotten why they learned the steps. We pass ingredients without looking. We coordinate timing without speaking. It's a muscle memory of domesticity that feels hollowed out.

"How was your day?" He stirs the pasta water, his back to me.

"Fine. Yours?"

"Productive."

That's it. That's all we have now. Fine and Productive.

Dinner is silent except for the scrape of forks against porcelain. He's made my favorite—carbonara, perfectly executed, rich and creamy. The care he takes with everything, even now, even broken, makes my chest ache with a dull, throbbing pressure.

"It's good," I say. An offering. A white flag.

"Thank you."

That night, I lie in bed staring at the dark ceiling. Down the hall, behind the closed door of the master bath, the shower runs.

It runs for a long time. Then stops. Silence.

The image intrudes, unbidden and sharp: Is he touching himself? Is he leaning against the tile, eyes closed, thinking of me? Thinking of the Red Room?

Stop. Don't think about that.

But I can't stop. Because despite everything—the manipulation, the lack of consent, the violation—some broken, wired part of me still wants him.

I shift in the cold sheets, my body aching with a phantom hollowness. I don't just want the sex. I crave the weight of him. I crave the dominance. I crave the obliteration of my own will, the silence that comes when he takes control and I just have to be.

I squeeze my eyes shut, digging my nails into my palms. I fought so hard for my freedom. I fought to get away from his control.

And I hate myself because, in the dark, I would give anything to kneel again.

CHAPTER 58
DAY 136

"CAN WE TALK?" JULIAN EMERGES FROM HIS STUDY. IT'S LATE. PAST TEN. I've been reading—actually reading this time, some mystery novel that doesn't require emotional investment.

"About what?"

"Everything. Nothing. I don't know." He runs a hand through his hair—a rare gesture of agitation. "I feel like we're sleep-walking through this. Moving around each other, saying nothing that matters. And I can't—I need to try to explain."

He's holding something—a leather notebook, fingers tight around it like it might escape.

"Explain what? How you justified violating my consent?"

"No. That's indefensible." He moves into the room, doesn't sit. "I want to explain why. Not to excuse it, but so you understand what was driving me."

"I've read your notebooks. I understand obsession just fine."

"Not all of them." He looks down at the journal in his hands. "This is the final one. From the day I arrived at your ranch with the ultimatum through... now. Every thought, every justification, every moment of doubt. How excited I was when the drugs worked. How that excitement turned to something else. How I realized I wanted what you felt to be real, not manufactured."

"Why would I want to read that?"

"Because it shows the erosion. Of my certainty. Of my control. Of everything I thought I knew about us." His thumb traces the leather spine.

"Julian—"

"I wrote about wanting to die when I saw your face that day. When you realized what I'd done." His voice cracks slightly. "I wrote about these last days of careful distance. About sharing your childhood bed and not being able to touch you. About how giving you space might be killing us both, but I don't know what else to do."

The notebook trembles slightly in his grip.

"It wasn't just obsession." His voice is raw. "It was fear. I wanted you for seventeen years. Planned, waited, built everything toward the moment I could have you. And when you were finally in my house, in my space—I panicked."

"Panicked how?"

"I saw you building walls. Saw the fear in your eyes, the resistance in your body language. Every day, I kept thinking, 'She's going to leave. She's going to walk out before she even gives us a chance.'" He starts pacing. "So I... accelerated things. Lowered your inhibitions so you'd explore what I knew was there."

"You took my choice."

"I know. God, I know. But in my twisted logic, I was giving you freedom. Freedom from your father's voice in your head, from society's expectations, from your own fear. I thought if I could get past your defenses, you'd see what we could be."

I set down my book. "And it worked. That's the fucked up

part. I did explore, I did surrender, and I became everything you wanted. But it was built on violation."

"Yes."

"So what do you want me to say? That I forgive you? That I understand?" I shake my head. "I can't. Every time I start to soften, I remember what you did. How you stole my agency to feed your obsession."

"I don't want forgiveness." He stops pacing and faces me directly. "I want you to know that I see it. See what I did, what it cost. I thought I was being clever, strategic. Really, I was just a coward who couldn't risk rejection. If I could go back—" He moves closer, not crowding but present. "If I could make one different choice, I wouldn't have given you that first dose. Because at least then, if you stayed, I'd know it was real."

The words land heavily between us. Honest, raw, too late.

"But you can't go back." A whisper. "Neither can I. So what do we do now?"

"Keep trying? Keep failing? Keep hoping something shifts?"

"That's not a plan."

"No."

Despite myself, I almost smile. "At least you're honest about it."

"I want you to read this." He moves to the couch and sits on the opposite end from my chair, the notebook in his lap. "And then I want to talk about it, if you're willing. You can ask me anything. About the notebooks, the drugs, my obsession. Complete honesty, no filters. Maybe if you understand fully, you'll be able to... I don't know. Process it."

I should refuse. Should tell him to leave, that his explanations don't matter. But curiosity wins.

"When did you decide? To use the drugs?"

"Three months before I bought your father's debt. I'd been

researching protocols, working with the chemist. But the decision to actually do it—that came when I saw you at your father's funeral."

The memory surfaces—standing by the grave, numb with grief. "You were there."

"In the back, yes. You didn't see me. But I saw you. Saw you completely alone, carrying everything. Your father's business partner was there, and he cornered you after and tried to buy the ranch for pennies. You said no, walked away with your head high, but I saw your hands shaking."

I remember that. The predatory offer, my desperate refusal.

"I wanted to intervene," Julian continues. "To chase him off, to offer you genuine help. But I knew you'd refuse. Knew your father had probably warned you about me on his deathbed. So I decided —if I couldn't help you as an equal, I'd engineer a situation where you had no choice but to accept my help."

"And the drugs made that help more palatable."

"In my mind, yes. In reality, I was eliminating your ability to reject me." He leans forward, elbows on knees. "I told myself it was strategic. That I was being smart, using every tool available. Really, I was just terrified of hearing you say no."

"Have you ever heard no? In your life? Or do you just acquire whatever you want?"

"Plenty of people say no to me in business. I'm used to negoti-ation, to pushback." His voice drops. "But from you? No. I've never heard you say no and mean it. Even in high school, when you laughed off my homecoming invitation—that wasn't no. That was 'I want to, but I can't.' I saw it in your eyes."

"Arrogant assumption."

"Accurate observation. I've been reading your body language for years. I know the difference between true rejection and forced refusal."

The certainty in his voice should anger me. Instead, it just makes me tired.

"So you thought you'd... what? Drug me into admitting what I secretly wanted?"

"Essentially, yes. And it worked. That's the worst part. It worked exactly as I planned. You explored, you submitted, you became everything I dreamed about, but the foundation was poisoned, so none of it counts."

We sit in heavy silence. His confession hanging between us, honest and horrible.

"I'm not going to forgive you."

"I know."

"And I don't know if I'll ever trust this. Us. What we had."

"I know that too."

"So why tell me? Why explain? What's the point?"

He looks at me then, and his eyes are devastated. "Because I love you. And even if that love is twisted and wrong and built on violation—it's real. And you deserve to know the depths of it. Even if it only convinces you that you're right to leave me."

The honesty cracks something in me. "Damn you, Julian."

"I know."

"Damn you for making me want to understand. For making me—" I stop, biting back words.

"Making you what?"

"Want you still. Despite everything. I want you so badly it hurts."

He goes very still. "Clara—"

I stand abruptly. "Don't. I shouldn't have said that."

But he's standing too, closing the distance between us. "Why not? If we're being honest—"

"Because it doesn't change anything. I can't want you and not trust you. Can't crave your dominance and hate what you did. Those things can't coexist, and it's destroying me."

"Then let it destroy us both." His hand cups my face—first touch in days that's not accidental. "I'd rather burn with you than exist in this hell."

I should pull away. Should maintain the boundaries we've been so careful about. Instead, I lean into his palm, craving the contact despite myself.

"This is a bad idea." The words are barely audible.

"Probably."

But we're already moving together, drawn by a gravity neither of us can fight. His mouth finds mine—desperate, claiming, tasting like grief and need. I kiss back just as desperately, fisting his shirt, pulling him closer.

We don't make it to a bedroom. Right there in the living room, we destroy each other again.

He lifts me, shoving my skirt up. No gentleness, no careful consideration—just raw, desperate need. I wrap my legs around him, pulling him closer, biting his lip hard enough to hurt.

"Clara—" His voice is wrecked.

"Don't talk. Just—" I pull him into another kiss before he can respond.

His hands are everywhere—rough, desperate, relearning my body. When he enters me, it's not gentle. Not loving. Just raw need, both of us trying to feel something real through the numbness.

I come fast, crying out against his shoulder. He follows seconds later, groaning my name like a prayer or a curse.

Afterward, we stay tangled together, breathing hard. His forehead rests against mine, hands gentling on my hips.

"That was—"

"Don't." I cut him off. "Don't analyze it. Don't make it mean something."

"Clara, we just—"

"I know what we just did." I push him back. My legs shake as I stand. "And it doesn't change anything. My body still wants you. That's not news. But it doesn't fix what's broken."

His face falls. "I know."

"So let's just... not. Not talk about it, not assign meaning to it. It was just—" I smooth my skirt, avoiding his eyes. "A release. That's all."

"If that's what you need to believe."

"It's what I need to survive this." I head for the door. "Goodnight, Julian."

He doesn't correct me on the name. Just watches me leave, still disheveled from what we did, looking lost.

I make it to my bedroom, close the door, and wait for him to enforce the rule. To knock, to insist I sleep in the bed with him, like the contract demands.

He doesn't come.

For the first time since our agreement, he's letting me sleep alone. The freedom should feel like victory. Instead, it feels like another kind of loss.

That's when the tears come. Not sad tears—frustrated, angry ones. Because the sex was good. Perfect, even. Physically, we still fit like we were made for each other.

But emotionally?

Emotionally, it just proved how completely fucked we are.

My body will always respond to him. Will always crave his dominance, his control, his possession. But my mind can't trust it. Can't separate genuine desire from chemical conditioning.

So we're trapped in this hell—wanting each other, having each other, and feeling more alone afterward than before.

CHAPTER 59
DAY 137

I WAKE TO SUNLIGHT SLICING THROUGH THE BLINDS, THE KIND OF COLD, merciless light that doesn't let you hide. My head feels heavy. My chest hollow.

The bed is mine again.

Empty.

Last night crashes back—the desperate sex, the hollow aftermath, the way Julian touched me like he was trying to erase a sin neither of us could name.

The hollow quiet after, when he left me without enforcing our sleeping arrangements.

I dress without thinking—one of his shirts, my hands shaking as I button it—and pad barefoot down the hall.

In the kitchen, centered on the counter like an offering or a confession, sits the leather notebook.

No note. Just the journal, waiting.

My heart pounds as I pick it up.

His scent lingers in the worn spine—cedar, smoke, control. I open it, and his handwriting stares back at me, clean and deliberate.

My heart stutters, palms slick as I turn the first page.

Julian's Private Journal

The letter has been sent. Seven days until I see her again. Seventeen years of preparation distilled into one week of her desperation. The ranch is mine—every acre, every debt, every blade of dead grass. But that's just paper. What I want is Clara on her knees, calling me Mr. Blackwell like she should have at seventeen.

Nathan thinks I'm obsessed. He's right. I've built an empire to bring one woman to heel.

The lines blur on the second read, meaning clawing its way through the fog. My throat closes.

Seventeen years. He planned this—every move, every manipulation, every step that led me to the moment I stood on my porch with his letter in my shaking hand.

Every word slices deeper. He wanted me on my knees. He built an empire for this—for me. My stomach twists. I press my palm against it, willing back the nausea.

Not for love. For ownership.

And yet, even now, my pulse doesn't slow. It races. Because part of me already knows—he was never lying about the obsession. Only about what it cost him.

I keep reading even when I want to throw the journal across the room. Even when tears sting, and my hands tremble so badly the pages shake.

Day 0 — The Proposition

She's more beautiful in her rage than my memory allowed. Standing on that porch, fighting tears, hands shaking as she held my letter. I gave her the terms: one year of complete submission or lose everything.

The dress arrived—red, like blood, like surrender. She'll wear it to the gala. She'll sign the contract. She has no choice, and we both know it.

The champagne is already prepared with the first dose. Nathan says 0.5mg is conservative, but I want her to be aware for our first time. Want her to remember choosing this, even if the choice is an illusion.

The breath leaves my lungs in a strangled sound. I reread it, then again, tracing the words with my fingertip as though they'll change if I touch them enough times.

They don't. The page blurs. The champagne...

My stomach twists violently. That night—the warmth spreading through me, the strange calm, the way I couldn't stop responding to him.

He drugged me.

On purpose.

My hands shake so hard the journal slips, pages fluttering like wings before I clutch it back to my chest.

He planned every word, every touch, every lie.

And yet... the idea that he wanted me aware, wanted me to remember choosing—it's so twistedly Julian it hurts.

Day 1 — The Contract

She signed it. My hand over hers, guiding the pen, her body trembling against mine. The champagne worked perfectly—just enough to soften her edges, make her pliant. She called me Mr. Blackwell. Came apart under my hands like she was designed for it. This morning, she looked at me with such confused hunger. The drugs are working, binding her to me chemically while her mind still fights. Perfect.

His breath on my neck. His hand guiding mine across the page. His voice telling me to trust him.

A sob tears from my throat before I can stop it.

He described my violation like an experiment.

But beneath it—God help me—there's reverence too. He wanted me pliant, yes, but also fighting. He loved that my mind still rebelled. Loved my defiance even as he drugged it away.

The way he looked at me. Not like a possession. Like a man terrified he'd break the very thing he wanted to keep.

Day 5

The orange juice delivery system is flawless. She drinks it every morning, grimacing at the taste but obeying. 0.75mg now. Her responses are intensifying—pupils dilating when I enter a room, breath catching when I command her. She's started anticipating my needs without being told. Years of research are paying off. Nathan wants more data, but all I care about is the way she kneeled yesterday without being asked.

A SOB CATCHES IN MY THROAT.

The orange juice.

Every single morning.

He watched me obey—watched me trust him.

And still, I can't stop the way my body remembers those mornings: the steady calm that followed, the quiet satisfaction when he'd touch my jaw and whisper *Good girl.*

Was that real? Or just chemistry?

Day 15

She begged for the cane last night. Actually begged. "Please mark me, Mr. Blackwell. I need to wear your bruises." The drugs make her suggestible, but the desire has to exist first. I'm simply removing her inhibitions, her father's voice, and seventeen years of denial. She's becoming what she was always meant to be: mine.

MY EYES BLUR WITH TEARS.

That night—the trembling, the tears, the ache that turned to heat. I thought I was reclaiming power. Thought I was choosing.

But I wasn't.

Not completely.

And yet his words... *the desire has to exist first.*

He believed in me. Even in his manipulation, he saw something true beneath it.

Day 30

A month. She crawled to me this morning, asking how she could serve me. The transformation is complete—or seems to be. But something sits wrong in my chest. When she looks at me with those dilated pupils, is it Clara or the chemicals? Nathan says it doesn't matter, but it does. I want HER submission, not drugged responses.

FOR THE FIRST TIME, I PAUSE. MY ANGER WAVERS. HE KNEW. HE HATED himself for it. My fingers hover over the ink, smudging the word *HER*.

He doubted himself. He questioned everything.

It's the first hint of the man I've seen since—the one who stopped dosing me. The one who looked at me like I was something sacred, not conquered.

DAY 45

I watch her in the garden, humming while she tends her mother's vegetables. Happy. She seems genuinely happy. But is it real contentment or pharmaceutical harmony? The question haunts me. I've achieved everything I planned, but victory tastes like ash when I wonder if the woman in my bed is Clara or my chemical creation.

MY CHEST TIGHTENS.

He saw me. Even then.

Not a puppet. Not a possession.

Just... me.

And it broke him.

***

DAY 60

Two months. She told me she loves me last night. Unprompted. The words I've waited seventeen years to hear, and I can't trust them. How much is the drug? How much is real? I'm lowering her dose without telling Nathan. Need to see what remains when the chemicals fade.

***

I CLOSE MY EYES.

I said it. I meant it.

He didn't trust my love because he couldn't trust himself.

***

DAY 90

Three months. She's radiant—submission has made her glow. But I've been watching carefully as I've slowly reduced the doses. Her personality, her fire, it still breaks through. She still challenges me, still has that sharp tongue when pushed. The drugs enhance, but they don't create. What we have is real. It has to be.

***

MY THROAT CLOSES AROUND A SOB.

He didn't stop because he was caught—he stopped because he couldn't bear the possibility that what we had wasn't real.

***

DAY 117

Made the decision. Stopping the morning doses. Told her I was listening to her. The relief on her face gutted me. She trusts me while I've been drugging her. Nathan thinks I'm insane, but I need to know—what survives without the drugs? If she stays submissive, stays mine, then what we built is real.

I can't breathe.

The morning he stopped. That day—the taste of plain juice, the way I smiled at him, thinking he was kind.

He stopped because he needed to know if I was still his when he didn't control me.

And I was.

God help me, I still was.

Day 120

Three days weaning off the drug. She's irritable, restless. Classic withdrawal. But she still kneels when told. Still calls me Mr. Blackwell. Still comes only with permission. The conditioning holds. Nathan's wrong—this isn't just chemical dependency. This is us.

I slam the book shut, press it against my chest, breathing hard, shaking my head because it shouldn't matter—it can't matter—but somehow it does.

Because even now, even knowing everything, my body remembers the peace of his voice, the safety of his touch. My heart rebels against logic.

I hate that a part of me believes it. That my body still aches for him even while my heart burns with betrayal.

I press the back of my hand to my mouth and force myself to keep going.

DAY 124

She heard everything. The phone call with Nathan. The complete betrayal on her face—I'll carry that image forever. She knows about the drugs, the club, all of it. But she didn't run. Stayed for the contract, for her ranch. Even through her rage, she obeyed when I commanded her to the Red Room. I told her I love her. She didn't believe me.

MY VISION SHATTERS WITH TEARS. EACH ENTRY CUTS DEEPER, HIS VOICE unraveling from arrogant precision into something fractured, human, afraid.

He's wrong. I did believe him. I just couldn't survive believing him then.

The pages start to shake as I turn them.

DAY 127

Last dose. She asked for space. I gave it to her—no commands, no expectations, just coexistence. I've destroyed us trying to create us.

I clutch the journal to my chest, choking on the sound that escapes.

Destroyed us trying to create us.

Yes. That's exactly what he did.

And what I let him do.

Day 128

First day completely clean. She spent it at her ranch. I moved into her childhood home—manipulated the situation to stay close while pretending to give space. Her bed is comically small. We lay there rigid, pretending we don't want to touch. This is torture, but at least I'm with her.

My pulse races. That night. The silence between us, heavy and fragile, filled with everything we didn't say. He called it torture. I called it mercy.

Maybe it was both.

Day 130

She's reading my journals. All of them. Seventeen years of obsession laid bare. She could run screaming. Instead, she pressed against me in that tiny bed and said she misses what we had. Not forgiveness, but not condemnation either. We're in purgatory, but at least we're here together.

EVEN THEN, HE WAS WAITING FOR ME TO DECIDE WHETHER TO SAVE US OR burn it all down.

DAY 131

She knows everything now. Every manipulative thought, every obsessive plan, every desperate attempt to own her completely. And she's still here. Still fighting her need for my dominance. Still calling me Julian instead of Mr. Blackwell, which hurts more than her anger. The drugs are gone, but the hunger remains—hers and mine. We're either going to rebuild from this, honestly, or destroy each other completely. Either way, I regret nothing except hurting her. She was always meant to be mine. Now I just have to prove I'm worthy of being hers.

HIS HANDWRITING IS DARKER, PRESSED HARDER INTO THE PAPER, LIKE THE words cost him to write them.

The last sentence blurs before my eyes, the words swimming as the tears finally spill over—hot, uncontrollable, splattering the ink until it runs like blood across the page. My chest aches with something too big for breath, too raw for language.

He was never going to stop until he had me—every part, every secret, every fractured edge—and yet somewhere along the way, he broke himself open too.

Between the lines of dominance and obsession, there it is: the moment the control stopped being about power and started being about need. He realized what it cost. Realized that love built on control is only real if both surrender to it.

Together.

I close the notebook with shaking hands, pressing it to my

chest as if it might still be warm from his touch. The silence in the room feels alive, vibrating with everything we've done to each other.

He ruined me.

Saved me.

Loved me in a way that scorched me from the inside out and left something unrecognizable in its place.

But the truth is inescapable. Every nerve he rewired still hums with his name, every heartbeat a betrayal of the fury I thought I still had. And underneath it all, the truth pulses through me like a second heartbeat—terrifying, inevitable, absolute.

Neither of us can survive without the other. Not because of the drugs. Not because of the contract. Because our wounds recognize each other.

Our damage fits.

It's sick and beautiful and wrong, and it's the only thing that feels real. I want to hate him. I want to undo it. But all I can do is clutch the ruined journal to my chest.

"Please... let there still be something left to save." The words escape into the quiet. Because if there isn't, I'll drown in the pieces of what we were—and what, God help me, I still want us to be.

For a long time, I just sit there, shaking, tears running unchecked down my face. He destroyed me. Manipulated me. Took my choices and turned them into his masterpiece of control.

And yet... every entry bleeds with longing. With guilt. With love.

The same love that's been carving me open since the day he walked back into my life.

I understand him now in a way I didn't want to—how he needs control the way I need to breathe, how he confuses possession with protection. And how, even knowing that, I can't stop wanting him.

We're both broken in complementary ways.

He destroys to keep. I surrender to survive.

And somewhere between those extremes, we've built something that looks like love.

Not pure. Not perfect. But real.

I wipe my cheeks and close the notebook gently.

"I'm still here." The words drift into the silence.

Because, for better or worse, neither of us knows how to live without the other.

And maybe—just maybe—that's where our redemption begins.

The notebook slips from my shaking hands, falling open on the floor with a muted thud. Pages fan out, fluttering like dying wings, and something white slips free—a folded envelope, thick cream stock, my name written across the front in his sharp, deliberate handwriting.

Clara...

CHAPTER 60
DAY 138

THE SIGHT OF THE LETTER STILLS ME. FOR A MOMENT, I JUST STARE, MY pulse roaring in my ears. Then I sink to my knees, reaching for the letter as if it might vanish if I hesitate. The paper is warm from where it was pressed between the pages, faintly smelling of him—cedar, ink, and something darker.

My thumb trembles as I break the seal.

Inside, his handwriting cuts across the page in clean, even strokes that still somehow shake.

Clara,

I'm poisoning you.

Not with chemicals. By existing in your space. Being a constant reminder of how I took your choice and called it love.

Every breath we share feels like a lie I keep forcing you to live inside. I told myself I was protecting you, saving you, loving you the only way I knew how—but the truth is, I've been undoing you piece by piece.

Watching you fade into someone quieter, smaller, more careful. That isn't who I fell in love with.

Maybe the only loving thing left is to let you go.

So I am.

The contract is void. The ranch is yours—your name, your deed, your freedom. I've already filed the transfer. No lawyers. No conditions.

I won't come back unless you want me to. This is surrender.

Because the man who swore he'd never bow to anyone found the one person who brought him to his knees—and in that surrender, I finally understand love.

You once told me that control was my religion. Maybe this is my blasphemy.

I love you. I will love you until my last breath, but I can't keep watching you wither in a cage I built with my own hands.

Be free. Be whole. Be yours.

—Julian

THE LETTER TREMBLES IN MY HANDS. EACH LINE FEELS LIKE A BLADE carving through the remnants of anger I thought I still had, leaving only a gaping, bleeding wound. Him writing this—alone, in the dead of night, controlled even in his grief, his heart bleeding out in neat, disciplined script.

He's really gone.

I press the paper to my chest, crushing the expensive stationery against my skin, a broken sound escaping before I can stop it. The room tilts. The air feels thick, viscous, impossible to breathe. My pulse pounds in my throat as if my body refuses to accept what my mind already knows.

He hasn't just gone to the office. He has removed himself from the equation.

No contract. No rules. No him.

I look around the study. The walls that once felt like a cage now feel like a void. The open door doesn't look like an exit; it looks like a mouth screaming into nothingness. Every breath tastes like loss. His scent lingers everywhere—in the leather chair, in the curtains, in the ghost of his touch still imprinted on my skin.

He said he couldn't keep watching me fade. He said he was poisoning me.

But only now, without him, does the crushing truth hit me: I haven't just disappeared into him. I was anchored by him.

"No," I whisper, the word scraping my throat.

I sink fully to the floor, the letter crushed in my fist, my tears dripping onto the ink until his name blurs into a dark smudge. I curl into a ball on the Persian rug, right where his feet would be if he were sitting in his chair.

"Julian..."

It's barely a whisper, more breath than sound. A prayer to a god who has abandoned his temple.

"Don't let this be how we end."

But the room stays silent. The house offers no comfort. There is no heavy footstep coming to check on me. No strong arms to lift me up. No voice to tell me to breathe.

Only the echo of my heartbeat answers—hollow, uneven, breaking apart inside the space he's left behind.

I am free. And I have never felt more trapped.

CHAPTER 61
DAY 138 — HOURS AFTER THE LETTER

THE FLOOR IS COLD AGAINST MY CHEEK. I'VE BEEN HERE SO LONG MY tears have dried, the letter crumpled in my fist. The ranch house echoes with his absence—every corner, every shadow shaped by memories of him here, invading my space while pretending to give me distance.

Be free. Be whole. Be yours.

But who am I without him? The drugs are gone, have been for days, and still I ache for his control. Still, my body remembers his hands like phantom bruises.

I pull myself up, legs shaking. The mirror across the room shows a stranger—hollow eyes, tangled hair, wearing one of his shirts like armor against the emptiness.

No. Not a stranger. Me. The real me, without chemicals or contracts or commands.

And she's furious.

The rage comes suddenly, volcanic. I grab the nearest thing—a coffee mug, my favorite one—and hurl it against the wall. It explodes in a shower of ceramic, the sound cathartic.

Another follows. Then a plate. A vase of dead flowers. Seventeen years of his obsession, months of manipulation, and he thinks he can *leave*? Give me freedom like a gift when he's already rewired my soul?

"Coward!" I scream at the empty house. "You absolute fucking coward!"

My phone is in my hand before I think. His number glows on the screen. One call and he'd answer—he always answers. But what would I say? Come back? Stay? Go? I hate you? I need you?

All true. None sufficient.

Instead, I grab my keys.

DAY 138 — MIDNIGHT

His estate looms against the darkness, all sharp angles and black glass, exactly like him. Security lights flood the driveway as I screech to a stop. The gates are open. He probably watched me leave the ranch on some app, tracking me like he tracks his investments.

I storm up the steps and pound on the door with both fists. "Julian. Open this fucking door."

Silence.

"I know you're in there. I know you're watching through your cameras like the control freak you are."

The door opens so suddenly I nearly fall forward. He catches me, steadying me with hands that shake slightly.

He looks destroyed. Stubble shadows his jaw, his usually perfect hair disheveled, wearing only pajama pants like he'd given up on the armor of his suits. His eyes are rimmed red.

"Clara—"

"Shut up." I push past him into the foyer. "You don't get to talk yet."

He closes the door, leaning against it like he needs the support. "You shouldn't be here."

"You don't get to tell me where I should be anymore. You voided the contract, remember?" I spin to face him. "You gave me my freedom. So I'm using it to come here and tell you exactly what I think of you."

"I deserve that."

"You deserve more than that." I'm shaking with rage and something else—something that feels dangerously like grief. "You drugged me. Manipulated me. Turned me into your perfect submissive through chemistry and control."

"I know."

"You planned it for seventeen years. Seventeen! Built an empire just to own me."

"Yes."

"And then—" My voice cracks. "Then you *leave*? You poison me with need, reshape my entire existence around you, and then you walk away?"

"Because I love you." His voice is raw. "Because watching you suffer in a cage I built was killing us both."

"Love?" A harsh, bitter laugh. "You don't know what love is. Love doesn't drug people. Love doesn't manipulate and control and—"

"You're right." He pushes off from the door, moving closer but still maintaining distance. "I don't know how to love normally. I only know obsession. Possession. Control. It's all I've ever known."

"Your mother tried to warn me."

"My mother is terrified I'll become my father." His jaw tightens. "Maybe I already have."

"Your father?"

"Controlled everything through fear and money. Died alone in this house because everyone either feared him or wanted his fortune. Even my mother... she loved him, but she also fled the moment she could." He meets my eyes. "I swore I'd be different. That when I found love, I'd protect it, nurture it, keep it safe. Instead, I became him. Worse than him. At least he never drugged my mother into compliance."

The pain in his voice catches me off guard. "Julian—"

"The withdrawal isn't from the drugs, is it?" He cuts me off. "It's from me. From us. From what we built, however poisoned at its foundation."

I want to deny it. Can't.

"I feel it too." He continues. "Like someone carved out my chest. Like I'm suffocating on empty air. Every instinct screams at me to go to you, to take you, to make you mine again through whatever means necessary."

"Then why don't you?"

"Because that's not love. That's addiction." His hands clench at his sides. "And you deserve better than being someone's drug."

"What if I don't want better?" The words escape before I can stop them. "What if I want you?"

He goes still. "The chemicals—"

"Are gone. Have been for days." I step closer. "And I still dream of kneeling for you. Still wake up wet from memories of the Red Room. Still feel phantom leather around my throat."

"That's conditioning. Stockholm syndrome. It's not real."

"Fuck you." The words are quiet but fierce. "Don't you dare tell me what's real. You don't get to decide that anymore."

"Clara—"

"I read your journals. All of them. Even the ones you hid. The teenage poetry about my laugh. The detailed plans for our future you wrote at nineteen. The pages and pages about wanting to protect me, provide for me, worship me. And the drawings, oh the drawings... the x-rated ones you thought I'd never see. The ones where I'm wearing a collar, crawling to you, spread out, tied up. The whispers of desires that only a teenager could dream up, yet held within them the echoes of the man you would become."

"Those were fantasies—"

"Those were love letters to someone you hadn't even kissed yet." I'm close enough now to see his pupils dilate. "You loved me before you ever touched me. Before the drugs. Before the contract. You loved me at seventeen when I laughed at you, and you love me now when I hate you."

"Yes." The word is barely breath.

"And I..." I force myself to say it. "I responded to you before the drugs. The week before your twisted contract proves it. I still came to you. Secretly wanted you. Started falling for the broken, obsessive, brilliant disaster that you are."

"That doesn't excuse—"

"No, it doesn't." I cut him off. "Nothing excuses what you did. But it does mean that underneath the violation, there's something real. Something that existed before the chemicals and persists after them."

We stand there, inches apart, both breathing hard. The old electricity crackles between us, the pull that's always existed, drug-enhanced or not.

"I can't trust you."

"I know."

"I might never fully trust you."

"I know."

"But I also can't..." I swallow hard. "I can't be free of you. Not because of conditioning, chemicals, or contracts. Because you're carved into my bones. You've been there since I was seventeen and laughed to keep from crying. Since you asked me to prom five times and I said no five times, and we both knew I was lying."

His control finally cracks. "Clara—"

"You want to give me freedom? Fine. I'm free." I reach up, frame his face with my hands. "And I'm using that freedom to choose this. To choose us. Not the version you manufactured, but whatever we can build from the ruins."

"You don't know what you're saying—"

"I'm saying you're mine as much as I'm yours." My thumb traces his lower lip. "I'm saying your obsession has always been matched by my own. You built an empire to own me? I stayed in this dead town partly because I knew you'd eventually come for me."

His breath shudders. "That's insane."

"Probably, and definitely unhealthy." I lean in until our foreheads touch. "But it's also true. We're both broken in complementary ways, remember? You need to control. I need to be challenged. You need someone strong enough to handle your intensity. I need someone who sees all of me, not just the nice parts."

"I violated you."

"Yes. And that will stand between us. A scar that won't heal clean." I pull back to meet his eyes. "But I'm choosing to build something on scarred ground. Question is—are you?"

His hands finally, finally come up to cover mine. "You'd forgive me?"

"No. Not yet. Maybe never completely." Ruthless honesty. "But I'd try to build something new with you. Something where my submission is a gift, not theft. Where your dominance is earned, not forced. Where the power exchange is real because we both choose it with clear minds and open eyes."

"That could take years."

"Then we take years."

"I might fail. Revert to old patterns."

"Then I'll call you on it. Fight you. Leave if I have to." I search his face. "But I'll try if you will."

He kisses me then—not dominant, not commanding, just desperate. Like a drowning man finding air. I kiss him back with equal desperation, tasting salt and whiskey and the bitter truth of us.

When we break apart, we're both shaking.

"We need rules." His voice is rough. "New ones. Ones we both agree to."

"Yes."

"And therapy. Professional help. Someone who understands... this." He gestures between us.

"Agreed. Now," I step back. "Show me the room where you've been sleeping."

He leads me through the dark house to a guest room. Not the master—that surprises me. The bed is wrecked, sheets twisted, pillow stained with what might be tears or sweat or both.

"You haven't been sleeping."

"Neither have you."

"No."

We stand there, awkward as teenagers. Then I make a decision. I pull off my—his—shirt, then my jeans, standing in just underwear. Not seductive. Just real.

"I want to sleep." My voice is steady. "Just sleep. Next to you. No sex. No power games. Just... proximity. Can you handle that?"

His throat works. "No."

The honesty of it stops me cold.

"I can't sleep next to you." His voice is rough, raw. "Not after days without you. Not with you standing there, choosing to be here. I need—" He stops, starts again. "I need to fuck you. Not as your master. Not with games or control. Just as a man who's been dying without you."

The words send heat straight through me. "Julian—"

"Tell me no, and I'll respect it. I'll suffer through it. But don't ask me to pretend I don't want to be inside you right now."

I'm across the room before I finish thinking, crashing into him, our mouths meeting in desperate hunger. No dominance, no submission, just raw need. He lifts me, and I wrap my legs around him, both of us tearing at the remaining clothes between us.

We don't make it to the bed. He takes me against the wall, both of us gasping, clutching, absolutely feral for each other. It's not pretty or controlled—it's seventeen years of want finally unleashed without artifice.

"Fuck, Clara." He groans against my neck. "I've needed this. Needed you."

"Then take me." The words come out breathless. "Not as my owner. As my equal."

He drives deeper, and we both break apart in minutes, too desperate to last. We slide down the wall, tangled on the floor, breathing hard.

"Again." A demand.

"Again." An agreement.

This time, we make it to the bed. Three more times before we finally collapse, exhausted and raw and more honest than we've ever been.

"This doesn't fix us." A whisper into the darkness.

"I know."

"We might destroy each other trying."

"Probably."

"But we're going to try anyway."

"Yes."

I shift closer, just enough that our arms touch. He releases a shuddering breath.

"Clara?"

"Yeah?"

"The morning I woke up with you kneeling by the bed... that wasn't the drugs. I checked the data after. You hadn't been dosed in three days."

My chest tightens. "I know. I checked too."

"It was real."

"I know. Complicated and twisted and problematic, but real."

His hand tightens on mine. "I love you. The real you. The fighter who challenged me in the kitchen. The woman who threw that mug at the wall—yes, I saw the security footage. Yes, I installed cameras you didn't know about." No attempt to hide his guilt at that invasion. "You could have walked away clean, but came here instead."

"I love you too." The admission comes easier than expected. "The obsessive disaster who kept journals like a lovesick teenager. The control freak who tries so hard to protect that he crushes. The man who gave up everything to set me free, even though it was killing you."

"We're insane."

"Completely."

"But we're doing it anyway."

"Yes. We are."

A pause, then: "Can we stop talking and get back to fucking? I've been jerking off to memories for days, and now you're here, real, in my bed—"

I shut him up by rolling on top of him, and we stop talking for a long, long time.

CHAPTER 62

365 - ONE YEAR

"You're cheating," Dr. Martinez says flatly.

We sit on opposite ends of her plush beige couch, trying to look innocent. We're terrible at it. Julian shifts, adjusting his tie, looking everywhere but at the therapist. I pick at a loose thread on my jeans.

"We did the vanilla date." Julian's protest is immediate, though it lacks conviction. "Dinner at Le Coucou. A walk in the park. No power exchange. No protocols."

"Until the parking lot," I mutter under my breath.

Julian shoots me a glare that is 100% dominant male. "You asked me to fuck you."

"I asked you to kiss me," I correct, turning to Dr. Martinez. "He pinned me against the Escalade, grabbed my hair, and—"

"You called me Sir," Julian interjects, crossing his arms. "You dropped your voice an octave and looked up at me through your lashes and said, 'Take me home, Sir.' You triggered the response."

"You had your hand around my throat before I even finished the sentence," I counter.

Dr. Martinez—who is currently on her fifth session with us because we broke the first six therapists with our... specifics— sighs deeply. She takes off her glasses and rubs the bridge of her nose.

"You're supposed to be practicing normal intimacy," she reminds us, her voice weary. "Equal partnership. Reciprocity. Not defaulting to your D/s dynamic every time you find yourselves alone."

"We tried." My hands spread helplessly. "But it's like... breathing. It's gravity. Even without the drugs, without the contracts, without the fear... we just fall into it."

"She submits," Julian finishes, his voice dropping lower. "I dominate. It's not a performance anymore. It's who we are."

"It's what you've conditioned yourselves to be," Dr. Martinez corrects gently. "The question is whether you can have a healthy relationship within that dynamic, or if you need to break it entirely to find equality."

We look at each other. The silence stretches, heavy and knowing. The answer is obvious to both of us, even if our therapist disagrees.

"We can't break it," I say quietly. "We've tried. The last four months of equality... they've been safe. But they've made us both miserable. We're starving."

"Then you need to rebuild it," she says, putting her glasses back on. "Consciously. With boundaries. With safety. With genuine consent that isn't clouded by chemical manipulation or financial coercion."

She looks between us. "The Red Room."

The air in the office changes. Julian stiffens.

"We haven't been back," he says sharply. "Not once since... since the letter. Since I left."

"Since I found out," I finish.

Dr. Martinez leans forward. "Do you want to go back?"

The question hangs between us. The Red Room—where everything was both most honest and most violated. Where I discovered myself and lost myself simultaneously.

"Yes." The whisper tears out of me. "But I'm terrified."

"Of me?" Julian asks, pain flashing in his eyes.

"Of us," I admit. "Of what we become in there. Of how easy it is to lose the line between Clara and the submissive."

"Then maybe," Dr. Martinez suggests, "that's exactly where you need to go. To reclaim it. To make it yours by choice instead of by force."

Later that night, we stand in the hallway. The house is silent, save for the hum of the HVAC. The heavy oak door of the Red Room looms in front of us.

"You can say no." Julian says it for the tenth time, his hand hovering near the knob but not touching it. He looks pale, the weight of his past crimes pressing down on him.

"I know."

"You can leave anytime. The door will not be locked."

"I know."

"The safe word—"

"Is 'freedom.'" I meet his eyes, steady and sure.

"And I'll respect it." The words come quickly, desperate. "Always. The moment you say it, everything stops. I won't be... him. I won't lose control."

A slow, dangerous smile curves my lips. I look at this man— this careful, repentant man who has spent months atoning for sins I have already forgiven.

"I don't care what *Julian* will do," I say softly.

He blinks, confused. "Clara?"

"What happens next..." I step closer, my voice dropping to that submissive purr I haven't used in months, the one that bypasses his logic and hits his lizard brain. "That's up to Mr. Blackwell."

His entire body goes rigid. His pupils blow wide, swallowing the iris, his breath catching as if I've just shot pure heroin into his veins.

"And Mr. Blackwell," I continue, trailing a finger down the placket of his shirt, "never let me use my safeword. He pushed and pushed until I broke, until I was sobbing and begging, and still he didn't stop. Because he knew better. He knew what I needed better than I did."

"Clara..." His voice is strangled, a warning and a plea. "Don't."

"You've been Julian for months now." My murmur is soft, deliberate. "Careful, considerate Julian who asks permission and respects boundaries and treats me like glass. And that's been necessary. Important. But it's not feeding that part of you, is it? The dark part. The part that wants to own me so completely that safewords become meaningless."

His hands are shaking at his sides. "That's—we agreed—safety—"

"We agreed to try being normal." I press my body against his, feeling the hardness of him, the tension radiating off him like heat. "We failed. Julian might be who you are at dinner parties and therapy sessions. But in there?" I nod toward the Red Room. "In there, you're Mr. Blackwell. I don't want Julian in that room with me."

"This is dangerous." The words come on a breath, his control fracturing. "What you're suggesting—"

"Is exactly what we both need." I turn toward the door, my hand resting on the cool metal of the handle, then look back over my shoulder. The excitement thrumming through me makes my voice breathy, needy. "Open the door, Mr. Blackwell."

The change in him is instant. Visceral.

He closes his eyes for a second, inhaling deeply. When he opens them, Julian is gone. His spine straightens, his shoulders square, and that dangerous, absolute control slides over him like armor. The repentance vanishes, replaced by possession. When he speaks again, his voice has dropped to that commanding register that once ruled my every breath.

"Ask properly."

The words send liquid heat straight through me. My knees actually wobble—not from chemicals or conditioning, but from pure, undiluted want.

"Please, Mr. Blackwell," I whisper, my eyes locked on his. "Open the door."

He steps forward, crowding me against the wood, his breath hot on my neck. "If we go in there, the negotiation ends. I will use you exactly how I want, for as long as I want. Is that clear?"

"Yes, Mr. Blackwell."

"Your safeword exists." His hand wraps around my throat, his thumb pressing into my windpipe, just enough to claim. "But we both know you won't use it."

"Yes, Mr. Blackwell."

He releases me, reaches past my shoulder, and twists the handle. The door swings open.

The scent hits us first—leather, cold air, and memory.

I practically vibrate with anticipation. This—this is what we've been missing. Not the careful, therapeutic sex. Not the vanilla attempts at normal. This electric space where he becomes the savage monster I crave, and I become the willing victim he needs... it's what we need to thrive.

"Inside." A command. "Knees. Now."

My knees hit the floor, the impact echoing through me like a heartbeat.

The air in the Red Room feels different from what I remember.

It's no longer a prison. It's a temple. My pulse quickens, not from fear, but from recognition.

He circles me slowly, the sound of his boots on the floorboards deliberate, controlled. His gaze drags over every inch of exposed skin, heavy as a physical touch. When he stops behind me, the silence stretches, taut and trembling.

Leather slides—familiar, sacred. A belt, a cuff, a sound that sends goosebumps racing across my skin.

"I've missed this." The words are quiet, spoken almost to himself. The voice isn't Julian's—gentle, hesitant, human. It's Mr. Blackwell's—measured, powerful, absolute. "You're offering yourself because you want to."

"I very much do," I whisper to the floor. "I need this. Need you like this."

He exhales—a sound that's part relief, part surrender to his own nature. Then the soft brush of leather grazes my wrists, not yet binding, just teasing.

"Then let's stop pretending we're something we're not."

I nod once, trembling.

"Good girl." A dark, hungry smile. Home.

The sound of the lock sliding into place fills the air, final and familiar.

And as he reaches for the restraints, as his touch steadies and claims and redefines me all over again, the truth of what we've rebuilt settles into my bones.

This isn't about breaking or saving anymore. It's about choosing the darkness—together.

CHAPTER 63
TWO YEARS — DAY 730

"How's therapy?" Julian's mother asks over lunch, cutting into her poached salmon with precise, surgical movements that remind me instantly of where he gets his need for control.

We are at Le Bernardin. The tablecloths are crisp white, the crystal sparkles, and we are pretending to be a normal family.

"We broke another one," I admit, reaching for my wine.

She laughs, that knowing, low laugh that says she understands her son better than he thinks she does. "How many is that?"

"Twelve."

"Thirteen." Julian's correction is immediate. He's drinking sparkling water, his gaze tracking a waiter who moved too close to my chair. "You're forgetting Dr. Henderson."

"He lasted one session," I argue. "He doesn't count."

"He counts." Julian won't let it go. "He sent a formal letter via courier declining to continue treatment. Something about 'fundamental incompatibility with therapeutic norms' and 'ethical concerns regarding codependency.'"

His mother sets down her fork, wiping her mouth delicately. "What exactly are you doing to these poor therapists?"

"Nothing," we say in unison. It comes out too quickly. Too synchronized.

She raises a skeptical eyebrow. "Julian."

"They ask intrusive questions," he says defensively. "They want to unpack the dynamic. We don't want to unpack it. We just want to... maintain the machinery."

"Clara told the last one that submission was her love language," Julian adds, throwing me under the bus without hesitation. "The therapist nearly choked on her herbal tea."

I kick him under the table. "You told her dominance was a form of supreme caretaking."

"It is."

"That's not what she meant by 'caring behavior,' and you know it."

His mother watches our bickering with amusement, sipping her Chardonnay. "But we're getting better," I lie smoothly. "We made it six whole sessions with Dr. Martinez before she fired us."

"Progress," his mother says dryly, but there's a genuine fondness in her eyes. "And the ranch?"

"Thriving." The word comes out bright, eager. "Twenty horses now. Fifteen kids in the program. We just got approved for a state grant to expand the stables."

"Which I'm not funding." Julian's bitterness is palpable. He stabs a roasted potato. "She won't let me."

"It's mine," I remind him. "My project. My success. If you pay for it, it becomes your project."

"I offered to donate anonymously—"

"You already did that once," I cut in. "Fifty thousand dollars through a shell company registered in the Caymans. 'Equine Welfare Solutions LLC'?"

His mother nearly drops her water glass. "Fifty thousand?"

"The horses needed winter shelter," Julian says, shrugging as if that explains everything. "The contractor she hired was too slow. I expedited the process."

"You can't help yourself, can you?" His mother studies him, shaking her head. "You have to control everything, even her independence."

"I prefer to think of it as aggressive support."

"You prefer to think of yourself as benevolent," she says sharply. "But we both know better."

The table goes quiet. The air thickens slightly.

"Mom—"

"I'm not criticizing." She reaches across to pat his hand, her rings clicking against his watch. "I'm observing." Her brow arches toward me, sharp and assessing. "He didn't try to buy your ranch again, did he?"

"No." I take a sip of wine, hiding a smirk. "But last week, he had the entire kitchen at the ranch house ripped out and replaced with a professional-grade chef's kitchen while I was out for the day. He said I needed 'an upgrade' because the stove burner stuck."

"I was trying to make things easier for you," Julian defends. "That stove was a fire hazard."

"So I made things 'easier' for him," I say, my voice deadpan. "I changed every password he has. Email, banking, trading platforms included. It cost him three million in missed trades before his IT team could sort it out."

His mother throws her head back and laughs, delighted. "Good for you."

"She's vicious," Julian mutters, glaring at me. But there's no anger in it. There is only pride. Deep, terrified, reverent pride. "Magnificent, but vicious."

"She'd have to be, to handle you," Evelyn replies, still chuckling. "Your father would have hated her."

"He would have tried to destroy her," Julian agrees, nodding. "He couldn't stand anything he couldn't break."

"Which is why he died alone, and you won't." She stands, smoothing her linen skirt, gathering her purse. "Don't break each other too badly, children. I'd like grandchildren eventually. And I don't want them raised by wolves."

"Mom!"

"What? I'm not getting younger. And despite this insane thing you call a relationship, you're less miserable than I've ever seen you." She kisses his cheek, then leans in to kiss mine. "Though, do try to keep at least one therapist for more than a month. It looks bad on the insurance forms."

After she leaves, sweeping out of the restaurant like a queen, Julian and I sit in comfortable silence. The waiter clears the plates, terrified to interrupt us.

"Your mother thinks we're insane," I say, tracing the rim of my glass.

"My mother knows we're insane." He reaches across the table, palm up. An invitation, not a demand. But the weight of the command is there, underneath the skin. "She also knows I'm worse without you."

"And I'm worse without you."

"Which makes us perfect for each other."

"Definitely."

I place my hand in his. His fingers close around mine—possessive, firm, grounding.

"Ready to go traumatize therapist number fourteen?" he asks, checking his watch. "We have an appointment at three."

"Actually," I say slowly, "I thought we might skip therapy today."

His eyes darken with interest. The boredom vanishes. "Oh?"

"The Red Room's been empty for three days," I murmur, leaning forward so only he can hear. "I've been too busy with the grant paperwork. You've been too busy with the merger."

"Has it?" His thumb strokes across my knuckles, finding the sensitive spot between the tendons. "How neglectful of Mr. Blackwell."

The name sends heat straight through me, rushing to my center, even here in public, even after all this time. It acts like a Pavlovian bell.

"Extremely neglectful," I whisper. "Someone should be punished for that."

His pupils blow wide. The Julian who eats lunch with his mother vanishes. The predator takes his seat.

"Someone should," he agrees, his voice dropping to a low rumble. "Someone should be reminded exactly who she belongs to."

We pay the check and leave with indecent haste, ignoring the dessert menu. His hand rests on the small of my back as we walk to the car—heavy, guiding, claiming.

Don't break each other too badly, his mother said.

Too late for that. We're already broken.

But as he opens the car door for me, his eyes promising a beautiful, ruinous afternoon, I know the truth. We're broken in ways that fit together perfectly.

If you liked CRUEL OBSESSION,
You will love TWISTED OBSESSION

A Dark Billionaire Romance

"Kael Draven saved her sanctuary. Lila Chase saved his soul.
Together, they'll burn down everything else."

When an environmental lawyer must sell her soul to the timber
baron she despises to save her wilderness sanctuary, she discovers
his price includes more than her body—he wants to chemically
rewire her brain to crave his dominance.

Enemies to lovers. Forced proximity. Morally gray billionaire.
Dubious consent becomes enthusiastic consent. Touch her
and die.

TO MY READERS

You're here. You made it to the end of my very first book, and that means more to me than I can say. Stepping into this author world was equal parts terrifying and exhilarating. I wanted to write the kind of stories that set your pulse racing, that make you ache and swoon, that remind you love is strongest when it's tested by fire.

If you found pieces of yourself in these pages — if you held your breath, if you whispered *just one more chapter* at midnight, if you felt too much — then I've done what I set out to do.

This is just the beginning. There are more dangerous love stories waiting, and I want you with me for every single one. Come join me at **FreyaLocke.com** and sign up for my newsletter — that's where I share what's next, bonus content, and secrets I only whisper to my readers.

. . .

Thank you for trusting me with your time and your heart. I can't wait to tell you the next story.

With all my love and mischief,
Freya Locke

To save her forest, Lila strikes a bargain with a man who doesn't negotiate mercy—and Kael intends to bind far more than land before he's finished.

RUTHLESS OBSESSION

Damian Stryker & Avery Donovan

Damian destroyed the monster who hurt her, but salvation comes at a cost—and Avery must decide whether true surrender can exist without lies.

DARK OBSESSION

Colton Wolfe & Ivy Monroe

Colton dismantled her father's empire piece by piece, and now Ivy is the final acquisition—eight years of obsession coming due.

TWISTED OBSESSION

Nathan Cross & Sera Winters

She's determined to expose his dangerous research; he's determined to prove her desire is darker than her fear—and neither of them plans to lose.

SAVAGE OBSESSION

Sebastian York & Chloe Henderson

To save her brother, Chloe signs a contract with a man who doesn't forgive debt—and Sebastian always collects in full.

Start at the Beginning

Begin with **CRUEL OBSESSION**, or read the Obsession Series in any order—each novel is a standalone with its own dark romance, guaranteed HEA, and no cliffhangers.

Visit: www.freyalocke.com

ABOUT FREYA LOCKE

Freya Locke writes dangerous love stories where desire burns as hot as danger. Her books peel back the layers of control, exploring the raw edges of power and surrender, and proving that love—real, fierce, undeniable—thrives in the fire.

She is drawn to tortured heroes, because redemption is sexier when it's hard-earned. Her heroines are brilliant and strong, even when vulnerability cuts close to the bone. And her stories are laced with tension sharp enough to hurt, because the best love stories cut before they heal.

Freya believes the right book should keep you up too late, make you squirm, and make you feel just a little too much. If that's what you're looking for, you've found your next obsession.

This is just the beginning. More dangerous love stories are on their way, and she can't wait to share them with you.

THE END